Blood

Book 2 of the Avatars of Ruin

Also by Tej Turner

The Janus Cycle
Dinnusos Rises

<u>Avatars of Ruin</u>
Book 1: Bloodsworn

The Last Days in Existence is Elsewhen

Blood Legacy

Book 2 of the Avatars of Ruin

Tej Turner

Elsewhen Press

Blood Legacy
First published in Great Britain by Elsewhen Press, 2022
An imprint of Alnpete Limited

Elsewhen Press, PO Box 757, Dartford, Kent DA2 7TQ
www.elsewhen.press
British Library Cataloguing in Publication Data.
A catalogue record for this book is available from the British Library.
ISBN 978-1-911409-89-2 Print edition
ISBN 978-1-911409-99-1 eBook edition

Designed and formatted by Elsewhen Press

For Chuck Ashmore

Contents

Map of Sharma and Gavendara .... *viii*

Prologue:

   Gazareth's Night 1

Chapters:

   Shemet...37
   Recruited 63
   Sleeper Agents 75
   The Institute 95
   Lighter Burdens 113
   Squad Three 125
   The Mission 143
   Transferred.......................................157
   Setting Forth.....................................165
   Outlaws 179
   The Ruena 199
   Gavendara 229
   New Objective 247
   The Pillars of Parchen............................271
   Flash...293
   The Lost Squadron 317
   An Old Friend 339
   Boom..363
   A New Terrain 377
   Lord Galrath......................................391
   Flight..407
   A War Coming......................................433

Gods & Godesses of Sharma & Gavendara *454*

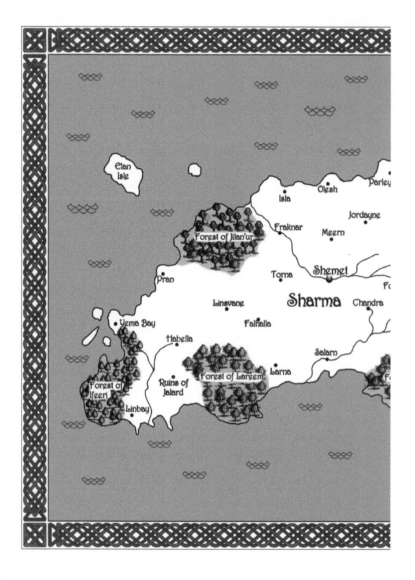

VALLESHIAN MOUNTAINS

Vallesh
Lartung
Perna
Izt
Velu
Warling
Malachi
Shreevay
Llamaleil
Kadar
Darlesh
Mordeem
Rhumania

Gavendara

Marinda
Lishar
The Folds
Beed
Barlech
VALANTIAN
MOUNTAINS
Suule
Chillin
Dohgan
ort Valen
Passerskeep
Falam
Holliston
Sarok
Dotto
LEVIAN
MOUNTAINS
Korst

orest of Freema
Inez
Farnesh
Pallila
Halesh
Palu
Yemalla
Babuton

Babu'an Jungle

Prologue

Gazareth's Night

(Eighteen Years Earlier)

Meredith was tending to the plants.

It was summer, but the sky was cloudy and the air was cool. This was typical for the place Meredith lived. It was just a stone's throw away from the sea, after all.

Parleyban was its name, and it was not so much a village as a sprawl of hamlets and farms spread across the breadth of three valleys in the northern reaches of Sharma; safe from the turbulent tides that tore at the coast, but at the mercy of the chilly, bitter winds which also came with them.

Meredith had never actually seen the ocean up close – to venture too near was dangerous – but she had glimpsed it a few times whilst walking around the outer rim of Parleyban. It was a sight that conjured awe and existential disquiet within her in equal measure. She often found herself returning but not quite knowing why.

This day, however, Meredith was occupied. Her aunt had tasked her with maintaining her herb garden. A chore that Meredith enjoyed and was content within, but the serenity of it came to an end when a panic-stricken woman came running to the house with a child dangling from her arms and tears in her eyes.

"What's wrong?" Meredith called, dropping her spade as she recognised the woman. It was one of the weavers from the village, and the child was her son.

"It's Colben!" the woman yelled as she raced towards her. "A bee stung him! He's not breathing!"

"Bring him in!" Meredith said, opening the gate and ushering the woman to follow. "Quick!"

As they ran towards the house, the door swung open. It was Pativa, Meredith's aunt, who must have been alerted by the woman's cries.

"Put him there!" Pativa said, gesturing to the treatment table in the middle of the room. The woman carried the boy over, and Meredith got her first proper look at him. His face had turned purple.

Pativa placed a hand upon the boy's throat, and Meredith witnessed green energy stream from her palm as she summoned upon her Blessing. A moment later, the boy's mouth gaped open, and he lurched, gasping for air.

"What are you *doing!?*" the mother asked.

"Get back!" Pativa exclaimed, and the fretful woman leapt away. Her eyes, though, never left the figure of her son's trembling body. "I need room! What happened to him?"

"He was stung!" the mother cried. "That bloody Vivil and her bee-keeping! I told her that one day–"

"Bee sting! That is all I need to know!" Pativa interrupted her, and the other woman placed a hand over her mouth. Most people in the village found Pativa intimidating, but Meredith knew her aunt better than most people. Beneath the austere persona lived a gentle soul; she was only stern when she needed to be.

Pativa turned to her niece and softened her voice. "He's had a bad reaction to a sting, and it's inflamed the inside of his throat," her words came out as a hiss – probably so that Colben's mother wouldn't overhear. "I am using my *viga* to keep his airway open, but I don't fancy keeping this up all day. We need a solution. What would you suggest?"

Meredith's heart rate quickened as she realised that this was a real life-or-death situation, and her aunt was using it as an opportunity to test her. Pativa had never given her such a grave responsibility before.

Meredith's initial thought was gherdleroot, but she just as quickly dismissed it; an infusion would help Colben breathe for a short spell but do little to remedy the cause of the problem. Lodebane was the next alternative that entered her mind, but that came with the possibility of some volatile side effects, and its use on a boy so young

2

was fraught with complications.

"Nefia leaf!" Meredith realised. "If you keep his throat open long enough for him to drink it, it will counter the venom... maybe if I add some varverry, it'll get into his blood quicker and soothe the inflammation too?"

Pativa nodded. "You are correct. Get to it!" she decreed, pointing towards the hearth.

*   *   *

They managed to get the potion down him and, a few minutes later, the boy was breathing without Pativa's aid. He even dropped into a peaceful sleep, thanks to the addition of garanwort Meredith added to the potion she made him.

Meredith then sat down and busied herself grinding up hartlewood leaves and alomelosis roots in a pestle and mortar to make a soothing paste to apply to the swollen area on his shoulder where the bee had stung him. Pativa took the mother – who by now had calmed down a little – aside to speak with her.

While Meredith massaged the ointment to his skin, she looked at the boy's face and realised that it didn't seem so long ago that she had assisted with his birth. Seven years. Back then, she had been just a young girl, fetching blankets and warming pails of water at the hearth whilst the soon-to-be-mother cried out with each contraction, and Pativa – positioned between her legs – guided the process, coaxing her to push the baby out.

Meredith was eighteen years old now, and she did far more than merely fetch blankets and water these days. She was on the cusp of becoming a Devotee of Carnea in her own right.

*   *   *

Pativa wanted Colben to stay for the night so she could keep an eye on him, and his mother refused to leave his side. By the time Meredith had finished tending to him, it was mid-afternoon, so she made her way home.

When she stepped out of Pativa's house, the chilly breeze once again hit her. She pulled her coat tighter around herself to keep in the warmth and began to make her way down the path.

When Meredith reached the bottom of the hill, she passed the one part of Parleyban that could almost be considered its concourse; a collection of merchant houses, a few cottages, and the only tavern. She greeted a few of the villagers as she passed but refrained from getting into any conversations. It had been ingrained into Meredith from an early age to live an inconspicuous existence. Meredith's family had many secrets – the fact that they were from Gavendara alone could cause them much trouble – so she wasn't allowed to get too friendly with other people.

After crossing the bridge, Meredith became shadowed by woodland. She skirted her way around the side of the hill. The trail that snaked its way through the trees was familiar – she trod it almost every day between her home and Pativa's place.

As she was making her way, she caught the sound of twigs snapping behind her, followed by footsteps.

"Hello Meredith," a familiar voice said.

She turned around and saw it was her cousin, Jediah. She smiled at him.

No matter how many times Meredith saw Jediah, he never ceased to fascinate her. There was something unearthly about him. His eyes were violet – more strikingly so than any wildflower she'd glimpsed during her trips around the local meadows gathering herbs – and his skin was so pale it almost seemed to glimmer in the sunlight. Ebony curtains of gossamer hair curtained his face.

He caught up with her, and they walked side by side. When they were younger they had been of similar height, but now he was almost a foot taller than her.

"Have you just been to the village?" Meredith asked him.

4

He nodded his head and smiled. "Father sent me to collect these," he explained, raising a handful of books.

Meredith nodded. Her uncle Godrei was a scholar under the patronage of several benefactors, who often sent him old texts in need of translating. Jediah seemed to have inherited his father's passion. No doubt he had just spent half of the day sat beneath a tree leafing through them before he was obliged to hand them over.

"How was your day?" he asked.

Meredith sighed. "One of the boys from the village was stung by a bee. Don't worry," she added when his expression became concerned. "He's okay."

"Not much to worry about with you and Pativa around..." he said encouragingly. "The villagers say you couldn't find better medicine women even if you went to Shemet itself."

Meredith wasn't so sure of that. She had never met any other Devotees of Carnea aside from her aunt. And besides, it wouldn't have mattered how skilled they were if the boy had not got to them in time. Stings could kill very fast when people reacted badly.

Meredith almost explained this to Jediah but thought better of it. She didn't want to bore him.

"You don't visit us much anymore..." Jediah commented a few moments later. "You should come over sometime. I think my parents would like to see you..."

Things change, Meredith thought. *People grow up*.

She shrugged. "I've been busy learning with Pativa. And anyway, I kind of thought that with you, mother, and Carmaestre... well... I just don't want to get in the way..."

"Why would you say that?" Jediah asked. He stopped, grabbed Meredith's arm, and Meredith saw that he was frowning. "You're still family, Meredith. So what if you didn't inherit our Blessing. You can *heal*. You've done more good for the world than we have so far."

Meredith nodded. She knew it. After years of feeling like she was a failure, being taken under her aunt's wing had finally given her the sense of value that she had lacked before. Becoming a Devotee of Carnea felt like her purpose now. Her calling.

But still, it cut Meredith off from the one thing in the world she wanted most.

*   *   *

When Meredith and Jediah reached her house, her little sister ran out to meet them.

They lived on the top of the hill, so Carmaestre's hair was caught by the breeze, rippling behind her in dark, almost snakelike tresses. Like so many of their family, Carmaestre possessed distinctive violet eyes and pale skin. She was very much the image of how Meredith imagined their mother looked when she was young.

Carmaestre collided into Jediah's arms.

"Jediah!" she exclaimed. "Where *were* you today?" She pulled away, and her eyes went to the stack of books cradled beneath his arm. "Don't tell me you've been reading some boring old books, again!? Mum's going to have you strung from the chimney!"

"They're accounts from the Feudal period!" Jediah defended himself. "I have–"

"*Bor-ing*!" Carmaestre crossed her arms over her chest. "How come you came together?" she said, looking at Meredith. "I hope you're not turning into a bookbrain too! He's missed *four* of Mum's lessons this tean cycle!"

Meredith shook her head. "No... I just came from Pativa's. We bumped into each other. Besides, I don't think you can solely blame the books, Carmaestre," Meredith said. "Jediah had a rebellious streak *way* before he knew how to read!"

Jediah grinned at Meredith. "Remember that time Nagella was trying to teach us how to *psyseer*, and we snuck away when she had her eyes closed?" he asked.

"When we hid behind that tree?" Meredith finished for him, and they both laughed. It had taken Meredith's mother most of the day to find them and, when she did, she gave them both a hiding.

"Mum tried to teach you to *psyseer*?" Carmaestre narrowed her eyes at Meredith.

Meredith nodded.

"Your Mum used to teach Meredith too," Jediah said, putting a hand on Meredith's shoulder.

"*Really*?" Carmaestre's eyes widened. "When?"

"When you were just a wee girl," Jediah replied. "You probably don't remember."

Meredith turned her eyes to the ground. Thinking about that period of her life brought back a deluge of memories. Some were fond ones, but others were painful and triggered feelings of shame.

When Meredith was younger, her mother tried to teach her the Blessings of their family alongside Jediah, but all Meredith achieved from hours of desperately trying to bend her magic against its nature were headaches. Most of the members of Meredith's family had an aptitude for a wide range of sorcerous techniques, but Meredith was not one of them. Her Blessing was a different kind. She could heal, and it was a gift she inherited from her father's lineage. As well as her hazel eyes.

Carmaestre seemed to notice the turn in Meredith's mood and came to her rescue by grabbing her hand. "How was it at Pativa's today, Sis? Did you learn much?"

Meredith nodded. "Yes. Do you know Colben? He got stung by a bee..." she began to explain, but she could tell her sister wasn't interested – or even listening – so she drew the story to a premature end.

"On that note, I will take my leave," Jediah said, dipping his head at the two of them as he stepped away. He began to walk in the direction of his home. "Best make myself scarce before your mother catches me."

"Don't go!" Carmaestre said, grabbing his arm. "Stay for supper. I'm sure Mother will–"

"Father needs these," Jediah said, holding up the books he'd collected. "So I best get going. I'll visit tomorrow, though. Promise."

"You'd better!" Carmaestre said as she let go reluctantly. "Come, Meredith," Carmaestre then said, linking arms with her. "Let's go inside."

They made their way towards the house. It was a pretty little cottage surrounded by trees. Meredith suspected that the previous owners, whoever they might have been, had made an effort with the garden – because it contained a diverse variety of flora – but Meredith's family had left it untended during their occupancy, and it had become a wild jumble of overgrowth competing for space. Once in a while, their father would trim away at the edges so that they could at least reach the front door, but that was all. Meredith did occasionally muse over making it a project for herself to renovate it, but she never quite found the time. She already had her work cut out tending to Pativa's garden, let alone all those hours she spent foraging for herbs.

When they entered the house, Carmaestre rushed straight over to their mother to tell her about her encounter with Jediah. Meredith removed her boots and hung her coat on the rack before she entered the kitchen and sat at the table.

"But he said he'll come tomorrow!" Carmaestre said, with great animation, while their mother tended to the meal she was cooking over the hearth.

Nagella, their mother, shook her head. "He's frivolous, just like his father! Where either of them gets it from escapes me…" she shrugged and then saw Meredith was there, and her face softened. "Hello, darling," she said, walking over and kissing Meredith on the cheek. "How was your day?"

"It was fine," Meredith replied. She didn't elucidate. Her mother often displayed an interest in Meredith's vocation, but Meredith suspected she was merely trying to be courteous. After years of fruitlessly pressuring her daughter to demonstrate gifts she didn't naturally possess, Nagella had spent the latter part of Meredith's life overcompensating. Meredith understood her mother was likely trying to make up for all those years of anguish she had caused, but it sometimes felt a little suffocating.

A few minutes later, their father Stanvel came home,

and the four of them ate together. As usual, Carmaestre and Nagella dominated the conversation whilst Meredith and her father ate quietly.

Meredith often thought her mother and father an odd pairing. Her mother, like many in her family, had an otherworldliness about her. She had those same strange violet eyes. She was also obsessed with a lifelong goal that she had set for herself to see the arcane legacy of her family come to fruition.

Meredith's father, on the other hand – with his broad shoulders and sandy hair – was much more mundane. He was a quiet person. A local woodcutter and fisherman whom Nagella mated with shortly after she moved to the village. Most people thought him simple, but Meredith suspected there was more to him than people assumed. He had startling green eyes, and they spoke volumes more than his lips ever did.

Despite the contrast between them and the fact that they never seemed to have much to say to each other, Meredith sensed that her parents loved each other dearly.

After they had finished their meal, Nagella turned her gaze to the window and smiled.

"I have a surprise for you all…" she announced.

"What is it?" Carmaestre asked, her eyes lighting up. "Are we going to Jordayne again?"

Nagella silenced her by raising her hand. "No, Carmaestre. Calm down. I would like you all to come with me outside."

Meredith and Carmaestre turned to each other with shared curiosity. Neither of them had any idea why their mother would ask them to do such a thing at this time of the day, but they followed her regardless.

Nagella opened the door. It was unusually dark that night, but the light from within the house lit up the front of their garden.

"Look up," Nagella said, pointing at the heavens.

Meredith did so and saw lots of stars glistening above her. Teanar – the largest out of the moons – was nowhere to be seen, and Lumnar existed as a mere crescent. The third moon, Lunid, was almost full but steadily creeping towards the horizon and soon to be swallowed by the hills.

"Teanar has just reached his vanishing phase," Nagella said to them. "We will see darkness twice more before he appears again." She then pointed to Lumnar. "*He* is in his final stage of horning and will not shine tomorrow."

Finally, Nagella turned to the hills on the west, where Lunid was rapidly dropping from the sky. Lunid was not only the smallest but the most fleeting of the lunar brotherhood. On long winter nights, one could sometimes watch Lunid disappear only to re-emerge in the early hours of the morning.

"It will be not long after this time tomorrow when he flies away again," Nagella said. A radiant, almost reverent sentiment then illuminated her violaceous eyes.

Meredith sucked in a breath when the implications of what her mother was saying became realised.

Tomorrow, there will be no moons in the sky, and their world will turn dark. Such an event was rare. So rare that Meredith had never seen it before.

She had certainly not thought it would happen so early in her lifetime.

She knew what it meant, though; their village – like everywhere else in Sharma – would mark the occasion by holding a festival.

One known as Gazareth's Night.

*   *   *

"You did well yesterday, Meredith."

Meredith lifted her eyes from the book she was reading. It was the next day, and Pativa had just sent Colben and his mother back home. The boy had made a speedy recovery and woke up that morning quite restless.

"You taught me," Meredith replied, feeling her cheeks turn red. Compliments embarrassed her because she didn't know how to respond to them.

"Yes, I did," Pativa agreed. "And yesterday, you

proved yourself worthy of all the time I have invested in you. You are almost ready. Within a year, you could move somewhere and tend to a community of your own."

Meredith opened her mouth to reply but found herself struggling to find the right words. The thought of moving somewhere else made her nervous. She didn't know where she would go.

"Have you given it any thought?" Pativa asked.

"No..." Meredith admitted. "I haven't..."

Pativa's eyebrows narrowed as she scrutinised her niece. "Most young striplings like you have heads brimming with ideas of where they want to go and what they want to do. The majority are destined to be unfulfilled, of course, but it is healthy to have dreams and aspire to something. *You* are one of the ones who truly has options, Meredith."

Pativa waited for a response, but Meredith still didn't know what to say.

"What about Jediah and Carmaestre?" Pativa asked. "You're close to them, aren't you? Maybe you could leave with them once they're mated. The thought of parting with them makes you feel sad. I can tell. You haven't been yourself since they were Promised."

"No!" Meredith found herself blurting. She didn't know why; it was just her knee-jerk reaction. She then sighed and shook her head. "I don't desire to go with them. It would be... strange. I don't know what I want to do, Pativa. I wish things could just stay the same. *Why* do they have to move away?"

"They have to go," Pativa said firmly. "They can't get mated and start a family here. People would talk."

The mention of them starting a family conjured an image in Meredith's mind. Carmaestre and Jediah, surrounded by an entourage of children; all with pale skin, black hair, and purple eyes. Her sister had that unflappable smile upon her face as she wrapped her arms around Jediah and rested her chin on his shoulder. An idyllic cottage with a sea view behind them.

And twinned with it was the fear that Meredith would

grow old alone. Just like Pativa.

"I know…" Meredith said. She would never admit it, but a part of her hated her mother for pressuring her sister and cousin to elope. Nagella's determination to see the prophecy of their bloodline come to fruition bordered on obsession.

Jediah and Carmaestre could never start a family in Parleyban. They would have to move somewhere new, where no one knew of their kinship. It was said that people who mated with those of the same blood risked bearing sickly children. Her mother claimed that this was not the case for them because of their divine ancestry, but Meredith doubted people would believe them if they tried to explain that to the villagers. Their bloodline was a closely guarded secret.

"I can't go with them, Pativa," Meredith said. "It would feel like I was clambering onto the back of *their* wagon. I want to find my *own* path… Don't worry about me. I just need time to think it through."

"You get to choose who to love," Pativa said. "Be glad of that, Meredith. Your sister hasn't been given any options… young girl she is, as well."

"Carmaestre is happy with it," Meredith replied, feeling defensive for her mother despite her own mixed feelings. "I think she wants to mate with Jediah. And she *is* the right choice. She's got the family Blessings. The legacy is strong in her."

"Let's just pray to the gods that she stays that way…" Pativa said. "She's young to shoulder such responsibility…"

*   *   *

Meredith ate supper with Pativa that afternoon, which came as a welcome respite. Meredith felt much more at ease with her aunt than her immediate family. It was always peaceful at Pativa's place. There was no pressure to fill the air with pointless chit-chatter. Pativa was the only member of the family with whom Meredith could sit with in complete silence without feeling awkward.

In her time, a number of people had told Meredith that she held a resemblance to her mother, but she didn't believe it. With her chestnut hair, hazel eyes, and ability to heal, it was her aunt whom Meredith thought she took after. Growing up within such an enigmatic family could be alienating at times. Meredith wasn't sure how she would have coped without Pativa.

They left for the village when the sky was beginning to turn hazy, and when they arrived, the celebrations had already commenced. Merveln, the owner of the tavern, had hauled some kegs outside for the occasion and was selling cups of ale. The path through the middle of the village had been lined with large candles, and children were playing.

As she walked through it all, Meredith heard snippets of conversation. Most of the villagers were busy speculating whether the festival would actually occur and they would truly see a moonless sky. An elderly man mentioned a false alarm that happened years ago; a night when everyone *believed* it was going to happen, but Teanar unexpectedly began to wax just as Lunid was due to vanish.

Meredith looked up at the sky. Her mother's prediction seemed promising; Lumnar had vanished since yesterday, and the only object in the heavens – apart from the stars – was Lunid, who was making his gradual descent.

Just then, Carmaestre ran to them.

"Aunt Pativa!" Carmaestre squealed as she collided into her.

Meredith was forced to cover a hand over her mouth to hide her amusement; Pativa was not one for physical displays of affection, but she was doing her best to hide her discomfort. Carmaestre, on the other hand, was utterly oblivious.

"I haven't seen you for *ages*!" Carmaestre exclaimed as she pulled away.

"Hello, Pativa," Nagella said, greeting her next. Instead of forcing her into an embrace, she merely patted her on

13

the arm. "It's good to see you again. I trust Meredith has been behaving herself?"

"She's doing very well," Pativa praised. "I'll make a Devotee of her yet."

The two older women chatted. It had been a while since they had last seen each other, so they had much to catch up on. Meredith left them to it and walked over to greet Jediah and his mother, Leylee. They were standing by a tree, and Jediah had a hand on her shoulder. They looked more like brother and sister than mother and son. Leylee was supposed to be only a few years younger than Nagella, but she was small, had an almost girl-like figure, and seemed to have not aged a single day in all the years Meredith had known her.

"Mother," Jediah whispered into her ear. Leylee was staring at a group of kids who were playing a few yards away with a faint and distant smile on her face. She seemed fascinated by them. "It's Meredith. Say hello to Meredith."

Leylee dreamily rolled her head and looked at Meredith. Of all the members of their family, Leylee had the most hypnotic eyes.

"Hello, Aunty Leylee," Meredith said.

Leylee smiled. "Hello, Meredith. It is pleasant to see you."

"Where are the others?" Meredith asked, looking around and realising that both of their fathers were missing.

"Godrei has left us…" Leylee whispered. "He is squiddling again."

"He's just entertaining some kids back there," Jediah elucidated, thumbing behind his shoulder. "He brought out his hat, cards and everything. You know what he's like…"

Meredith laughed. "I wish to see…"

"Sure! We'll come with you," Jediah offered, turning to his mother. "Won't we."

"Mum!" Meredith called. Nagella, Pativa and Carmaestre had huddled together and were still chatting.

"We're just going to watch Godrei. He's telling stories again."

Nagella rolled her eyes. "Must you encourage him?"

"I don't think he needs much encouraging," Pativa said dryly.

"But Jediah. The Festival!" Carmaestre said, looking up at the sky. "It'll start soon."

"We have a while yet," Jediah smiled. He pointed to Lunid, which was still glowing in the sky. "And we're not likely to miss it. The sky isn't going to run off anywhere!"

Carmaestre giggled, and she skipped over to kiss her betrothed on the cheek. "You're funny! Just look after my sister, okay?"

"Will do."

Jediah guided Leylee by the hand through the crowd of villagers, and Meredith followed. They skirted around a few buildings and trees until they came across a cluster of people gathered by the side of the river. In the middle of the throng was Godrei and, at the moment Meredith arrived, he was busy juggling glowing orbs of light while the children around him clapped and cheered. Even the adults standing at the back had smiles on their faces as they watched.

Leylee became instantly enthralled by her husband's display, racing to the back of the crowd and clapping her hands gleefully.

Godrei eventually brought the spectacle to an end by tossing the spheres into the air and making them all vanish in a flash of light. He then took a quick bow, and the children chanted for more. He pretended to be nonchalant – and in need of coaxing – but it was no secret, from the smile on his face, that he was enjoying himself and just riling up the crowd.

"Tell us another story!" one child called out.

"Juggle knives!" another one yelled. "Like last summer!"

"Sing The Rhyme of Lord Ropert!" wailed a small girl.

Godrei gestured with his hands for them to quieten, and

some of the parents intervened. Once the children had calmed down, Godrei turned his head up to the sky.

"The Night of Gazareth looms upon us," he said. His voice was almost like a whisper, yet Meredith could still hear him. "So, it is time for me to tell you the story behind this eve of festivities. Who wants to hear the tragic tale of Verdana and Gazareth?"

There followed an eruption of applause, and some of the children squealed in delight. Meredith turned to Jediah, and they grinned at each other; this was one of their favourite stories. It had been told to them countless times since they were children but never lost its intrigue. "Tell me of my foremother!" Leylee cried out, turning several heads. Jediah grabbed her shoulders and made a hushing sound to her ear.

"Yes!" Godrei said, his vivid blue eyes lighting up as he pointed to his wife. "Verdana is the mother of humanity. The sacred deity to which we *all*," he said, casting gaze across the circle of people around him, "owe our existence. But her tale isn't merely one of grandeur. She went through much strife before she ascended to the glory that she is today!"

Everyone stared at the cloaked man in rapt attention as he began the story.

"Lania, Ignis, Vaishra, and Ta'al," Godrei began, listing the four primal gods. "Earth, Fire, Water, and Air. This world we live upon is their creation. Lania and Vaishra were the first. Sisters, created side by side. Lania was the earth: serene and stable, the ground we rest upon, whereas Vaishra was the oceans: mercurial, fluid, all feeling, ever-moving," he engrossed the audience into his tale further by making dramatic movements of his arms, rocking them back and forth like waves of the sea as he described Vaishra.

"Their existence was a peaceful one, at first, but one that lacked exuberance until the dawning of the first day. When Ta'al stirred up the seas with the first breath of wind, and Ignis appeared as a ball of fire in the sky…"

Godrei summoned a glowing orb of fire from his hand

and sent it floating above the heads of the crowd.

"Vaishra and Ta'al fell in love, as was destined, and, with their love, they created Manveer. A weather god who ruled over the clouds and rain. From that day on, the two of them lived in harmony," Godrei explained, and then his expression darkened, and his voice went gloomy. "Ignis and Lania fell in love too, but their relationship wasn't so amicable…

"The first time Ignis lit up the heavens, Lania raised herself to meet his warmth. From this first union, molten earth burst forth from within her. This was Lania's first offspring, and his name was Vuule. He ruled over the mountain highlands, between the land and blue. But, after this first act of creation, the harmony between Lania and Ignis became turbulent. Their love was tumultuous. When it was dark, Lania missed his light, but in the midday heat, his passion seared her.

"One night, the winds of Manveer caressed Lania, and she could not resist the cool breath of his touch after a day of Ignis's fiery intensity. The weather god made love to Lania, stirring up dust from the ground into a sandstorm."

Particles of light burst from the palms of Godrei's hands, causing many eyes to widen. He manipulated the glowing orbs of magic he had conjured, willing them to swirl around him as he spun his body into a dance. The crowd clapped and cheered.

Eventually, Godrei's dance came to an abrupt finish, and he drew to a halt. The shimmering particles he had created with his magic fell like rain, coalescing into three separate piles.

"The evidence of Lania's act," Godrei said, gesturing to the three mounds at his feet. "At sunrise, Lania tried to hide them from Ignis, but his light illuminated them…"

With a wave of Godrei's hand, the three mounds at his feet began to glimmer with blue light.

"Lania pleaded the fire god for forgiveness, and Ignis could never resist his love. He let her three children live but cast them up into the sky." Godrei continued, furthering the visual demonstration by waving his hands and making the shimmering piles of dust by his feet rise into the air and coalesce into orbs. They swirled around him. "And, from that day, they were charged with the task of illuminating the welkin in Ignis's absence. He bid each one to take a different route through the sky. So that they could spread their watchful gaze upon Lania in times of darkness."

Godrei shook his head. "But there was one flaw in Ignis's plan. Every now and then – perhaps only once or twice each generation – there is a fleeting moment where none of the moons is present, and the world is plunged into darkness. During these moments, Lania is free from their eyes.

"And it was on such a night," he continued. "That Lania met Gazareth. He was one of the Others. A new tribe of gods who threatened the tranquillity the Ancients maintained over the world. Lania had been warned by Ignis to stay clear of them but, when she laid eyes upon Gazareth for the first time, she fell in love with him. He was charismatic, mysterious, and enticing. He seduced her in the darkness, and, by the morning, he was gone. It wasn't long after that when Lania realised that new life was growing inside her.

"She gave birth under a dark night when only Lunid was in the sky. The first body to emerge from her womb were a pair of conjoined twins, which she named Flora and Fauna. Despite being joined, they were fair-haired and comely, like herself, so she disguised them as the sires of Ignis."

Godrei paused for a brief moment to let that statement hang in the air. When he did continue again, his voice took on a darker tone.

"But, as soon as the third child crawled out from her, Lania looked at the newborn and knew she could never disguise her as a child of Ignis. With her dark hair and alien splendour, there could never be any doubt she had the seed of the Others within her. Lania named her Verdana and hid her in a cave deep underground, hoping that Ignis would never find out.

"For a time, peace continued. Flora and Fauna grew to be extremely beautiful, and they brought abundant life to the world. But Lunid," Godrei said, pointing at the small moon as it edged its way closer to the horizon. "Had witnessed the birth, and he was scared of Ignis's wrath. Eventually, the fear of his master prevailed, and he told him."

Godrei clapped his hands together, and sparks of energy burst into life, fulminating around him and colliding into each other. "Igniting the Great War between the Gods! The Ancients and The Others fought each other! Lava spewed from the mountains! Thunder tore across the skies! Rocks fell from the sky!" he exclaimed whilst manifesting illusions to demonstrate each event. "Waves from the ocean rent the land asunder! Nowhere was safe!"

And then, Godrei clapped his hands together again, and the magical display came to an abrupt end. The air around them darkened, and Meredith looked towards the horizon and saw that only a horn of Lunid was visible now. The rest of it had vanished behind the hills.

"By the end of the war..." Godrei said. "Almost all of the gods were weakened. All of them, except for Vaishra and Verdana. For Verdana had never left her cave, and the goddess of water could not find it within herself to fight. In the morning, the two of them emerged and saw the desolation around them. Vaishra took the younger goddess under her wing. The world saw its first autumn; the trees lost their leaves, the animals hid in their burrows, the sky became covered in clouds, and the air turned cold. But it was during this time of desolation that Verdana brought something new to the world. She created humanity, and the other Ancients were too weak to stop her.

"And that," Godrei finished. "Is the story of Gazareth's Night."

*   *   *

Lunid vanished shortly after that, and the Festival began. Godrei's audience dispersed. Most made their way to the main street of the village. Meredith, Jediah and Leylee followed the congregation, reuniting with the rest of their family outside the tavern, where it seemed the entire population of Parleyban had gathered.

It wasn't often Meredith had an opportunity to socialise with the other villagers, so she made the most of it. But she had, as usual, to be very careful about what she said when it came to matters of herself and her family. Her father let her drink a few cups of ale that night and, by the time Meredith had finished her fourth, everything began to turn hazy.

Someone had built a bonfire by the side of the river, and Meredith went and sat by it, along with her family and some of the other villagers. She leant back and looked at all the stars twinkling above her. She was fascinated by them. She had never seen so many before.

When Meredith sat up again, she noticed that Leylee was staring into the flames. Her lips were moving, and at first, Meredith thought she was trying to say something, but when she leant closer to listen, she realised that none of it was coherent.

"Leylee," Meredith said, placing a hand on her shoulder. "Are you okay?"

Leylee looked at Meredith briefly and then turned back to the fire. "The darkness will bring ruin," she said. "But that's not all. The fire… it speaks…"

Meredith looked around to see if she could find any other members of her family, but it seemed that whilst she had been staring at the sky, they had all wandered off.

"I seek answers…" Leylee whispered.

She crouched on all fours and crawled towards the fire.

"No!" Meredith yelled, wrapping her arms around her aunt's waist and trying to pull her back, but her aunt was surprisingly strong for her size. Leylee reached the fire and placed a hand on the charred embers.

Meredith let out a scream. "Help!" she cried. "Help!"

Her uncle then appeared.

"Leylee!" Godrei exclaimed as he grabbed her by her shoulders. "What are you *doing*?!"

He tried to pull her back, but Leylee struggled against him, her hands clawing at the air like a cat.

"Stop it!" she wailed. "I need to know! I need to know!"

Nagella and Pativa appeared after that, and Leylee kicked and fought. It took the efforts of all four of them to pull her away from the fire, but once they did, Meredith looked around them and noticed that dozens of villagers had witnessed the incident and were now staring. Some of them began to whisper to each other.

"Let's get away from here..." Nagella said, grabbing Leylee.

Meredith helped the others guide Leylee away from all the people.

"Her hand is burnt," Pativa said, examining Leylee's palm once they had privacy. "It shouldn't scar if I treat it soon..."

"Why did you do that?" Godrei said, his eyes glistening with concern. He placed his fingertips under Leylee's chin to make her look up at him, but she turned her head away and sobbed.

"You've drawn a lot of attention to us!" Nagella narrowed her eyes at Godrei. "Why weren't you watching her!?"

"She's been better recently!" Godrei argued. "I don't know where this has come from..."

"I need to get her back to mine!" Pativa interrupted them all. "You two can argue another time! I need to treat her!"

"I'll come with you," Godrei said.

"Do you want me to help?" Meredith offered.

"No," Pativa shook her head as she and Godrei began to lead Leylee away. "It's just a burn, Meredith. You enjoy the Festival."

Meredith then found herself alone with her mother.

"The lineage of our family is not always a blessing," Nagella said as they watched the three of them walk away. "A part of me is glad that you have been spared from it all, Meredith…" She shook her head. "She used to be the most gifted of us all, you know. Me and your sister, we have the magic, but Leylee… she could *see* things."

"She said something bad was coming…" Meredith whispered.

Nagella shook her head. "Pay it no worry. Leylee had so much potential, but she lost herself in dreamland. You can't take much she says seriously, these days."

* * *

When Meredith made her way back to the street, the festival had transformed so dramatically it was a little unsettling. Most of the children had disappeared by then, and the candles were starting to dwindle. Meredith almost stepped upon two people who were on the ground together, and she leapt back, shocked to realise that it was a man and a woman, and he was between her legs, thrusting into her. A mere few feet away, two other people were pressed up against the wall of a building, their mouths joined and their hands exploring. All around her, pairs of villagers were locked in intimate embraces and tearing each other's clothes away. Meredith stared at the scene with her mouth hanging open, barely believing her eyes.

She remembered a lesser-known tradition of Gazareth's Night; it was an occasion where men and women could pleasure with any one of their choosing, without reprisal from their mated or betrothed.

Meredith had thought it no more than a myth until then. She had certainly not been expecting a turn as dramatic as this.

She was pulled out of her stupor when she saw her sister. They ran to each other.

"Meredith," Carmaestre exclaimed. "What happened to Leylee? I heard something!"

"It was just a burn. Pativa and Godrei are looking after her," Meredith replied.

"But someone said–"

"Don't worry about her. She'll be fine," Meredith said, touching Carmaestre's arm. "Do you know where Jediah and the others are?"

Carmaestre shook her head.

"Let's go home then," Meredith said. "I think I've had enough of this Festival…"

Carmaestre hesitated and looked around them. "I don't think I want to go home…" Carmaestre said, unable to look Meredith in the eyes. "You know what tonight is… I'll be mated soon. One man for the rest of my life. Tonight is the one night I can…"

Meredith opened her mouth to object, but her sister had already turned and begun to run away. "See you in the morning, Meredith."

*   *   *

After a quick search of the village, Meredith could only find her father, whom she discovered pressed up against a tree with a woman who was not her mother. Meredith turned away from the sight in dismay and decided that she'd had enough. She pulled one of the candles from the ground and began to make her way home.

The walk back to her house was a familiar one – Meredith made it almost every day – but it felt like a different world in the darkness of the festival. The tiniest sound caused her heart to race. Her candle cast barely enough light for her to see the ground beneath her feet, so she had to step carefully to not trip over any of the roots or undergrowth. She missed the moons.

The ale she drank finally got the better of her, and she lost her footing. Meredith stumbled and tried to regain her balance only to fall, landing on her back.

The candle went out, plunging her into darkness. Tears streamed from her eyes, and she let out a wail, striking the ground with her fist.

She lay there for a while, feeling very sad but not knowing why.

Eventually, Meredith became aware of a ball of glowing light hovering further down the pathway and looked at it. It was floating towards her. As it got closer, she saw Jediah's face.

"Meredith?" he said, pausing a few feet away. He stared down at her. "Are you okay?"

"I'm fine," Meredith said, wiping her cheeks with the back of her hand and forcing a smile. "I just fell."

Jediah held his hand out to her, and she reached for it. He helped pull her back onto her feet.

"I heard something happened to my mother," Jediah said. "Were you there?"

"Don't worry," Meredith replied. "It's just a burn. She's at Pativa's. With Godrei. They're looking after her."

"Oh…" he said. "What are you doing here, then?"

"I was just walking home," Meredith said.

"I've had enough of the Festival too…" Jediah admitted. "Shall I walk you?"

"Yes," Meredith said, feeling a wave of gratitude. "Thank you."

With an arm around her shoulder, he guided her through the trees. Meredith felt safe now she was with him – the light he summoned lit up the way, casting the trees with an eerie glow.

"Where's Carmaestre?" Jediah asked.

Meredith closed her mouth tightly to stop herself from saying anything. She shook her head.

"I think I know…" Jediah said. "Try not to judge her, Meredith. It's Gazareth's Night."

"It doesn't bother you?" Meredith asked.

"Our mating was arranged," Jediah stated. "They say that love comes in time with such pairings, but I haven't given it much thought yet in all honesty. I just want to…" He paused. "Enjoy being young. Whilst I can."

"I will miss you," Meredith admitted.

"I will miss you too, Meredith…" Jediah said. He then stopped, and they looked at each other. Jediah opened his mouth again to say something else but hesitated. A nervous sensation crept into Meredith's spine and made its way into her chest. Whatever was going on between the two of them that moment, she desperately wanted to stop it. But she couldn't. She stared into his eyes and found herself unable to look away.

He leaned forward, parting his mouth. Meredith closed her eyes.

Their lips met. Meredith kept her eyes closed. As if, by not looking, she would make what they were doing less real. Less wrong. Jediah pulled her in closer, and Meredith felt the warmth of his body against hers.

She couldn't resist him anymore, and some crazed part of herself she didn't even know existed took over.

*   *   *

The things which happened next were a blur. They were on the ground, and Meredith pulled away Jediah's tunic because she craved to feel his bare flesh against hers. Neither of them was experienced or knew what they were doing. It was clumsy yet blissful and perfect in every way.

It was only when it was over – when Meredith opened her eyes to see Jediah looking down upon her, with his naked body pressed against hers – that she fully realised what had just happened.

"What have we done?" Meredith whispered into his ear.

*   *   *

They lay together for a while and stared up at the stars. Meredith never wanted it to be over, but she knew that it would not be long until Lunid appeared again, and this moment would become a secret she could only hold in her memory.

"I love you, Meredith," Jediah whispered. "I always have. The day that your mother Promised me to Carmaestre was… difficult for me."

"You shouldn't say that," Meredith said as she stroked his chin. "We need to forget this happened."

"But why should we?" Jediah flinched, looking at her. "You are the oldest. It should have been *you*. That's the way it was always done."

Meredith ran her hand across his chest, and her fingers came across the chain dangling from his neck. She looked at the purple stone attached to it. It was softly glowing. The Stone of Vai-ris. The precious family heirloom.

Meredith's mother said that it once belonged to the goddess herself. That Gazareth gifted it to Vai-ris when the Ancients condemned her to live a mortal life.

"Why do you think it hasn't chosen someone for so long?" Meredith asked. It had been eleven generations since the Stone last awakened and someone from their family had inherited the powers of Vai-ris. In that time, it had passed through many hands, but its powers remained dormant. Jediah had been bequeathed the artefact by their grandfather when he was a baby.

Jediah sighed. "I don't know..." he said. "I don't think it has anything to do with arranging marriages to strengthen the damn bloodline, though. Maybe the powers of Vai-ris are just not *needed* in the world at this point in time, and, when they *are*, it will happen."

Good luck telling Carmaestre that, Meredith thought. Her sister seemed to believe that if she got her hands upon the Stone, she would find a way to awaken it. Once, she'd said to Meredith that when she and Jediah were mated, the heirloom would belong to her as well. Meredith had tried to explain to her that it probably didn't work like that, but when Carmaestre got things into her head, they were often hard to drive out.

"We should go," Meredith said, reaching for her clothes. "I don't want Lunid to catch us."

*   *   *

The following morning, Meredith left the house early because she couldn't face her mother and sister. She went straight to Pativa's place.

"How's Leylee?" Meredith asked her aunt.

"She's fine," Pativa replied. She was sitting at the table. "She and Godrei left a while ago. You just missed them."

Meredith noticed there was a pot simmering over the hearth and recognised the smell wafting from it. Neytherleaf; a herb with contraceptive properties.

Neither of them said anything when Pativa filled herself a cup.

A few minutes later, Pativa left the house to make a trip to the village, and Meredith drank some of it herself. The first time, it came back up, so she poured herself another.

*   *   *

After that night, Meredith did her best to avoid Jediah – the sight of him was too painful for her to bear. Whenever her mother invited Godrei and the family over for supper, she made excuses not to be there. She spent more and more time at Pativa's place, honing her craft, and she received much praise for all the hard work she poured into it.

One day, Meredith was walking home and passed Leylee at the bridge. Her aunt had a basket cradled beneath the crook of her arm and was smiling to herself in dream-like contentment as she made her way towards the village. It was the first time Meredith had seen her since the Festival, so she greeted her as they crossed paths.

Leylee's eyes lit up, and she skipped over to Meredith.

"Hello Leylee," Meredith said.

Leylee looked Meredith up and down and then placed a hand upon Meredith's belly.

"You will have two," Leylee whispered. "One will have my eyes and live between worlds. The other... his destiny is clouded... uncertain."

Before Meredith could voice any of the various questions going through her mind, her aunt's expression turned sour. She slapped Meredith across the face.

"That is for the strife you bring upon us!"

And then Leylee walked away, and Meredith stared at her. Too shocked to respond.

She didn't tell anyone about the meeting. By the time she reached home she wasn't even sure what exactly happened herself.

*   *   *

Two aeights later, Godrei and Leylee came to Pativa's for lunch, and Meredith could not find an excuse to be absent.

By this point, Meredith had begun to suspect she was carrying a child because she had missed her bleeding.

She worried that Leylee would tell everyone, but Meredith's hazy-headed aunt seemed to have returned to her usual blithesome self and didn't say anything.

When they left, Meredith retreated to her room and buried her face into her pillow. It was at this point that the gravity of her situation dawned upon her. She knew that it was still early enough for her to get rid of the life growing inside her – and do so with little risk to herself – but, for some reason, she couldn't bring herself to do it.

*   *   *

"You're pregnant," Pativa said.

Meredith froze with the spade in her hand. They were in the garden, pulling out the weeds, but Pativa had stopped and was now staring at Meredith with her arms folded over her chest.

Meredith tried to think of a reply but stammered. She knew there was no point trying to lie.

"How do you know?" Meredith whispered.

"I am a Devotee of Carnea," Pativa said flatly. "There isn't a bump yet, but your breasts have swollen." She stepped forward. "I have to say, I'm surprised. It was at the Festival, wasn't it? Don't worry, Meredith, people won't judge you. Quite the opposite, actually. Children conceived on Gazareth's Night are said to be special. But I have to ask; why didn't you drink some of that neytherleaf? When I left the house that morning, I left plenty enough of it in that pot so that you could drink some without causing yourself embarrassment."

"I tried…" Meredith whispered. "But I felt sick, and it wouldn't stay down. I tried and tried again. On the fourth time, I thought some of it stayed… but I guess it wasn't enough."

Pativa's face softened, and she put a hand on Meredith's shoulder. "You have to tell your family, Meredith. You know what they're like. They will know about it soon anyway. If your mother found out that I kept something like this from her, she would not be best pleased with me…"

The knot which had been ever-present in Meredith's belly recently tightened. Events were spiralling out of control, but she knew her aunt was speaking sense. This wasn't something that she could ignore. It wasn't going to go away.

"And the father?" Pativa said. "Who is he, Meredith?"

"I'll tell the father myself," Meredith moaned. "Please, Pativa. Give me some time with that one…"

* * *

The next thing Meredith knew, her aunt marched her back home, and together they told her family the news. Pativa was supportive, and she held Meredith's hand as she coaxed the announcement out of her.

Meredith knew that her aunt loved her – and was merely doing what she thought best – but, during that moment, she despised her.

Her family were surprisingly approving. Carmaestre ran over from the other side of the room to wrap her arms around her.

"Oh, Meredith!" Carmaestre exclaimed. "It was on Festival night, wasn't it? You dark old horse! Who is the daddy? He best be handsome! Tell me!"

"Meredith wishes to tell the father *first,* before she reveals…" Pativa stated firmly. "So try not to let word get out in the village about this just yet."

"I won't! You can trust me!" Carmaestre said, grinning. "Oh my gods! This means I'm going to be an auntie, doesn't it!" She turned to Nagella. "Can Jediah and I wait till she has had it before we leave?"

"We will discuss that later…" Nagella said measuredly. "Stop smothering her, Carmaestre! Give her some room," Nagella then gave Meredith a warm embrace. "Festival children are said to be special," she said. "This family has been blessed…"

Her eyes then went to Meredith's stomach, and there was something guileful in her expression.

Meredith had an inkling of what it was that her mother was thinking.

In Nagella's mind, a 'blessed' child would be the perfect mate for one of Carmaestre and Jediah's offspring.

Another way for the descendants of Vai-ris to strengthen their bloodline.

Meredith suddenly felt very sick, and she ran out of the door to empty her stomach in the garden. Pativa followed her and placed a hand on her back.

"Morning sickness…" Pativa said with a grimace. "It's started…"

*   *   *

The next day Meredith was at Pativa's, and she heard a loud thumping on the door. At the time, Meredith was sitting at the table with a book in her hand, pretending to read; she was not taking in any of the words because her mind was elsewhere. Pativa got up to answer it.

"Pativa!" Jediah panted as soon as she opened the door. He was out of breath from running. "Where's Meredith? I need to see her!"

Meredith froze at the sound of his voice. There could only be one explanation for this sudden appearance.

He knew.

"Yes, Jediah," Pativa said. "Is something wrong?"

"I need to speak to Meredith," Jediah said, stepping

inside. Meredith tried to keep her eyes glued to the table as he strode into the room, but she could see him in the corner of her vision. He was staring at her.

"Would you like some tea?" Pativa asked. "Maybe linden flowers and–"

"Meredith, I want to talk to you. Alone," Jediah said.

All Meredith could do was shake her head. She couldn't even look at him.

"I'm going to hazard a guess and say that Carmaestre told you the news?" Pativa said, crossing her arms over her chest. "We were going to wait for a while, but that girl has always had a loose tongue... You need not worry, Jediah. She's in good hands. We're all going to help her."

Jediah shook his head. "Meredith! Look at me. Why won't you look at me? We need to talk!"

"Oh my gods!" Pativa exclaimed. She slapped her hand over her mouth in sudden, terrible realisation, and her face whitened in dismay. She looked at both of them in horror. "It's *you*! Isn't it? Oh no. Please..." She then abruptly shook her head. "No, it can't be... tell me it isn't true..."

*   *   *

Meredith took a sip from the calming tea Pativa had made.

The three of them had gathered around the table. Jediah was to her right, and Pativa sat opposite her. None of them wanted to be the first to speak. Meredith just stared at her lap.

Pativa was the first to break the silence.

"How did this happen?" she asked. "What the blazes were you thinking?!"

Meredith turned her eyes to the window.

"It was the Festival..." Jediah said.

"I guessed as much," Pativa said. "And we all know the rules of the Festival, but I am not sure your family will quite see it that way, considering the circumstances..."

"We need to tell them," Jediah said, placing his hand on Meredith's. When he first touched her, she almost flinched but stilled herself. It felt strange, especially in the presence of Pativa, but Meredith needed the comfort. "I know they will be angry. But I don't care."

Pativa shook her head sternly. "You can't, Jediah. And you know it. You are Promised to Carmaestre, and she is Blessed. There has always been something... tempestuous about Carmaestre... and I am not sure what she would do."

"I am Blessed as well," Jediah reminded her. "I can protect us. I know it'll be hard. But we just need to explain to them–"

Pativa shook her head again. "There is also Nagella to consider, and you cannot pitch yourself up against her as well. However powerful you are. Meredith, your mother loves you more than you will ever know, but the legacy of Vai-ris has *always* come first. She would never let the two of you mate." Pativa then looked at Jediah. "The best you could possibly hope for is that after the initial anger of what you have done has blown over, she will *still* force you to elope with Carmaestre. She may even try to Promise Meredith's child to one of Carmaestre's when they are older."

"No," Meredith shook her head violently. "They would be brother and sister! That would be... *no*!" Meredith held her stomach protectively. "I will move away..."

The moment she spoke those words, Meredith put a hand to her mouth. The thought of running away scared her, but the consequences she faced if she stayed terrified her even more. Even if she and Jediah tried to keep it a secret, Meredith would still have to live the rest of her life within the chains of her mother and living a guilty secret. She could suffer through it if it avoided tearing the family apart but, as soon as Meredith thought about the child within her – one whom her mother considered 'blessed' – she knew she couldn't do that. She wanted her child to be free from all of this. To not be forced into mating someone they didn't even know was their part-sibling.

"I'm going to have to go…" Meredith sobbed. Tears streamed from her eyes. Her own words shocked her, but she knew they were true. It was the only way out of this.

"I'll come with you," Jediah said.

"No," Meredith shook her head. "You can't, Jediah. It will tear everyone apart. Forget about me."

"I can't!" Jediah said. "Even if I wanted to, I couldn't. I don't want Carmaestre. I want *you*! I can't lie anymore. I haven't even been able to look her properly in the eye since that night. I can't live with anyone but *you*, Meredith. I love you!"

He touched her face, and Meredith looked into his eyes. For a moment, everything else disappeared. She forgot that Pativa was there, watching. She loved him more than anything in the world. She knew that now. The love she had for her sister and the rest of her family had forced her to repress those feelings, but now that he had said it, she couldn't deny it anymore. She had a part of him growing inside her.

He leaned forward and kissed her, and she succumbed. She had been dreaming of the feeling of his lips every day since that night. She gave in to him.

And she knew that, from that moment, there was no going back.

When the kiss ended, Meredith turned her head and abruptly became aware – and conscious – of her aunt's presence again.

Pativa sighed deeply and ran her hands through her hair. "You two have put me in a very difficult position…" she said, looking at them. "The thought of crossing your mother and sister scares me to death, and the two of you running away together will leave no doubt in their minds over what has happened… but you are right. There is an innocent life growing inside you, and they deserve to be free from all this. You are like a daughter to me, Meredith, and ever since Jediah was Promised to Carmaestre, I have seen the change in you. Despite the brave face you put on, I knew that you were deeply unhappy. It was one of the reasons I taught you medicine. I hoped it would distract you. That you would find a mate of your own. But I just saw the way you looked at Jediah and, despite the terrible situation you are in, I have never seen you so happy."

Meredith wiped the tears from her eyes. Everything Pativa had just said was true. Meredith had never felt so loved in her life.

"I want better for you, Meredith..." Pativa said, reaching for her hand. "Which is why I am going to help you."

*   *   *

Four days later, Meredith rose early. She silently dressed and filled her bag with some of her possessions. She was careful with what she chose, as she knew these were the last things that she would be able to take with her. Over the last few days, Meredith had smuggled many of her belongings to her aunt's place. A little at a time to avoid suspicion. She couldn't take everything she owned, though. She was going to have to leave most of it behind.

On her way out of the house, Meredith tiptoed into her sister's room. Carmaestre was sleeping peacefully. Meredith crept up to her bedside and ran her fingers through her hair. She kissed Carmaestre's forehead.

As Meredith left, she knew that, despite the overwhelming love she held for her sister, after this day, Carmaestre was going to loathe her until her last dying breath.

Meredith could never see her again.

It was only when her house was out of sight that Meredith let herself cry. She rubbed the tears from her eyes as she walked through the trees, thinking about how she had never got the chance to say farewell to her father. She would never get a chance to explain. She had not spoken to her mother properly for a long time. She had been avoiding her as much as she could out of fear that she would sense Meredith's guilt.

When Meredith reached Pativa's place, her aunt and

Jediah were waiting for her outside the house. Jediah was wearing a pair of leggings and a brown tunic. Meredith looked at him longingly, barely believing that she was so lucky that she would get to spend the rest of her life with him.

He was worth all of this.

She embraced Pativa. When she pulled away, her aunt smiled reassuringly, but Meredith sensed she was afraid. It was a great risk her aunt was taking. No one could predict what Nagella would do if she found out that Pativa had aided them. It almost made Meredith change her mind, but then she thought of the child she was carrying.

Meredith then heard hooves padding across the ground and turned around to see Leylee guiding a black stallion from around the back of the house. Meredith gasped at the sight of her.

"Don't worry," Pativa said, touching Meredith's arm to reassure her. "Leylee turned up this morning. She knew, Meredith… somehow. She said she will keep it a secret, and she wanted to say goodbye."

Leylee smiled as she neared them and kissed Meredith on the cheek. "He is my gift to you…" she said, patting the horse's snout. "Take care of him. He likes apples and carrots and grass and when you stroke his mane." She then put her mouth to Meredith's ear and whispered. "Head south and then head west. And then south again. Keep going until you find a village with a brook lined with willow trees. They are in need of a medicine woman so they will accept you. One day, you will meet a man there. A handsome one. He will be from a place far away, too. His eyes will have the colour of clouds. He will guide your children to their destiny."

Leylee then breezed over to Jediah and whispered into her son's ear too. Whatever it was she said to him made his eyes widen for a brief moment, and then his face became sombre. When he realised that Meredith was looking at him, he pretended to smile.

"Let's go…" Pativa said, picking up their bags and

leading them over to the horse. "We will walk you down the hill, but no further. Leylee and I *must* be back home before they notice you are gone, or they will know we helped you."

*   *   *

Meredith held on tightly to Jediah's waist as he spurred the horse into a trot by flapping the reins. She turned around and looked at both her aunties. They were waving, becoming smaller and smaller. Tears leaked from Meredith's eyes and were stung by the cold wind. Eventually, the sight of the two women vanished.

"You're good at riding," Meredith commented as Jediah leaned forward, and the horse quickened its pace. She had always thought her cousin an indoorsy type of person, but he appeared to be guiding the horse with ease.

"Leylee made me take lessons when I was younger," Jediah said over his shoulder. "I hated it, but she said it was important. That, one day, I would have need for it…"

"What did she say to you?" Meredith asked. "Just before we left? She whispered something into your ear."

"Nothing…" Jediah said. "She was just saying goodbye."

Even then, Meredith knew that he was lying. But she had a strong feeling it was because he was trying to protect her.

Chapter 1

Shemet

Bryna woke up with a sudden lurch.

The sensation of being in the saddle of a horse – rocking back and forth as the creature galloped across the terrain – ended with the dream, and Bryna's mind sputtered back into the world of the waking. With a sharp intake of breath, she brought a hand to her chest as the vision's revelations became realised.

Whether her mother had sent those memories to her from the spirit world – where she now rested – or some divine force had gifted them to her from the *aythirrealm*, Bryna did not know. It was a peculiar experience for her to witness the events surrounding her conception. To finally see the faces of a family her mother had always been so secretive about.

Bryna had never known anything about them. Not even her father, who died shortly before she was born.

Before that dream, her family had been an abstract idea without meaning. Bryna had always known that she must have grandparents and other extended family members but, because she had never known them, she never had cause to think of them much or even consider the possibility that she may have missed out by not knowing them. During that dream, Bryna had particularly identified with Leylee – as she knew that sometimes it was hard to focus upon the mundane reality around you when subject to visions and sensations from the other side. She also knew what it was like for people to think you strange.

The resemblance between Jediah and Bryna's brother – Jaedin – was uncanny. Bryna's twin was the spitting image of their father in almost every way. Apart from the eyes. Those Jaedin appeared to have inherited from Stanvel.

Bryna's hand went to the Stone of Vai-ris hanging from her neck. She and Jaedin were never part of Nagella's plan but, after all the strife her ancestors had been through, the precious family heirloom had awakened again. Bryna had inherited the powers of Vai-ris.

But they came at a price. It had claimed her mortality, her freedom, and often her sanity.

She closed her eyes for a few moments and concentrated upon storing as much information from the dream as she could, in case it held any relevance which would serve her in the future. She wanted to fully comprehend and understand the things she had seen so that they wouldn't cloud her mind, like an incessant whirlwind kicking up dust in a storm. Focussing on the present was sometimes a heavy task when you were the Descendent of Vai-ris. When Bryna first awakened to her powers, her consciousness had been so foggy that, for a while, many thought she had lost her mind.

The present was that Meredith was dead. She was murdered by the Zakaras. Along with the rest of the people of the village Bryna grew up in. Bryna, and the small party of people she was with, were the only survivors. Carmaestre was now a bitter and twisted woman who would stop at nothing to destroy Bryna and regain the family heirloom. Carmaestre had helped create the Zakaras. A new species of monsters that now threatened the world.

Bryna reorganised these facts and then rested her head again. She closed her eyes. She needed to rest. She was in for a long day tomorrow, and she didn't want dreamland to catch her again.

*   *   *

In the morning, Sidry dressed swiftly and crawled from his tent, discovering that most of his companions had risen long before him. The twins, Bryna and Jaedin, were sitting on the grass eating breakfast while Kyra was busy dismantling her tent. Sidry caught Bryna's eye, and she smiled at him. He was just about to walk over to speak to her when a hand grabbed his shoulder.

"Sidry!" Rivan boomed, twisting Sidry round to face him. Rivan's dark hair was still wet from his morning wash in the river, and he was drying himself with a scrap of linen. "You've only *just* dragged yourself up? We've almost reached Shemet, Sidry! *Shemet!*"

Rivan pointed to the outline of the city ahead of them. He was excited, and he had good reason to be. After all the turmoil they had been through, they were finally about to enter the streets of Sharma's capital city. A place they would, hopefully, be safe.

In truth, Sidry was excited about seeing Shemet too, but he was also anxious. And he was dealing with feelings of guilt; to feel excited right now felt like an insult to the people who were no longer with them.

Sidry found it hard to understand Rivan sometimes. It seemed that nothing ever daunted his friend. Even when the Zakaras laid waste their village – and they lost their families, their homes, and everything they had ever known – Rivan had not let it affect his stride. He had met every challenge which came after that without hesitation. They were the same age and had been friends since before Sidry could even remember but, with his bold confidence, it had always felt like Rivan was a little older than him.

"Why didn't you wake me?" Sidry asked.

"I tried to," Rivan shrugged. "You kept making all these groaning noises. You best get ready. I think Baird wants to leave. And, to be honest, so do I."

Sidry hurried back to their tent and packed his possessions. It didn't take him long, for he didn't own much. Not anymore. He had left most of it behind when they fled from Jalard.

*   *   *

Once everyone was ready, they began to make their way along the river.

For the first half of the morning, the only activity Sidry saw was the occasional farmer tending to their crops or the odd chariot rolling past them. The city was just a shadowy outline in the background, the sun too low to make out most of its features.

As they drew closer, they passed some homely cottages by the side of the river – many of them with mills annexed to the side, spinning with the current. The city opened up around them. The riverside became a dock lined with rowboats. Men and women stood on the prows, yelled out tariffs for rides to numerous parts of the city. The other side of the road became a succession of merchant booths. It began to get very noisy.

"We're finally here!" Rivan said. "This is Shemet!"

"Aylen would have liked to see this," Sidry said, thinking of their friend, dead almost two aeights ago.

Rivan's dauntless disposition slipped for a moment, and Sidry saw sadness in his eyes. "He died to kill Shayam," Rivan said. "We won. Just keep that in mind… it helps. We saved Fraknar."

Sidry suppressed a cold shiver as he thought about Fraknar; all that remained of that town now was a land of ruins and a small number of survivors picking up the pieces. They managed to stop Lord Shayam, but it came at a heavy cost.

Aylen was no longer with them. And now, even though they had finally reached the capital, it was to warn the Synod that their nation was in grave danger.

"Shayam was just one of many," Sidry reminded him "There is a war coming."

They rode on in silence for a while, and Sidry took in more of the scenery around them. The sheer magnitude of Shemet's landscape was intimidating for someone who grew up in a village as remote as Jalard. There were structures in the distance that dwarfed all the architecture Sidry had ever seen.

At some point, he found his eyes drawn to one building in particular. It was on the other side of the river, fashioned from stones so large Sidry couldn't fathom how its builders had managed to haul them there, let alone assemble them. Rows of pillars lined its façade, and beyond its opening, an eye-catching statue of a bare-chested woman rested within the atrium.

"It's a temple for Lania," Jaedin said.

Sidry turned to the young man riding just ahead of him. "Really?" he asked. "How do you know?"

Jaedin pointed to the gap between two of the pillars, where three young women had gathered. "The priestesses are wearing brown. Brown is the colour of earth, and thus, it is Lania's colour."

"What about the one over there?" Sidry asked, pointing to another temple further upstream, which was smaller and capped with a domed cupola. This one didn't have a statue, but symbols were etched all over its outer walls. A congregation of men dressed in auburn robes were outside, chanting a hymn Sidry did not recognise, and incense burned from a large censer, clouding the air around its entrance.

Jaedin studied it for a while. "I think that is a temple of Manveer..." he eventually said. "The robes those monks are wearing are in his colours. Manveer is usually represented in reds and browns. Brown for the earth, and red to resemble lava; a glowing, red liquid which is known to erupt from mountains when he is angry. They say that it burns everything in its path until it eventually cools down and turns into rock. Imagine seeing that! Oh wait... I recognise those symbols on the outer wall. It is written in Ancient. It says–"

"Alright, Jaedin," Rivan groaned. "We get the point. It was just a question... no need for a lecture."

Sidry had actually been quite interested in what Jaedin had to say but decided to let it rest. It dawned upon him then that, after their recent experiences – travelling mostly through the wilderness and being forced to use their wits, strength and cunning to get by – they were now in a place where Jaedin held more dominion. He was educated and already knew much about this city.

"Okay, smartass," Rivan said a few moments later. He

pointed at a series of colossal buildings ahead of them that towered above all the others and dominated the backdrop of the city. "Could you tell me what *they* are?"

"I think that yellow building is the Synod," Jaedin replied. "It is made from sandstone, and almost three hundred years old. Inside is the Solus, which is the biggest chamber of any building in the known world. It can fit all of the Synod's two hundred Consil members."

"There's two hundred Consil members?" Sidry asked.

Jaedin nodded. "More. And those steps at the front of the building are where citizens queue for petitioning."

That's where we are heading, Sidry thought.

"The other buildings behind the Synod probably belong to the Academy," Jaedin continued. "The library, lecture halls, training grounds, residential areas, war rooms, other things. I am not quite sure which ones are which…"

"They're quite close to each other," Sidry noted.

Jaedin nodded. "The Academy is run and funded by the Synod. It is not just a centre of learning either; many of the Synod's Consil members are graduates from the Academy. There are also army barracks somewhere behind all of that. I don't think you can see them from here though."

"Oh my gods!" Kyra interrupted as her horse caught up with them. "Is that *really* the Academy, Jaedin?"

Jaedin nodded. "I think so."

"So, you've *finally* reached it," Kyra said, winking at Sidry and Jaedin. "Better late than never, 'ey?"

Anger swelled up in Sidry at that comment – he didn't appreciate *that* being a topic of jest – but he held his tongue because it was very possible Kyra had been trying to get a rise out of him.

It was whilst Sidry and Jaedin were on their way to the Academy that they were kidnapped… and then everything else happened. Sidry still had scars all over his body from what those people did to him.

Despite everything they had been through, Sidry still found Kyra irritating at times.

"I think Sidry and Jaedin will have more to be worrying

about than that damn Academy after we arrive…" Rivan grunted.

"I figured that…" Kyra shrugged. "*I* would still like to see the place though… maybe duel some of their oh-so-talented '*Chosen*'."

"They've had years of training over you…" Rivan said. "I wouldn't fancy your chances."

"We've slain hundreds of Zakaras and saved the world," Kyra bragged. "I doubt some *boys* who've been playing with sticks in a cosy little training ground are going to be able to keep up with us."

"I didn't say beating them would be a problem for *me*…" Rivan said.

"Oh my…" Kyra let out a sardonic sigh. "Was that a *challenge*?"

"As I have tried to drill into your thick skull a few times now," Rivan responded. "I think we're going to have a lot more to be dealing with than that ruddy Academy once we arrive at that Synod… but I guess if we *do* get some spare time at some point I'd be happy to show you how it's done."

Sidry sighed. But he didn't make a show of it – and it was genuine. It seemed that, no matter how much Rivan and Kyra had been through together, their rivalry endured, and neither of them would change.

"Quit it, you two!" Baird muttered and gave both of them one of his stony glares. It was an expression that was usually enough to evoke even Kyra's reticence. "We'll be at the gates soon. *Behave!*"

Baird then turned back around and continued riding. He was at the head of the group, as usual, with Miles beside him. Sidry stared at the back of Miles' head and narrowed his eyes. He wondered if Baird would make good on his promise and hand him over to the Synod once they arrived. When Miles first confessed to being a spy for the Gavendarians, Baird had only kept him alive because of the valuable information he held. He had fully intended to make him face trial for his crimes once they reached Shemet.

Since then, however, Miles had aided them through many of the ordeals they endured and been granted increased freedom in return. Was that enough for Baird to consider him redeemed?

Sidry hoped not.

"Are you okay, Sidry?" a soft voice said, pulling him out of his thoughts.

He turned his head and realised that Bryna had levelled her horse beside him. She looked at him, and as usual, Sidry found himself both flustered and magnetised by her peculiar beauty. Her face was pale and smoothly shaped, and her black hair seemed to glint with hints of purple when it caught the sunlight. It was her eyes which he found the most alluring, though. Those eerie and enigmatic irises often felt like they were looking *through* you rather than at you.

"I'm fine," Sidry lied. "How are you?"

"Relieved," Bryna replied. "Our journey is almost over... I will feel safer once we're at the Synod. You look sad, Sidry. Are you thinking about your parents?"

"How did you know?" Sidry asked, and an antsy feeling crept up his spine.

He had been thinking about his parents. All morning. He kept trying to push them out of his mind, but they lingered in the back of his consciousness.

It was like Bryna could read your thoughts sometimes, and it made him a bit uncomfortable.

"I was there the day you left for the Academy," Bryna reminded him. "Me and my mother came to wish Jaedin farewell, but no one came to say goodbye for you. I remember it... I also remember when Baird asked where your parents were, and you didn't answer. You seemed sad. I wanted to comfort you – make you feel better – but I didn't know you well enough."

"You remember that?" Sidry asked. The idea that Bryna had noticed him back then made him feel strangely honoured. She had always seemed unapproachable in Jalard. Her, the daughter of the medicine woman, and him, the son of a humble farmer.

Bryna nodded. "Why weren't they there?"

"Don't you already know?" Sidry asked.

"I don't know everything…" Bryna said. "Only what I can see and what the spirits tell me."

"Have my parents ever…" Sidry hesitated. "You know… spoken to you?"

"No," Bryna shook her head. "Not that I can remember…"

"What about in Fraknar?" Sidry asked, remembering all the familiar faces he had glimpsed that night when Bryna summoned souls of the dead. "There were so many… and some of them were from Jalard."

Bryna shook her head. "Maybe, Sidry… but it is as you said. There were many, and I am sorry, but I do not remember them all." She placed a hand on his arm. "The ones who come back are the restless ones with unfinished business. If I have not heard from them, it means they are at peace."

But it would be nice if they had thought to give me a message, Sidry mused, feeling neglected. *Some kind of goodbye…*

"You still haven't told me why they weren't there…" Bryna pressed.

"They didn't want me to go," Sidry whispered. "I am an only child." ***Was** an only child…* he corrected himself. "After my mum had me, she never had any more. Your mother said she'd gone barren. And my parents had a farm. It was my grandfather's before it was theirs and his father's before that. They wanted me to stay so I could look after it, but I never wanted to be a farmer. Not really. I did enjoy Baird's lessons but always thought I would just end up on the farm. And Rivan and Kyra were better than me anyway. But when I was Chosen by the Academy… well… it felt like a dream. I never thought it would happen but, when it did, I wanted it more than anything. I was selfish…"

"No, you weren't," Bryna said. "You had your own path to follow. If you stayed, you would have died with the others. The gods wanted you to live."

Does that mean they wanted my family and everyone else to die? Sidry thought, but didn't say it.

They rode in silence for a while.

"I still mean what I said, Bryna," Sidry whispered. "I don't care what you are. I still… care about you. And it is different to how I care about everyone else. You said before that you couldn't get too close to me because you wanted to be there for Kyra – that you thought that her seeing her friend happy with someone else might hurt after what happened between her and Aylen – but she's fine…" Sidry said, gesturing at her. Kyra was riding a dozen or so paces ahead of them, grinning as she chatted away with Jaedin.

"Do you really believe she is happy?" Bryna asked. "She lost her family. And then Dion. And then Aylen as well. Look closer… when Kyra smiles, and when she laughs, it doesn't always reach her eyes…"

*   *   *

After they crossed the river and reached the centre of the city, the roads became more crowded, and Jaedin had to concentrate very hard to navigate his horse through all the people.

The novelty of seeing Sharma's capital city for the first time had worn off, and he was beginning to feel disenchanted. He had read many books about Shemet – ones that detailed its rich history, its grand architecture and temples – and it had painted a picture in his mind of it being a centre of opulence.

But the reality was turning out to be somewhat less glamorous. Monumental buildings seemed to be outnumbered by shanty ghettos. Jaedin had imagined the citizens of Shemet to be erudite beings – educated, and finely dressed – but the street they were currently passing through was filled with sots and rag-clad peasants. Some of them were even sitting in the doorways of dishevelled buildings begging for money. The cloud of incense, wafting from one of the nearby shrines, didn't quite overcome the putrid smell of a sewage system that couldn't keep up with the demands of the population.

"Where is Fangar, anyway?" Rivan asked, looking around them. "I haven't seen that cavecrawler for a while."

"He went on ahead," Jaedin said. "He will meet us at the Synod later."

Fangar could never stay sitting upon a saddle for too long without growing frustrated, so earlier that morning he sold his horse to a farmer on the outskirts of the city so he could race on ahead.

"You don't think he's done a runner, do you?" Rivan asked.

"No!" Jaedin said and then realised that his reaction had been a little too explosive, so softened his voice. "He wouldn't do that…"

"Why don't you use your power to speak to him?" Rivan suggested. "Just to make sure he's not done a runner on us."

"The Stone of Zakar doesn't work on Fangar," Jaedin reminded him. "He's *not* a Zakara."

"He sure looks like one…" Rivan muttered, but Jaedin ignored him. While it was true that Fangar could shapeshift into a similar form, Fangar was not like the rest of them. He was still human in many ways. He had thoughts and feelings, and he still – unlike the other Zakaras – possessed free will.

It irritated Jaedin that the others still couldn't bring themselves to trust the man. He was a little wild by nature, and he could be unpredictable at times, but he helped them defeat Shayam. *That* was what Jaedin felt was most important.

Besides, it was partly the danger of Fangar which Jaedin found darkly irresistible.

"Someone could easily disappear in this city if they wanted to," Rivan said, surveying the scene around them. "Maybe, now we've helped him kill Shayam, we're no use to him anymore. He's left us."

"*No*," Jaedin shook his head. "You are wrong! Fangar

can smell me. That's how he found us in the first place, and it is how he will find us again…"

Rivan grunted sceptically.

Shortly after, the road became less clamoured, so Jaedin spurred his horse on ahead a little so that Rivan could no longer antagonise him. It seemed that the closer they got to the Synod, the cleaner the streets became. The buildings in the district they had just entered were grander and clad with marble. It almost resembled the Shemet Jaedin had always imagined in his head.

"Reality never quite meets expectation, does it…" a voice beside him commented.

Jaedin turned. Miles was now riding beside him.

"You only ever told me about the Synod and the Academy. The library. The temples," Jaedin replied. "You never mentioned the poverty, the dirty streets, the *smell*."

"I tried to. Actually," Miles chuckled. "But you were always much more interested in all the other stuff…"

Miles had an expression of fond nostalgia on his face, but Jaedin didn't know how to feel. Those years he spent in Miles' study – learning history and lore – had been happy for him too. But now, he knew them to be a lie. Even then, Miles was a spy.

"I know why you've come to talk to me, Miles," Jaedin said flatly. "So there is no need for pleasantries. Don't worry. If Baird hands you over to the Synod, and you face trial, I will keep your secrets."

"As sharp as ever, I see…" Miles said, smiling grimly to hide his nerves. Jaedin could see in Miles' demeanour that he was deeply anxious over what fate was to befall him when they arrived.

"No, I am just beginning to learn what you're really like," Jaedin said. "You've barely spoken a word to me for almost two aeights, so it wasn't hard to figure out that when you finally got round to it, you had a motive."

For a fleeting moment, it seemed that Jaedin's words had hurt him. Miles turned his eyes to the ground.

But Jaedin didn't know whether this display of guilt

was genuine or contrived. Jaedin had come to understand, during the past year, that Miles was an artful manipulator.

"Is it not possible for you to consider the notion that, maybe, the reason I haven't spoken to you since you and Fangar have become... involved... is because it is difficult for me?"

"I don't believe it," Jaedin said. He and Miles had kissed once. It wasn't something they ever talked about, but it lingered between them.

Jaedin used to suspect – wish, even – that Miles had feelings for him that mirrored his own, but Jaedin didn't believe that any more. He knew all too well now that Miles was very willing to play with people emotionally to achieve his goals. Jaedin wasn't going to let that happen to him again.

"If you truly have such a low opinion of me, then why aren't you going to tell them what you know?" Miles asked.

Jaedin sighed. In truth, he didn't know why. He didn't trust Miles anymore, but his former mentor still had a hold on him. One from which he wished he could free himself.

Miles was responsible for Aylen's death, and he had been much more instrumental in the creation of the Zakaras than he had previously admitted to the others, but Jaedin could not bring himself to hate him, no matter how hard he tried.

"If the others knew the full truth, they would kill you. And that would be a waste. You have valuable information, and you are more useful to us alive. It's purely pragmatic. Nothing more," Jaedin lied as he drove his horse forward, ending the conversation.

*   *   *

They reached the outer walls of the Synod shortly after. They were imposing and grey, rising out from the city and towering over twenty feet high.

Despite Jaedin's fervent denial when Rivan voiced his

concerns, he was relieved when they found Fangar waiting for them by the gate. The rogue was leaning against the wall with his arms folded across his chest. He smiled at Jaedin as they reunited.

"You took long enough…" he uttered.

"Too many ruddy people!" Jaedin complained. "The streets were packed."

"That's why I took the more direct route," Fangar responded, and he gestured to the 'path' of rooftops he had leapt across.

Jaedin smiled. "I bet the residents were happy…"

"None of them saw me," Fangar shrugged. "*You* could have joined, you know…"

Jaedin grimaced. Like Fangar, the things Shayam did to him had changed him in ways that were both a blessing and curse. Jaedin tried to keep his abnormalities hidden, though.

"You know I can't do that…" Jaedin whispered.

"You can't cage yourself up forever," Fangar whispered back. "Once you free the beast, it all becomes easier. Trust me."

"Wait here while I talk to the guards," Baird said as he dismounted. He then walked over to speak to the pair of men on the other side of the gate. They were both clad in chainmail but, beneath the ringlets, they wore yellow tunics bearing the crest of the Synod. Jaedin realised that they must be members of the Synod Sentinels.

"Why don't they just let us through?" Kyra grumbled impatiently.

"We might have to wait a while to get anything out of those blethering idiots…" Fangar warned.

"You've already tried?" Kyra asked.

Fangar nodded. "All they say is, 'petitioning is closed for today'," he said, putting on a whiny voice as he mimicked them.

Jaedin watched as Baird argued with the two Sentinels. At first, they merely shook their heads, and their expressions remained impassive, but then Baird's face turned red, and the exchange became more heated. The soldiers turned to each other, as if uncertain.

Eventually, they moved aside, and one of them opened the gate.

"Looks like they learned a lesson today," Kyra grinned as she spurred her horse into motion. "Don't mess with Baird."

She guided her steed through the gate, sparing a moment to mock the guards with a derisory wave as she passed through. Jaedin followed her. He looked at the yellow walls of the Synod as he entered the grounds. He could barely believe he was finally *here*. Seeing it with his own eyes.

And it was while Jaedin was admiring this monumental building – one that he had always longed to see – that he became aware of a tingling sensation in his forehead.

He sucked in a breath, realising it was the Stone of Zakar.

The artefact was trying to warn him of something.

Jaedin closed his eyes and assimilated his mind with the relic, listening to its peculiar language.

He sensed four malevolent presences nearby.

There were Zakaras here.

Jaedin opened his eyes, and a heavy feeling settled in his chest. All of the relief he had felt over finally reaching safety left him.

Jaedin was tempted to act there and then; use his Stone of Zakar to delve into the minds of the creatures and find out what their intentions were. Or kill them, even. But he knew that exerting the artefact's powers would cause his eyes to glow, and that was a spectacle he wanted to avoid when he was out in the open if he could help it.

I need to tell Baird, Jaedin decided, but more Sentinels appeared. A dozen of them. They emerged from the side of the building and, before Jaedin had a chance to grab the attention of their leader, Baird spurred his horse on ahead to speak with them.

They conversed for quite some time whilst Jaedin and his companions waited in silence. Sitting upon the saddles of their horses.

Eventually, three of the Sentinels separated from Baird and began to march towards Jaedin and his companions, readying their spears. For a very brief moment, Jaedin's heart lurched in his chest, but then he realised that it was Miles whom the uniformed men were marching towards, not himself. They formed a triangle around the scholar.

"Off your steed!" one of them bellowed. "*Now!*"

Miles' face fell with dismay, and he carefully lifted his leg over the side of his horse and lowered himself. Their spears followed Miles' every movement as he dismounted, never wavering more than a few inches away from his neck.

When Miles' feet touched the ground, he stumbled a little as he found his balance. His legs were shaking.

"Come with us," the Sentinel said.

Even though this was what Baird had always promised he would do, it still caught Jaedin by surprise. He didn't know how to feel as he watched the Sentinels escort Miles away.

"The rest of you, off your horses!" Baird said once he returned, taking charge of the situation again. His face gave away none of his feelings. "They will be taken care of, and these men will guide you to your rooms. I want you *all* to remain there until you are summoned."

Jaedin leapt from his horse and ran over to Baird, realising this was his last chance to tell him about the Zakaras.

"Baird!" Jaedin called. "I need to speak with you!"

Baird frowned at him. "Jaedin. I know you worship the ground he bloody walks on, but he's a *traitor*!"

"No Baird," Jaedin said. "It's–"

"I don't want to hear it!" Baird hissed. "It was my duty to report Miles, and I don't need to justify myself to you! Oh, and one more thing. You and Fangar are getting separate rooms. I'm not having that–"

"Mine and Fangar's business is none of yours!" Jaedin retorted, feeling angry.

"You are seventeen…" Baird shook his head. "And look at *him*… it's not natural. I tolerated your behaviour when we were on the road, but we are at the *Synod* now. I won't have the people here thinking I–"

"A girl from our village got mated when she was *fourteen*," Jaedin reminded Baird. "It happened just a few aeights before the…"

"That was different!" Baird muttered.

"*How?*" Jaedin challenged. "Just because I… because Fangar and I are sodds? Let's face it, it's not because he's older than me. Your real problem is–"

"I don't need to hear this!" Baird rasped. He looked at the Sentinels – standing only a few yards away – self-consciously. "That man is *dangerous*, Jaedin. You think that he is like you? He's not even human…"

"You. Need. Me," Jaedin said between gritted teeth. He pointed to the band on his forehead. The one that covered his scar. "You want me to help *you* in the future? Well… I have news. If you make life hard for *me*, by the gods, I will make life difficult for *you!*"

From the way Baird's eyes widened then, Jaedin realised he had just angered their leader like never before.

"We will speak of this later…" Baird uttered and then turned and walked away.

"Wait! Baird!" Jaedin yelled, running after him. "There's something else–"

"Just *go!*" Baird roared. "Leave me alone!"

"There are *Zakaras* here!" Jaedin yelled.

Baird halted and spun around, looking at Jaedin with wide eyes.

"Why didn't you tell me before?!" he hissed.

"I only just sensed them…" Jaedin responded, shrugging.

"Do you know what they are doing?" Baird whispered. "Why they are here?"

Jaedin shook his head. "No," he said, keeping his voice low. "I could try to find out, but my eyes will–"

"Don't do that!" Baird said, casting a glance at the Sentinels nearby. "How many are there?"

"Four," Jaedin said.

Baird looked at the Sentinels again and muttered a

curse under his breath. "Four shouldn't be too much of a problem…" he said. "We've dealt with more than that before."

"We need to take them out," Jaedin said, firming his voice. "*Now*. Otherwise, they might spread."

"Can't you just kill them?" Baird asked, motioning to Jaedin's forehead. "You know… like you did in Fraknar."

"I could *try*…" Jaedin said. "But it depends on what kind of Zakaras they are. They might try to resist… and if they do, things could get messy…"

Baird nodded thoughtfully. "Okay… look, just go to your room and wait for me. I will come as soon as I can. We'll figure out what to do together."

"But–"

"Don't do *anything* till *I* come to *you*!" Baird interrupted him. "We are in Shemet now, Jaedin. Things are different here, and we need to tread carefully. We can't just rampage our way around doing as we please anymore."

"What if–" Jaedin began only for Baird to cut him off again.

"I don't have time for this!" Baird exclaimed, gesturing to the Sentinels. "They're *waiting*! Just… keep an eye on the Zakaras, okay! See if you can find out why they're here, but don't do anything that might cause a scene. Don't tell the others about it either, as I don't want people to panic. I'll come find you as soon as I can!"

*   *   *

The Sentinels escorted Jaedin and his companions to a smaller building around the back of the Synod. Jaedin walked with his fists clenched by his sides. The residual anger from his confrontation with Baird lingered.

There were Zakaras here, yet Baird wanted Jaedin to sit and wait.

The soldiers allocated Jaedin a small room on the second floor. As soon as they closed the door behind them, Jaedin slammed his bags on the floor and sat upon the end of the bed. He could still feel the presence of four Zakaras – they existed as dots of malevolent energy within his radius – and it unnerved him.

Jaedin closed his eyes and called out to the crystal. It shimmered, and he felt the uncomfortable – but now familiar – sensation of the scar on his forehead opening as he used the artefact's powers.

Jaedin attempted to delve into the mind of the Zakara closest to him so that he could discover its purpose, but something blocked him from achieving assimilation. The creature had a peculiar energy signature. One that Jaedin had not come across before.

Jaedin tried the same with the other three creatures, but they were all the same. They had all been enhanced.

Jaedin sighed. Enhanced Zakaras were harder – sometimes impossible – for him to control.

Jaedin was then startled by a noise nearby, and he opened his eyes. The red light glowing from the crystal faded, and the relic sank back into his forehead.

Jaedin looked to the doorway and saw that Fangar was standing there.

"You can sense them as well, can't you…" Jaedin said.

Fangar sniffed the air and nodded. "Come, Jaedin," he said, offering his hand. "Let's go hunting…"

*   *   *

When Baird entered the Synod he had been expecting the Sentinels to escort him straight to the Solus but instead found himself led to one of the smaller chambers in the upper floor where a mere three Consil members were waiting to meet him.

Baird scanned their faces. He knew the man in the middle well. Greyjor. The two of them fought together during the War of Ashes, but when it was over, Greyjor ventured into the political world of the Synod whilst Baird was sent to Jalard to train its boys to fight. Greyjor had steadily climbed the ladder since then, Baird had heard. Three years ago, they had even elevated him to Chief of the War Consil.

Baird couldn't help but notice that all those years Greyjor had spent in this building had filled his face and rounded his belly. They were around the same age, but Greyjor had let himself get out of shape.

"Where are the others?" Baird asked. He didn't recognise the other two Consil members.

"The Synod has adjourned for today, Baird..." Greyjor said.

"Well, call them back!" Baird said. "This is a very serious matter."

All three of them frowned at him.

"What makes you dare to assume you can speak to me this way?" Greyjor asked. He raised his voice, almost making Baird flinch.

Baird clenched his fists behind his back to help contain his frustration. *I am going to have to play by their rules to get them to listen to me...* he realised, reminding himself that these people did not know how critical their situation was yet. Baird had got so used to having the authority over his rat-pack of survivors whilst they were out in the wilderness that he had forgotten correct protocol. He was at the Synod now.

And here, Greyjor was his superior.

"Sorry..." Baird said, gritting his teeth as he swallowed his pride. He turned his eyes to his feet.

"Let us begin with some introductions then..." Greyjor said, gesturing to the man to his left. "This is Konard, who is one of the members of the Justice Consil. And Worac, who is one of my advisors."

Baird greeted them by slightly dipping his head and then turned back to Greyjor. "I apologise for my bluntness, but this is urgent. We are in grave danger."

"Your appearance has caused us much surprise..." Greyjor admitted, narrowing his eyes. "The Sentinels inform me that you have handed in one of your fellow tutors and accused him of being a spy for the Gavendarians. And you have also indicted him of aid to murder and abduction. I hope you realise that these are some very *serious* allegations you're making…"

"There's more," Baird said. "Please, Greyjor, summon the rest of the Synod. They must all hear this. Fraknar has been–"

"Fraknar?" one of the men beside Greyjor repeated. Baird had already forgotten his name. "Just a couple of days ago, we heard rumours…"

"They're true," Baird said. "Fraknar has been near destroyed. We just came from there."

"That's impossible!" Greyjor exclaimed. "How can Fraknar be destroyed? No armies have crossed the border. It would take–"

"I can assure you it has," Baird said gravely. "I saw it myself. Let me explain–"

"This is ludicrous!" Greyjor argued. "Have you lost your mind? First, your students turn down their places at the Academy, and now *this*. What is going on with you?"

"My students didn't turn their scholarships down…" Baird gasped. "I brought them here with me. They–"

"That's not what Ne'mair told us," Greyjor said.

"*Ne'mair*?" Baird repeated the name. "He's *here*?"

"Yes!" Greyjor replied, slamming his fist on the table. "Of course he is! He is a Consilar now."

"But I thought the representatives were killed…" Baird thought out loud.

"Poor old Bildac and Fenn didn't make it, of course," Greyjor said. "They were murdered by a pair of bandits while they were on the road – gods have mercy upon their souls – but Ne'mair survived to tell the story. Yes!"

"What story was it that Ne'mair told you, exactly?" Baird asked.

*   *   *

Jaedin and Fangar followed their senses, which led them across a courtyard and into the main building of the Synod. It appeared that most of the Consilars had finished for the day because the place was quiet, but there were plenty of

Sentinels posted around the vicinity. None of them, however, paid Jaedin and Fangar any heed. Jaedin guessed this meant that once people had managed to get into the grounds of the Synod they were all just assumed to have a warranted purpose and allowed to wander freely.

Jaedin and Fangar went up a staircase, and after reaching the second floor, Jaedin sensed that their target was close.

They didn't waste any time. Fangar pushed the door, and it swung open, revealing a large chamber filled with shelves of books.

A man was sitting at the far side of the room behind a desk. He jerked his head up and looked at them.

"Ne'mair!" Jaedin gasped, recognising his face. It was the man who came to escort him to the Academy last summer. Jaedin had assumed him dead.

The being who used to be Ne'mair smiled.

Jaedin called upon the Stone of Zakar and summoned its power. His field of vision turned into a monochrome dimension in shades of red. Within this crystal-sight, Jaedin could see Ne'mair glowing; confirming him as a Zakara.

Jaedin then tried to exert his will over Ne'mair – hoping that the closer proximity meant this would now be possible – but something blocked him.

"What did they do to you?" Jaedin asked. He reached for his sword, realising that they would have to kill this creature using conventional means.

"I don't know what you are talking about," Ne'mair said, feigning incredulity. He then directed his voice towards the door and yelled. "Guards!"

Shit! Jaedin cursed as he heard footsteps echo down the corridor.

Jaedin slammed the door shut and bolted it to buy them some time. Meanwhile, Fangar leapt across the room. Claws grew out from his hands while he was in the air, and he drove his fist into Ne'mair's chest as he landed. Ne'mair crumpled and fell back. He tried to yell out again, but his voice cracked as Fangar's claws tore through his ribcage. Fangar uttered a low growl and yanked his talons out. Ne'mair fell, a pool of blood already forming beneath him.

Jaedin stared. It seemed all too easy. Why wasn't Ne'mair summoning his Zakara form? Why wasn't he fighting back?

A nervous feeling knotted itself in Jaedin's stomach. Something was not right here.

Fangar carried on regardless, making another growl as he raked his claws again, severing Ne'mair's head from his shoulders. That was often the only way to guarantee a Zakara wouldn't rise again.

And then the door burst open. Jaedin spun around.

Three Sentinels appeared in the doorway. They stared at the scene before them in utter disbelief; from the bloody remains of Ne'mair's body to his dismembered head and then to Fangar, the clawed man-beast standing over him.

"I... I can explain–" Jaedin began.

"Drop your weapon!" one of the Sentinels yelled as he ran towards Jaedin, pointing his spear. Jaedin was so shocked he didn't know how to respond. He couldn't even bring himself to move.

"Drop your weapon!" the Sentinel repeated. This time more forcibly.

"But–" Jaedin tried to explain, but the man drove his spear into Jaedin's shoulder. Jaedin cried out, blinded by pain. His sword fell, and it landed with a clang.

Jaedin turned his head and stared in horror at the sight of the spear embedded in his flesh.

But nothing could prepare Jaedin for the horror of what happened next.

Fangar leapt across the room, coming to Jaedin's aid in the blink of an eye. It was just like the time back in Fraknar, when Jaedin was in danger. Fangar's claws became a whirl of grey, tearing into the Sentinel's abdomen.

Fangar then pulled his talons out, and the Sentinel placed both hands to his gut. He looked down in disbelief as blood began to stream down his legs and puddle at his feet. He was silent at first, but some of his organs slipped between his fingers, and he screamed, desperately trying to hold them in place.

"Fangar!" Jaedin cried out, tears stinging his eyes. "What have you done?"

Back in Fraknar, when Fangar had come to Jaedin's rescue, the threat to Jaedin's life had been from a Zakara. Not a human.

"He hurt you!" Fangar rasped. "I won't let anyone hurt you! *Ever!*"

The other two Sentinels – still standing in the doorway – looked at Fangar, and Jaedin feared they were going to try to fight him too.

But they were saved by a familiar voice.

"Halt!" Baird yelled as he appeared, shoving his way past the Sentinels as he entered the room. A trail of men Jaedin didn't recognise followed, and they all stared at the scene in horror. Their eyes lingered upon Fangar.

For a moment then, Jaedin saw Fangar as they must have seen him. He had partially shifted into his Zakara-like form. His skin was dark and leathery. His talons were long and sharp and covered in blood. Even his face was not the same as it usually was; his jaw had become elongated and wolf-like, with pointed teeth.

"Arrest them!" one of the men yelled.

Fangar growled. His body convulsed. His jaw bulged open with a crack as his teeth grew even longer. His legs protracted. His eyes turned black.

"Stop it!" Jaedin screamed, desperate to stop the situation from escalating. "Just stop! Fangar, *please!*"

Fangar turned to him with his monstrous, almost unrecognisable, face.

"Please," Jaedin begged. "If you don't fight, they won't hurt you…" Jaedin then turned to Baird. "Will they?" he said with a hint of challenge in his voice.

"Retract your claws, Fangar!" Baird ordered. "You have my word that they will not hurt you if you *stand down*."

Fangar looked at Jaedin one more time, as if he was fighting some inner battle with himself, and then he relented. His body jerked a few times, and his bones made creaking noises as he reverted to human shape. Some of his clothes were torn and, in the process, draped to the floor in slithers. The guards in the corridor muttered to each other as they watched the strange spectacle.

"What are you waiting for!" the man next to Baird yelled once it was over. He pointed to the half-naked man standing where a monster had been, trying to sound commanding, but his hand was shaking. "Take them away!"

The Sentinels warily crept towards Fangar and formed a circle around him. Once they had gathered, there was a pause. It seemed that none wanted to be the first to lay their hands upon him.

"Do it!" the man yelled. "*Now!*"

Two of them grabbed Fangar's hands and pulled them behind his back. Then, they began to march him towards the door.

Three more Sentinels came for Jaedin. Two restrained him whilst the third held the spear engorged within Jaedin's flesh in place. Jaedin spared a moment to look at it and winced, only now noticing how much blood he had lost. It covered his tunic and leggings and his boots. As they carried him out of the room, it left a trail.

When Jaedin passed Baird, the man looked at him in dismay.

"This is just the beginning, Baird..." Jaedin whispered. "These Zakaras are not normal, and there are three more."

Chapter 2

Recruited

"We shouldn't be doing this…" she said.

"Why not?" Astar asked as they walked hand in hand through the meadow. In truth, Astar found the whole hand-holding stage in courtship a little cloying, but he knew from experience that girls liked it when you appeared to be sensitive.

Her long eyelashes flickered with guilt, but she continued walking with him all the same.

Her name was Kadey. She was the baker's daughter and Astar's latest fascination. A while ago, she had been just a girl he occasionally crossed paths with in the village. She used to giggle a lot, and her hair had always been a little messy. Her face was less round now, and her features more womanly, which drew Astar's attention to her twinkling blue eyes and the redness of her mouth. Her once unruly hair was now tied into a braid that curved around her neck and rested on her collarbone.

Astar had been lusting over her for a few tean cycles now, but there was just one problem.

"Rochela," she said. "I can't do this to her. She's my closest friend."

Astar suppressed a groan. From the moment he asked Kadey if she would like to join him for a walk around the hills together, the implications had been clear. So why did she accept only to now start acting all coy?

"I haven't spoken to Rochela since the summer," Astar said.

"But she still cries over you…" Kadey admitted, turning away from him.

"She will get over it. Kadey, look," he said, turning her around to face him. "There is something I want to tell you. I finished with Rochela because… well because I liked *you*. Okay? And it just didn't feel right. It wasn't fair on *her*."

It was only partly a lie. Astar *was* looking at Kadey when he was courting Rochela – that much was true. He looked at a lot of girls.

"We need to tell her…" Kadey whispered.

"No," Astar said, shaking his head. The last thing he wanted was more drama. "That would just hurt her feelings. You don't want to hurt your friend, do you?"

"No," Kadey agreed. "So, maybe we should just be friends? Get to know each other for a while? Wait until Rochela has–"

Astar tuned out and stopped listening to her. He was getting bored now.

He decided to aid this pursuit by other means.

He drew upon his magic, channelling the fiery energy of his Blessing at Kadey, using it to alter her perception.

He had already been using some of it. Astar rarely ventured outside without casting a glamour around himself to make his face more handsome and his frame a little taller and broader.

This time, he added some highlights to the scenery. He made the grass around himself and Kadey greener and the flowers more prominent and colourful. He made the branches above them dance with the sunlight, and their leaves float down like snow. He made imaginary birds sing.

Astar had tested many of his illusions out on girls before, and he had gradually learned, from trial and error, that a romantic setting vastly increased his rate of success.

He applied some more gift to his eyes. Making them shimmer with sincerity as he reached over and caressed the side of Kadey's face.

"I don't think I can," he whispered.

And a few moments later, he had his lips pressed against lovely Kadey, the baker's daughter. She ceded and let him press his body up against hers as his tongue explored her mouth.

He had her now.

There was no illusion Astar knew to make himself good at lovemaking; *that*, he had gleaned from experience.

But Kadey pulled away, having second thoughts. "Wait!" she gasped. "No! I can't!"

Astar amplified his illusions. The meadow became more radiant, dotted with purple flowers. He unfastened his tunic and made Kadey see smooth skin and pectoral muscles that were much firmer and defined than the ones he naturally possessed.

Her eyes widened with desire as she admired him. Astar took a step closer.

She then shook her head. "I'm sorry!" she cried as she turned and fled. "I can't do this!"

* * *

Astar walked back to the village. Alone, frustrated, and pondering over whether Kadey was still a worthy pursuit. He was confident that, given time, he could seduce her, but how much time was he willing to invest?

There were other girls in the village. Salda was always giving him dally eyes, so he knew he struck a good chance with her, but she wasn't as pretty as Kadey, and it would probably be a bit *too* easy. There was also Naleen, but she was friends with Betsy, which would only put Astar back into the same situation he was in with Kadey and Rochela. Maybe he should try to spark things up with Betsy again. He'd stopped courting her because he grew bored, but that was over a year ago now.

As Astar approached the village, he heard someone call his name and turned to see a young boy running over to him.

"Astar!" the boy yelled as his little legs hurried over to him. "*Wait*!"

Astar smiled. "What do you want to see today, Namji?"

"Last night, Daddy told me a story which had a tiger in it," he said. "What do they look like?"

"I don't know," Astar said. "I have never seen one. They are from the jungles of Babua, and I have never been there."

"Show me! I want to see!"

Astar couldn't conjure an illusion of something he couldn't picture in his own mind, but he was rather fond of the excitable young boy, so he improvised. Astar drew upon his *viga* and crafted the visage of a cat but made it bigger and with springier legs and a fuller jaw of teeth. He then covered it in black and orange stripes.

"If you ever see a real one, you should run away, you know…" Astar said to him.

"I know," the kid said as he stepped closer to get a better look at it. "But this one isn't real. It doesn't scare me!"

"Oh really?" Astar asked, raising an eyebrow. He then made the illusory cat stretch its hind legs and utter a growl. The boy froze, and his eyes widened. Astar then made the creature leap, and Namji fled, screaming.

"Sshh," Astar urged, quickly dispelling the illusion and placing a finger to his lips. Kids often asked him to entertain them with his magic, but some of their parents disapproved because they feared his Blessing.

"That's not fair!" the boy exclaimed.

"I thought you *weren't* scared?" Astar grinned. "Anyway, I must be off now, little fella–"

"I'm not that little," he said indignantly.

"Right. You're not…" Astar conceded, ruffling his hair. "Stay out of trouble."

"Show me an elephant!" he demanded.

"Next time," Astar promised as he waved.

When Astar reached the main village, he made for the keep, passing by the market. The day was drawing to its end, so the vendors were in the process of packing away their wares. Llamaleil was known to most of Gavendara for its primary exports – mutton and wool – but many of its farmers also grew grain and vegetables, so there was a lot of domestic trade within the community.

As Astar reached the drawbridge, he heard a

commotion. Two men were arguing with the guards outside the gatehouse.

"I don't care if his *Lord* is busy. I want this sorted! Once and for all! Now!" one of them exclaimed.

The other man crossed his arms over his chest. "Leave them be..." he said. "We'll come back and talk to him tomorrow."

"*Tomorrow!*?" he retorted, his face turning red. "And leave you to *steal* from my plot in the meantime?!"

"What is the meaning of this?" Astar interrupted them. He amplified his glamour as he strode up to them to make himself seem more imposing.

Both of them turned to him in surprise. "Oh, if it isn't the lordling's son," the angry one spat. "You're not Lord yet, kid. So leave out!"

"No, I am not," Astar conceded. He placed a hand on his chest and looked the man in the face to make sure he knew he was not in the least intimidated by him. "But I *will* be someday, so I would ease that tongue of yours if I were you. Now, tell me. What is all this about? Why are you making a disturbance outside *my* father's keep?"

"He is stealing my crops!" he accused, pointing to the man next to him.

"I paid a lease for that land," the other defended, lifting his head. "Fair and square."

"Is your name Killan by any chance?" Astar inquired, turning back to the other.

The angry one's eyes widened disconcertedly for a moment, and then he nodded his head.

"And your plot is just outside Little Lama?" Astar clarified, and Killan nodded again. Llamaleil was what they called the village which surrounded this fortress, but in truth, all the farmlands for miles around it were part of Llamaleil's demesne and governed by Astar's father. Some of the other villages and hamlets, over time, had acquired nick-names the locals used for simplicity.

"Yes, it is," Killan admitted.

"I thought so," Astar nodded. "My father *did* warn you that you were farming past your allotted tract during the inspections last year, did he not? You were told that if you wanted to carry on over-extending, your taxes would be increased. This man here – who I am guessing is Waldin, your neighbour – recently paid a year's fee for it."

That'll teach you to try and belittle me, Astar thought to himself when Killan's face fell.

Astar had been assisting his father with Llamaleil's administration for a few years now, so he was familiar with the affairs of its people. And he also had an uncanny ability to record and remember information – a skill which his tutor picked up on when Astar was young. For most people, memorising information was an arduous process involving recitation and repetition, but Astar had always been able to store a picture of it in his mind, meaning he could recall information to the tiniest detail after a mere glimpse.

"I was ready to harvest this morning, and he bought that plot *yesterday*!" Killan exclaimed, pointing at the other farmer, whom Astar now knew to be Waldin. "He waited till *my* crop were ready and then scurried over to your father like a little rat and bought the land. I've been tending that land for over a season. It's not right!"

Astar studied Waldin and noted that he *did* have a rather smug air about him.

"Come back tomorrow morning, and you can both speak to my father then," Astar decided. "Until then, I don't want *either* of you touching that plot of land. You understand? If I hear of any more trouble, you may start to see wolves and all manner of other creatures prowling around outside your homes… might make it a little tricky spotting the *real* ones when they come for your lambs."

The men both scowled, but neither of them argued; Astar's ability to make people see things that weren't really there was well known within the community.

"Can you let me through now?" Astar yelled to the guards on the other side of the portcullis. Two of them rushed forward and began pulling on the ropes.

Astar made his way straight across the central

courtyard to one of the buildings near the southern side. When he entered the main living chamber, Veldra, his nanny, was sitting by the fire making repairs to a pair of leggings with a needle and thread. She looked up at him with her shrewd blue eyes.

"Stop that!" she screeched. "*Now!*"

Astar cursed under his breath. He had forgotten to revert his glamour again. He usually dispelled it before entering his living quarters, but he had been using it so much in the last couple of years that it was almost becoming second nature to keep it running. This scenario wasn't new; Veldra always scolded him when she caught him using his magic in such fashion.

He did as she said and dispelled the illusion.

"I held yer in me arms an' cleaned an' fed yer as a tyke," Veldra reminded him as she turned her eyes back to her sewing. "So, if yer think ol' Veldra will put up with yer lil tricks, yer wrong! The gods gave yer a gift, Astar. If that's all yer can think t' use it fer, than y' don't deserve it."

There weren't many adults Astar let boss him around these days, but Veldra was an exception. His father was a very busy man, and it was therefore his nanny who raised him. Barely five feet tall and with an arched back and skinny frame, Veldra was far from an imposing figure, but Astar had been rapped with her walking stick enough times during his childhood to respect her.

"I'm sure I will use it for something else at some point in the future..." Astar said. "But for now, what's the harm?"

"Y' shou' be happy with wha' yer have," Veldra said, looking at him. Her face was craggy with age and lined with wrinkles, but her eyes retained that virulent sharpness. "Y' look like yer mother, Astar. That's more a gift than any of the tricks yer pull."

Try telling my father that, Astar thought wistfully.

"What's cook making?" Astar asked, trying to change the subject. He thought he caught the smell of roasting duck when he walked past the kitchens.

"How's damn'd I know?" Veldra replied. "Ever' time I try talk to tha' man he stares me baffled."

Astar did not let his amusement show. He knew exactly why. Veldra was from the far-flung mountain ranges of Valleshia, and many of the people around here had problems understanding the way she spoke. She had been his mother's nanny, and moved to Llamaleil with her when she wed Astar's father.

"Where is my father?" Astar asked. "I need to speak with him."

"In his study," Veldra replied. "He was lookin' fer yer while back…"

Astar made his way over to the western tower and climbed two flights of the spiralling staircase to reach his father's study. Just before he entered, he paused to perform the usual ritual for when he was preparing himself to be in the presence of his father; drawing upon his *viga* and using his Blessing to change the colour of his eyes, removing the flecks of green from his irises to change them from hazel to chestnut brown. He then subtly altered some of the features of his face.

All to make himself less resemble his mother.

When she died of The Ruena, all those years ago, it took years for Astar's father to be able to stand being in the same room, let alone speak to him. Astar eventually learnt that using his gift to alter his looks made it easier for the two of them to interact with each other.

Once Astar was ready, he knocked upon the door.

"Come in," his father said.

Astar opened the door to find Lord Oren sitting at his desk.

Astar thought his father a peculiar fellow. Lord Oren became the liege of Llamaleil at a very early age after his own father died prematurely. That very sudden departure threw him straight into the deep waters of being Lord to one of Gavendara's oldest regencies. He never had time to prepare for the wealth of responsibilities that he suddenly found dropped upon him. Perhaps that explained his aloof nature, lack of social skills, and the fact he never even made an effort to *look* the part. Oren presented himself modestly for a Lord. His hair was messy, and he rarely ever bothered to have his clothes flattened properly. Apart from a few grey streaks in his hair, he looked young for his age, and many women from other noble families had tried to win his affection over the years to no avail. Astar doubted his father would ever let himself move on.

"Oh, it's you…" his father said, peering up from his scrolls and ushering Astar into the room. "Please, come in."

"Killan and Walden are arguing over land," Astar informed as he shut the door behind him. "I told them to come back tomorrow."

His father shook his head and breathed an exasperated sigh. "I'll just leave a message for them with my guards and send them home. I warned Killan he had overextended his plot a while ago, and now Walden has paid for it."

"I think it's more complicated than that," Astar said, folding his arms over his chest. "That Walden is a crafty little snake – I don't like him at all! He waited till the day that crop Killan had been tending to was ready, *then* he bought it from you."

"The law states that the land is now his," Oren said.

"Yet we both know that what Walden did was sly…" Astar argued.

"So what would you do?" Oren asked, looking at his son.

Astar realised his father was testing him.

"Let them split the harvest from that plot between them," Astar proposed. "Then, after that, the land is fully Walden's."

Oren narrowed his eyes. "In an ideal world, yes," he said and then turned back to the parchment he was writing on. "But if you start making concessions, there'll be no end to it. Did you know that Sharma has a gods-awful system where several 'Elders' run each tiny little village," he laughed heartily. "Can you imagine that? All of them sat around, twiddling their thumbs, agonising for hours over *every* matter which comes their way… it's no wonder they never get anything done over there. This is Gavendara, son. And here we don't pander. Trust me, one day this will be yours, and then you'll understand."

Astar looked down at the unruly jumble of papers, scrolls and books cluttered across his father's desk. That was not a day he wanted to come anytime soon.

"Anyway, son," his father said, picking up one of the pieces of parchment before him. "This came earlier, from the capital, and it concerns you."

Astar raised his eyebrow. "From Mordeem? What does it say?"

"They want you," his father said. "At the Institute."

"The Institute?" Astar repeated. He was surprised. Like many Blessed noble sons, Astar had been offered a chance to live and study there when he was younger but declined. "But I'm too old. It must be a mistake."

"It's all changed," Oren shook his head. "The Institute and the army have merged and expanded. People with special abilities, such as yourself, are being summoned. Not just nobles, either."

"What's going on, father?" Astar asked.

"Keep this to yourself," his father motioned a finger to his lips. "But rumour has it that there is a war coming. It will probably be common knowledge soon, but they want to keep it on the hush for now."

"Sharma?" Astar said, his eyes widening. "Why attack Sharma now? They tried that years ago and lost."

"I don't know, exactly…" Oren shrugged. "Some of King Wilard's advisors seem confident that we can win this time. Anyway, if your tutor did what I paid him for, you'll know that Sharma's lands are much more fertile than ours. They have forests and trees everywhere! While our province remains one of the few places in Gavendara which produces a good bounty, in some of the others the poor are going hungry."

Astar sighed. He knew this. But still – a war? He was not sure if he liked the idea.

"Grav'aen has been instated as the facilitator of the Institute *and* the army," Oren added. "This letter came from the man himself. He has a particular interest in you."

"I thought Grav'aen was trying to find a cure for The Ruena?" Astar asked. His father was an associate of Grav'aen's and had been donating money to that project for years. Astar didn't know much about it as they were very secretive. "You said they were making progress…"

Oren shook his head. "Grav'aen began that project over fifteen years ago," he reminded him. "And he has now realised that it is a fruitless pursuit. Sharma is free from The Ruena, Astar. Not one of their people has perished from it, so they think it's our *land* which is the problem. We are dying. Slowly but surely, Gavendara is dying. Last year's reports showed that people are now falling from The Ruena faster than the rate of birth. Do you know what that means?"

Astar looked down at the table. He knew what it meant. Gavendara was a proud nation, and not many would let their despair show, but The Ruena was a gloomy presence in the back of everyone's minds. Barely an aeight went by without a report landing on his father's lap that another member of the Llamaleil community had perished. Astar doubted there was a single soul now who had not lost at least one friend or relative from it. The experience of watching his mother slowly waste away was one of Astar's earliest memories.

"When do I leave?" Astar asked.

Chapter 3

Sleeper Agents

"You know… if I were to guess that one of us would one day end up in the clink for being disorderly, it wouldn't be you I'd put on that side of the bars…" Kyra said as she peered into the cell.

Jaedin looked up at her from the dingy pallet he sat on. He was a sorry sight. He had not even bothered to fully dress; clad in only a pair of dirty leggings. Kyra found her eyes drawn to the bandage on his shoulder.

"I see Jaedin's got himself his first war wound," Kyra said. She was trying to humour him in the hope she could lift his spirits. She didn't like seeing her friend sad. "That means you're a man now. Let's have a look."

"I would rather not," Jaedin mumbled, shifting uncomfortably and turning his eyes to the floor.

Kyra dragged a chair over and sat. She had not seen Jaedin this low for a long time. The traumas they experienced over the summer changed them all, but none of them quite as strikingly as Jaedin. It turned him into a fighter and he did things to survive that people would have previously not thought him capable of. He became surer of himself. When the other boys picked on him, he began to deal it back rather than turning the other cheek. Only two days ago, she had watched him defiantly argue with Baird outside the steps of the Synod – and not even Kyra had the guts to stand up to their steely mentor very often.

But the young man sitting before her now, bearing such a solemn expression, reminded her more of the old Jaedin. The one who was scared of the world and seemed only interested in experiencing it through books. Kyra had been fond of that Jaedin, too. Her love for him was unconditional. With everyone else gone, he and Bryna were the closest thing she had to family now.

But Kyra knew that the angry Jaedin – the one who had learned to fight back – was much more likely to survive what was to come.

Kyra leant towards him a little. "Don't worry, Jaedin. You'll be out of here once this gets straightened out."

"Fangar killed a man," Jaedin whispered. "We've never killed a man before. Apart from Shayam, of course, but that was different. That Sentinel was just doing his job. He thought me and Fangar were…"

"I know…" Kyra said. Baird told her what had happened, and it came as quite a shock. "Baird has been talking to the Synod… he said that Ne'mair's blood wasn't red. It was brown. Like a Zakara. The Synod can't ignore that."

"They have spent the last two days *talking*?" Jaedin said. His expression became angry, and he clenched his fists. "There are three other Zakaras out there! I can still *feel* them. I thought that once we got here, we would be safe. Baird promised us we would be safe…"

"Can't you just kill them?" Kyra whispered. "You know… with your mind. Like you did in Fraknar."

It would hurry things on a bit, Kyra added to herself. All this waiting around while Baird tried to convince the Synod of what was right before their eyes was frustrating for her too.

He shook his head. "I can't."

"Why?" Kyra asked.

"It's hard to explain…" Jaedin said, folding his arms over his chest. "Do you… remember what they did to Dion?"

At the mention of that name, a cold shiver passed down Kyra's spine. She didn't flinch, though. "What of it?" she asked, turning to the window. She shrugged in an attempt to hide the feelings that name conjured within her.

"He was different to most Zakaras," Jaedin reminded her. "Shayam did something to him…"

Kyra swallowed a lump in her throat. She knew better than anyone how different Dion was when he turned into a Zakara. The monster which hid underneath his skin tried to rekindle the romance she'd had with the real Dion. She was kept in confinement for days, under its mercy, and it tried to break her. It said it wanted to see if reproduction between humans and Zakaras was possible, and then, when Kyra refused, he threatened to turn her into one. Kyra did not even want to think about what would have happened to her if the others had not stormed the encampment and rescued her, but she often had nightmares about it.

She had never told the others that part of the story.

"But we still killed him," Kyra said, trying to think of positive things. One of their small victories. "Do you remember when Aylen stabbed him!" she laughed as she thrust an imaginary spear into the air.

Her laughter came to an abrupt end when she remembered the rage Aylen had in his eyes as he plunged the spear into Dion's head, over and over again. She saw that memory in a new light now.

Back then, Kyra had no idea that Aylen was in love with her. Looking back, it must have been obvious.

He was dead now, too.

"So…" Kyra said, wanting to change the track of her thoughts. "What about it? Are these Zakaras the same?"

"Similar," Jaedin said gravely. "These Zakaras have been enhanced. Even more so than Dion was. I could still *see* into Dion's mind, and I could influence him too, but it was just much more difficult than it is with most Zakaras. Think of it this way: Zakaras are more or less brain dead. Their minds are empty. That makes them the perfect mercenaries because they follow orders without question. Myself, and the other people who possess the Stones of Zakar, can use their powers to control hundreds of *normal* Zakaras all at once because they put up no resistance. Dion was different, though… Shayam used his Stone to awaken parts of his mind and gave him access to the *real* Dion's memories. He was much more intelligent than a normal Zakar, and could, to some extent, imitate Dion's behaviour. Zakaras which have been enhanced are not only more cunning, they are also better at pretending to be human. But the downside is, the more they are enhanced, the more immune they become to telepathic commands from the stones. They are harder to control. Are you following me?"

"I think so..." Kyra said.

"The Zakaras that are here are even more enhanced than Dion was," Jaedin said. "I can't even get a glimpse into their minds, let alone control them."

"We need to find them," Kyra whispered.

"Don't get yourself locked up like me..." Jaedin warned. "None of us will be any use if we're all behind bars. We need to get one of them to show its true form and *then* kill it. If that doesn't convince the damn Synod, I don't know what will..."

*   *   *

After three days of being confined within a small cell, the door finally opened.

Miles looked up and blinked a few times as silhouettes appeared in the doorway. His eyes were still adjusting to the sudden influx of light into the chamber, but he could see that they were Sentinels. They urged him to rise to his feet and he complied, obediently placing his hands behind his back so they could bind his wrists together.

A part of him was relieved – another, filled with dread – that the waiting was finally over, and he was going to find out his fate.

As they escorted him through the corridors and across the courtyard, Miles mentally prepared himself for what was to come. He had been utterly alone for the last few days. Even his meals had been anonymously passed to him through a hatch in his cell. Miles had used this time well by scheming answers in his mind for every question they could throw at him.

When they finally reached the Solus, dozens of faces stared down at him from the terraces above. The Sentinels guided Miles towards a small pew. He didn't have a chance to admire the architecture. He had always wanted to see Sharma's great dome-shaped monument to meritocracy, but this was far from an appropriate moment for that.

Miles was very aware that many eyes were now watching him – and they were the eyes of people within whose hands lay his destiny – so he began to consciously think about his body language and how he could use it to convey a certain mien about himself. He turned his gaze downwards to give the impression of a man wracked with guilt and shame. It was against everything his noble upbringing had taught him, but he knew that the way he came across during these moments could prove important. Miles was on thorny ground, and he was going to need more than clever rhetoric to win this battle.

They unbound his hands. Once they were free, Miles made a show of wincing and rubbing his sore wrists so that all the Consil members watching would see how much discomfort the binds had caused him. He wanted to evoke their sympathies.

It was only when a voice from above addressed him that Miles finally allowed himself to look up and face his judges: three people sitting on a parapet before him. He guessed they were to be his interrogators. Above them, the aisles were full of faces; it seemed that the entire Synod had come to observe his trial. Many of them had quills in their hands and were already taking notes.

The man in the middle rose and addressed the room. "Fellow Consilars, we are now to begin the initial hearing for one Miles of Suule, Assigned Tutor for the village of Jalard, of the south-western region. He has been accused by one of his fellow tutors of treachery and aid to abduction." He then looked down at Miles, his eyes narrowing. "My name is Linden, and I am the Chief of the Justice Consil. The lady beside me is Selena, of the Diplomacy Consil, and the gentleman to my right is Vancer, of the War Consil."

Linden then sat again and reached for his quill. "How do you plead to these charges?"

"Guilty…" Miles said.

Linden blinked and looked down at Miles again. "Is there anything else you would say for yourself?" he then asked after a pause.

Miles nodded. "Yes. I am willing to tell you everything. I have known this day would come quite some time… and back then I vowed to come clean and do everything in my power to help you once it came."

Linden narrowed his eyes, and Miles could tell that this was not the kind of answer he had expected to hear. Selena, the woman beside Linden, whispered something into his ear, and he nodded.

"Miles," Selena said, turning her eyes to a sheet of parchment in her hands. "When you entered Sharma, you had refugee status. It was shortly after the War of Ashes, and you claimed you were from Sulle and had no other choice but to cross over the border because you were born to a Sharmarian father, and this caused you to suffer such severe prejudice that you were no longer safe in Gavendara… we have recently been informed that this is untrue. That you are not actually from Sulle, but instead of noble lineage. Is this correct?"

Miles cursed inwardly; Selena drawing attention to his heritage would not do him any favours. Sharma was not an oligarchy anymore. The Synod was founded, through social reform, hundreds of years ago, and it was now ingrained into the psyche of Sharmarians to demonise the collective of Lords that ruled over Gavendara.

If Miles were to win these people over, he would need to turn this around somehow.

He turned his head down in shame. "It is true," he admitted. "That other story was part of the cover I was forced to use to achieve my mission."

"Which noble family are you from?" she asked. "I have studied Gavendarian culture and history – it is one of the reasons Linden invited me to sit here during this meeting – and I would like to know your lineage."

Miles held back a smile: he had been waiting for her to ask such a question because he had prepared the perfect answer for it. "Any titles I once had a claim to are forfeited," he said, composing his face into a solemn expression. "When I betrayed my people, I disgraced my family and lost any claim to an inheritance. If I were to be recognised on Gavendarian soil now, it would spell my execution. 'Miles of Sulle' was a lie – that is true – but my title now is simply Miles. Miles of No Land."

All three of his interrogators stared at him, and there followed a brief pause, filled only by hushed murmurs of people in the upper aisles whispering to each other.

"And how, exactly, is it that you betrayed your people?" Linden asked.

"By helping Baird and two other young men who were captured by Shayam escape," Miles replied. "And I also was of some assistance in putting an end to the siege of Fraknar."

"Impossible!" Vancer, the man next to Linden, exclaimed. It was the first time he had spoken, and rage was evident in his eyes. "This whole story about the–"

"*Vancer*! Let him speak!" Selena raised her voice, surprisingly stern. She turned back to Miles and explained. "We are still waiting for our riders to return from Fraknar... to verify what happened there." She cleared her throat. "Miles... this kidnapping you helped them escape from was one you helped orchestrate, was it not?"

"That is true," Miles nodded. "I was in a very difficult situation... I had to carefully choose the precise moment to betray the people I worked for to limit the overall damage they would cause to Sharma."

"That is a very ambitious claim..." Linden murmured. He turned back to his list of questions. "Tell me, Miles, at what point did you *decide* that you were going to turn against your people?"

"Not long before I crossed over the border," Miles replied.

"That was over ten years ago..." Linden said flatly.

Miles nodded. "Correct."

"So, you are claiming that you had a sudden change of heart, but it took you a full *ten years* to act upon it,"

Linden asked and turned to the Consilars beside him and chuckled. Other people in the room began to laugh as well. "I would very much like to hear this tale."

This was the moment that Miles had been waiting for; a chance to be given free rein in his testimony. He shifted to not solely address the three judges before him but the entire Solus.

"In my former life, back in Gavendara, I worked for a man by the name of Grav'aen," Miles said. "Who was trying to find a cure for The Ruena... I worked for him for altruistic reasons. Because I wanted to bring an end to the disease and save lives," Miles said. He paused for a moment and was satisfied to hear a silence in the room that he hoped was akin to sympathy. The Synod was all too aware of the contagion that marred the lands of their neighbours, yet refused to send aid. Miles knew this and hoped that any guilt some of the Consilars may feel over this matter would work in his favour.

"With no one to help us, we became desperate," Miles continued. "And we began to turn to the most obscure places to find a solution. In the mountains of Valleshia, to the north of Mordeem, a complex of ancient temples had recently been unearthed. Carved into its walls, we found instructions to arcane procedures which, they claimed, could be used to make people stronger. We wanted to save our families, and as farfetched as it seemed, we had nothing to lose...

"These procedures were conducted in a series of ritual experiments and resulted in the creation of creatures we have come to call 'Zakaras'. *That* was when I had a change of heart... I joined Grav'aen's cause, initially, because I wanted to save lives, but it became clear to me, as time passed, that Grav'aen was making weapons. And that his true purpose was to use these creatures to invade Sharma. To steal your lands which are free from The Ruena."

By this point, the room had gone silent. Everyone was staring at him with rapt attention.

"I feel obliged to explain to you the full extent of the danger the Zakaras present to you..." Miles said, noticing that this was the kind of information that seemed to seize their attention most aptly. "Among the things which were found during the excavations that took place in the Valleshian Mountains were ten crystals. It was later discovered that those in possession of these stones could control Zakaras telepathically. That, and the fact those who are killed by Zakaras, turn into ones themselves – further increasing their numbers – make them the perfect weapons."

"And you helped create such creatures..." Linden asked, wide-eyed.

"I was just a scholar. I had no involvement in *that* side of things," Miles lied. "But I did witness what some of the *others* who worked for Grav'aen were up to, and the first time I saw what they had created..." He made a show of shuddering and pulling a pained expression. "I *knew* I had to stop them... so I made a vow to do everything I could...

"I have been informed that you had an incident inside the very walls of this building just three days ago," Miles then said. Baird had come to visit him on the first day of his confinement and told him all about the incident with Jaedin and Fangar.

"Two of our men were murdered," Vancer said through gritted teeth.

"And Ne'mair's blood?" Miles said. "It wasn't red, was it? It was more of a brown colour?"

"Yes..." Linden admitted, shifting uncomfortably. "We did notice something unusual about the colour of his blood. His body is being examined by our physicians."

He is afraid, Miles realised, reading Linden's body language. *That is why they are so loath to react... because the truth frightens them...* Miles felt an alarming wave of dread pass through him as he realised that all this bureaucracy was just a shield against a reality that they were too terrified to face.

Miles' faith in a nation governed this way, enduring what was to come, weakened.

"If he did not transform into this true form, I doubt

your physicians will find anything too peculiar… besides the colour of his blood," Miles said. "I beg you; make haste and take action. Jaedin possesses one of the Stones of Zakar, and he has sensed three other Zakaras in your vicinity."

"Your advice has been noted," Linden said. "But we will not pass judgement until we have the facts. I'm not going to let a murderer roam my castle and kill people until we have *proof*."

"How is Jaedin?" Miles asked softly. "I heard he was wounded…"

"The prisoner was examined this morning, and he…" Linden hesitated. "He seems to be making a rather swift recovery."

Miles stared at Linden and had a sneaking suspicion as to why he seemed so uncomfortable at the mention of Jaedin.

Could it be that fusing Jaedin to The Stone of Zakar had also gifted him with the ability to regenerate himself?

That procedure achieved results more remarkable than we could have ever imagined! Miles thought, feeling a wave of excitement at such a revelation.

"What do you have to say about the alleged attacks on the peoples of Jalard and Fraknar?" Vancer said.

"By the gods, I swear I had no way of knowing what would happen to Jalard," Miles said, placing a hand on his chest. "And when we heard word of what was happening in Fraknar, I did everything in my power to help put an end to it. Baird, who I am sure you have already spoken to – and is a man of great integrity – will vouch for me on that."

"I am not buying this…" Vancer said, folding his arms across his chest. "You *claim* that for ten *whole* years, you knew what it was they were planning, and yet you only acted against them *after* it occurred. Your story has too many gaps…"

"I was in a very precarious situation," Miles said. "Grav'aen is an exceptional Psymancer… and he has ears everywhere–"

"If you warned us, *we* could have done something!" Linden said.

Miles shook his head. "He has ears even here, in this chamber…" he said, causing many within the dome to gasp.

"That is a very serious accusation…" Vancer uttered.

"I am not accusing anyone…" Miles said. "If there *is* a mole in this building, Grav'aen was discreet about it, and I do not know their identity. All I can say is that I *do* know he has mysterious ways of knowing about things that happen within these walls…"

People began to mutter to each other, and Miles was satisfied to notice many eyes making a suspicious sweep of the room. This was good, he realised. Any distrust between them would divert focus away from him.

"You still haven't sufficiently explained to us why it is you waited so long to act," Selena said, looking down at her notes.

"Jaedin possesses a Stone of Zakar now. When the armies of Zakaras march across your border, he will be infinitely valuable to you," Miles said. "And Baird and Sidry can now summon the avatars of gods. Those are *three* weapons of immense power that will be on your side during the war to come. That was always my plan. I let Shayam perform those experiments on them… and only *after* that did I help them escape."

For a few moments, the entire chamber was silent.

"Baird gave us an account of the things they did to him…" Linden grimaced. "Are you admitting that you let *that* happen?"

"Yes," Miles said, turning his eyes down to his feet again. "It was the hardest thing I have ever had to do, and there is not a day which goes by that I am not deeply ashamed of myself." He then made his voice croak as he said the next bit. "But yet… it was the *only* thing I could do. To ensure your nation had a fighting chance in what is to come."

"I can only thank the gods that he and the other two young men survived…" Linden muttered.

"I have regularly thanked them as well. Believe me…" Miles whispered.

Miles then pulled an expression of shame: hoping that all of the people watching saw him as a man who was so deeply sorry for his crimes that he was willing to die. He hoped it would convince them to give him another chance.

Because he wanted to live.

"Do you have anything else to say for yourself?" Vancer asked.

"Only that I am willing to submit to any judgement of your choosing," Miles said. "As I explained earlier: from the moment I realised just how wrong the things Grav'aen was doing were, I pledged to do everything I could to thwart him. Now that this deed is done, I can finally live an honest life. And I wish to do so in *your* service. I am yours to do what you choose. That is my purpose now. I would like to help you further if you would permit me…"

"If that is all," Linden said. "Then I call this session adjourned. Take him back to his cell."

*   *   *

That morning, Bryna set off to visit the Academy Library.

It wasn't difficult to find. The Academy grounds were adjacent to the Synod, so she merely needed to stroll through the ornamental gardens between them. Once she reached the other side, she recognised the library almost immediately, with its golden arch looming over its entrance and marble-clad walls.

She was a little worried that they might ask questions – that they wouldn't let her in – but no one paid her any heed nor bother. After walking around for a while, she found the history section and slipped a few tomes she thought Jaedin would like to read beneath her coat. Bryna knew that her brother would likely be losing his mind with boredom whilst trapped within that cell. She wanted to surprise him later on when she went to see him.

This was not the only reason she had come to visit this place, though.

It took her a while to find what she was looking for. Bryna did not understand the bizarre cataloguing systems libraries used. Jaedin had tried to explain it to her once, back in the modest collection their village held in Miles' study, but she could never quite comprehend the logic behind it. She wandered for a while, eventually stumbling upon a shelf of books in a dark corner that looked promising. It appeared to be an unfrequented place, for it was rather cluttered, and the books there were not properly organised; even Bryna knew that the books within the same subsection of a library were supposed to be arranged alphabetically.

She scanned through the titles, selecting ones that seemed relevant, and piled them beneath the crook of her arm. By the time she had gone through all of them, the pile was heavy. She made her way over to the nearest table and began to leaf through them.

Most of them were not very useful and barely mentioned the name 'Vai-ris'. One of them merely referred to her as '*Verdana's rejected daughter, a woman of darkness*'. Bryna wanted to know more.

'*Vai-ris was born from an act of lust between Verdana and her father, Gazareth,*' another read. '*This incestuous act caused a grave deformity, and for this, she was cast out from the realm of the gods.*'

This didn't sound right to Bryna. Incest was frowned upon between humans but was not uncommon between gods. Jaedin once told Bryna you should always check the legitimacy of sources, so she examined the cover, discovering it was written less than ten years ago, and the writer had no academic references. Bryna placed it on her discard pile and moved on to the next.

She found what she was looking for later in the afternoon, in a book which was so old the spine had almost worn away. A whole page of text, with 'Vai-ris' as the heading.

The deity Vai-ris began her tragic tale as a member of the divine family, but her existence escalated tensions that were already apparent between the two factions of the gods.

It is commonly said that Gazareth was her father, but I have performed extensive research and concluded that this assumption does not have much basis. The earlier texts state that Verdana refused to name the father of her child, but the Ancients could tell (from Vai-ris's alien splendour) that her father was almost certainly one of the Others. Gazareth was referred to as a suspect but never actually confirmed as being her father.

From the moment Vai-ris was condemned to live a mortal life, her story disappears from most grimoires. The only other primary source I have ever encountered with any mention of her after that point is from an annal I found in Gavendara's national library in Mordeem. I could not discern any reliable date of publication – for it was written in Ancient script and, almost certainly, from a calendar which has been lost in time – but it gives an eye witness account of a sorceress who helped a clan conquer a large region in the western mountains of Gavendara. The witness claimed to have met the sorceress in person, describing her as having 'ghostly eyes, of no mortal origin' and the ability to raise the dead back to life. The clan this sorceress was affiliated with was said to synchronise their attack strategy with the time of the year where she was said to be most powerful; when summer turns to autumn. Every spring, they would recuperate while her strength dwindled.

She is described as never taking any particular man as her mate, but she must have had at least one lover, for she fell pregnant. She was then said to have predicted her own death, claiming that, because she was the descendant of Vai-ris, the act of bringing new life into this world would tear the remaining thread of her mortal existence.

The baby was said to have slid out of her with her very last breath.

There were a few more details. About how the clan fell into decline after her death, and other such things. Bryna read the page to its very end but barely registered the closing minutiae. Once done, she closed the book, got up from her chair, and left the building.

As she walked back towards the grounds of the Synod, her throat tightened, but she did not cry. The book had only confirmed something that, deep down, she already suspected. She was a walking corpse. Only Jaedin knew the entire truth of what happened to her back in Jalard.

She stared at the ground as she walked and did not realise someone was in her path until she bumped into them.

"Sorry!" she squeaked as she shifted aside.

She looked up and saw it was Sidry.

"Bryna?" he said, seeming a little bemused. "I was waving at you…"

"Sorry," she repeated, running a hand through her hair. "I was miles away. I–"

"Are you okay?" Sidry asked, his eyebrows furrowed with concern.

Ever since Bryna was a child, she had always found herself incapable of lying. She often kept secrets, but that was different. Sidry had asked her a direct question, and he was watching her, waiting for her reply.

Bryna turned away and said nothing, hoping that he would forget he asked.

The next thing she knew, a pair of arms closed around her shoulders, and she found her face buried in Sidry's chest. She gasped for a moment in disbelief, realising that no one, besides Jaedin and Kyra, had dared to come this close to her since she had been reborn.

This was different, though. Sidry was warm, and Bryna had always felt so cold since that day.

For a time, Bryna enjoyed Sidry's warmth, but it ignited a longing within her. One which made her abruptly aware of the revelation still fresh within her mind. She pulled away.

"Thanks," she said, looking up at him and smiling nervously.

Sidry was so kindhearted. She could never let him know how much she wished she were able to return his affections.

"Are you going to tell me what's wrong?" Sidry asked.

"I can't," Bryna whispered, shaking her head. "But thank you. It is… pleasant to see you."

"Jaedin woke up this morning," Sidry said. "Kyra just went to visit him."

Bryna nodded. She had sensed her twin waking up well before Baird took the trouble to inform her. She reached into her cloak and showed Sidry the books she'd smuggled out of the library.

"I got these for him," she said. "I thought it would be nice for him to have something to read… I hope he likes them."

Sidry smiled. "You know your brother well…"

Bryna nodded. "He is sad right now. I want to make him happy."

"And what about *you*, Bryna?" Sidry asked. "You're always looking out for other people. Are *you* happy?"

Bryna turned her eyes away, wishing that she could lie. She didn't want to trouble people. "I must go…" she said and began to walk. "He'll be wondering where I am."

Sidry caught hold of her arm as she passed him. "You know I am here to help you, right? If you are ever upset, or in danger or worried… I just want you to know that I am there. Someone needs to take of *you* too, Bryna."

She nodded. "I… understand," she whispered. "Thank you, Sidry."

*   *   *

When Baird appeared outside the bars of Jaedin's cell, neither of them said anything at first. The burly ex-soldier crossed his arms over his chest and looked at Jaedin with a stony expression. Jaedin met his gaze defiantly. He did not flinch.

"What were you thinking?" Baird uttered.

Jaedin had been expecting Baird to be angry. He had been scolded by the former soldier so persistently that it was what he had learnt to expect from him, but it was not anger Jaedin perceived from Baird this time. It was something wearier.

"I tried to warn you," Jaedin replied. "You wouldn't listen…"

Baird sat in a chair.

"I don't want to listen to your excuses…" Baird said. "That is not going to get us anywhere. I want you to tell me everything you know about those damn Zakaras."

Jaedin sighed. "There are three of them…" he began.

Baird nodded. "I know. Kyra came to see me earlier. She said that you believe they have been made stronger or something. How is this possible?"

"The Stones of Zakar can be used to enhance Zakaras and awaken parts of their minds. Like what Shayam did to Dion, remember?" Jaedin explained. "When this is done, the Zakara becomes more cunning and intelligent. They can even have modes of behaviour instilled into them."

"Does this mean *you* can do this too?" Baird asked.

Jaedin frowned. "I hope you're not asking…"

"I'm not asking you to create new Zakaras!" Baird hurriedly added. "Gods, what do you think I *am*… I'm talking about the ones we *find*. You just said that you can teach them to behave. Does this mean we could make them–"

"No!" Jaedin exclaimed. The thought of such a thing filled him with revulsion.

Jaedin did know how to do such a thing; he had gleaned many such techniques concerning the Zakaras from Shayam just before Kyra killed him. "It's evil!"

"But what if–"

"*No!*" Jaedin yelled. "I'm not discussing this *any* further!"

Baird huffed and crossed his arms over his chest. Jaedin could tell from the disgruntled expression on his face that he was far from considering the matter over. "Baird, listen..." Jaedin said, attempting to steer the conversation back in a more productive direction. "What has been done to the Zakaras here is much more advanced than anything I believed possible. They have been altered so much I couldn't get into their minds at all, at first... but earlier today, I did it. Only for a moment, but I got inside one of their heads."

"What did you find out?" Baird asked. "Who are they?"

"I don't know..." Jaedin said. "I couldn't sustain the connection for long enough, but I found out a little... and it's very bad. Someone has not only granted them fully-functioning minds, but they have also..." Jaedin then paused as he tried to figure out what words to use whilst explaining such a thing to someone like Baird. "It's... like someone has trained them. Like dogs, almost. Someone has written a sequence of actions into their heads. They have a plan."

"What is it?"

Jaedin shrugged. "As I said, I wasn't in there long enough to find out. Also," he added. "I realised something else earlier. I don't think what happened when we arrived was an accident. Ne'mair didn't fight. He didn't shift into his true form. He *let* us kill him. The one thing he *did* do, however, was call for the Sentinels. I think they wanted me and Fangar to kill Ne'mair. They knew it would cause trouble between us and the Synod. By keeping me locked up in here, the Synod is playing right into their hands. You need to convince them to let me out," Jaedin then said. "The Zakaras are still out there. I can help you find them."

"I will try, but you killed an innocent man," Baird said. "It's going to be hard to get you out of here after that stunt."

"I know..." Jaedin said. "But... that doesn't really matter anymore. This is more important. Unless we kill the rest of those Zakaras soon, a lot more people are going to die."

"You killed an innocent man!" Baird repeated, raising

his voice. "And now you want to carry on as if nothing has happened!? Do you feel no guilt?"

"Yes," Jaedin nodded. "At first, I did. I thought about it a lot. Those days I was bed-ridden, it wasn't because of this wound," Jaedin pulled a face at the bandage wrapped around his shoulder. "It was because I was upset. I felt so much guilt and shame for what happened that I couldn't face *anyone*..." Jaedin shuddered as he remembered that feeling, and he had to make a conscious effort to not fall back into that place again. He swallowed a lump in his throat and then looked at Baird. "But then... after I came round, I found out that since then you and that bloody Synod have done *nothing*! Nothing but *talk!* Whilst Zakaras roam freely! I'm angry now... what in the gods' names is wrong with you all!?"

"I have been trying to–" Baird began.

"Every minute you and your Synod drones waste endangers the lives of *everyone!*" Jaedin said forcibly. "My regret for what happened – and my sympathy for these Synod people – is beginning to wear *very* thin..."

"*Jaedin!*" Baird exclaimed. "How can you say such a thing?! You are here because you disobeyed my orders! If you'd just waited–"

"*NO!*" Jaedin raised his voice. "You are *not* placing all the blame on me! *You* are in the wrong this time, Baird!"

"How *dare* you!" Baird roared. He rose from his chair, his face red with fury. If there had been no bars between them during that moment, Jaedin suspected that Baird might have even struck him.

But there were bars.

And, also, something about the way that Jaedin saw Baird had changed now. Something that used to be there, whenever Jaedin was in his presence, was missing.

"You don't scare me anymore..." Jaedin realised. It was a startling revelation, and it came out as a gasp.

"What's got into you?" Baird frowned. He looked at Jaedin as if he didn't even know him. "Have you gone mad?"

"No... I've just grown up..." Jaedin realised, feeling

strangely calm and apathetic as he looked his former leader in the eyes. Seeing him in a way that he never had before. Baird's jaw dropped. "I have grown out of *you*..." Jaedin shook his head. "You know, I was always scared of you... and you were always making me feel so shit and useless about myself. I *hated* you back then, but at least I respected you. I knew, deep down, that if it weren't for you, I would probably be dead. I thought you always had the right answer. I did *everything* you said because, no matter how nasty you were, I trusted you. You pushed us so hard to get here, Baird. And you promised that, once we got here, we would be safe. I worked so hard to please you..." Jaedin's voice croaked. "And you were *always* shouting at me."

Jaedin paused for a moment to gather control of his voice again.

Baird just stared at him, speechless and aghast.

"When I tried to warn you that we were in danger, you didn't act..." Jaedin said softly. "You seemed more concerned about what your precious friends from the Synod would think about me and Fangar. You acted like I was bothering you for telling you about the Zakaras, but I came to you because I thought you always had the right answers... and you let me down. And now you are shouting at me. Again! For doing what *you* should have done in the first place. You are always shouting, Baird, but shouting isn't going to work on me anymore. I've lost my respect for you."

Chapter 4

The Institute

After two aeights of riding, Astar reached the outskirts of Mordeem.

He bypassed the bustling centre. Astar had seen Mordeem enough times by now for the novelty to have worn off, and these days he only ventured into the heart of the city when he needed to. The Institute grounds were on the other side, so Astar rode around the outer rim of hills that surrounded it.

As soon as he arrived at the Institute, Astar was struck by how different the place was from how he remembered it. Astar had visited these grounds for a few short spells during his younger days to mingle with other young nobles and use its library. It had always been a rather exclusive establishment, as one needed to either be wealthy or exceptionally gifted to be invited. That seemed to have changed since Astar's last visit. It wasn't just visibly busier; Astar could feel a change in the air.

Astar went to the portico and showed the woman there his letter of invitation. She gave it a quick scan and told him to report straight to Grav'aen's office on the second floor of the main building.

"Come in," a voice called before Astar even reached the door.

Astar opened it to see Grav'aen standing by the window.

Astar had never met Grav'aen in person before, and he was not at all what he had expected. Short and stocky, with a broad face and dimpled chin. His scalp was completely shaven, and he had a big red scar in the middle of his forehead. Astar didn't know where he had got that disfigurement from, but he tried to not look at it for too long. One of the biggest surprises was how elegant his attire was. Astar had heard that Grav'aen was hedgeborn: that he was one of those plucky individuals who somehow rose from humble origins to create their own wealth. He had even – rumour said – found a way to fund his studies at Mordeem's University.

"Welcome, Astar," Grav'aen said, flashing a perfect set of white teeth when he smiled. He ushered him inside. "Please, shut that door behind you."

Astar closed it.

Grav'aen then stared at him with a distant look in his eyes, and Astar felt a strange sensation. It started as a pressure in his skull, and then the discomfort grew and grew until Astar involuntarily fell to his knees and let out a groan. He clawed at his hair and screamed. It felt like thousands of ants were crawling around inside his head.

When it was over, he heard a chuckle and opened his eyes to see Grav'aen standing in the same place with a hand to his chest. He was laughing with an arrested chortle.

Astar felt violated, and he didn't even know why.

It was as he rose back to his feet that he realised that something was missing. His glamour – the favourable mirage he almost always shrouded himself within – had vanished.

"Your little tricks won't work on me," Grav'aen said when his chuckling finally subsided. "Sorry about that, I couldn't help myself... No harm done. I was just curious what you *really* looked like."

Astar was far from amused and made no effort to hide it. There was no point in trying. If all the rumours Astar had heard about Grav'aen – concerning his aptitude for Psymancy – were accurate, attempting to hide his thoughts was futile.

"You have a remarkable gift," Grav'aen said, fingering his chin as he studied Astar. "I think we could have much use for you here," his eyes then widened. "Oh... and you are a reminreaper too..."

"A what?" Astar asked, placing a hand on his hip.

"A reminreaper," Grav'aen repeated. "It's what they call people like you, whose minds recall things with ease.

You can look at something and store a picture of it in your mind, like that," he snapped his fingers. "Can't you? That's a useful skill. Many of your kind can land themselves positions in libraries and other such places very smoothly... I think we can find a much better use for *you*, though. Do you have any skills in armed combat?"

"Some."

Grav'aen studied him in silence for a few more moments, and Astar felt pressure in his skull again, but this time it was gentler. Grav'aen smiled. "You are a fair hand with a spear, I see. Good choice. Specialising in a weapon with a long range is smart when you are on the smaller side."

Astar scowled. It had been years since anyone apart from his nanny had thought of him as small. His glamour usually took care of that.

"Please, try not to be too angry. Take it as a compliment," Grav'aen said, and the feeling of his presence in Astar's mind receded. "I only do this to the recruits who interest me... I promise that, from now on, as long as you are not brought to me for bad behaviour, I will stay out of there." Grav'aen tapped a finger to his temple. "Now the question is... what should I do with you?"

Grav'aen then returned to his desk, pulled out a sheet of parchment, and dipped his quill in a pot of ink. "I am assigning you to Squad Six," he said. "The physical training here is focussed within small groups, as it is my belief that familiarity between the students and their instructors makes progress more personalised and productive. Physical training is what most of your days will consist of..." He scratched his head. "Now... what else..." he pondered out loud. "You seem to have a good grasp on how to use your Blessing already. And it is quite a rare one, so I am not sure if any of the mages I have at hand would be of much help to you anyway. There are people at the university who study aspects of the psyche, though. I think attending some lessons with them might

97

teach you more about *how* the human mind works and better inform you how to apply your abilities. You will need to ride to the university into the city for that... let's say one day out of every aeight..."

He continued waffling for a while as he wrote onto the parchment, and Astar watched as his new routine was mandated for him.

"There we go," Grav'aen eventually said, scribbling his signature on the bottom. "Show this to someone downstairs, and they will lead you to your lodgings. Your horse has already been taken to the stables, and your belongings should be waiting for you in your room."

"Is there a war coming?" Astar asked as he accepted the rolled-up parchment.

"Save that conversation for another time..." Grav'aen replied. "I think you already know the answer, Astar. Gavendara cannot carry on the way it is."

*　　*　　*

Astar was then escorted to another site a short walk away from the main grounds. One filled with old, barrack-style wooden buildings with slate roofs. The guards led him into one of them and down a rather dismal looking corridor.

When Astar reached his allotted room, a man was waiting outside it with his arms folded over his chest.

"Are you Astar?" he uttered, looking him up and down with a sour expression on his face. The fact that he was bald made the wrinkles on his forehead even more noticeable when he was frowning. Astar took an instant dislike to him.

"Yes. Astar, son of Oren of Llamaleil," he said.

The man sneered. "Don't think that bein' noble swine makes you special here..." he said. "Fought much?"

"Some," Astar said. "I was trained by one of my father's handmen. I am good with a spear and sword. And I can draw a bow."

"We'll see..." he said. "I've heard many a Lord's brat make such claims."

"I will make sure to not disappoint you then..." Astar said backhandedly. He stared the man in the face and didn't flinch to make it clear that he would not be browbeaten.

"I'm Frast," he said flatly. "And I will be in charge of your training. Gods help me... You do what I say, when I say. I don't take well to grief. Have I made myself clear?"

Astar disrelished this man's manner, but another encounter with Grav'aen was something he wanted to avoid at all costs, so he nodded.

"A bell will ring at dawn. That's when you wake up. The second bell means breakfast. If you're not in training hall number *three* by the fourth bell, pack your bags and go back to whatever swamp you came from."

Astar had no idea where he was supposed to go to eat breakfast or where any of the training halls were, but he had a feeling this man didn't favour questions, so he nodded again.

"This is your room," Frast then said, thumbing behind his shoulder just before he strode off. Astar watched him leave, wondering what madness had convinced him to come here in the first place. Then, with a heavy sigh, he opened the door.

It was basic but clean. And Astar was relieved to see that he at least had his own fireplace and bathtub. His bags had been carried and left in a jumbled pile upon the floor.

He began to unpack.

*   *   *

Astar's ears rang with the clang of bells shortly after dawn, and he pulled himself out of bed with a groan. He readied himself for the day, stepping out into the hallway at the exact same moment as a few of the other people who shared his corridor. They made their way towards the stairs, and Astar followed them out of the building and towards the eatery.

Astar was expecting the food to meet standards similar to the dismal setting, but it appeared that the Institute wanted their trainees well fed, at least. Porridge, various fruits, milk, boiled eggs, cured meats, and potatoes smothered in rosemary and garlic were available, spread out across one long table. On a second table, a selection of bread and cheese was rapidly disappearing. Astar filled his plate, and a woman handed him a steaming cup of honeyed tea.

Astar walked down the lines of benches, looking for a place to sit. It seemed that most of the other youths were already familiar with each other, and none of them felt inclined to welcome a newcomer. Astar sat down at an empty table in the corner of the room and ate alone.

"New here?" a young man asked as he plonked his tray opposite him.

Astar nodded. "I came from Llamaleil."

The young man shrugged and sat. He began to tuck into his food, making no attempt at further conversation. Astar couldn't tell whether it was because he had never heard of his home or was just not interested. His messy black hair obscured his eyes, and he had the kind of face that made it hard to tell if he was sneering or not. Astar wasn't sure what to make of him. The red tunic he was wearing was of regal bearing, but his eating manners and everything else about him did not match someone who came from that kind of upbringing.

"Where are you from?" Astar asked.

"My name is Dareth," he said. "Don't worry where I'm from. You wouldn't know it."

"You new here as well?" Astar asked.

"I got here a few aeights ago," Dareth replied. "Most people are new here."

"Do you know where the training halls are?" Astar asked.

"Most of them," he nodded. "What one are you looking for?"

"Number three."

He nodded. "I'll show you if you like."

"That would be great. Thanks."

"What you here for?" Dareth asked.

"For training… and–"

"No," Dareth interrupted. "I mean, *why* are you here? Why were *you* picked?"

Astar smiled. "I have a gift. A Blessing. I can make people see things."

"Really?" Dareth raised an eyebrow. "What kind of things?"

"Whatever I want," Astar said. "Why are you here?"

"I…" Dareth began and then hesitated. He cast a look around them to check if anyone was listening and then opened his mouth to speak again but changed his mind. He shook his head. "I can't tell you…"

"What?" Astar asked. "Why?"

"I'm not allowed to," Dareth replied guardedly. Astar could tell from the look in his eyes that he *wanted* to, though. He had a stocky, warrior-like frame about him, but Astar sensed that there must be something more.

"Is it magic?" Astar asked. "Some kind of gift?"

Dareth laughed. "No… nothing like that. Anyway," he said, rising and leaving his empty tray on the table. "Do you want me to show you to the training halls or not?"

Dareth pointed out some of the buildings to Astar and explained what they were as he guided him through the grounds. His manner was blunt, but Astar soon realised that was just his awkward way of being friendly. Astar was beginning to like him.

"And that is training hall three," Dareth said, pointing to a large building that looked more like a barn.

"Thanks," Astar said, giving his new friend a nod of approval. "Which squad are you in?"

"I don't have one…" Dareth shook his head. "I do jump in with other training groups every now and then, though. Anyway, I best go. Grav'aen wants to see me."

He has secrets… Astar realised, but he knew that he was unlikely to find any of them out this soon.

Astar strolled into the building. It was a bit more impressive from the inside than its rather depressing exterior had made him believe. It held a large open chamber, as well as a few small storage rooms tucked away into the corners. A girl with a long mane of thick blonde hair was sitting on a chair a few yards away with her feet resting on the table. Astar walked over to her.

"Is this where Squad Six is meeting?" he asked.

"I hope so…" she replied, turning and smiling at him. "Why? Are you fresh meat? What is your name?"

Astar couldn't help but stare at her for a few moments before he replied. She was possibly one of the most striking girls he had ever seen, with long eyelashes and dimples on each side of her mouth.

His opinion of this place was beginning to improve.

"Astar," he said, making sure his magic was doing its job of casting a favourable haze about himself. He considered amplifying it, but there was something very shrewd and perceptive about this girl's sapphire blue eyes, and he had a feeling she would notice. "Son of Lord Oren of Llamaleil."

"Yeah… I had a feeling you were a lordling," she said dryly.

"And you're not?" Astar asked, realising he had assumed she was because of the self-assuredness she had about her.

She laughed. "No. Far from it. I'm as common as they come… but I was raised at the Institute."

"Here?" he said, realising that she must have a remarkable gift if she had been taken in as a child.

"Not here," she shook her head. "The *real* Institute. They moved us older ones to this dump a few aeights ago. Don't tell me you're so naïve you haven't figured out that we've basically been conscripted?"

"How do you know about that?" Astar asked. He thought that the rumours of war were still just whispers between the noble families.

"Well, this place *was* an army barracks a short while ago," she said, looking up at the ceiling. "How much subtler can you get? Oh, I almost forgot. My name is Elita, by the way," she said, extending her hand.

Astar shook it. Her grip was strong, and apart from a few callouses, her skin was soft.

She pulled him in, drawing him closer so that their faces were inches apart. "Don't think that just because I'm common and you're a lordling that I'm going to let you in my breeches easy," she then said.

"If you're common, then why have I never met a girl like you before?" he asked.

"Because there are no other girls like me..." she whispered.

They were interrupted by a group of rowdy young men stepping into the hall. They were so busy chatting with each other that they didn't even notice that there was a newcomer at first. Astar quickly deciphered that most of them were warrior-types – rather than Blessed – from the manner with which they carried themselves. A barrel-chested giant walked slightly ahead of the others, and Astar guessed – from his bearing and poise – that he was their leader. He had the darker skin tone of someone descended from the tribes of Gavendara's southern province, Babua.

"You've been assigned to this squad?" he asked when he noticed Astar. He looked him up and down.

Astar nodded.

"I'm Bovan," he said, shaking Astar's hand. His grip was tight, and he looked Astar right in the face. It was subtle, but it was certainly a warning. It said, *I am the alpha male here. You're welcome in my pack if you accept that.*

"Astar of Llamaleil," he replied curtly.

"Where is that?" Bovan asked.

"It's to the west," one of Bovan's cronies answered. He was a little less stocky than the others and finer-dressed. "It's where much of Gavendara's wool and mutton comes from." He then came over to greet Astar, shaking his hand. "I am Lonel, third son of Urion of Narleywood."

Astar didn't know where Narleywood was, so he guessed it must be a small regency. He refrained from asking at risk of causing offence.

"So, we have ourselves a sheepherder..." Bovan sneered. Some of the other men at the back laughed.

Astar glared at him. Llamaleil was one of the largest regencies in Gavendara, and his family had a legacy they could trace back over eight hundred years. He opened his mouth to make a retort but was cut short by Frast marching into the hall.

"Astar! Got your ass out of bed *and* dressed yourself, I see. Impressive, for a lordling," he said as he joined them, causing everyone, including Elita, to laugh.

"While you clearly got out of the wrong side of yours..." Astar muttered.

"Nijax," Frast barked, and one of Bovan's cronies stepped forward. "You're up first. Let's see what the rookie's made of."

"What weapon?" Nijax asked.

"Up to him," Frast turned to Astar. "What do you fancy, sonny?"

"Spear," Astar replied. First impressions can be lasting, and he planned to make them all see that he was someone to be reckoned with.

Frast directed Astar to a small room with a selection of wooden weapons with blunted points. Astar tested the weight and balance of a few, but none came anywhere near the comfort he felt with his own spear locked away in his room. He settled on a shorter one with a thick shaft. Nijax went straight for the largest on the rack.

A few moments later, they were standing twenty yards apart in the centre of the main chamber, and Frast and the rest of the squad had formed a ring around them to watch. Elita waved at Astar as Frast counted down.

When the count was over, Nijax rushed in, his spear swaying from side to side as he charged. Astar twisted from his opening thrust and skirted around him. He swung for Nijax's shoulder, but the other man blocked. Wood met wood, and Astar's spear jarred in his hands. He tried to hold his ground, but Nijax was stronger and sent him reeling.

Astar knew that he couldn't let Nijax press his

advantage, so he caught his balance on the back of his heels and sidestepped. Circling him, Astar leapt back into the fray, twirling his spear around in an attempt to distract the eye, but Nijax saw the blow coming and dodged.

Astar took a few steps back and reconsidered his tactics. So far, he had only used basic manoeuvres because he was testing Nijax's skill level. Astar didn't want the next opponent Frast threw at him to know the full measure of his technique – he greatly believed that keeping people in the dark about your full potential gave you the edge of surprise.

He was going to try and win this first bout without even using his magic if he could.

Astar upped his game a little. He drove forward and flashed his spear in a sequence of lunges and drives, trying to get within Nijax's range. Eventually, he did and chanced a blow to Nijax's thigh, but the young man was as sturdy as a tree and barely flinched. Nijax fought back then. Aggressively. The air whistled with the force of his blows. Astar blocked every one, but each came at a price. Nijax was stronger than him. He was beginning to wear Astar down.

But Astar had discerned two things by this point: he was more skilled than Nijax, and he was faster. So, he began to use both to his advantage.

He began to favour twisting and skirting around the thrusts of Nijax's spear instead of blocking them. He danced around him. Eventually, Astar saw an opening and landed a blow to Nijax's side. If they were wielding real weapons, it would have inflicted a grave wound and resulted in Astar's victory, but Nijax evidently had a high pain threshold and didn't acknowledge it.

They both took a step back and circled each other. Sweat beaded Astar's brow. He knew he would have to finish this soon, or he wouldn't have enough energy to defeat the next person Frast threw at him.

He resorted to magic. Channelling *viga*, he focussed on the tip of Nijax's spear and sparked an illusion of flames.

Everyone in the hall gasped.

Nijax stared at his weapon, his eyes widening as fire danced all the way down the shaft to lick at his hand.

He dropped it, and Astar was upon him, driving his elbow into his gut and toppling him over.

Nijax fell flat on his back, and Astar pointed the end of his spear to his neck.

"What is it with these little lordlings and their cheap tricks?!" Frast groaned. "*Fine!* Let's even the playing field and send in one of your own then, little mage. Lonel!" he called. "You're up!"

Nijax limped back to the others and was shortly replaced by Lonel, who, like a typical noble, chose a sword as his weapon. Astar did the same, swapping out his spear so as to not have an unfair advantage over him.

Astar entered this skirmish a little more carefully than the last. He had no idea what kind of Blessing Lonel had. The young noble was a skilled swordsman though, so at first they merely jousted with their weapons.

Astar found an opening, but a flash of light repelled his blow. A sphere of blue energy manifested around Lonel.

He can shield! Astar realised. It was a fairly common ability among those who were Blessed, especially among the noble houses. Astar had duelled with such people before and knew that the only way to get past was to wear them down until they ran out of *viga*.

Astar summoned upon his own magic and created a doppelganger of himself. Everyone gasped, and Lonel's eyes widened as two Astar's approached him from opposite sides.

Lonel flashed his sword in frantic motions, trying to fight both of them off, but Astar was fast, and his mirror image was even faster. They both circled Lonel to distract his eye and make him forget which one was the real Astar, and Astar took advantage of Lonel's confusion, striking at his shield over and over again until Lonel's *viga* ran thin and Astar broke through.

Lonel was honourable in his defeat, and the two of them shook hands. Frast, however, seemed furious. He scowled and crossed his arms over his chest.

"Elita!" he yelled. "Your turn."

Astar had a feeling this was going to be a much tougher challenge. Elita must have a powerful gift to have been taken in by the Institute as a child.

Everyone whispered to each other as she strolled into the centre of the room.

"Illusions, hey?" she said coolly as she halted twenty paces away from him. She had a short wooden sword in her hand. "That's cute. *My* scits are *real*."

"I look forward to seeing it…" Astar winked.

"Are you ready?" Frast yelled.

"Always," Elita yelled back over her shoulder.

As Frast counted down, Astar cloaked a shroud of invisibility around himself and left a doppelganger to stand in his place.

Astar then crept away, hiding from view in the far corner of the room. But, to the others – including Elita – it seemed that Astar had not moved at all.

He wanted to hang back and observe. Find out what exactly it was Elita could do before he stepped into the ring for real.

Once the count ended, Elita clenched her fists by her sides, and a gust of wind engulfed the air around her, billowing her hair.

She's Blessed by Ta'al, Astar realised.

Astar continued observing. Although, he made sure to keep the doppelganger of himself convincing by amplifying the illusion. He made them seem to try to fight their way through the gale Elita had conjured to reach her, hair and tunic flapping with the wind as they laboured for each step. When the illusory Astar finally reached Elita, she ceased the winds, and the two of them began to spar. Astar made the image dodge and skirt around her blows rather than block, though, as he knew that if her sword passed through his mirage she would realise it wasn't real. He wanted to learn the extent of her gift before he went in to finish her off.

She displayed remarkable agility as she ducked and

spun around the thrusts of his spear, always with a smile on her face. At one point, she directed her free hand towards Astar's doppelganger, and forks of blue light flared from her hand like thunder tearing across a sky. Astar made his replica fall flat on his back as if stunned.

She's more than just Blessed by Ta'al, he realised. *I'm going to have to surprise her to win this…*

He made the image of himself split into two, making it seem like he was performing the same trick he had used on Lonel. Both of the mirages leapt back to their feet and circled her from opposite directions. Astar had to concentrate very hard to make both of them seem convincing as they closed in on Elita from each side.

Elita burst into life again. She was giving it her all, twirling her sword around in agile motions to evade the dual attackers. More forks of lightning flared from the palm of her free hand, but both her physical and magical assaults passed through Astar's mirage as if they were dust. She spun around. Frantic. Trying to decipher which of them was the *real* Astar.

Neither. The real Astar was invisible, and closing in on her. When he was just a few feet away, he implemented his last, final diversion and made one of his illusory doppelgangers cry out in pain and topple over, seemingly wounded. The other mirage vanished.

Elita held her sword up to the air, victorious, and smiled at the figure of Astar's body convulsing on the floor. She then lowered the sword to his neck.

"That's all you've got?" she teased. "I was expecting more from you…"

"Glad to meet your expectations," Astar replied as he lifted the veil and revealed himself.

Astar had crept up behind her, and he now had one arm wrapped around her collar and the side of his training sword held to her throat. She jerked in surprise, which made her body press up against his. Everyone in the hall gasped.

"That trick will only work on me once…" she whispered.

"I have plenty more," Astar said as he released her.

Frost was vexed about the situation and possessed no inclination to hide it. He stared at Astar, the wrinkles on his forehead tightening until they crumpled together.

"Bovan!" he yelled, summoning the giant waiting at the sidelines. "It's down to you now…"

Frost then turned back to Astar. "And no damn sorcery this time! I want to see what you're *really* made of."

Astar felt nerves creep up his spine, but he did not let his nerves show.

He knew what was going on here; Frost was punishing him for being too good.

Bovan strode up and poised himself ready. Even from twenty paces away, he visibly towered over Astar. His arms were broader than most men's thighs.

I'll lose this without my magic. For sure… Astar realised as he eyed up his opponent. Astar desperately wanted to win this.

Even if it was just to piss Frost off.

*I **could** try to use my magic on him without Frast knowing…* Astar then thought.

A couple of years ago, Astar discovered that he was capable of isolating his illusions – making it so that only those he specifically targetted could see them – but it was a technique he had never had much reason to practice before.

It would be risky, he thought. *If Frost catches me, he'll make my life a misery. He'll have me cleaning the latrines. Or something worse.*

*But I **did** come here to learn…* he decided, as he drew upon his *viga*. *Let's give it a try…*

He channelled a thread of his magic at Bovan so that the young man alone would be the only one subject to the sequence of illusions Astar was about to implement.

By the time Astar had established the link, the countdown was over, and Bovan was charging. Astar threw himself back into the present with a jolt, opening his eyes barely in time to see Bovan's sword swoop down upon him. He ducked and rolled.

Bovan was faster than he looked. Astar had barely landed back on his feet before he had to evade another blow. This time he twisted out of range. Bovan was on him again. Their weapons met, and Bovan was so strong the force send Astar's feet skidding across the floor. He retreated.

The few short moments before Bovan squared up to him again gave Astar a chance to start conjuring illusions. The link he had established with Bovan was still there.

But Astar knew that, if he were to stand a hope of pulling this off, he would need to be subtle – anything too dramatic would give him away – so he focussed on small changes. He altered the angle of his blade, making Bovan see it in a different position than it actually was.

Bovan's weapon bore down upon him but, thanks to Astar's misdirection, Astar blocked in such a way to gain an opening. He poked the giant in the ribs, and Bovan groaned.

Astar withdrew and took this moment as a chance to consider his tactics. Bovan put a hand to his chest and then looked at Astar with a peculiar expression – as if he knew that something was wrong but couldn't quite put his finger upon it.

He advanced on Astar again – a little more cautious now – and swung his blade. Astar blocked, but Bovan was still seeing Astar's weapon from a distorted angle, which gave Astar the chance to catch him off balance. He struck, catching Bovan with another blow, this time to his leg.

Bovan yelled out and retreated a little, frowning as he did so.

Astar knew he needed to finish this soon – to avoid drawing too much suspicion – and pressed his advantage. Their blades met again. Bovan was stronger, so it took all of Astar's determination to hold his ground whilst devising his next misdirection. He crafted an image in Bovan's mind of himself remaining in the sword lock.

But the real him slipped away, leaving Bovan almost toppling over from the sudden weight missing beneath his sword. Astar twisted around him and made a finishing blow, thrusting the flat of his boot into Bovan's back, sending him falling flat on his face.

From the shocked gasps which came from the other side of the hall, it was clear to Astar that what he had just done – defeat Bovan in armed combat – was unheard of within Squad Six.

The giant groaned as he rolled over, and Astar could see, from the cold anger in his eyes, he knew that Astar had somehow duped him.

Astar had made his first enemy at the Institute.

But it was worth it. Elita rushed over to congratulate him.

Chapter 5

Lighter Burdens

"Why aren't you ready?" Rivan asked when he strode into Sidry's room to find him clad in a loose-fitting tunic and white leggings – which was hardly fitting attire for a day duelling in the fields.

"I can't go…" Sidry sighed. "The Synod want to see me."

"Really? *Again*? They don't want me as well, do they?" Rivan groaned. The thought of having to sit through another one of their inane interrogations made him want to tear his hair out.

"No," Sidry shook his head glumly. "It's just me and Baird they want to see today. We've been called in."

"Are you *sure* they don't want me?" Rivan asked, scratching his head.

"Yes. They were quite specific," Sidry said. "Just me and Baird this time… Look, Rivan, just go to the fields without me. I'm sure you'll find someone willing to spar you."

"Why do they only want you and Baird, though? You don't think that it has something to do with the…" Rivan hesitated and motioned to Sidry's forehead. "The…"

"The Stones of Gezra," Sidry finished for him. "Yes, Rivan… I think it probably has everything to do with that."

"Are you okay?" Rivan asked.

Sidry had always been uncomfortable with the idea of being made a spectacle. Rivan knew that. The ritual that fused him to the Stone of Gezra left him covered in scars, and he was extremely sensitive about them. So much so that, ever since then, Sidry had only ever changed his clothes or bathed when he was in utter privacy.

Despite these things, Rivan couldn't help but feel envious sometimes. When Sidry summoned his Avatar, he became near-immortal – and yet, he spent much time lamenting about it.

Rivan often wished that it had been him for whom fate had chosen such a heavy burden, for he was certain he would have put those powers to greater use than Sidry.

It wasn't something he would ever speak out loud, though.

"Look on the bright side," Rivan said, pushing those thoughts to the back of his mind again. He knew they were unreasonable. "If they want to see… well, you know… what you and Baird can do… that must mean they're starting to listen."

Sidry feigned a smile. "I know, Rivan. Look. I'll be okay. Just go out and enjoy yourself. I'll tell you how it went later."

"Are you sure?" Rivan asked. The thought of leaving his friend to face something like that alone left Rivan guilty.

"Just go…" Sidry said. "I'll be fine. I Promise."

"Okay. Well… I'll come see you later, I guess," Rivan said, just before he left.

It's out of my hands, he thought as he shut the door behind himself and made his way out of the building.

Reaching the Synod had been a disillusioning experience for Rivan. He thought that the revered establishment would have lightened their burdens but, so far, they had only made them heavier. He didn't feel safe here – not since Jaedin had revealed that there were Zakaras among them. Most of Rivan's days had been spent being interrogated by Consilars who kept asking him the same questions over and over again, yet not believing any of his answers. He had lost his temper on more than a few occasions, and no real progress had been made.

This was the first day the Consilars had left Rivan to his leisure, and it was Veyday. The day of rest. The Academy was closed for lessons, but its training fields were still accessible for those who wanted to use them.

It was a peculiar feeling for Rivan to wander the

grounds of the Academy. The place had been his life-long aspiration. Being an unwanted child had driven him to do his utmost to gain a scholarship there so that he could prove his worth to his parents, but now his parents were dead. He didn't know how to feel. A part of him still idolised the Academy – he always would. But, in another sense, he felt like he had outgrown it.

The first thing Rivan saw when he reached the fields were a pair of students pummelling their fists into punching bags filled with grain, and he couldn't help but look down upon them. What Kyra said when they rode into Shemet was true; whilst these Academy students had played joust in a controlled environment, Rivan had slain monsters; saved them from an evil they didn't even know existed yet.

If his adventures were truly over, Rivan wouldn't mind settling down here and living out his lifelong dream of training at the Academy, but a bigger part of him wanted to take on something *real* again.

Rivan groaned when he spotted Kyra in the archery fields. He should have guessed that she, too, would jump at the very first opportunity to visit this place.

It appeared she had already made friends. Rivan tried to walk past without being seen, but it was too late. Their eyes met, she opened her mouth, and that annoying voice of hers rang through his ears.

"Rivan! I was wondering if you would show up," Kyra called. The boys around her looked over at him. "They have a beginner's lane here!" she taunted, pointing to one of the targets on the other side of the field. "Shall I teach you how to draw a bow?"

"I thought you said everyone from your village was a master hunter?" one of the boys asked Kyra, jokingly.

"Most of us are," Kyra bragged. "But there are always a few who lack the grace… anyway, move out of my way," she said as she shoved past him. "I'll show you how it's done."

She nocked her arrow and loosed. It hit the centre of the ring and one of the boys whistled. She then loosed a second arrow. And a third. All of them struck true.

"Alright… We get the point. You're fair with a bow," one of them conceded.

"What about with a sword? Or spear?" another of them cut in, shouldering past his friends. "I bet you three lannies I can beat you in a duel. Any weapon."

"Good idea," Rivan said. They all looked at him. "Where do you go to spar here? I'll happily show you how fast she falls on her face."

Rivan crossed his arms over his chest and gave Kyra *that* look. They didn't need words to goad each other.

"Bring it on!" Kyra said, smiling.

"The duelling cages are this way," one of them said, thumbing behind his shoulder. "Follow me! We'll see what you western clodhoppers are made of…"

Rivan smiled as they all collected their bows. Despite everything, he had missed this. Competition. Banter. It would be interesting to see how talented these Academy fledgelings *really* were.

And any opportunity to show Kyra up was always a bonus.

"She's a bit of a rare bird, isn't she?" one of the boys sidled up next to Rivan. He then whispered into his ear. "Nice tits as well."

Rivan flinched. The thought that anyone could ever find Kyra appealing in that way had always perplexed him.

"Oh… sorry…" the boy then said, noticing something in Rivan's expression. "I didn't mean… look, don't worry. I'll leave her alone if you and her are–"

"Oh Gods! *No!*" Rivan interrupted him repugnantly. "*No! No! No!* It's not… Look man, no offence, but I'd rather stick it in a bee's nest! You can *have* her!"

"Oh, he can. Can he?" Kyra butted in. "I wouldn't hold your breath… either of you. Anyway, Rivan. Can I speak with you a moment?"

"What do you want?" Rivan asked irritably.

"*Rivan,*" Kyra reiterated, and there was something sobering about her tone. "I want to talk. *Alone.*"

"Fine…" Rivan groaned as he fell back with Kyra to the tail of the crowd.

"Don't fuck this up for me!" Kyra warned once they were out of earshot.

Rivan grinned. "What's the matter, Kyra? Afraid I'm going to show you up? You said before you–"

"Look, Rivan. *You* may be thinking that this is all fun and games – and maybe that is all you're interested in," Kyra whispered. "But *I* am doing something important, and I don't want you to get in my way."

"Oh, important work is this?" Rivan snorted. "Look, Kyra. I've been cooped up indoors with those bloody Synod morons for *days*. I just want to–"

"Is that *all* you can think about?" she asked. "Don't you remember what Jaedin said? There are *Zakaras* here. What if one of these guys is one of them?"

Rivan stared at her, realising that, underneath all that bravado she had been brandishing, something else was going on.

"I'm trying to suss them out, Rivan," Kyra whispered. "Zakaras are never quite the same once they've turned. You know that. They're quicker, stronger, and even when they disguise themselves as human, there's still something not quite right about them. Can't you see what I'm doing?" she asked, gesturing to the group of young men leading them towards the cage. Rivan looked at them, but now in a different way. He suddenly became aware of the reality. That it was perfectly possible that any one of them could be among the Zakara infiltrators Jaedin had warned them about. "That's why I'm fighting them. To see what they're made of."

"Okay, okay! I get your point," Rivan agreed. "So what's your plan?"

"Fight them," Kyra replied simply. "Not each other. I'll kick your ass some other time if you want it so much, but right now, we have more important things."

"Okay, so we fight them and see if any of them are unusually fast or strong, or… well, I reckon I could tell just by looking them in the eye, to be honest. We should also watch out for the quiet ones. Zakaras are usually a bit brainless."

"Not these ones," Kyra shook her head. "Haven't you spoken to Jaedin yet?"

Rivan shook his head. He had thought of going to visit him but not quite got round to it. Rivan no longer hated Jaedin like he used to, but he couldn't help but feel that an encounter between the two of them alone would be awkward. They had never been friends. All the time they had ever spent together had been a matter of survival rather than choice. They were completely different people.

And yet, Rivan still felt a little guilty.

"Jaedin said they have been enhanced. Or something. I don't quite get what he was on about, but the point is, be wary…" Kyra said. "These are not your usual Zakaras here, Rivan. They are smarter, and I think they're going to be harder to suss out."

"Okay…" Rivan said, eyeing the boys walking ahead of them – now seeing them all as suspects. "Let's do this."

*　　*　　*

It wasn't too long after Rivan left that Sidry heard a knock at the door. He got up from his chair and answered it to find Baird on the other side.

"Are you ready?" his mentor asked.

Sidry nodded, although he didn't feel it. Nerves were fluttering around in his stomach.

"I think something's happened," Baird said when Sidry closed the door behind himself. They began to make their way down the stairs. "There's been lots of people running around the Synod today. They're all talking in whispers."

"Do you think they believe us now?" Sidry asked.

"I don't know," Baird shook his head. "Sidry… I think there must be a reason for it being just you and me they want to see today. Do you understand what I am saying?"

"Yes," Sidry said, swallowing a lump in his throat.

"If they ask you to show them the Avatar of Gezra, you must do it," Baird said. "We need to make them believe."

A pair of Sentinels met them at the entrance of the Synod and escorted them to a small chamber on the upper floor, where three Consilars were waiting. Sidry recognised two of them, but the third was a blonde-haired woman he had never met before.

"Hello Baird," Greyjor said. Sidry had spent many hours being interrogated by this man over the last few days and, during that time, he had grown accustomed to his face bearing a hostile expression. Now, there was something much more disconcerted about his demeanour. The same was true of the other two people with him; it was clear, from the solemn expressions on their faces, that they had just received dire news.

"We have… just heard back from our scouts," Greyjor began. "They arrived this morning, and their reports are… well… to be quite frank, concerning…" He inhaled deeply and peered at the sheets of parchment on the table before him. "Our scouts have confirmed that there has indeed been grave devastation to the township of Fraknar… what is left of it, at least. Gods have mercy on their souls…"

"It was the Zakaras," Baird said. "Just like we've been trying to tell you all this time… Greyjor. It is time to act. We need to–"

"We believe you," the blonde woman next to Greyjor said earnestly. "We just need to smooth out some of the details…"

She then turned to Sidry and smiled thinly. Sidry could see, from the glassiness in her eyes, that she had not too long ago been crying. He hoped that meant that, behind her dutiful mien, she was a compassionate woman. "Sorry, I forgot to introduce myself. I am Selena. You are Sidry, aren't you? We made a request for you to come here with Baird."

Sidry nodded.

"I'm going to cut to the chase," Selena said. "Gods forgive us… it is clear that we have wasted enough time as it is. On behalf of the Synod, I wish to apologise for the way we have received you so far. Please try to understand that some of the things you have told us are very—"

"Are we really going to believe *all* of this?" Vancer interrupted, gesturing to the reports. "There's tales here of ghouls taking to the sky, and all sorts!"

Sidry shifted uncomfortably in his seat. He had been interviewed by this man a few times previously as well, and had taken a strong dislike to him.

"There are several reports of a girl," Greyjor said, adopting a calmer tone than his peer. He gave Vancer a hard stare before turning back to Baird. "A sorceress. One who appeared to be using some form of necromancy. Do you know anything about this, Baird?"

Bryna… Sidry thought, his heart lurching within his chest. *They mean Bryna.*

He turned his face to his lap so that his expression wouldn't give anything away.

Bryna had asked them all to keep her identity as the Descendant of Vai-ris a guarded secret.

"Vancer is right. On that count, at least," Baird said, through gritted teeth. "You know what word of mouth is like, Greyjor. People talk, and each time, the story changes a little, and the details get muddled. A few of those who helped us fight Shayam that night had Blessings which they put to use. But I didn't witness anything as dramatic as what you've just described."

"Isn't one of those girls you brought back with you a witch?" Greyjor asked, narrowing his eyes.

Baird nodded. "Her mother was a Devotee of Carnea. And, well, as you likely know, that kind of thing usually runs in the family. You should have a file on Bryna's mother somewhere, as she was also a registered tutor. Her name was Meredith. But like I said, I don't think Bryna is of much interest to you. When we went out to battle, she stayed behind to help with the wounded."

Sidry was surprised at how easily his mentor delivered the lie. He didn't even flinch.

"Okay. Well, that just leaves the matter of you two..." Greyjor said. "What is behind this claim that you can summon celestial forms? Ones which can leap over the walls of a castle!"

"The tales our scouts have brought back certainly seem to support it... but I have to confess that I find some of the details hard to believe," Selena said.

There was a brief silence.

"Can you give us some kind of demonstration of this power you claim to have?" Greyjor asked.

Baird turned his eyes up to the ceiling. "We can. But not in here."

Vancer burst into a ripple of laughter and slammed his palm upon the table, making Sidry jump. "Hear that!" he chuckled, turning to Greyjor. "They *can't* show us! How convenient!"

"I can't show you the avatar of a god in this room!" Baird yelled back.

"The avatar of a god!" Vancer exclaimed. "Did you hear him? An avatar of a *god!* Well, I guess it would be useful to have a couple of those hanging around. How about some unicorns as well, while we are at it! That would fill our stables!"

"That is quite enough, Vancer!" Selena said, rising from her chair and gathering her papers. "Come with me, Baird..." she said. "I'm taking you to the Solus."

"The Solus?" Greyjor repeated, frowning at her. "You can't! There's a meeting–"

"We have wasted more than enough time with your ruddy meetings!" she retorted.

"Selena!" Greyjor yelled as she left the table and made her way towards the door. "Stop this now! You are breaching–"

"I can't care!" she said over her shoulder. "Baird! Sidry! Are you coming with me?"

"First bit of sense I have heard from any of you!" Baird said as he got up to follow her.

"Get back here! *Now!*" Greyjor roared, his face turning red with vehement rage.

Why is he so angry? Sidry wondered. It just seemed so irrational.

Sidry then had a sudden epiphany.

He's one of the Zakaras! he realised. *One of the infiltrators!*

It all made sense. Why had Sidry not thought of it before? Ever since they had arrived, it had always been Greyjor slowing everything down for them. Keeping their meetings contained within quiet little rooms instead of making them public, and sowing the seeds of scepticism.

And now, when the truth was becoming harder and harder to deny, he was *still* desperately trying to keep it contained.

"Are you coming, Sidry?" Baird's voice interrupted his thoughts.

"Yes..." Sidry said, feeling an urge to get as far away from Greyjor as possible. He leapt from his chair and rushed to catch up with them.

"I need to talk to you!" Sidry said to Baird once they were clear of the room.

"Not now..." Baird replied as the two of them raced to keep up with Selena. She was leading them down the stairs. "We must do this *now*, Sidry. While we have the chance."

He thinks I'm just trying to get out of showing them my Avatar, Sidry realised.

"It's *important*, Baird!" Sidry hissed. Baird looked at him again, slowing his step. "What is it?" he said, hushing his voice. "Tell me."

"Greyjor," Sidry whispered. "I think he is one of the infiltrators."

Baird drew to a complete halt and frowned at him. "Why?"

Sidry paused before responding, realising that he didn't have much in the way of justification for his theory. "I just *do*," he said. "Think about the way he has been. It's like he's against us."

The two of them were interrupted by Selena's voice. "Are the two of you *coming*?" she called.

Sidry looked down the steps to see that she was holding a door open, waiting.

"We'll talk about this later..." Baird murmured to Sidry and then grabbed his arm. "Let's go!"

The rest of their march to the Solus was all a blur. All Sidry could think about was Greyjor. He recalled every interaction he had ever had with him in his mind with terrible new clarity, and it only convinced him more of his suspicions.

Eventually, Selena swung open a final pair of doors, and Sidry found himself being led right into the centre of a massive circular chamber. Sunlight shone brightly from the skylight in the middle of the domed ceiling, illuminating all the people sitting in the pews above.

"Selena?" a man stood within a parapet said. "What is the meaning of this? We are holding council."

"I'm sorry, Jared," Selena said as she stepped onto the dais. "But this is an emergency. It can't wait."

She then turned to Baird. "Show them," she said and then walked away, leaving just Sidry and Baird alone on the platform.

The entirety of the Solus was staring down at them. Many of them seemed disgruntled at having their meeting interrupted.

"Sharma is in grave danger," Baird raised his head to address the rows of people sitting above them. "And I have been trying to warn you about it for too long. You know now that Fraknar has been destroyed, but yet you *still* refuse to act! You can't accept the evidence which is right before your eyes!"

Baird tore off his tunic, and there were a series of gasps as he revealed the scars that covered his body. Sidry knew the symbols and markings on his mentor's flesh all too well; they were identical to his own.

"I am just a soldier!" Baird declared. "I don't understand the things which were done to me. Or the evil which has been unleashed upon this world. All I know is everything that I have seen since. And *you!*" he exclaimed, pointing an accusatory finger across the room.

"Are sitting here in your little chairs *talking!* Doing *nothing* to help! People will die if you don't act soon. By wasting time, you disrespect every soul from Fraknar and Jalard who were killed by the Zakaras!

"So now…" Baird said, his voice lowering as he turned his head down. "I am going to show you…"

He clenched his fists, and a sudden flash of light engulfed the room.

When it was over, Baird was gone, and another being was standing in his place.

One only had to look upon an Avatar of Gezra – with its glimmering skin that more resembled armour than flesh – to know it could only be celestial in nature. Its mighty stature towered several feet higher than the tallest of men.

Baird spun around in one fluid, graceful motion, and the two slits which were now his eyes looked at Sidry. He didn't need to say anything. Sidry knew it was his cue.

He called upon the crystal in his forehead, summoning its power. White light encased his body.

They cannot deny the truth now, Sidry thought, as he transformed.

Chapter 6

Squad Three

When Astar reached the food hall that morning, he was disappointed to find that Elita had already claimed a place at another table. One full of young men.

He watched as one of them leaned over and whispered something in her ear. She laughed and did that thing she sometimes did when she was flirting; tilting her head and flicking a lock of her blonde hair over her shoulder.

Elita had proven herself to be Astar's most ambitious challenge to date, but that had only inflated his desire for her. Every conversation the two of them had shared, since Astar had arrived at the Institute, had become a game. One of coquettish words and playful gestures. Elita always gave him just enough encouragement to keep him trying, but never relented.

Astar filled his platter with food and pretended not to see her as he claimed one of the nearby tables, but he could have sworn that, as he walked past, she looked at him from the corner of her eye.

He began to eat alone. As usual. Astar was yet to make any friends at the Institute. Bovan had made it clear to the other members of Squad Six that Astar was their enemy ever since that first day when he defeated him in a duel.

It was not something which bothered Astar all too much; he would rather be feared than liked.

"We're fighting today," Dareth announced as he dropped his platter on the table.

"We're fighting?" Astar repeated quizzically.

"Well… maybe. Sort of," Dareth said as he stabbed a knife into a sausage and brought it to his mouth. "You're part of Squad Six, aren't you? I've been told to report to your group."

"Why?" Astar asked.

"Not sure. They didn't say…" Dareth said.

Astar stared at Dareth for a few moments and, as usual, wondered how much the young man wasn't telling him.

He had grown to enjoy Dareth's company during their occasional exchanges over breakfast. The young man had a sour candour to him Astar appreciated and, furthermore, Astar wanted to get to the bottom of his secret. He had been subtly trying to whittle it out of him but so far Dareth had divulged nothing too revealing.

Maybe seeing him fight today would give him more clues.

"How are you finding this midden of a place?" Dareth asked.

"Boring," Astar murmured.

"Find something to entertain yourself with then," Dareth suggested.

"I'm working on it," Astar said, eyeing Elita.

"There's a watering hole by the stables," Dareth suggested. "Some of the other students spend their evenings there."

"What's it like?" Astar asked.

"Not sure," Dareth shrugged. "Never been. It's too far from my room."

"Where *is* your room?" Astar said. This was yet another surprise. As far as Astar knew, all of the students lived in the same block of boarding houses. Which happened to be close to the stables.

"I live on the other side of the grounds. By that stupid library," Dareth replied.

"Really?" Astar said. That was where most of the teachers and trainers lived. "Why do you live there?"

"I just do," Dareth said guardedly.

"Are you going to tell me where you're from yet?" Astar probed. He still couldn't place Dareth's accent. It was unlike any that he had ever heard. His vowels sounded lazy.

"It's none of your scitting business!" Dareth snapped, catching Astar by surprise. "What's with all the questions? You're not a soddy or something, are you?"

"What do you mean?" Astar said, somewhat taken

aback by the young man's overblown reaction. "What's a 'soddy'?"

"A soddy," Dareth repeated. "You know... a *sodd*. Men who..." He hesitated and pulled an awkward expression. "Do things with each other."

"I've never heard that word before," Astar raised an eyebrow. "And for the record. No. I am one hundred per cent going to rump that girl over there."

Dareth turned around.

"Don't *look* at her!" Astar exclaimed.

"Why?" Dareth asked.

"Because if she catches you looking, she'll know I'm talking about her! Gods, Dareth! What are you *doing*?" Astar said, slapping his forehead.

"She's not that special..." Dareth shrugged. "What you being all weird about it for? Either she likes you, or she doesn't. You shouldn't waste your time."

"You know nothing about women, do you..."

"I don't let them run my life," Dareth shrugged.

"And you think *I'm* the sodd?" Astar laughed.

Dareth scowled.

He has something against... sodds, Astar realised. *Even the way he says the word sounds harsh. Like he is spitting it out. It must be some kind of regional slang. Maybe, if I can find out where it is from, it'll be a clue as to where* **he** *is from.*

"You done?" Dareth grunted after he had cleared his platter.

Astar nodded and then followed him out of the mess hall. They walked towards the training grounds. Dareth seemed to have got himself into a mood, so neither of them talked for a while.

"Look – I'm sorry for snapping at you," Dareth eventually said when they neared the outbuilding. "It's just... something happened to my home, and I don't want to talk about it... I don't have a home anymore. It's gone."

"Oh... I'm sorry," Astar said. This was the first hint of tender emotion Dareth had ever expressed in front of him, and it was surprising. "I'm just nosey."

They entered the run-down building together, and most of Astar's squad were already there. Including Bovan, who greeted Astar with his customary sneer. Elita was sitting in the far corner and seemed intent with carrying on with her elusive act that day, giving Astar no invitation to join her.

"Friendly group you have here," Dareth muttered when Bovan narrowed his eyes at him.

"You don't know what you're missing out on…" Astar said dryly.

"We have something different for you today," Frast bellowed as he entered. He marched straight into the middle of the assembly and crossed his arms over his chest. "I did warn Grav'aen that *most* of you aren't ready for this, but he insisted, and, unlike *some* of you," he spared a moment to glare at Astar. "I know how to follow orders.

"You will be duelling against members of Squad Three," he announced after scanning the room to make sure he had their attention. "To be frank, I don't think many of you are a match for them, so I urge you, *try* not to get yourselves too bloodied up. If not for me, then for the cleaners who'll be wiping up the mess…

"You'll be paired up–" Frast began but was cut off when a series of shadows appeared at the door.

Squad Three entered. The drum of their footsteps echoed across the entire hall, and Astar found something about that sound unsettling. He looked at their feet and noticed that they were all marching in perfect unison. Left foot, right foot, left foot, right foot.

"Pretentious gits…" Astar muttered.

"Be careful," Dareth whispered. "You *don't* want to piss these guys off. Trust me…"

As they came closer, Astar realised that there might be some truth to that. Their trainer was a lithe figure. He seemed too young and fresh-faced to be the leader of such a physically imposing group. They visibly dwarfed him. Even the smallest of the members of Squad Three were on a par with Bovan when it came to size.

They all had deadpan expressions on their faces, and there was something strange about their eyes. Like they were out of focus.

"Greetings. My name is Nevara, and this is my Squad," the small man at the front said, gesturing to the youths assembled behind him. They halted as one and stared blankly at whatever was directly in front of them.

He is **weird**... Astar thought as Nevara and Frast shook hands. Nevara had a brightly patterned shawl wrapped around his head, obscuring his hair and anything above his eyebrows.

"Today, we will be staging inter-squad battles," Nevara then said, his eyes wandering across the hall as he sized everyone up. The way he spoke, and even his poise, gave Astar the impression that he was more of a scholar than a warrior. It made Astar doubt how efficiently he could have trained the youths who stood behind him. "Frast and I will each select a candidate in turn to duel one another. All weapons and techniques are permitted."

Astar was greatly relieved by this news, and he and Elita grinned at each other. Frast all too often forbade them from using magic.

"Samex," Nevara then called, and one of the members of his squad dully lifted his head. "Please select your weapon."

Frast ran his eyes across the members of his squad contemplatively, and his gaze honed in upon one of the members of Bovan's gang.

"Kierium," Frast decided. "You're up."

They're pitching their weakest first, Astar realised as the two combatants went to the weapons rack. Kierium was one of the underdogs of Squad Six.

Astar and Dareth claimed seats on a bench at the side of the hall while the two combatants prepared.

The first duel didn't last for very long. Kierium blocked the first three swings but was struck by the fourth and fell flat on his back. Samex fought like an automaton. His expression was placid and, even when he won, that countenance didn't change. He merely turned and walked away.

Astar began to feel nervous. If this man really was the least prolific member of Squad Three, they were in trouble.

Frast picked Nijax for the next battle, and he faced off against a young woman with red hair and big arms. Astar often held female warriors in high regard because there were fewer, and, what they sometimes lacked for in terms of strength and size – compared to their male counterparts – they frequently more than made up for in swiftness and grace, but this giantess was an exception to that rule. Her biceps were even thicker than Bovan's and, much like her predecessor, she fought in a routine and monotonous manner, swinging her wooden claymore in a series of massive blows that eventually sent Nijax tumbling over.

Nijax lasted little longer than Kierium did.

"We're getting our asses kicked," Astar whispered to Dareth.

"You're faring better than most," Dareth replied through the side of his mouth. "Squad Three are... a bit different."

He knows something he's not telling me, Astar realised, reading his friend's guarded expression. He opened his mouth to ask but was cut short by the next brawl beginning.

Frast's summons came in an increasingly frustrated tone as he bellowed each name, but Squad Three sent each member of Squad Six hobbling back to the bench within moments of their spar beginning. Only one from Astar's squad triumphed, and that was Larius – one of the more apt members of Bovan's gang – and he came out of his narrowly-won victory limping and in a much sorrier state than the young woman he defeated. Lonel managed to stay standing longer than most of the others by using his shielding ability but, as soon as his *viga* ran dry, his opponent sent him sprawling.

"Elita!" Frast then roared.

The calling of her name made Astar realise that they were down to the last three members of Squad Six now. After Elita, there was only himself and Bovan left.

Elita casually swaggered towards the weapons rack, picked a sword without much deliberation, and made her way to the middle of the room.

As soon as her opponent was ready and Frast blew the whistle, Elita discarded her weapon and extended her palms. Blue static flared from her hands, and the charged bolts of energy rippled in the space between herself and the barrel-chested warrior before her. He gritted his teeth, and his entire body trembled.

He managed to stand his ground for a surprising amount of time before Elita's magic sent him reeling in a fit of convulsions.

"Bovan!" Frast then yelled. He seemed a little happier now. "You're up."

He's saving me till last! Astar realised in surprise.

By making such a gesture, Frast was admitting Astar was the most accomplished member of Squad Six.

It was something Astar had already known. But still, the fact that Frast was *acknowledging* it was something he had not anticipated.

Astar looked at his mentor, but Frast was too busy leering at Nevara.

I see... Astar thought, noticing the contempt in his trainer's eyes as he glared at the leader of the other squad. *He hates Nevara even more than he hates me...*

Frast did eventually look back at Astar, and when their eyes met, Astar did not sense the usual malice and disdain emanating from his mentor but something more abstract.

Astar understood. He and Frast still despised each other – that much was clear – but, at that moment in time, they shared a goal. An understanding.

By sight alone, Bovan's opponent was the mightiest yet. A hulk of a giant named Darek. The whole room went silent in anticipation as he and Bovan prepared to face each other.

Nevara had barely brought the whistle to his mouth before they both charged. Their weapons shrilled through the air but, just before they collided, Bovan dodged around him. Bovan then spun around and arched his sword at Darek's legs, but Darek leapt out of range.

They ran at each other again, and this time the boom of their weapons meeting was so loud some of the spectators jumped. They spun around each other, swinging and blocking in such rapid motions it was almost too fast for the eye to follow. Darek was undeniably the stronger of the pair, but Bovan had better technique.

Nearing the end, Bovan caught a blow to the ribs that sent him falling back, but he managed to recover his balance before the next strike came and dived out of the way.

He then darted back in again from the side, catching his opponent by surprise and knocking his weapon out of his hands.

By the skin of his teeth, Bovan had won.

"Astar," Frast said. "It's you now."

"Good luck," Dareth whispered as Astar got up and walked over to the rack to choose a weapon. He selected his favourite spear whilst his brown-haired, dull-eyed opponent grabbed a wooden broadsword.

Astar could feel everyone staring at him as he made his way to the marked spot in the middle of the hall. He prepared his wits for the battle, summoning threads of his magic and priming himself with *viga* so that he could ensnare his opponent with illusions.

When the whistle blew, Astar manifested four identical copies of himself. Three of them fanned out to his right, while the fourth darted to the left. Astar made them all copy his motions perfectly as he pointed the tip of his spear towards his adversary and slowly advanced.

Some of the people watching gasped and muttered to each other. This was the most sophisticated illusion Astar had ever let them see. He had been keeping the fact that he was able to sustain this many individual doppelgangers a secret. One saved for a special occasion.

But his opponent paid none of the doppelgangers any heed. He fixed his eyes upon Astar. The real Astar.

Shit! How does he know this is me? Astar wondered.

Astar made two of his copies leap in an attempt to startle him, but the young man just ignored them. He did not even flinch.

Astar panicked. He sent a flurry of illusions. A wall of fire rose from the ground, and another copy of himself leapt across the flames. Astar even cast a shield of invisibility around his actual self, but it was all vain. His opponent strode across the flames like they were water and swung his wooden training sword at Astar, striking his arm.

Astar cried out, falling to his knees. He dropped his weapon. All of his illusions vanished, apart from the usual shroud of glamour he always had wrapped around himself, and he only just managed to sustain a tenuous hold on that through the myriad of pain.

Just like all the others before him, Astar's opponent displayed no pleasure in his victory. He simply turned and marched away.

He didn't see my illusions... Astar realised.

"Get up, Astar!" Frost roared, his face turning purple. "You're in the way!"

Frost's voice tore Astar back to reality, and he realised that he had been shamefully beaten.

Astar crawled onto his feet, trying to keep his head held high to retain a shred of his torn dignity. He found himself unable to look any of the members of Squad Six in the eye, especially Elita. The pain in his shoulder was agony.

"And now for the final bout. Vivian!" Nevara announced, and a sturdy woman from his squad stepped forward.

Another bout? But there's none of us left... Astar thought.

"Dareth!" Frost called.

Dareth! Astar realised as his friend got up from the bench

He's not even picking a weapon, Astar thought as he watched Dareth take a spot in the middle of the room. *Why hasn't he got a weapon?*

When the duel began, Dareth clenched his fists, and what followed was a flash of white light that almost sent Astar falling back off the bench. It was blinding.

When Astar's sight returned, a glowing being with three horns upon its head was standing in the spot where Dareth had been.

*   *   *

What was that thing? Astar thought, later that evening.

He had made a very swift and humble exit from the training hall that day and went straight to his room without eating any supper. He'd been sitting on the end of his bed ever since. Brooding.

Astar summoned a memory of that creature in his mind again. No matter how many times he studied the image, he could never quite believe that it had been *real*. Its three horns. The shimmering hue of its body. The azure crystal on its forehead. It was a wonder that the young woman pitched against it didn't flee at the sheer sight of it.

The duel was over within moments, and yet Astar was convinced that Dareth had been holding back.

*Just **what** is your secret, Dareth?* Astar wondered as he examined the being's oval, almost featureless face from memory. It had just a few grim lines where its nose, mouth, and eyes should be.

Nothing to Astar's knowledge came close to offering any form of explanation for what he had seen that day. He regretted leaving the training hall so hastily after the skirmishes were over and missing a chance to quiz Dareth about it, but he felt so shamed by his mortifying defeat that he needed to get away.

Astar knew he had lost much of his esteem that day. A part of him felt tempted to pack his bags and head home.

But he couldn't bring himself to do it. By giving up and

leaving, he would only lose more face.

And besides, Astar had another riddle to solve. Dareth was not the only mysterious presence that haunted the Institute now. What Astar had just seen had convinced that there was something strange going on with Squad Three too. There was something unnatural about its members, from their abnormal strength to their deadpan faces and dull eyes. Even their manner. It was like they had no souls.

But Astar knew that his suspicions were wholly subjective and unsubstantiated. He couldn't act upon them.

Astar had never known someone to be immune to his Blessing before. That was something else that eluded explanation. Even Grav'aen had *seen* Astar's illusions before he had encroached upon his psyche and brought them to an end.

Astar's thoughts kept weaving around in circles, and his head began to ache.

Eventually, he exhaled loudly, grabbed his coat, and headed for the door. He thought of that watering hole Dareth told him about and decided to head there. He was tired of spending every evening alone in his room, reading books and ruminating. Besides, a drink might help calm his nerves.

Astar used his magic to cast a shroud around himself as he ventured outside. It wasn't quite invisibility; more a haze to make himself less noticeable. Astar often used it when he ventured to places he might be recognised and didn't want to be disturbed.

It didn't take long for Astar to find the tavern. It was a sullen, nameless building not quite far enough from the stables to be entirely free from the scent of straw and manure. Even the dimly lit interior had a makeshift appearance, and the tables and chairs were jumbled and mismatched. Astar lifted his magical shroud when he reached the bar and caught the attention of the scrawny-looking serving man who poured him a flagon of ale from a pitcher.

"So, the lordling has decided to grace the little people with his presence…" a familiar voice said.

Astar turned his head and saw Elita had sat next to him. She grinned.

"He was hoping for a quiet drink…" he mumbled back. He was not in the mood for Elita and her ribbing.

He brought the flagon to his lips and took his first gulp but then spat it back out.

"Gods!" he gasped. "What *is* this stuff?"

"Yeah, it tastes like pigs' bile," Elita said, clinking her drink against his and then taking a large swig. "But it *is* free!"

He braved another taste, and this time managed to swallow. It tasted strong. So strong that he hoped he wouldn't have to drink too much of it to muddle his head.

"Your friend is interesting," Elita commented.

"If you're fishing for an explanation for that… *thing* we saw today, then I'm afraid you're going to walk away disappointed. I hardly know the guy myself. He's secretive."

"I bet…" Elita said before slugging down more ale. "Strange day, huh?"

Astar nodded. "I think there's stuff going on here they're not telling us about."

"Oh, for sure," Elita agreed. "Remember, I *have* been here longer than you."

"What's with those guys from Squad Three?" Astar asked her. "There's something not right about them…"

"They're the favourites," Elita shrugged. "I once knew one of them… he and I were… well," she smiled to herself. "Anyway… he was an incredible fighter. Better than Bovan. Better than you. But, one day, poof," she clicked her fingers. "He was moved to Squad Three. And then he changed. And it feels like I don't really know him anymore. He's not the same person. Oh, did I mention he was the one who kicked your ass?"

She jabbed Astar's arm. Right on the spot that the blow had been dealt.

"Ahhh!" he flinched. "Don't do that! It bloody hurts."

"I know..." Elita grinned. "That was the point."

"Your boyfriend... did he–"

"Boyfriend!" Elita slammed her pitcher on the counter and laughed. "Haha. He was far from that, Astar. I don't do boyfriends."

"Whatever," Astar groaned. "I don't care. Just tell me. Is he Blessed or something?"

"No," Elita shook her head. "Definitely not. He was a warrior through and through. Strong. Not bad in the sack – may I add – but apart from that, a little dull in the head. There was nothing remarkable about him. Why you ask?"

"He couldn't see my illusions," Astar said.

"I gathered that one..." Elita said dryly. "Now I have a question for you, Astar. What about the rest of the Squad Three? Could *they* see your illusions?"

"I don't know," Astar shrugged. "I didn't think to try it out."

"Well, maybe that could be something to test out sometime," Elita said cryptically. "But be careful, Astar. They keep things secret here because that's how they want them to be... people who are too inquisitive tend to mysteriously go missing. *Or,* they get transferred to Squad Three."

"Did you just admit you're concerned for me?" Astar asked.

"Not exactly concerned," she denied. "But I have to admit... you do make life here more interesting."

"What happened to you, Elita?" Astar said.

"What do you mean?"

"You..." he hesitated, trying to find the right way to word what he was thinking. "Just... the way you are. How can you be so carefree and just *you*? I've never known anyone like you."

"I've already told you," Elita said, reaching between his legs. "There are no other girls like me."

"Stop," Astar said, as his manhood stiffened against his will.

"Why?" she whispered in his ear. "I know you want me."

137

"You're just teasing. Like you always do," Astar said.
"Maybe this time I'm not teasing…"

*   *   *

As soon as the door slammed behind them, they were
fumbling each other's clothes away, sending them
cascading to the floor. Astar could feel Elita smiling as he
kissed her mouth. She unbuttoned his tunic and pushed
him onto the bed. He laughed as he fell back. He was
used to blushing, bashful virgins. He was not used to a
girl taking control.

She untied her lacings, baring her breasts before she
leapt upon him. He took them in his hands and then rolled
his tongue over her nipples. Her body was everything he
imagined it would be. He was so excited that it was a
relief when she finally loosened the cords of his leggings
and let him free.

She crawled onto his lap and guided him inside her.
They looked each other in the eyes. He loved seeing the
expression on her face change as he entered her. He loved
that she was pleasured, and it was *him* who was doing it.

Elita, what are you doing to me? he thought as she
began to rock back and forth, making him throb.

They climaxed three times that night before she had
finally had enough of him. And when it was over, Astar
watched her sleep for a while.

He had bedded many women before, but nothing had
ever been quite like that. He had never let any of them
sleep beside him afterwards, either. He usually made an
excuse so that they would leave.

He kissed her forehead before pulling the covers over
them both and closing his eyes.

*   *   *

When Astar woke the following morning, he was alone.
He jerked upright from his bed and looked around the
room, wondering if it had all been a dream, but the smell

of her still lingered, and his discarded clothes lay strewn across the floor. Hers had vanished.

Why did she go? Astar thought.

He then smacked his forehead, realising the fatal error he had just made.

There was a reason Astar never let girls sleep beside him afterwards. His glamour – the magical haze Astar always shrouded himself within – faded when he slept.

Elita had seen him as he truly was.

He cursed.

*   *   *

He found her at the eatery, sitting alone.

"Can I sit here?" he asked when he reached the table.

She looked up at him and smiled. "Oh… you have that… thing," she waved her finger around his outline. "Back now, I see…"

He scowled but sat opposite her anyway. She continued eating. He just stared at her. Eventually, she noticed and looked up at him.

"Oh no…" she groaned. "You want to have *the talk,* don't you?"

He didn't know what to say. Although they were now both dressed and sitting a few feet apart from each other, it still felt like he was exposed. She had seen him as he truly was, and he could tell, just by the way that she was looking at him, that she now thought of him differently.

"Look, Astar…" she said, dropping her bread onto her tray. "*If* that is even your real name. I don't do boyfriends – I already told you this – but, if I ever *did*, I like my men with a bit of backbone. You hide… and I'm not into that."

He turned away. He wasn't used to this – it was usually *him* giving someone else the brush. Astar desired her more than any of those girls put together, and he didn't even know *why*. She vexed him almost interminably.

"We had great sex…" she then said. "So, let's just remember it for what it was and try not to get all awkward and angsty about it."

"So we… what? Be friends?" he asked.

"I guess so…" she shrugged.

He scratched his head. "I haven't done that before…"

"I'm okay with it if you are," Elita said. "What I said yesterday was true. You *do* make life here more interesting. Even if you are a tad smaller and less… impressive than you make yourself seem. Oh, don't scowl like that!" she laughed. "Don't worry, I'll keep your secret."

"Now eat," she said, reaching for her fork. "You're making me nervous."

*   *   *

Astar felt apprehensive about facing the rest of his squad again, so he made sure to amplify his glamour to lend his face a confident expression when he entered the training hall that morning.

Everyone stared when he and Elita walked into the building together, and none of them made any effort to hide the fact that they had just been talking about him.

Astar realised his situation was even worse than he had imagined. He had lost their respect. Something that would be hard for him to win back.

"Oh, look! He's back on his feet now!" Bovan mocked, making his friends laugh.

"Ignore him…" Elita whispered. "He's just trying to bait you…"

"Go back home, sheep boy!" Bovan raised his voice. "You're not cut out for this place."

"Come here and say that!" Astar yelled back, ignoring Elita's advice. He squared up to Bovan, clenching his fists. "Go on! I dare you!"

"You think I'm scared of *you*?" Bovan smirked, crossing his arms over his chest. "We all know your illusions are nothing but trantles now!"

"Oh really?" Astar asked, feeling his face turn hot with rage. He drew upon some of his *viga,* creating an illusion of a dagger in his hand, and threw it at Bovan's head. Bovan flinched when it neared his face but resisted the urge to duck or raise his hands. It passed through him.

"See!" he yelled over his shoulder to the people watching their confrontation. "They're nothing more than cheap tricks!"

"I would hold your tongue if I were you!" Astar warned.

"Or what?" Bovan retorted. "I'm not scared of you, *little lordling.*"

Astar channelled more of his magic and created a wall of fire at Bovan's feet. Bovan's eyes initially widened at the sight of the flames, but then he lifted his foot and stamped upon them.

"See!" he declared. "Just ignore them! They're fake! They can't hurt you!"

Astar knew that this was his last chance to redeem himself; if he let Bovan get the better of him now, his reputation would never recover.

He was no match for Bovin physically. The only possible way he could come out of this on top – and regain the respect of his peers – were if he could somehow get Bovan to respect his illusions again.

And to do that, he would need to do something far more sophisticated.

Astar created a clone of himself to stand in his place, cloaked his actual self in invisibility, and slunk out of harm's way.

"You think I can't hurt you?" Astar's clone roared, unleashing a sword from its belt.

"Ha!" Bovan pointed at the mirage. "That's not even a real sword!"

Astar sent the clone charging at Bovan, with the phantom sword raised high. Bovan seemed determined to ignore the blade – but he still appeared to believe that it was the real Astar who was running towards him – so he raised his fists and lunged.

The clone of Astar bore its weapon down upon one of Bovan's legs. The next thing everyone saw was the blade cleaving through Bovan's thigh, dismembering his leg in one clean stroke.

The hall went silent. And Bovan's eyes went to the bleeding stump where his leg used to be.

And then he fell. He rolled across the ground, covered in his own blood. Screaming. His tormented eyes went to the remnants of his leg, lying a few feet away.

He cried out. So blinded by the imagined pain he *thought* he was experiencing, he lost all will to ignore Astar's illusions. Astar summoned a family of snakes, and they zigzagged across the floor towards Bovan, raising their necks as they approached. Their forked tongues emerged out from their open mouths, and they hissed.

"Astar!" Lonel yelled. "Stop it! He's scared of snakes! Stop!"

But by the time Astar had heard – and had time to heed to Lonel's warnings – it was too late. Bovan's mind had gone into such a state of blind terror that he no longer needed Astar's illusions to make him panic. Somewhere, between it all, he had drawn a dagger, and he was now thrashing it around himself in a frenzy. Patches of red began to appear around his tunic, and these were not illusions. Bovan stabbed at one of the vipers he was convinced was crawling over his body, and the blade tore into his chest.

Chapter 7

The Mission

The door opened, spilling light into the room, and Miles looked up to see four Sentinels standing outside.

"What is it?" Miles asked.

"Get up," one of them said.

Miles scrambled out of his nest of blankets. He knew that there could only be one reason for them to come and drag him out of his cell again.

It was time to face his judgement.

Miles spared a quick moment to brush his hands over his clothes to straighten the creases in a vain attempt to accord himself some dignity. He had grown thin from the meagre meals they had provided, and he was conscious of the fact he'd acquired a strong odour in the lengthy time since he had been allowed to bathe. A thick, itchy beard covered his face.

"Put your hands behind your back," one of the guards said.

Miles complied, and one of the other escorts manoeuvred around him to bind his wrists. Miles kept his head down and didn't complain.

Over an aeight had passed since Miles had faced questioning in the Solus. Back then, he had felt confident that he had done a decent job of painting a picture of himself as a reformed collaborator, yearning for redemption.

But that felt like a long time ago now. Ever since, he had been kept in complete isolation, with no knowledge of anything outside his cell. During his confinement, his thoughts had wandered and grown bleaker with each cycle.

Miles mentally prepared himself for the worst as they guided him towards the Synod. He knew that death was the most likely sentence for his crimes. He stumbled a few times because his legs had grown weak, and the glare of the sun hurt his eyes.

Miles had never felt so wretched in his life.

He was not guided into the Solus like last time, but instead, to his great surprise, a small chamber on the upper floor. There were five people there waiting for him.

"Bring him here," one of them said, pointing to a seat on the other side of the table. "And lose the binds."

The Sentinels unfastened the ropes around Miles' wrists, and then Miles was allowed to walk freely towards his chair.

"Miles," the blonde woman said. "Do you remember me?"

He nodded. "You're Selena," he recalled, smiling thinly.

She began to introduce the others, but Miles didn't care to bother remembering their names. He was flustered. He had thought that the next time he saw the light of day he would be escorted into the Solus again and given a verdict but instead found himself in this rather discreet gathering.

"What do you want from me?" he asked, interrupting her.

She paused and pursed her lips. Miles could tell she'd been planning to broach the purpose of this meeting gently, but he was in no mood for pleasantries. He was impatient. He had been locked up for an excruciatingly long time and wanted to know his fate.

"The Synod has discussed your case at great length since your trial," she said, pushing a sheet of parchment in front of him. "And we have an offer for you."

"What is this?" Miles asked.

"Your pardon," Selena said. "If you choose to sign it."

"What is the catch?" Miles asked, knowing there must be one. He lifted it to his face and began to read. It didn't take him long to glean the general gist. It was clear from the opening paragraph.

"You want me to be a spy?" he gasped, unable to hide his surprise.

A couple of the men beside Selena flinched at that word. They didn't seem very comfortable with the idea.

"We want you to go to Gavendara," Selena said tactfully. "To gather information…"

"And what would happen to me if I chose to refuse this offer?" Miles said, testing the waters.

"We have… not quite decided yet…" the side of her mouth twitched. "We are hoping it will not come to that."

Miles sighed. He could tell, from the tentative expression on Selena's face, what the outcome would likely be if he turned this down. "So, it is either this or the gallows?" he said flatly.

"That is a possibility," she admitted.

Miles turned his gaze back to the written pardon and read some of the finer details. He found its idiom a little fustian, but it didn't take him long to decode it. "You want me to find out what is going on up there, basically."

"Armies, positions, movements," she said. "And see if you can find any evidence that they are creating more Zakaras too."

"And how do you know you can trust me?" Miles asked, folding his arms over his chest.

"We don't," Selena replied. "We are giving you a chance to prove yourself to us. If everything you claim is true, then our situation is bad, and our options are limited. You know the lay of the land. You know the people."

"You will not be going alone, either," a man next to her said. "You will be watched."

Miles leant back and considered all of this for a few moments. Of all the possible outcomes that he had plotted in his mind, this had not been one of them.

A spy? Miles almost laughed out loud at the irony of it. It did make sense in a fashion. Secretly playing both sides had become somewhat a lifestyle for him.

The thought of venturing into Gavendara again terrified him, though. Miles had never thought circumstances would force him to face his country of birth again, nor risk encountering the people he had betrayed.

"You do realise if I were to be recognised by the wrong

people out there, it would spell my death," he said. "I am a wanted man. They would kill me."

Selena blinked a few times, and Miles caught a brief flicker of empathy in her eyes. A little.

"Yes…" she said. "In fact, it is the very reason we are placing this trust in you. Your situation is our only assurance that you will not cross us. If you return, you will earn your pardon. You will be safe here."

Death. Or probable death, with a slim chance of salvation, Miles thought gloomily, as he stared down at the space at the bottom of the parchment they were expecting him to sign. The idea that he had a *choice* was a farce.

"So, what is it, Miles?" Selena asked, pushing a quill towards him.

*   *   *

Kyra was in the garden outside her lodgings, performing her morning routine, when Rivan disturbed her.

"What you want?" she asked, continuing with her sit-ups. She pulled her body up from the ground until her chest touched her thighs and then flattened her back on the grass again.

"Baird said they want to see us," Rivan said.

"When?" Kyra groaned, not even bothering to ask who this particular 'they' were. 'They' were all the same to her. Officious Consilars. 'They' had all proved themselves to be varying degrees of useless, and Kyra considered them nothing more than a nuisance.

It had been a few days since her last questioning by them, and she was glad for it.

"Now," Rivan said.

She rolled onto her upper back, pushed her palms against the ground to launch herself back to her feet. She enjoyed flouncing tricks like that in front of Rivan as he lacked the dexterity for them.

"So, do you know what they want from us this time?" she asked as they began walking.

146

Rivan shrugged. "Not really. Ever since their scouts came back from Fraknar, they've been secretive. I think they've stopped picking their asses now though, as things seem to be moving along. Baird keeps mentioning this woman called Selena. Says that she's stepped up to the mark and been helping."

"About time someone did..." Kyra muttered. "What about Greyjor? Has Baird done anything about *him* yet?"

Rivan shook his head. "No. I don't think Baird has the guts. Apparently, Greyjor is a big figure in the Synod and has lots of influence. I don't even think Baird is all that convinced he even *is* one of the Zakaras anyway... it's just Sidry."

Kyra nodded. She didn't like Greyjor either, but when Sidry confided to her his suspicion that he might be one of the Zakaras, it somewhat jarred with her. Greyjor had been dubiously unhelpful to their cause, yet everything about his manner and the way he acted seemed too calculated for him to be a Zakara. Even an enhanced one.

The thought that there were still three of those creatures somewhere within these grounds disturbed her. Kyra and Rivan had fought almost half the Academy students by then, but none had proven themselves suspicious yet. Kyra was avoiding the place now because some of the boys had tried to get amorous with her. She had spurned them all away, often violently. The thought of male attention turned her stomach after what happened to Aylen and Dion.

"Why won't they just set Jaedin free?!" she exclaimed. "They *know* the Avatars and the Zakaras are real now, so what are they waiting for? If they just let him out, he could find them!"

Rivan shrugged, but she could tell from the way he clenched his jaw that he was just as frustrated about the situation as her.

When they reached the Synod, the Sentinels frisked them to ensure they weren't carrying weapons. A practice they had only adopted recently – after the incident with Jaedin and Fangar – and that never failed to infuriate

Kyra. This establishment had been warned there were infiltrators among them yet remained arrogantly sure that their Sentinels were enough to ensure the grounds were safe.

Kyra didn't have so much faith. None of them had ever even seen a Zakara, and for all they knew, the Sentinels themselves could be compromised. She had taken to the habit of concealing a dagger within a strap on the inside of her thigh. None of them had ever found it.

A pair of Sentinels led them to a room on the upper floor.

"What are *you* doing here?" Kyra asked when she saw Miles' face. He was not bound and dirty like the last time she saw him. He had shaved his beard and clad himself in a fresh set of new clothes.

"Hello Kyra," a woman said, walking over to greet her. Kyra looked around the room and realised that she was the sole Consilar present. The only other two people in the chamber were Bryna and a very disgruntled-looking Baird. "If you come and sit down, I will explain everything to you."

Kyra glared at Miles. Her feelings towards him were complicated. She didn't loathe him quite like she used to, but neither could she find it within herself to completely forgive or trust him. At this moment in time, she was angry. How had *he* managed to wangle his way out of the clink while Jaedin remained incarcerated?

"I trust this means that you'll be releasing Jaedin soon?" Kyra said to the woman icily.

"If it were down to me, he would be out by now. Believe me…" she muttered under her breath, and Kyra sensed she was being sincere.

"You must be Selena," Kyra said. It was a relief to finally meet the only member of the Synod who appeared to be sane.

"Yes, I am," she said, shaking Kyra's hand and smiling warmly. "I am a specialist in Gavendarian culture and history, but recently I've been put to more… pressing duties. And you must be Rivan," she said, extending her hand to the figure beside Kyra. "Now, please take a seat, and I will explain to you why you are here."

Kyra claimed a chair. This already felt very different to all the other meetings she'd attended recently.

"I would, first of all, like to request that anything said here today stays within this room," Selena said, eyeing all of them. "Officially, this meeting will never have happened, and everything said will be completely off the record. The reason why Miles is here," she turned to the traitor. "Is that we are sending him on a covert operation, and I would like the three of you to be his guides."

She pointed to Rivan, Kyra, and then finally, Bryna.

"You *can* say no," Baird advised. He glared at Selena, making his opinion on the matter clear.

"What exactly do you want us to do?" Rivan frowned.

"We need information," Selena said. "Army placements. Movements. Numbers. Anything you can find."

"Your main job, though, is to cut my throat if I try to run off back to my Gavendarian family, who cherish me so dearly…" Miles said dryly.

"Now that is a reason to go if I ever heard one," Kyra muttered as she folded her arms across the table.

"We also want to know if you spot any signs of Zakaras. Or anything else unusual," Selena said, steering the conversation back on course. "And what Baird just said is true. You are perfectly within your right to turn this down. Nobody would think any less of you for it. This is a very dangerous mission. I want you to understand that. There is a chance you will not return."

"Why us?" Rivan asked.

Selena hesitated before making her reply. "This is all completely off the books," she reminded him. "And the three of you are neither members of the Synod, nor the Academy, and… well, forgive me for being heartless enough to mention this – but you do deserve our honesty – you have no family left, either, so there is less chance of people noticing you are gone. Not only that but, from what I have read – about the ordeals the three of you have been through – you *do* have the skills we are looking for."

"We are also disposable," Kyra finished flatly.

Selena looked at her.

"Come on…" Kyra said. "Admit it. It's true. Baird and Sidry are your secret weapons and need to be kept safe, but we mean much less to you. We're loose ends. If *we* disappear, who cares."

"Like I said before," Selena spoke after a long pause. "You *can* say no. We can find someone else."

"See!" Baird declared, flattening his palm upon the table. "They're not interested. Go find other people to do your dirty work."

"I never said I wasn't interested," Kyra said.

Baird's eyes widened.

"Are you sure?" Selena asked. "You know that there are risks? I don't want you to go if–"

"As their guardian, I refuse!" Baird interrupted her. "I didn't drag them all the way here, barely alive, for you to send them on a suicide mission!"

He cares more than he ever dared admit, Kyra realised.

"They are, under law, of adult age," Selena argued back. Her manner was calm and controlled compared to Baird's. "And are therefore permitted to give their own consent."

"I don't like this," Baird mumbled, shaking his head. He looked at Kyra. "Don't do this. You've already been through enough. You're safe here."

"Safe?" Kyra repeated, raising an eyebrow. "In what world are we *safe* here? With Zakaras stalking around, and them lot," she waved a hand at Selena. "Doing scit all about it? What about when an army of them cross over the border? Will we be *safe* then? If people do nothing, then we are *all* dead."

"Let someone *else* do this," Baird pleaded. "Kyra, I have spoken to the Academy, and they're willing to take you and Rivan in. Isn't that what you've always wanted?"

Baird looked at Rivan, but the young man seemed far from convinced.

"We're bored," Kyra said. "I've already brawled half of those Academy brats, and I'm better than most of them. You need to stop thinking of us as children, Baird. We haven't been children for a while now. Ever since the Zakaras came – they took that away from us. We're adults, and we can make our own decisions. And this," she turned back to Selena. "Is *my* choice."

"Rivan," Kyra said, nudging him in the ribs. "Are you in?"

He grunted and nodded. "Sorry, Baird. But I think this is something we should do. I hate this place. I need to get out of here before I end up rippin' one of their heads off. Sorry Selena," he added. "You're better than the others, but the rest have been scittin' useless till now," he turned back to Baird. "Doing something... it keeps my mind away from everything that happened. It stops me thinking about it."

"I will come, too," Bryna said. It was the first time she had spoken. "I can help take care of them."

The irony of Bryna's words was clearly lost on Selena; Bryna's secret identity was still a closely guarded secret. Kyra guessed that it was probably her known skills – those in medicine – which had earned her invite to this mission.

A part of Kyra felt tempted to try and talk Bryna out of going, but a bigger part wanted her company. She would feel safer with Bryna there, and she would also be glad to have at least one friendly face on the journey.

It would perhaps make her slightly less likely to end up stabbing Rivan too. Or Miles.

"You will leave tomorrow," Selena said.

*   *   *

"You can't go!" Jaedin exclaimed when his sister told him.

"Yes, I can," Bryna said. She tucked a lock of hair behind her ear and looked at her twin. "I... feel that it is right. That I am *meant* to go. And I will come back. I promise."

151

Jaedin narrowed his eyes at her. His sister's cryptic premonitions were rarely wrong, but that did not do much to ease his concern.

The solid fact was that she was crossing into enemy territory.

Jaedin had never been able to bear being separated from his sister for too long. The only other time they had ever parted ways had been disastrous for both of them.

Bryna reached between the bars and placed a hand on Jaedin's arm. "Let's not fight. Please. Not just before I leave. I came to see you today because I have an idea... I think we may be able to communicate while I am gone."

"How?" Jaedin asked.

"Just close your eyes," she whispered. "Attune to your *psysona* and *psycalesse* with me. I want to try something."

Jaedin complied and eased himself into a relaxed state. He soon felt a tingling sensation. It was Bryna's *psysona;* a being of pure energy and the source of her magical self. Her *viga* was violet and aphotic. It reminded Jaedin of that moment during sunset when the sky turns dark, and everything feels charged. It was very different to the source of his own *viga,* which always assumed a leafy green.

Despite the disparity, the essence of their combined *psysonas* fused effortlessly. Ever since they were born, they had been connected on a deep and arcane level. Jaedin had believed it to have withered when they got older, but during this moment – as their *psysonas* melded together so easily – he realised it had never really faded. It had just become less salient. When they aged – and their thoughts became ever less innocent and ever more intimate – they subconsciously blocked each other out.

Hello Jaedin, Bryna's ethereal voice rippled through his consciousness.

Bryna! he channelled back. They had done this to communicate with each other when they got separated during the siege of Fraknar. *Why are we doing this again?*

I want to try something. Just relax...

He felt a tug deep within the core of his being. It was uncomfortable, and if anyone else besides his twin had been so invasive, Jaedin would have resisted. But he trusted Bryna. He felt a lurch in his navel and deep within his *psysona* too. A part of him was twisted into a cord and wound itself around Bryna, tying their essences together.

Look, Jaedin, she said. *Open your eyes.*

When he did so, Jaedin saw his own face but through Bryna's eyes. He watched his own eyes open, and he took a double-take at the sight of himself.

He was somehow fully aware of both his own sensory perceptions and Bryna's, all at the same time.

It was disorientating and made him feel dizzy at first.

What is this? he thought. *What have you done?*

It worked! I wasn't sure if it was possible, but I wanted to try, Bryna thought back. They both shut their eyes again to blank out the world and better concentrate on the inner sanctum of their joined psyches. *This is how we can stay connected, Jaedin*, she explained. She tugged upon the psychic thread which now linked them.

Will this still work when you leave? Jaedin asked.

I think it will... Bryna replied. *It is possible because we are twins.*

But won't it be a bit weird? Jaedin asked. He didn't like the idea of his sister knowing his every thought. Especially the ones which involved Fangar.

*I will try to stay out during **those** times*, Bryna thought back, knowingly.

If Bryna could have seen Jaedin's face that moment, it would have been crimson, but she didn't need to. She could *feel* him blushing. She could feel his embarrassment and everything else he was thinking.

He pushed those thoughts away.

*And you can shut **me** out, if you like*, Bryna added. And then, to demonstrate, she summoned a chasm of walls around her consciousness. Jaedin felt them rise and solidify around him, blocking him from knowing Bryna's most inner thoughts. He remained connected to the sanctum of her psyche, but he was now only permitted to know what Bryna allowed him.

Jaedin mimicked her, drawing threads of his *viga* and forming them into a shield.

There, Bryna sent a telepathic message over to him. *Now we can talk this way, and you don't need to worry about me seeing what you and Fangar get up to…*

And I won't see those thoughts **you** *have about Sidry…* Jaedin sent back smugly. He had glimpsed those for a flicker of the moment, and they came as a great surprise.

You… shouldn't have seen that, Jaedin, Bryna said.

Yeah. I think we can both agree that it's much healthier with these shields up. We're not children anymore…

No… she thought back wistfully. *We're not…*

And then Jaedin felt Bryna pull away. He was alone again.

He opened his eyes, and he and his twin were back in the room. Back in the material world again. Separated by bars. It took a few moments for Jaedin to ground himself.

Can you hear me? Bryna asked. It almost made him jump, experiencing her voice echoing through his mind when he wasn't Psymancing. Jaedin could feel the psychic link she had woven between them ripple as he received the telepathic message from her.

Jaedin nodded.

I will contact you each night after we leave. To make sure this still works when distance grows between us, Bryna whispered into his consciousness. *If it does, it will be useful. You can report to the others. Pass on messages. Tell them how the mission is going. You should reconcile with Baird, Jaedin*, she added. *We need to stick together.*

Fat chance of that happening… Jaedin thought. But he kept that one private.

Bryna then reached for Jaedin's hand. They couldn't embrace with the bars between them, but it was still a warm farewell. *Bye Jaedin…* she said, looking him in the eyes. *We will see each other again. I promise.*

*　　*　　*

When Bryna turned her back on her brother, tears streamed from her eyes. She shut Jaedin out of her mind so that he wouldn't know the terrible string of emotions she was feeling. She needed to be strong. For him and herself. For everyone.

She went back to her room and began to prepare for the journey.

The Synod had provided Bryna with everything she needed for the mission. Clothes, provisions, a small tent. There was some extra space in her travelsack, so Bryna packed her medicine bag too.

Bryna then spread the rest of her possessions across the bed and stared at them for a while.

I am going to have to leave these behind, she thought sadly. They were the remaining vestiges from Jalard. The only things she owned in the world. Everything else had burned in the fire.

Tears came again. Bryna didn't fight them. She sobbed. Wiped her eyes. Her other hand went to the Stone of Vairis, and she held it to reassure herself.

Bryna had not told any of the others yet, but her magic was waning. The Festival of Verdana was the night of the year where the spirit world was closest. Back then, she had been so replete with *viga* that it had been practically bursting out of her, but now the season was changing, and, with each passing day, the spirit world became more distant.

Shemet itself was still a source of power for her – each death that occurred in the city charged Bryna with energy – but what would she do when they were out in the mountains? Without her magic, Bryna would be vulnerable.

She jumped when she heard a loud rapping upon the door. She knew who it was before she opened it.

"Bryna!" Sidry exclaimed, entering the room and grabbing her shoulders with peculiar urgency. "I just heard about the mission!"

He pulled her into his arms and held her so tight she could feel his heart beating through his chest. He was warm. She wanted to press herself against him and forget the world. Forget that she was leaving in the morning.

"Don't go!" he pleaded, pulling away slightly but maintaining a tight grip on her shoulders. "You can't! Bryna, you–"

Bryna grabbed his neck and pulled his mouth towards her. Their mouths touched. He gasped and stared at her.

Then he kissed her back.

Chapter 8

Transferred

After the incident with Bovan, Astar spent the rest of the day hiding in his room, reliving everything that had happened. He remembered all the blood and the way it had taken half of the squad to wrestle that dagger out of Bovan's hands. The look on Frast's face when he arrived.

He kept trying to figure out how it had all gone so wrong so quickly. At what point should he have stopped? It was a tormenting cycle.

Astar was utterly convinced that someone was going to come to punish him. He tossed and turned in his bed all night, waiting for Frast, Grav'aen, or someone else to knock on his door, but no one came.

Eventually, sunlight crept through the window, and Astar had no other choice but to get up and prepare for the day.

It was a small mercy that on this particular one – in his aeightly program – he was scheduled for lectures at the University. Astar rode to the city, skipping out on breakfast at the Institute to sup at an inn on the outskirts of Mordeem. He was too ashamed by what he had done to be seen by any of his peers yet.

Most of the seminars Grav'aen had chosen for Astar focussed on the philosophy of cognition and the human mind. Usually, Astar found them interesting, but he was too distracted to take much of it in that day. He couldn't stop worrying about what he would have to face when he returned to the Institute.

When his lectures were over, Astar had a personal one-to-one with one of the professors that he dragged out for as long as he could by dissecting minute details from the various theories he had been learning. Eventually, the elderly scholar drew the meeting to an end, so Astar went to the library and studied well into the evening.

He didn't dare arrive back at the grounds of the Institute until it was dark, and he went straight to his room.

It was only out of sheer exhaustion he managed to sleep that night. He rose the following morning with a sense of dread. By then, it had been two days since the incident with Bovan, and Astar still had no idea what consequences he was going to face for it. He knew he would find out soon though, as he was scheduled for training with Frast that day.

As Astar made for the mess hall, he considered using his magic to make himself less visible but decided against it. He knew he would have to face everyone again at some point and figured that he might as well get it over and done with. It was early, so the place was mostly empty and, for the first time since Astar had enrolled, he got to have first pickings of the food.

The tables around him gradually filled. Astar had been anticipating hostility, gossip, and stares, but, overall, he was surprised by how little attention his appearance had drawn. He did catch a pair of boys from his squad gawking at him at one point but, once they realised Astar had noticed, they sheepishly turned away.

"I was wondering if you would show up..." Elita said as she dropped her platter beside his.

Astar almost jumped.

She frowned at him as she sat herself down. "What's got you all cowed?"

Astar put a finger to his lips, hating the way she was speaking so loudly. He was trying to keep a low profile.

She shook her head and laughed. "Oh, Astar. Are you *really* that full of yourself? You're hardly the first here to get into a bit of a scuffle."

"*Really?*" Astar asked. "No one cares?"

"Oh, some of Bovan's friends want nothing more but to break that buttery face of yours, but you've made quite sure that they're all too scared of you now..."

"So... I'm not going to get into any bother about it?" Astar asked. A part of him was relieved, but a much larger one was appalled by the idea the Institute wasn't going to reprimand him for what he did. He knew he deserved it. Didn't the people who ran this place impose any sense of responsibility?

"Oh, I'm sure Grav'aen has something in mind. And Frast is going to make your life a living nightmare for losing him his little prodigy."

Astar spat out his tea. "What?" he asked. "Losing Bovan? What do you mean? He hasn't left, has he? Or–"

"You haven't heard?" Elita asked. She shook her head. "Bovan's fine. In fact, he's made a bloody miraculous recovery, if you ask me. But he's not in our squad anymore. He's been transferred."

"Transferred," Astar repeated. "Where?"

Elita looked him in the eyes. She didn't need to say anything more.

"Squad Three…" Astar muttered under his breath.

"Why are you looking so glum?" Elita asked. "Bovan's gone, and now everyone in Squad Six fears you. Apart from me, of course. You're number one now. Congratulations," she tapped her cup against his. "Isn't that what you always wanted?"

Astar turned away from her. He was tired of Elita's tone. And all of her back-handed comments.

Mostly because they were true; to be the undisputed paragon among his peers had been Astar's goal ever since he got here.

But he had not wanted to get it like *this*.

He ate the rest of his breakfast in silence, studying every face which entered the eatery. When Bovan entered, Astar got up and raced to him.

"Bovan," Astar said.

Bovan dully lifted his head, and they stared at each other. There was something peculiar about the look in Bovan's eyes. None of the bravado and arrogance he used to carry with him was there anymore. It had been replaced with something bleak and empty.

Could what Astar did really have broken his spirit *that* much?

"I…" Astar began. He struggled to find the right words.

"I just want to say that I am sorry. For everything… I didn't mean… I mean, I only wanted to…"

Bovan just stared at him.

"If there is anything I can do for you, let me know," Astar finished, feeling somewhat unnerved by Bovan's lack of response.

Bovan smiled thinly. There was nothing bitter or loathing about his expression. If anything, he seemed apathetic.

Everything about this whole exchange felt wrong to Astar.

Bovan walked away and sat at a table filled with other members of Squad Three. Astar watched him.

That creature – whatever it was – *looked* like Bovan, but that was where the familiarity ended. Something was missing. Something just wasn't right. He had been moved to Squad Three now and, already, it seemed he had become possessed by the same mysterious aura as the rest of them.

Astar remembered what Elita said to him that night at the tavern. Could it be possible that *all* of Squad Three were immune to his illusions?

He decided to test that theory out.

Astar knew he was already in enough trouble for abusing his Blessing as it was, so he crafted an illusion of something small and innocuous. A butterfly. He sent it fluttering towards the table where the members of Squad Three had gathered, but not a single one of them appeared to notice it. They all just carried on spooning mouthfuls of plain oatmeal to their mouths, so Astar amplified the illusion a little and sent the butterfly swerving right in front of some of their faces. Yet still, none of them paid it any heed.

Finally, Astar became more daring and burst the butterfly into flames right in the centre of their congregation. They didn't even flinch.

Astar ran out of the mess hall, feeling a need to get away.

That experiment had not given him any answers, only created more questions.

Astar now knew as a certainty that there was something strange going on in this place, but any form of explanation eluded him.

Once Astar had recovered his nerves, he stopped and caught his breath. He considered finding Elita to confide in her about this new revelation but decided against it. He didn't want to go back into the mess. Not when there were members of Squad Three still there.

"Are you Astar?" someone said as they approached him, interrupting his thoughts. Astar looked up. It was the woman who had greeted him at the entrance when he first enrolled at the Institute.

He nodded.

"You need to report to Grav'aen," she said.

"Oh…" Astar ran a hand through his hair nervously. "Right *now*? I'm due for–"

"Yes," she nodded. "He wants to see you as soon as possible. It's important. Follow me, please."

As she led Astar towards Grav'aen's office, a sense of dread struck him, and it lingered. He remembered Elita's words.

They keep things secret here because that's how they want them to be… people who are too inquisitive tend to mysteriously go missing.

I'm in trouble… he realised. He was about to be in the presence of a Psymancer who could read his thoughts.

And Astar's thoughts were riddled with suspicion.

Astar tried to push them to the back of his mind. Tried to forget his recent discovery about Squad Three. Tried to dismiss the encounter he had just had with Bovan. He hoped that maybe, just maybe, if he did not think about these things when he was in the presence of Grav'aen, the wieldy Psymancer wouldn't notice them.

But it was an impossible task. By trying so hard, Astar was, if anything, probably going to draw even more attention to his thoughts.

If only I could cast an illusion around my mind! he thought.

And then the idea came to him that, perhaps, he *could*.

It certainly wasn't anything Astar had ever attempted before, but that didn't necessarily mean that it wouldn't work. Astar knew his situation was dire. He had nothing to lose.

He experimented as he walked, channelling threads of his *viga* to create an image of the thoughts he would *like* Grav'aen to see. Anxiety over the trouble he was in. Regret for what he had done to Bovan. Fear of Grav'aen himself. And Frast. A little bit of lust for Elita in the background too. Just to make it more realistic.

Astar shut out all the suspicions he had concerning the Institute and Squad Three.

By the time Astar had finished devising his thought-mirage, he was outside Grav'aen's office. The woman left, and Astar made a quick prayer to Gazareth for this experiment to work.

And then, he knocked on the door.

"Come in," a voice called.

Astar entered the room to find Grav'aen sitting by the window. To Astar's great surprise and relief, the man smiled at him.

"Hello Astar…" he said.

"Grav'aen," Astar said, dipping his head slightly. "I'm sorry for what I did. I will take any punishment you see–"

"Wait, wait," Grav'aen raised his hand. "Don't worry about that for the moment… Astar…"

Astar felt Grav'aen's telepathy creeping into his mind. It felt gentler this time – which Astar hoped was because his own magic was interfering with it – so Astar fed his illusion more *viga* to make sure it held. He also added some supplemental thoughts of discomfort as a reaction to Grav'aen's presence in his mind.

"I can see that you are deeply sorry for what you've done," Grav'aen said, and then the sensation of his probing faded. "You are an important student to us, Astar. And I am afraid it is for a much more serious matter that I have summoned you here today. Can you sit down, please?"

Astar frowned. His relief over not being caught out by

the man's telepathic tricks became entwined with worry. What could this news be?

He sat.

"There is no easy way to tell you this," Grav'aen said, his mien uncharacteristically sympathetic. Astar even got the impression that it was genuine. "It's your father, Astar. I have just received word that he has The Ruena."

"The Ruena?" Astar gasped.

Grav'aen nodded. "I am truly sorry."

Astar felt the blood drain from his face.

"I am going to give you some time off. So you can go see him," Grav'aen said. "I know this must be difficult for you... what with your mother and all..."

Astar nodded. He felt like he should be sad – like he should cry – but he couldn't. He was concentrating so hard on sustaining the illusion, he didn't have any room for the news to sink in yet.

"I have already arranged for your horse to be prepared," Grav'aen said. "So go pack. Leave as soon as you can."

Chapter 9

Setting Forth

When Miles appeared outside his cell, Jaedin didn't even recognise him at first. Jaedin's former mentor had shaved his beard, leaving just some carefully trimmed stubble around his mouth and chin. A new hat obscured his hair, and he even had a pair of riding boots on his feet that matched the lofty coat draped over his shoulders.

"Someone doesn't want to be recognised," Jaedin said dryly.

"I'm guessing you've heard..." Miles said. He fidgeted, knotting his hands together. He didn't seem comfortable in his new garb yet.

Jaedin nodded, making no effort to hide his feelings when their eyes met. The unfairness of this arrangement – Miles bequeathed a new wardrobe and trusted with a clandestine mission, while Jaedin remained incarcerated – sparked an obvious but unspoken tension between them.

One which lingered thickly in the air.

"Look... Jaedin," Miles broke the silence. "I know a part of you must hate me right now... but I am leaving. And I just wanted to say goodbye."

Jaedin carried on staring at him.

"I..." Miles hesitated. "Are you okay?"

"I'm fine," Jaedin said, feeling a lump in his throat. It made his voice croak. Why was he letting himself get emotional? He *hated* Miles. For everything he did and the snake-like way he always managed to wriggle out of the snags he got himself into.

"Just try to behave yourself, Jaedin," Miles advised. "If you play by their rules and don't get yourself into more trouble, I'm sure you'll be out of here soon."

"What do you think I've been doing all this time?" Jaedin asked. He walked up to the bars and clenched his

165

fists around them. "I could bend these open if I wanted to. You've seen what I can do. So could Fangar, but I made him promise not to. Neither of us are normal anymore thanks to *your* people."

Jaedin then pulled back and paced his cell a few times to suppress his anger. He caught Miles looking at him and glared back.

"Don't leave it like this, Jaedin," Miles pleaded. "After all we've been through… I might not make it back."

Yeah, but maybe this is just another one of your schemes, Jaedin thought. *Maybe, as soon as you get over that border, you'll just switch sides again.*

The child in Jaedin – the part of him which had grown up under Miles' guidance – wanted to trust his former mentor more than anything, but that person was now just a distant voice in the back of Jaedin's psyche. Everything Jaedin had endured since then had hardened him, and he was determined not to let himself suffer another crushing betrayal.

Jaedin sighed and stepped back up to the bars. When he saw Miles' face up close, he found himself reminded why he had always felt so drawn to him. He was not classically handsome, but that didn't matter to Jaedin. He grew up in a small village, and Miles was the only male he could ever relate to. He had a certain charm about him. It was mostly his eyes Jaedin had always liked; they were ghostly, grey, and mysterious.

"Just promise you'll look after Bryna and Kyra for me," Jaedin said. "And Rivan too," he added. "That you'll do everything you can to keep them safe."

Miles nodded. "I *do* care about them too, you know."

Do you really, though? Jaedin wondered. He scratched his head; as usual, confused about almost everything where Miles was concerned.

"I just want to say one thing. Before I go," Miles hushed his voice and leaned closer towards the iron bolts that separated them. "Baird is right. You need to stay away from Fangar."

Jaedin rolled his eyes. Why did everyone keep

sounding that old horn over and over again?

"That is not a matter of your concern…" Jaedin replied coolly.

"It is," Miles said. "Because I care. I watched you grow up. And I know I'm not your favourite person these days, but I *do* worry about you. More than you could ever imagine. And I know that you're infatuated with him, and you're young. But you've got to listen to me. He's *not* good for you. He's dangerous."

"Dangerous?" Jaedin repeated in disbelief. "He's saved my life! More than once."

"And killed an innocent man!" Miles said.

"While *protecting me*!" Jaedin yelled back. "And he almost died saving me in Fraknar too! Whereas *you* risked my life for your own gain! Why are you so afraid of him?"

"I'm not afraid of Fangar," Miles whispered. "I only fear him for what he could do to you…"

"Go!" Jaedin said, waving his arm. "Just go, Miles! I have nothing to say to you."

*   *   *

When Sidry awoke beside Bryna, at first, he thought he must be dreaming. She opened her eyes just a few moments after he did, and they stared at each other.

She's leaving, Sidry thought, and felt a pang in his chest.

They remained in each other's arms for a while, while the light glowing from behind the curtain gradually brightened. They remained still, but time was against them and rapidly passing.

Bryna swung her legs over the side of the bed in one graceful, fluid motion. She was still clothed. Their night together had been passionate, but chaste. At no point had they ever disrobed. They had merely held each other. Tightly and fervently. Occasionally, joining their lips and caressing each other to satisfy their affections. Sidry was too much in awe of Bryna to expect anything more. Just to hold her, and be in her presence, was enough for him. It had been blissful, dreamlike, and laden with melancholy.

The thought that he may never see her again was tearing him apart.

"Don't go," he pleaded one last time, even though he knew she was well beyond persuading.

"You know I have to," Bryna said, looking back at him and smiling faintly. It was only now that Sidry knew her more intimately that he could see through the brave veil she so often wore. He knew now that Bryna got anxious. Just like everyone else. She just didn't like to let people worry about her. She was more fragile than she would ever let people know.

But the fact that she hid it so well was, in itself, her strength.

"We'll meet again, Sidry. I know it. I can feel it here…" she said as she touched her chest.

She then kissed him one last time. "Come, Sidry," she whispered into his ear. "We must leave now."

"Let me carry your bag," he said, rushing over to the other side of the room to lift it. He used those moments whilst he had his back turned, to will away the moistening of his eyes. *He* needed to be brave for her, too.

They walked towards the stables, where the others were waiting. Sidry and Bryna were subjected to some knowing looks when they arrived together – particularly from Rivan and Kyra – but no one said anything. They didn't seem as surprised as Sidry expected.

The only other people who had come to see the four of them leave were Baird and Selena. Sidry had been expecting more Synod members to be present, but it seemed this quest was so clandestine that even most of the Consilars weren't being made privy to it.

A pair of stable hands loaded up the horses while everyone said their farewells. Baird was unusually emotional. Rivan went to shake his hand, but the former soldier pulled him into an embrace and patted him on the back.

Selena made a little speech. One which Sidry didn't care to listen to. He was too busy observing Bryna as she greeted her horse by running a hand through its mane.

"Forgotten your oldest friend now you have a girl?" Rivan asked sourly, stepping in front of Sidry and obscuring his view of Bryna.

"No," Sidry said, abruptly feeling guilty. "Of course not."

"Good," Rivan grunted as he crossed his arms over his chest. "And don't you *dare* say goodbye either, because we're coming back. *All* of us. You understand me?"

Sidry nodded and forced himself to smile. "Take care of Bryna for me. Please," he asked.

Rivan's eyes narrowed. "She's likely going to be the one taking care of *us*."

"I know…" Sidry said. "But… she's not the sort to admit it when she needs help, so keep an eye on her. Promise you'll do everything you can to stop her coming to any harm. Even if it is from herself…" Sidry quietly added. "And take care of yourself too while you're at it."

Rivan nodded and then leapt onto the back of his horse.

Sidry then bid Kyra farewell by patting her on the back.

"Make sure you visit Jaedin," Kyra said to him. "He's bored out of his mind in that cell."

Sidry nodded and then returned to Bryna to say his final goodbye. She had already mounted her steed.

"I love you, Bryna," he whispered once he was close enough for only her to hear him.

It wasn't something Sidry had planned to say. It just came out. He almost tried to take it back – put his other hand over his mouth in a gesture of revocation – but resisted because he didn't *want* to. It felt right.

"I love you too, Sidry…" she said. She spoke so softly it sounded more like a confession. "But I'm not sure if… there is so much I should tell you, but it's not the right time yet. I will find you. As soon as I come back, I will find you. We will speak then."

"Are we all ready?" Rivan called as he rounded up his horse and guided it to the gate. Kyra was quick to follow.

Bryna's steed seemed keen to keep up with its companions, and it spurred into a trot of its own accord. She waved at Sidry.

"Goodbye," she said.

*　　*　　*

The sun began to set before Astar and Elita had even cleared the western plains, but to their fortune, two moons were in the sky that night: providing more than enough light for them to carry on riding into the evening.

When they did stop, Elita gathered some wood and sparked a fire while Astar pitched their tent. By the time he had unloaded the horses and guided them to a nearby stream, Elita had settled by the flames.

He joined her, and they ate a supper of dry cakes filled with fruit and grains, along with some of the strips of smoked pig meat the Institute had provided them.

"Maybe we should hunt something tomorrow," Elita suggested. "I'm not sure how long I can live on this."

"I don't think we have time," Astar murmured.

Elita pulled one of the expressions that usually preceded a snide remark, but then seemed to reconsider and said nothing. She had been aberrantly courteous ever since Astar had received the news about his father.

She picked up a stick and poked at the fire.

"You still haven't told me why you came," Astar said, hating the silence.

She shrugged. "I fancied a break."

Astar stared at her. He had been surprised to find her waiting for him at the stables as he was about to leave. She told him that the Institute had given her permission to accompany him, but neglected to mention *why* she volunteered to do such a thing. Astar had been in such a rush to get going he didn't have the mind to question her at the time.

"What's the real reason, Elita?" he asked.

"Well, I couldn't possibly let Grav'aen's favourite rough it out on the road alone..." she said, her voice slipping back to its usual chiding tone. "There may bandits or raiders, and all other manner of thugs out here with a taste for a little lordling's purse. Or maybe even his back passage."

"We both know I am capable of taking care of myself," Astar said. "And I'm not Grav'aen's favourite, either."

"Oh, pur-lease," Elita retorted. "You somehow outsmart everyone with that tricksy magic of yours, and he, quite literally, let you get away with attempted murder!"

"I didn't try to murder Bovan!" Astar roared. "And *Dareth* is Grav'aen's favourite! He only let me go because my father is dying!"

That was the first time Astar had said it out loud, and it made it more real to him. He inhaled deeply and crossed his arms over his chest to warm himself.

My father is dying…

"I'm sorry," Elita said. Astar didn't reply. For some reason, he hated the way that she was telling him that she was sorry. It wasn't *her* fault that his father was sick.

"Do you want to talk about it?" Elita shifted herself around to face him.

"I don't need your sympathy," Astar said. "And will you stop with all this trying-to-be-nice stuff? It's just *weird*. Because you know what? I am not even that upset about it. Well, I am, but just… not as much as I should be."

"Why?"

"Because… my father… we've… well, we've never been that close. I don't know how to feel about it. I feel weird cause I *should* be upset, and the fact that I am *not* upset is what is making me feel shit. Maybe I will feel different when I get there and actually *see* him. But, at the moment…" Astar shrugged. "I'm more worried about the thought that I'm going to have to take over that damn keep. And the land. I know that I should think myself lucky. And I am, compared to most, but I just don't *want* it. Not yet, anyway."

"And yes," he finished, turning to her. "I did kill Bovan."

Elita frowned. "Bovan's fine, he–"

"Bovan's not fine," Astar cut her short. "He's part of Squad Three. Have you not spoken to him since? He's not the same. That *thing*… it's not *him*. They've done something to him. To all of them. They can't see my illusions."

Elita's eyes widened. "So you tried it?"

Astar nodded. "Yeah, I gave it a go in the mess just before I was summoned to Grav'aen's office. They didn't see a scittin' thing."

"So what are we going to do?" Elita asked after a pause.

"*Do*?" Astar repeated. "We're not going to *do* anything. I'm going to go watch my father die and spend the rest of my life arguing with farmers over turnips. And you're going to go back to the Institute and pretend you know nothing. That's what we're going to do."

"So selfish…" Elita muttered.

"What?"

"Selfish!" Elita yelled. "You! Telling me all of this stuff and then sending me back to Grav'aen. He'll do his freaky mind-shit on me and see that I know something's up. Maybe he'll move *me* to Squad Three too! How would you like that?"

"He won't transfer *you*," Astar said. "That squad seems to have a penchant for warriors, and you're too valuable to them for your magic. You're one of his best mages."

"It's still selfish," Elita spat. "I don't have a family. The Institute and the people there… they're the closest thing I have to a home. It's all I know."

"What happened to your family, Elita?" Astar asked.

Elita sighed heavily and poked at the fire again.

"They're fine. I think," she said bitterly. "I don't talk to them. Not since the Institute took me in."

"How long ago was that?" Astar asked.

"When I was six…" she shrugged.

"*Six*?" Astar blurted. "And you haven't heard from them since. Gods… *why*?"

She hesitated for a few moments. "Look," she turned

back to him. "I didn't always have control over my magic, and when I was little bad things happened around me..."

"What kind of things?"

"Just *leave* it, Astar."

There was a long silence, and Elita went back to stabbing the fire. Astar felt like he should say something supportive but couldn't think of anything.

"Don't you *dare* go feeling sorry for me!" she warned, pointing the stick at him. "I'm the first Blessed of Manveer the world has known for over three hundred years. So fuck my parents."

"Three hundred years?" Astar repeated, eyeing her.

She nodded. "My Blessing is rare. The last known person to be able to conjure the elements of both air and water was a woman called Farlenna of Diverspeak. She is mentioned in quite a lot of the history books from that period. Apparently, she could fly, but I think that's just a scittin' story."

"Have you ever *tried*?" Astar asked. The image of Elita sprouting wings and taking to the sky did put a smile on his face.

Elita shrugged. "I used to try to when I was a bit young and naïve... but, like I said, it's just stories."

Elita then shuffled up to him and rested her head on his shoulder. "Don't get any ideas..." she warned as she draped an arm across his chest. "This is just... friendly. And don't tell anyone, either."

He nodded and put an arm around her. He wasn't sure if she was telling the truth or if this was another one of her teases.

"So, Astar," she said. "What about *your* parents? Why isn't your mother around?"

"She's dead," he said.

"I'd guessed," Elita said. "But... as we're doing this whole opening up thing, why don't you tell me about her."

*   *   *

Jaedin awoke that morning with a sense of unease. He knew something was wrong but couldn't figure out exactly *what* it was at first. He paced around his cell for a while, feeling restless, and tried to calm himself down by taking deep breaths. He told himself that it must be nerves. His sister and friends had left on a dangerous mission, so it was only natural that he felt a bit anxious. He had been confined to this room for over three aeights by then, so it was only natural he was frustrated.

But in his gut, he knew it was something more than that.

Jaedin's prophetic skills were sluggish, but he was still Bryna's brother. They were of the same legacy. He was subject to the same arcane impetus which flowed through her, but lacked her finesse to grace its waves. The undulations swept over him. He was often able to sense them, but rarely able to break his head above the water and glimpse what lay beyond.

You're a disappointment, his aunt, Carmaestre, had screeched at him the brief time they met. *Most of our family inherit some form of talent, but it seems to have missed you. Trust Meredith to birth such a useless runt.*

Jaedin sat down on the bed and clenched his fists, feeling wretched. Everyone was either away or occupied, but he was stuck here. Now that Bryna had gone, she wouldn't even be able to sneak him books from the library anymore.

Zakaras roamed free, while Jaedin and Fangar remained imprisoned. Regardless of the fact that an innocent man had got caught in the middle, the situation still riled Jaedin. It was something he could never forgive the Synod for.

Jaedin had grown wearily used to the presence of the Zakaras now. Their proximity meant that his Stone of Zakar was constantly humming, its powers triggered by their nearness.

It was during that moment – whilst Jaedin sat on his bed, brooding – that he realised that something had changed in that regard. Something was missing.

He could only sense *two* Zakaras now.

He froze, his entire body stiffening.

Where was the final one? That third malevolent presence that, until this moment, Jaedin had always been able to sense?

Jaedin gasped. That could only mean that one of them had wandered out of his radius. Either that, or it had been killed. Jaedin doubted that it was the latter. Usually, when a Zakara died near Jaedin, he would feel a wave of its energy pass through him as they screamed their way out of this world. Surely such an occurrence would have awakened him?

If one of the Zakara's had strayed from the grounds of the Synod, that could only mean bad news. It could create more Zakaras and spread the contagion. Cause an unprecedented amount of damage.

"Hello?!" Jaedin called, running over to the opening of his cell and grabbing hold of the bars. "Help! Please! Someone help!"

He rattled the bolts for a while and carried on yelling until he heard footsteps. One of the Sentinels appeared.

"What's the matter, kid?" he asked, frowning.

"Get Baird!" Jaedin yelled. "Or one of the Consilars. Anyone! Please! I have something important to—"

The Sentinel crossed his arms over his chest and rolled his eyes. "Important, 'ey? Tell me; what discovery could you have possibly made in *there* which is so damn important?"

"You don't understand!" Jaedin said. "Just get someone. *Please!*"

"I can't leave my post till my shift ends, and that ain't for a while…" he shook his head. "Now, just sit and calm the blazes down!"

"There must be *something* you can do?" Jaedin asked. "What if there is an emergency? How do you get help?"

"I ain't ringing the bell for… well… whatever *this* is…" he said. "Now shut yer trap before I break it!"

"Scit you!" Jaedin exclaimed. He pulled at the bars, finally unleashing some of his abnormal strength, and they bent in his hands. The guard's eyes widened as Jaedin opened a gap in his cage. "I could get out of here if I *wanted* to! Whether you let me or not. I'm only here because I *choose* to be. So just bloody *go* and get someone! *Now*!"

The guard's whole demeanour changed then, and he took a step back. He unleashed his sword and pointed it at Jaedin. "Get *back*!" he roared.

"No!" Jaedin let go of the bars and raised his hands to the air. "I'm not going to *hurt* you! I just want–"

"Get back, you *freak*!" the Sentinels hands were unsteady, causing the blade to quiver. "Now!"

Jaedin stepped away and gritted his teeth, hating the fact that he was, once again, having to hold back. If Jaedin wanted to, he could break out of this cell easily. He could disarm that Sentinel within the blink of an eye and escape.

But Miles and Bryna had advised he behave and play by their rules.

Jaedin and the Sentinel glared daggers at each other. Jaedin could tell the man was terrified, and this was grave news. Jaedin had come to learn that when people were scared, they could be dangerous and unpredictable.

Jaedin needed to think of a way to reason with him before this got out of hand. He opened his mouth to speak again but was cut short.

There was a sudden flash of movement which swept the guard off of his feet. He screamed, and then there was a burst of red. It all happened so fast, Jaedin didn't even catch what happened.

When it was over, Jaedin gasped, and his hands went to his mouth.

The guard was pinned up against the wall, with Fangar's talons buried into his chest.

The man let out a twisted groan of agony, but it was short-lived. Fangar twisted his claws inside him and then ripped them back out. The guard fell, and four red trails ran from the holes in his body. He was already dead.

"F… Fangar," Jaedin stammered.

"Jaedin!" Fangar yelled, and he ran over to Jaedin's cell, ripping away two of the bars with a single motion of his hands and scrambling inside.

"What have you done?" Jaedin whispered.

"You were upset!" Fangar said. "I could smell it, so I came for you!"

"You *killed* him," Jaedin cried. "Why? Why did you kill him?"

Fangar regarded the corpse behind him with a frown. "He was going to hurt you…"

"No!" Jaedin shook his head. "He wasn't…"

"I don't care about *him!*" Fangar exclaimed, turning back to Jaedin and grabbing his shoulders. "I tried to keep my promise, Jaedin! I *did*. But it was too long. I *hate* being locked up. I *hate* it!"

He kissed Jaedin and pressed his body against his. To Jaedin's shame, he found himself responding. The feeling of Fangar's warm skin against his own again stirred a fever of sensations. How could he let himself become aroused during a moment like *this*?

"What are you *doing*?" Jaedin gasped.

"Fuck," Fangar uttered into his ear. "I missed you, Jaedin!"

He began kissing Jaedin's neck, and Jaedin closed his eyes and let out an involuntary moan. He had missed Fangar too. Terribly.

Jaedin almost gave in.

Almost.

Until Jaedin opened his eyes again and saw the dead eyes of the Sentinel staring at him.

"No!" Jaedin yelled, pushing Fangar away. "Fangar! You can't keep killing people!"

"But he was the enemy!"

"No, he wasn't!" Jaedin cried. "Shayam! Grav'aen! The Zakaras! *They* are the enemy!"

"Anyone who stands between us and them is the enemy!" Fangar rasped. "One of them got away. You felt it too, didn't you? How many more people will die because of that? Because of these stupid cunts here?"

"They're stupid," Jaedin agreed. "But they're not evil. Not in the way the others are. Him," Jaedin pointed at the corpse. "He wasn't going to hurt me. He was just doing his job. He didn't *know!*"

They were interrupted by the sound of a bell. It began to clang frantically. Jaedin and Fangar both turned their eyes to the sound and then looked at each other.

"Come!" Fangar said, grabbing Jaedin's arm and pulling him to his feet. "We must go! Now!"

"No!" Jaedin screamed, wrestling himself free from Fangar's grip. Fangar stared at him.

"*If* I come with you..." Jaedin said. "Then you must promise me something."

"What is it?"

"That you will not kill people anymore," Jaedin said. "Not unless it is unavoidable. Unless they really *are* the enemy."

"I will! I will!"

"Good!" Jaedin said. "And now, I have one more condition. Before we leave..."

"What?" Fangar asked.

Jaedin went to the window and twisted one of the bars until it broke off. He then pulled away another. "There are two people we need to find. These ones you *are* allowed to kill."

Chapter 10

Outlaws

A sense of deep unease passed through Bryna, and she drew her horse to a halt.

Jaedin... she thought, knowing it must be something to do with her brother.

Bryna had always been able to sense when Jaedin was in danger or pain, and now that they had forged a link between their psyches', that connection was even more acute.

What's happened? she called out, tugging upon the cord between them.

He didn't reply, but she could sense that he had heard her.

Jaedin!

Don't worry. I'm fine, he channelled back. He sounded flustered, and the sentiment behind the word 'fine' was ambiguous. These things made Bryna suspect that, even though it was true Jaedin had not come to any physical harm, he wasn't necessarily out of danger yet. With this form of communication, the messages were laden with undercurrents of feeling, making it impossible to lie.

Where are you? Bryna asked.

I can't talk right now, he said. *I will speak with you later!*

"Bryna?"

She opened her eyes and realised that the others had all stopped riding and were staring at her from the saddles of their horses.

"Are you okay?" Kyra asked with one of her eyebrows raised.

"It's Jaedin," she said.

"Jaedin?" Kyra repeated. "How do you–"

"Is he okay?" Miles asked.

"He hasn't come to any harm..." Bryna phrased her

179

response tactfully. "But something has happened."

"You were *talking* to him?" Miles said. "From this far away? How?"

"We…" Bryna hesitated, unable to find the right words to describe what she and Jaedin had done. She wasn't even sure if they existed. "It's difficult to explain. We wove a… connection. Before I left. We can speak mind to mind now."

Miles seemed genuinely impressed by that feat, but then his concern quickly took over again. "Is he with Fangar?"

"I don't know," Bryna shook her head. "He shut me out."

"Please tell me when you hear from him again," Miles said. "Tell him I wish to speak with him."

"I… can't promise Jaedin will wish to speak with you," Bryna responded. "But I can ask."

Miles had always been one of those people that Bryna found hard to read, but for a very brief moment then she felt a flurry of jealousy burst out of his aura.

"Tell me as soon as you find out anything more," Miles said and then turned his horse away and continued riding.

Bryna spurred her steed back into motion and wrapped her scarf tighter around her head to stifle the cold air. This was only their sixth day on the road, but already the landscape was markedly different. They were in the northern plains now, a terrain of hills blanketed with grass and a sparse population of trees. It was a barren place, but Bryna appreciated its disquieting beauty. She sensed it must have a long history, because parts of the forbidding landscape softly radiated with old energy. Earlier that morning, they had even passed some ruins: a series of crumbled walls and buildings that she guessed to be the spoils of one of their wars with Gavendara. Bryna didn't know enough about antiquity to be sure, though. She would have liked to have shown it to Jaedin through her eyes, but he had been sleeping. She missed her brother – it hurt that he had shut her out.

"Don't worry about Jaedin," Kyra said, appearing

beside her. "Fangar would kill an army before he let anyone touch him."

Bryna nodded. Kyra probably didn't know just how accurate her words were.

To Bryna, it wasn't surprising Jaedin had fallen for Fangar. It was only natural. The rogue was everything Miles was not. Physically apt. Ardently loyal. Impulsive. Brutal. Honest. Jaedin wanted something far away from the calculating mentor who manipulated and betrayed him.

Whereas Miles was one of those people Bryna found hard to read, Fangar was so transparent that, every time she looked at him, she saw into the core of his tortured soul. He was wild. Instinctive. His desire for revenge was maniacal, and his infatuation for Jaedin was his only anchor. A part of Bryna thought that its obsessive fervency was a good thing – because it would compel Fangar to do almost anything to keep her brother safe – but another part of her feared about the future Jaedin could have, caught in such an intense affair.

"I know…" Bryna said. "I just… the last time I saw him, he was so angry. With the Synod. And Baird. Miles too…"

"Can't blame him for that," Kyra remarked.

"I worry about what he might do," Bryna finished.

Kyra frowned. "Come on, Bryna. We're talking about Jaedin here. *Jaedin*. I mean, I love him and all, and he's got more grit than we ever gave him credit, but he's not exactly the type to go all maverick on us. And he's not stupid. Gods… he's the smartest of us all."

No. Miles is, Bryna thought, looking at him. Bryna was still not quite sure what side Miles was really on – or if he had even picked yet. *He's smart in a dangerous way. He knows how people tick. How to get what he wants out of them.*

"But we can't say the same about Fangar," Bryna said.

Kyra sighed. "If they get into any bother with that damn Synod, my loyalty stays with them. I'm sure Jaedin and Fangar can take care of themselves."

Bryna smiled. Her friend's rash pragmatism did sometimes have its unique wisdom.

"Anyway," Kyra said. "When are you going to talk to me about Sidry."

Bryna blushed.

"Ah," Kyra grinned. "I thought so... I have to admit that I have *no* idea what it is you see in him, but," she shrugged. "At least one of us has something good."

Bryna felt her friend's sadness. "I'm sorry," Bryna said. "I know that you and Aylen... well... actually, I *don't* know, but I guessed something occurred between you. I tried to stay away from Sidry – so that I could be there for you – but he's so sweet, and it just... *happened*. I don't deserve him."

"I wasn't in love with Aylen," Kyra said softly.

"No..." Bryna whispered, sensing what her friend said to be true. But there was a complex weave of other feelings emanating from her. "You weren't, were you... so, why are you so sad?"

"Aylen loved me," Kyra said and then paused. "I didn't know about it... or maybe I *did* know, but I just used him anyway. After we escaped from that weird camp. After Dion..."

Kyra screwed her eyes shut and tremored as if to shake off memories that disturbed her.

"Me and Aylen had sex," Kyra then said. "And I don't even know *why*. I was just so numb that I wanted to feel something. *Anything*. And I didn't want to die a virgin. But just before Aylen died, he told me he loved me... that he did what he did – and died – for me." Kyra then looked out at the mountains. "I think I would have learned to love him..." she said. "It was just one of those things which probably would have happened, you know? The only other boys I know are Rivan and Sidry, and – no offence – but I can barely stand them. And then there's your brother, but he feels like a brother to me too, and well... I'm not exactly his type."

For a moment, the tension eased, and they both softly laughed.

"I was... fond of Aylen," Kyra said. "And now I wonder what would have happened *if* he lived..."

She then turned her eyes to the ground, and Bryna sensed that something else was stirring in her mind that she was hesitant to voice.

"What is it, Kyra?"

"Since all this mess happened," Kyra said. "Two men have fallen for me. And now," her face went grim. "They're both gone."

"It's not your fault," Bryna whispered.

"I know," Kyra said. "I know it's crazy. But I can't stop *thinking* about it. Wondering if maybe there is something wrong with *me*. I mean, I'm seventeen years old, and the only two boys I have ever..."

She shook her head, and they carried on riding for a while.

"Okay..." Kyra turned to Bryna. "It's your turn now. Why did you say you don't deserve Sidry?"

"I..." Bryna hesitated, not quite knowing how to explain. Sometimes, it was much easier for Bryna to read other people's feelings than to do the same for herself. "He's so nice. And handsome. And he cares for me..."

"Half the boys in the village grew up fantasising about you," Kyra said. "*He's* the one who should think himself lucky."

"They did?" Bryna narrowed her eyes at her friend. She didn't get the sense that Kyra was lying.

Kyra nodded. "I mean... they were all too scared of you to act upon it, but trust me. I overheard *way* too much of their boy-talk. So, anyway, what's the other reason, Bryna? You've been acting weird ever since we arrived at the Shemet. Even more than usual."

Bryna made the mistake of looking into her friend's eyes. Kyra didn't need arcane abilities to know when her friend was hiding something.

"If I tell you, you've got to promise that you will not speak to anyone else about it. *Ever*," Bryna said. "Not even Jaedin."

"Not *Jaedin*?" Kyra repeated. It must have been the

first time she had become privy to a secret Bryna had not shared with her twin.

Bryna shook her head. "No. He would worry too much. He's got enough to deal with at the moment." She took a deep breath. "I went to the library and found out some things. About Vai-ris. About her powers. And the other descendants who lived before me."

"And?"

"I can't have children," Bryna said, making Kyra's mouth fall open. "Well, I *can*," Bryna corrected. "Technically. But if I do, I will die when it's born. I… I'm not sure if Sidry would still want me. If he knew."

"Are you sure?" Kyra asked. "There's lots of myths and legends which are crap, isn't there? I remember Jaedin telling me once about something called 'bad sources' or something."

Bryna nodded. "I think a part of me knew before I even read it…"

"There are teas and other things you can use to stop it happening," Kyra suggested. "I don't know why I am telling *you* this. You *are* Meredith's daughter."

"Yes…" Bryna said. "I know… it's just unsettling. The thought that if I should ever have children…"

"*Don't* then!" Kyra said firmly.

"But–" Bryna began.

"Just don't have kids," Kyra cut her short. "This world is in enough mess as it is without bringing brats into it."

Bryna didn't know why – for she had never even met her – but a part of her felt that by making such a resolution, she would be betraying her grandmother.

*　　*　　*

"Jaedin and Fangar escaped this morning," Greyjor said as Baird entered the room. He didn't bother beginning with any pleasantries.

Baird could tell, by the look on his face, he was furious.

"Yes," Baird said, placing his hands behind his back. "I came here as soon as I heard."

"And they killed *three* men…" Greyjor uttered between his teeth.

Baird frowned when he heard that number. He knew its relevance almost immediately.

Three. That was how many Zakaras Jaedin claimed he could sense.

But Baird guessed that there must be something else to this story. Jaedin was not one to go on a wild rampage. There must have been a catalyst for him to have suddenly decided to act.

"Who were they?" Baird asked, clearing his throat.

"Vancer," Greyjor replied. And at the mention of that name, Baird almost slapped his forehead.

Vancer! Baird thought. *Of course!*

He had been so preoccupied with Sidry's suspicions concerning Greyjor, Baird never paid the man in his shadow any attention.

"One of the members of the Holdings Consil," Greyjor continued. "His name was Ricard. I don't think you knew him. And a Sentinel, too. Kevlin. He was on duty watching Jaedin's cell just before the incident and was the first one to be murdered."

*At least Sidry was wrong about **you**…* Baird thought, turning his eyes back to his old comrade. It would have been an unpleasant business for Baird to kill a man he had once considered a friend. And Greyjor was one of the most senior of Consilars, so disposing of him would have come with some grave ramifications.

"They must have all been Zakaras," Baird said. "Was there anything unusual about the bodies?"

Greyjor frowned. "What are you trying to say, Baird?"

"Tell me, Greyjor," Baird's voice came out as a growl. He was losing his patience with this man. "Was there *anything* strange about the bodies? Don't bullshit me. I can ask others, and I *will* find out if there was…"

"Our physicians have commented that two of them had blood which was a little… off colour…" Greyjor admitted.

"Just like Ne'mair…" Baird mused.

"But this doesn't prove *anything*," Greyjor shook his head. "Having blood with a… slightly unusual pigment is no evidence that these men were monsters, Baird. It could just have been an illness or something. Our physicians are looking into it."

Baird stared at Greyjor in disbelief. Once again, realising just how much a man he had once known so well – even respected – now felt like a stranger.

Greyjor had seen the Avatars of Gezra with his own eyes. He had witnessed Fangar in his mutated form and heard accounts from several witnesses of what had happened in Fraknar. And yet, he was still failing to see reason or act.

Even worse, he seemed to be doing his utmost to stop *others* from doing so.

"And, anyway," Greyjor said. "Even *if* having brown blood makes someone a 'Zakara' – and those two men were what you *claim* them to be – that still leaves the lives of at least *two* innocent men whom Jaedin and Fangar *are* accountable for." Greyjor then reached for his quill and began to write upon a sheet of parchment. "I am sending search parties out into the city. Don't worry… we're going to find that brat of yours. And his pet."

"With all due respect," Baird said, between gritted teeth. "Do you not think at this time and hour, your men could be put to better use? Scouting villages? Defending the border? Protecting our *people*?"

"I *am* protecting my people," Greyjor said through the side of his mouth. "I am protecting them from two very dangerous outlaws."

"Jaedin is not dangerous!" Baird exclaimed. "It was *you* drove him to this!"

"I understand that these youngsters mean something to you," Greyjor said, in such a calm and officious manner that it made Baird want to throttle him. "Which is why I am going to pretend you didn't just raise your voice or try to intimidate me. Go cool your head, Baird."

*   *   *

Dear Baird,

Tell the Synod not to look for me. This is a big city, and you have seen what Fangar and I are capable of. They will never catch us.

When I first told you I could sense Zakaras within the grounds of the Synod, there were three. I woke up yesterday to discover that one of them had disappeared. Which can only mean it is on the loose. This is very bad. It is why Fangar and I did what we did.

The Synod needs to wake up. Before time runs out.

If you want to start an investigation, do this: find out who left the grounds the night before Fangar and I escaped. One of them is the infiltrator. Wherever that Zakara has gone can no longer be considered safe.

I am truly sorry another innocent man has died because of this, but the Synod need to understand that plenty more will follow if they carry on failing to act. They need to leave Fangar and me alone. While we are free, Shemet is safe from Zakaras. And I promise we will do everything we can to keep it that way.

When time is in need, I will return. But for now, do not worry about me.

I am sorry for the way things turned out, but the Synod are the ones who are at fault for what happened. Not us. I am holding them responsible for the Zakara that escaped.

Jaedin.

*   *   *

Jaedin placed the quill back in its holder and scanned the parchment. There were some other things he had wanted to say, but he knew it was very likely other people would read this letter before it reached Baird.

Jaedin wouldn't put it past the Synod to refuse to pass it on or merely dispose of it.

The door swung open, and Fangar entered the room.

"We best be off," the rogue said. "Some Sentinels just entered the bar and described a pair of fugitives that sound very much like *us*."

"Really?" Jaedin asked as he rose from his chair. Jaedin had been expecting the Synod to try to find them, but not this soon.

It appeared they *could* be efficient when it suited them.

Jaedin and Fangar were on the upper floor of an inn not far from the market quarter. Shortly after they escaped, Fangar had picked a few pockets and obtained enough money to buy them both a fresh change of clothes and a room for the night. Jaedin knew stealing from others was wrong – it was against everything his upbringing had taught him – but he didn't care. He was free again, and he had never felt more alive.

"Yes," Fangar said. He shrugged. He didn't seem worried.

He made his way to the window and swung it open.

"After you," he grinned.

Jaedin laughed. He knew now that what Fangar had been telling him all this time was true.

Leaping across rooftops. Sprinting as fast as his legs could carry him. Feeling the wind in his face. Living life on the run. No longer holding back because he was worried about people noticing he was abnormal.

It felt *good*.

As long as he was with Fangar, Jaedin felt like he was invincible.

Jaedin struck a dagger through the letter, pinning it to the table, and then he vaulted himself out of the window.

* * *

Baird felt a sense of trepidation when he heard a knock upon the door that evening. It wasn't often anyone came to see him in his room. Especially during this hour.

He got up to answer it, worrying that it was going to be more bad news.

"Selena?" he said, incapable of hiding his surprise when he saw her face.

"Hello, Baird," she said. "Can I come in, please?"

"Of course," Baird said, stepping aside.

She walked into the centre of his room, lifted her hood, and let her long blonde hair run free. Almost immediately, Baird found himself feeling conscious about the state of his living space. The rather basic room the Synod had provided for him contained no cupboards or drawers, so most of his possessions were scattered across the floor.

"It's about time they found you more adequate lodgings…" she said as if she had just read his thoughts. But it was more likely just his uncomfortable expression. "These rooms are just for visitors."

"I think they have bigger things on their minds at the moment," Baird shrugged.

She smiled grimly. "I came here to bring you something," she said, reaching into her coat and unveiling a rolled-up parchment. She handed it to him.

"What is it?" Baird asked.

"It's from Jaedin," she said. "One of the patrols just brought it back. They found it near the centre of the city."

Baird scanned the letter. "Have you read this?" he asked her.

She nodded. "I managed to intercept it before it was taken to Greyjor, but I *am* going to have to pass it on to him once you've read it… I just wanted to make sure you had the chance first."

"I see…" Baird sighed. "Gazareth's balls! What the blazes is he thinking?!"

"If what he says is true, then I believe he is thinking quite clearly…" Selena said. "He is at better hand to protect us out there than he was behind bars."

Baird looked at her, somewhat taken aback by her words. He had barely known who Selena was before he had been sent to Jalard all those years ago. She had certainly not been a person of any particular significance. She always came across as pleasant but simple; a woman who dutifully did everything by the book.

Baird was now beginning to realise that, behind her felicitous manner, was a woman of surprising grit.

"But what about *his* safety?" Baird frowned. "He's a seventeen-year-old boy! And that bloody Fangar! He is–"

"He's a young man who can break out of a cell with his bare hands and outrun trained Sentinels," Selena said. "And that Fangar has gutted two of our men for daring to stand in his way. I am sure they can look after themselves. You're just feeling protective because those youngsters you brought back from Jalard mean something to you."

Their eyes met, and residual energy from their previous argument over sending Rivan, Kyra and Bryna on a mission lingered between them.

Baird turned away.

He knew she was right. That her reasoning was, as usual, pragmatic and logical. And that he was letting his emotions cloud his judgement. That bothered him more than anything. The idea of 'family' had always been somewhat alien to Baird. During his time in Jalard, he had observed all the peculiar dynamics that children, siblings and parents had with each other. Witnessed enough of the strains and complications that often came with such relationships to think himself lucky to have grown up free from it all.

It was a sense of duty that compelled him to bring the survivors of Jalard back to Shemet, but somewhere along the way, he had become too involved. Baird had never intended to let any of them get under his skin, yet ever since he returned to Shemet, he had found himself terrified of losing them. Rivan, Sidry and Aylen felt like the sons Baird had never had. Kyra, for all that she was hard work, had a fire inside he never wanted to die. The most surprising revelation of all was how much Baird cared for even Jaedin, who had always been the most difficult of his rat pack.

"So, you're going to leave them to their own devices?" Baird asked.

Selena shrugged. "If it were down to me, we would have some effort put into tracking them down... but only as a token gesture. It would make the Synod seem weak to just let them off the hook, after all. I imagine Greyjor is going to have different ideas, though, and he has much more leverage on this matter than I."

Her expression then changed. "I don't trust him, Baird..." she whispered.

"Greyjor," he uttered.

She put a finger to her lips. "Careful, Baird. We don't know who could be listening."

Baird cast his eyes around the room warily – looking for any potential holes in the walls. He didn't spot anything, but he also knew that Selena was more aware of the ins and outs of this place than he was.

"Why?" Baird asked, lowering his voice.

She shook her head. "I don't know..." she whispered. "There's just something not right about him these days. The way he's been is so difficult. Even now. And Miles warned that there might be traitors among us. I don't know what to think anymore..."

He frowned. "This is a very serious allegation you're making..."

"I realise this," she nodded. "And that is why I haven't made it official. I have no evidence. And it is also why I came to you. You're... one of the only people I can trust."

Baird didn't like the way this conversation was going. He barely knew who this woman was until a couple of aeights ago, and now she was loosing heavy burdens upon him. Baird had always avoided the political world of the Synod – it was one of the reasons he opted to become a teacher when the War of Ashes ended – but, ever since he had returned to Shemet, it felt like he had been unwittingly dragged into its web of intrigues and chicanery.

Most of all, Baird didn't like what she was saying because it was bearing light upon suspicions that lurked in the back of his own mind.

"So, what do you plan to do?" Baird asked.

Selena sighed. "Nothing, for now. Greyjor may only be the Chief of the War Consil, but he has many of the other Chiefs under his thumb and reigns more influence than his position traditionally carries. Too much, in my opinion. But, believe it or not, Baird, there are others like me. People who aren't happy with the current situation – how do you think I managed to intercept that letter? – but most of them are too scared to openly speak out against him. All we can do, for now, is be vigilant and persevere. Try to do the best we can within our means. And, most of all, wait. Wait until we find evidence before we make any rash moves."

"What about what Jaedin said?" Baird changed the subject. "About finding out who left the grounds the night before he escaped? We need to track that Zakara down…"

She nodded. "It is already being looked into, Baird."

"Good," he said, once again impressed by Selena. He had underestimated her.

"And on that note, I shall leave," she said, pulling her hood back up and heading towards the door. "Come see me in the morning. I will tell you if we found out anything."

"Night, Selena… and thanks," he added.

"You do not need to thank me, Baird. It's my duty."

*   *   *

On the ninth morning of their journey, Bryna and the others caught their first view of the Valantian Mountains and paused for a while to take in the sight of it.

"Oh my gods," Kyra said. "Is that white stuff–"

"Snow," Miles finished for her, a nostalgic smile on his

face. "Yes, Kyra. There's snow on these mountains all year round."

"We've seen snow before…" Rivan said.

"When?" Kyra asked.

"I don't know," he shrugged. "I was young, but I kind of remember it… me and Sidry were throwing it at each other."

"You can pick it up?" she said. "I thought it was like dust?"

"You'll see…" he smirked.

Bryna eyed the sight, wishing she could show it to her brother. She had still not heard from Jaedin since their brief exchange.

She closed her eyes and sent out another call for him. *Jaedin. Speak to me…*

She sensed a fleeting impression briefly after – reassuring her that he had at least *heard* her – but nothing more. He was not ready to answer yet.

After a brief break, they continued riding. Everyone was in a somewhat quiet and contemplative mood that day. They kept turning their eyes to the mountain range looming before them. Bryna felt a complex mosaic of feelings from Kyra and Rivan; primarily wonder and excitement, but also unease and foreboding. The Valantian Mountains were legendary. Many myths surrounded them, and they were heavily embedded into the Sharmarian psyche because they were a natural defence against their traditional enemy, Gavendara.

Bryna's feelings echoed theirs. The sight of it, its beauty, almost took her breath away, but she knew its crossing was going to be taxing and potentially dangerous. Especially for her. She was not as physically apt as the others. It was going to be a challenge for her to keep pace.

The snow was also a reminder that winter was coming, and her powers continued to ebb. Bryna did not know how much she would be capable of by spring, but she knew for certain she would not be able to pull off anything close to the scale of what she did at Fraknar.

She knew she should tell the others about it, but she did not want to weaken their morale.

"We should leave an offering for Valan," she said.

"What kind?" Kyra asked.

"They say he likes precious stones and red wine," Miles said. "Certain types of food can be given, too. Nothing salty, though."

"That rules out most of our provisions…" Kyra said dryly.

"We'll think of something," Miles shrugged.

"Tell me a story about Valan," Bryna asked Miles. She wanted something to distract her thoughts for a while.

"There isn't much to say, really," Miles pondered out loud. His eyes went distant, the way they usually did when he was mustering from the library of information in his mind. "There are many tales. Ones about him giving aid to people passing through this realm. Plenty more about him punishing those who displease him. But his creation story is fairly simple: he is the son of Vuule – the mountain god – and Vaishra."

"The water goddess?" Kyra said. "That's a bit strange…"

"Well, his mountains *are* covered in snow most of the year," Miles reminded her. "He has several brothers and sisters who hold dominium over other mountain regions."

"What other mountains?" Rivan frowned.

"Most of them are in Gavendara," Miles said. "You don't have many mountains in Sharma. Yours is a land of forests and trees whilst Gavendara is colder and not as green."

"Sounds a bit dull," Kyra commented.

"It has its own beauty," Miles said, sounding a little defensive. "We have less abundance, and our soil isn't as fertile, so food is scarce, and winters are tougher… but we have more metals and mines. Much of your iron comes from Gavendara."

"That's crap," Rivan grunted. "We have loads of blacksmiths in Sharma."

"I assure you, it's not," Miles responded. "The *ore* your

blacksmiths burn is mostly from across the border."

"We *trade* with them?" Kyra exclaimed.

"Yes," Miles nodded. "We are taking a more discreet route for this occasion. If we had taken the passage through Fort Valen and the Toba Valley, however, we would have passed many wagons and caravans by now. There are even a few border villages where Sharmarians and Gavendarians live side by side. Even in times of war, there is still some measure of exchange. It goes both ways. Just as many of your metals come from Gavendara, much of our linen, cotton and other materials for clothing come from you."

"Don't you mean from *us*?" Rivan eyed him suspiciously.

"Just a slip of the tongue. Please excuse me," Miles grimaced. "Wherever my loyalties are *now*, I am still Gavendarian by birth. A part of me still cares for some of its people. I grew up there… it was my home."

Bryna heard a voice in her mind and drew her horse to a halt.

Bryna?

"Wait," she said. "It's Jaedin."

Where are you? she channelled back to him as she dismounted.

Don't panic, Jaedin replied. *I'm fine. I'm with Fangar.*

"Where is he?" Miles interrupted. "Is he okay?"

"He's with Fangar," Bryna muttered, turning away from the others. "Just give me a few moments."

She heard Miles let out a curse.

Are you at the Synod? she asked Jaedin.

No, he replied. *Things happened after you left. One of the Zakaras got away. Fangar and I escaped.*

Bryna's first instinct was to give him a firm reprimand, but she reconsidered. Maybe his actions weren't so foolish. If a Zakara was on the loose, the ramifications could be devastating.

What about the other two? she asked. *You said there were three.*

Fangar and I took care of them, but it all went wrong…

Fangar killed one of the Sentinels, and now the Synod is looking for us. Don't panic! We're okay. They won't find us. I sent Baird a letter.

"What's he saying, Bryna?" Miles asked, nudging her.

"He said that one of the Zakaras got away, so he and Fangar escaped and killed the other two," Bryna replied. She allowed Jaedin access to her eyes and ears so that he could see what she was telling them. "They are hiding out in the city now. The Synod is looking for them."

"Jaedin!" Miles said. "What the blazes were you *thinking*? You need to go back to Baird!"

Bryna, can I speak through your lips? Jaedin asked.

As long as you keep this civil, Bryna said, as she lifted more veils.

"No way!" Bryna found her mouth opening of its own accord. Even though it was still her own voice she could hear, the tone and persona behind it were discernibly Jaedin's. Rivan backed away, and Kyra's eyes went wide. "I'm *not* going back to that place. They are *fools*! We are better at hand to protect the city as we are."

"Jaedin!" Miles frowned. "This is not… like you. The city is dangerous, and so is Fangar! I am sure if you go back to Baird – alone – they will let you off! You'll be safer there."

Jaedin shook Bryna's head. "No, Miles," he said through her. "I tried to play by their rules, and thanks to them, a Zakara got away."

Walk away, Bryna, Jaedin said to her. *I've had enough of **him**.*

"Sorry…" Bryna said, assuming her own voice once again. "My brother wishes to speak with me alone a moment."

He's worried about you, she said to Jaedin as she walked away.

Whatever, Jaedin replied. *He lost his right to worry a while ago.*

I'm worried about you too…

*Do **you** think I am doing the wrong thing?*

I don't know, Bryna admitted. *I guess you **do** need to* *keep the city safe from the Zakaras. But Miles is wise to be worried. I mean, how are you going to live? Sleep? Eat?*

Fangar's with me, Jaedin said. *He's been living on the run for years.*

Bryna tried to conceal her own conflicted feelings towards Fangar. She knew he would protect Jaedin, but at what cost?

You don't like him either, Jaedin said, reading her thoughts.

No, she responded. *It's not that. I don't know. Just... be careful. Promise me.*

I will try, Jaedin said. *But I have to do everything I can to stop the Zakaras. That comes first.*

Bryna was then pulled out of her thoughts when she realised that Rivan was standing in front of her.

"Is that you or Jaedin right now?" he asked, keeping a wary distance.

"It's me," she replied. "But Jaedin can still hear."

"Can you..." Rivan began but then hesitated and shifted his weight from one foot to the other. He seemed a little uncomfortable. Like he didn't know how to address both her and Jaedin simultaneously. Bryna found it quite endearing.

I felt that, Jaedin said. *Don't give Sidry cause to be jealous...*

"Give messages to Baird?" Rivan continued. "From me. About the mission."

Jaedin groaned in Bryna's mind. *I guess...* he said. *As long as I don't have to actually **see** him in person. I'll figure out something...*

Some things are more important than your personal feuds, Jaedin, Bryna advised.

"Yes, he can," Bryna said. "But not in person. It would be... unwise for Jaedin to go near the Synod at the moment."

Why do you always have to be so ruddy tactful? Jaedin asked.

One of us has to be.

197

"Why are you grinning?" Rivan asked.

"Oh… don't worry," Bryna said. "Just twin-talk."

I need to go, Jaedin said. *But tell Rivan he's got the brains of a goose for me.*

I know you like him really, Bryna teased.

Not quite as much as you do, apparently, Jaedin said.

"Jaedin is leaving now," she said, ignoring the last comment. "But he sends his regards. Is there anything you would like him to pass on?"

"Not really," Rivan shrugged. "Yet, anyway."

Bryna nodded. *Bye Jaedin,* she closed her eyes again. *Speak to me soon.*

Alright, he replied. *Bye Bryna. Tell Kyra to look after herself.*

His presence faded away, and Bryna closed her eyes for a few moments to ground herself.

"He's gone now," she said.

"Are you okay?" Rivan asked. "You look a bit dizzy. Do you want a hand?"

"No," she said, though her feet wobbled as she took her first step. "I am fine. Thank you."

Chapter 11

The Ruena

When Astar rode into Llamaleil, he was surprised how little things had changed. It seemed that the pattern of life continued as usual. Astar didn't know if this was because the people were unaware of his father's malady, or they merely did not care.

"So this is your home," Elita said as they guided their horses towards the keep.

Astar nodded. Elita opened her mouth to say something else but then decided to keep whatever remark popped into her mind to herself. People were beginning to recognise Astar, and some of them waved as he rode through the market. When they noticed that Elita was with him, they stared and began to whisper to each other.

"I think they're under the impression I'm your mistress," Elita muttered. The idea didn't seem to bother her much; in fact, it appeared to be a source of great amusement. "Have you acquired yourself a bit of a reputation here, perchance?" she asked as she smiled sweetly at the crowds and theatrically waved.

"You're enjoying this, aren't you..." he said under his breath.

"Of course," she said. "Any opportunity to witness you squirm."

"Well, give it a rest," he muttered. "I'm not in the mood."

He spurred his horse ahead of her a little to distance himself for a while. After their time on the road together, she was beginning to irk him. Whenever she was courteous, it felt like pity, yet whenever she regressed to her usual quips, there was only so much of her derisive wit he could tolerate.

Most of all, she vexed him because, despite all this, he still wanted her. And she knew it too.

When Astar reached the gate, he had to clear his throat to get the guard's attention.

"No visitors today," the guard droned without even lifting his head. "Lord Oren is busy."

"Open the gate," Astar grunted. "*Now*."

The guard jumped at the sound of his voice. "Astar!" his face turned red when he saw who it was. "Sorry, Master! Right away!"

He rushed over and pulled at the rope. Astar found his hurried manner troubling. As heir to the province, Astar had always garnered some measure of respect from its people but very seldom fear.

It was as if this man already thought of Astar as his new liege.

Astar regretted not using his magic to make his return more inconspicuous as he rode into the bailey. His father's servants paused from their duties to stare at him, open-mouthed, and it wasn't shock nor surprise he could see in their expressions – for they must have anticipated Astar's return – it felt more like his presence made them nervous because they no longer knew how to regard him.

Brin, one of Astar's father's longest and most reliable manservants, seemed to be the only one to remember proper decorum and came to greet him.

"Welcome home," he said, smiling grimly.

"Thanks, Brin," Astar said and dismounted. "Can you see to these horses and have my bags taken to my room, please?"

"Don't worry. I will sort all out for you," Brin responded and then regarded Elita. "And what about the lady?" he asked.

Astar frowned, knowing that his response had the potential to escalate rumours which were likely already circulating. "Have someone organise a room for her in the guest quarters."

"I see…" Brin said and then ushered one of the stablehands over.

"Have food brought up to her," Astar then added. "And–"

"Don't worry about me," Elita said, touching Astar's shoulder. "I'll make sure they treat me right. You go and see your father."

"Thank you," Astar said.

He turned and made his way straight towards the western tower. On his way up the staircase, he passed a woman whom he recognised. It was Harnna, one of the local Devotees of Carnea.

"How is he?" Astar asked.

She hesitated. "He has The Ruena, Astar…" she replied with a grimace. "There's not much I can do but make him comfortable. I'm sorry."

Astar sighed. "Is he awake? I would like to see him."

She nodded. "He's coping quite well, all considering…" she said. "If you have need of me, send a messenger, M'Lord."

I'm not Lord yet! Astar almost yelled but held back. He took a deep breath to calm himself and thanked her.

He opened the door. Astar thought himself prepared for what was on the other side, but he wasn't. He had never witnessed anyone in the advanced stages of The Ruena before. He was very young when his mother died, and since then, his life within the walls of this keep had been sheltered from such things.

Lord Oren's face was almost unrecognisable. A distended protrusion of welling pustules and horrid growths. The degenerated flesh had swallowed one of his eyes, and it now drooped from the side of his jaw. He had covered most of his body beneath a blanket but Astar could see, from the bumps and shapes beneath it, that the deformities had reached almost every part of his anatomy.

"Father…" Astar whispered, and despite an entire lifetime of emotional distance between them, he found himself crying. He didn't even use his magic to veil his emotions like he usually did.

"Astar?" his father said softly. Astar was surprised to hear a voice coming out from somewhere beneath those features.

"What do you want me to do?" Astar croaked. He went to the bedside and hesitated.

What *could* he do?

"I don't want you to do anything, Astar..." his father wheezed. He coughed, and yellow bile ran down his chin. "You... will be Lord of Llamaleil soon."

No! I don't want this. I don't want Llamaleil yet! Astar thought but held back.

Instead, he nodded. He was a noble. He wouldn't stamp his foot like a child in front of a dying man nor refuse the duties which came with his birthright.

"You're not dead yet, father," Astar said.

*   *   *

On the morning of their fourth day scaling the Valantian Mountains, Rivan caught sight of a tower ahead of them.

"What is that?" he asked, pointing it out to the others.

"I don't know, but it doesn't look friendly..." Kyra said as she eyed it. "Look. There's a gate."

Rivan squinted his eyes and saw the rest of the large wooden structure ahead blocking their path. It was joined to the tower, and a row of spikes ran along the top that he guessed were there to stop people climbing over it.

"Nothing to worry about," Miles said. "It's just one of the watchtowers. Selena gave me the correct documentation, so they'll let us pass."

"Why is it there?" Kyra asked.

"To stop Gavendarians getting in..." Miles answered.

When they reached the gate, a guard came out of the tower, and Miles unravelled a scroll and showed it to him. The guard then went back inside and, a few moments later, the gate began to rise.

"Does this mean we're in Gavendara now?" Kyra asked once they passed through. Almost immediately, it began to close again. Rivan felt that there was something quite ominous about the whole experience.

"Not quite..." Miles said. "We have a couple of days riding yet until we are properly in Gavendara."

Kyra frowned. "How are we going to get in?" she asked. "Don't they have watchtowers as well?"

"No," Miles shook his head.

"Why not?" Rivan asked. He felt suspicious. He didn't like how Miles – with all of his knowledge – seemed to be taking charge of things now. It dawned upon him that it would be all too easy for Miles to mislead them and lure them into a trap. "Aren't they worried about being attacked?"

"Why would Sharma attack Gavendara?" Miles said. "Your lands are free from The Ruena... this border only really trickles in one direction, Rivan. Thousands would pass through one way if given a chance, but not many choose to go the direction we are."

"How did *you* get through, then?" Kyra asked.

"It wasn't easy, trust me..." Miles said.

They rode for the rest of that day mostly in silence, and the ascent became more challenging, so they had to concentrate on guiding their horses. They camped at night behind a small bluff on the side of the mountain, and the air had turned so cold Rivan was reluctant to leave the fire when it was his turn to retire to his tent to sleep.

The following morning, they finally reached the snowy peaks, and the ground turned white. Bryna and Kyra immediately became enchanted by the phenomenon. They both leapt from their horses to stamp their feet through the white layers, fascinated by the way they could leave footprints. Rivan crunched a sphere of it in his hands and threw it at Kyra, initiating a snowball fight that soon escalated.

Despite this light-hearted beginning to the day, the scaling of this final part of the mountain turned out to be much more arduous than Rivan expected. The higher they climbed, the more they found themselves under the mercy of cold, bitter winds that caused Rivan's neck to go stiff and his fingers throb. The air felt thinner. Drawing breaths of air didn't seem to satisfy Rivan's chest as much as they usually did.

Miles promised that if they made their way with enough haste, they shouldn't have to pitch their tents that night in the snow – a marvel which had swiftly lost its novelty – so they pressed on. Rivan often needed to coax his horse to get through some of the more laborious parts of the trail. It became narrower and more winding as it snaked through the rocky peaks and crags.

In the early afternoon, Rivan crested what he expected to be just another misleading ridge to find himself looking down upon the other side of the mountain. There were green hills in the distance.

"We've reached the top!" he announced.

"Really?" Kyra called back. "Thank the gods!"

She caught up a few moments later, reigning her horse beside him. "Does this mean we're in Gavendara now?"

"Almost," Miles said. He smiled fondly as he took in the view. "I haven't seen this for years…"

"Don't get used to it," Rivan warned. "You're not here for sport."

Miles' smile faded, and he turned his head down. "I know that…" he said.

"Do you?" Rivan asked. "Seems to me the closer we get the more I see those damned teeth of yours."

"Oh, give him a break, Rivan," Kyra said. "This *was* his home. You telling me you don't miss *your* home? I know I do…"

"Thanks, Kyra," Miles said. "For understanding…" he added when she frowned.

"Don't thank me," she said. "I don't trust you much either, to be honest. But I would rather focus on *proper* reasons. Anyway…" her voice then changed. "Let's get going… I plan on sitting by a warm fire tonight."

"What is that?" Rivan asked, pointing to what appeared to be a small settlement on the side of one of the neighbouring mountains.

"That…" Miles replied, squinting his eyes. "Is Passerskeep… it's a small town, but there is a garrison stationed there, so it is probably best we give it a wide berth."

"Where *are* you taking us, then?" Kyra asked. "You said we would be able to stop at a town tomorrow."

"Probably Sarok," Miles decided. "It's not too far from here, and it's an interesting little town. It's usually a safe place for... well, anyone really. Kyra is right, by the way. We best make a move if we want to clear the snow before nightfall."

Just as they were departing, Rivan noticed that Bryna's horse wasn't moving. She had a distant look in her eyes.

He sighed and rode up to her.

"Bryna?" he called cautiously. He never quite knew how to appropriately get her attention during moments like this because he was aware that her mind was so often swept away into that own little world of hers. A world Rivan knew near to nothing about.

"Bryna," he said again, this time more firmly.

She smiled. "Sorry..." she said and blinked a few times as her eyes cleared. "I was just showing Jaedin the view."

"Oh..." Rivan said. "It's just... well, we're heading on now."

"Don't worry," she replied as she gently tapped her horse's rump and rode towards him. "I won't hold you up any longer."

"How is he, anyway?" Rivan asked. "Jaedin, I mean... not the horse."

She laughed. "My horse is a she, and her name is Moongaze."

"Moongaze?" he repeated. The idea of naming a horse seemed a little silly to him, but he didn't say anything.

She nodded. "I call her that because sometimes I catch her looking at the sky at night... which is unusual behaviour for a horse, is it not?" she explained. "And Jaedin is well. Well, I *believe* so, at least. He is being a little secretive about what he and Fangar are up to at the moment. Although as his sister, there is probably some of that which I would rather *not* know," she finished, smiling sheepishly.

"Do you worry about him?" Rivan asked.

"Always," she nodded. "He is my twin. We entered this

life together, and I have always been able to feel it when he is hurt or happy or sad or in pain. At the moment, he is happier than he has been in a long time."

"That's good, isn't it?" Rivan said encouragingly.

"It's a strange kind of happy…" she mused. "It's wild and… I think he is in love, but I am not sure if it is good for him…"

Rivan didn't know what to say to that. He had never been in love. A few of the girls from Jalard had taken his fancy, but they all wanted more attention than he was willing to give them. The idea that Jaedin was in love with another man was also something Rivan found particularly hard to get his head around.

"You've never been in love, have you…" Bryna said.

Rivan flinched. He was not sure he would ever get used to Bryna's way of knowing what was on his mind. He sometimes wondered whether she could literally read his thoughts, or she was just insightful enough to guess. He was beginning to think that it was a bit of both.

"What's it like?" he asked.

She blushed. "I am not sure, to be honest," she said. "Me and Sidry only just… all I know is that when we left, and I said goodbye to him, I felt something pulling at me here," she touched her chest. "And I am still not sure if it's a good feeling or not."

"He told you to look after me, didn't he…" she then said, after a brief pause.

Rivan nodded.

"You are special to him as well," she said. "In a different way, of course, but equally valuable. So I will look out for you, too. He would be sad if you didn't come back."

Rivan was shocked, not just by her words but also by how much of a comfort they were to him. They put to rest some of the insecurities which had been lurking in the back of his mind.

Ever since Sidry had shown an interest in Bryna, Rivan had felt a little jealous. Sidry was the closest thing Rivan had to a family, and he worried such a strong attachment to someone else might cause a rift between them. Bryna had not only somehow picked up on these thoughts, but also found a graceful way to resolve them.

Rivan looked at Bryna in a way he never had before. He realised that she was even more remarkable than he had previously thought. He had just not noticed it before.

He then also realised he was happy for her. And Sidry. Because he could think of no one better to bring his friend happiness.

"It's a deal," Rivan grinned. "We'll look after each other…"

*   *   *

Jaedin went to meet Fangar in the yard which, over the last few days, had become their customary meeting place.

There, he found the rogue waiting for him: leant against a wall and with his arms crossed over his chest.

He began to quiz Jaedin with the usual series of questions.

"What did you find today?"

"Three silver and five lannies," Jaedin said, feeling quite proud of himself as he emptied his pocket into Fangar's hand. "I got these too. I think they're valuable," he added, opening up the sack and showing Fangar the collection of silver plates and cups he had looted. Jaedin then dug into his coat and retrieved a small necklace and jewelled bracelet.

"How did you get them?"

"I picked the money from pockets," Jaedin replied. It was strange to hear his voice bragging about such a deed. There wasn't even much guilt anymore. "The silverware was from someone's home. And the trinkets were from the market place."

"Did anyone catch you?"

Jaedin hesitated. "A woman *almost* did…" he admitted. "But I got away before she spotted me."

"And is that *all* you wish to tell me?" Fangar asked, narrowing his eyes.

Jaedin nodded.

"You lie!" Fangar rasped. "I was watching you! You were chased out of that house!"

"She never *saw* me…" Jaedin winced.

He had not thought that incident counted as being 'caught', so he'd tried to get away with not mentioning it.

"And to top it all off, you were just lucky at the market!" Fangar added. "That vendor figured out who it was straight after you left and told everyone! Now the whole trading district knows what you look like! And what *do* you look like, Jaedin?" Fangar demanded.

"I… I–" Jaedin stammered.

"You look like a wanted man! The Synod have posted descriptions of you all over the city. You're small. You have green eyes, black hair, and that bloody thing wrapped around your head. You're too distinctive!"

Fangar grabbed the scrap of linen Jaedin used to veil his forehead and tore it off.

Jaedin cringed as the ugly scar beneath it was laid bare. It felt strange to feel the air against it; he always kept it covered.

Fangar's face softened, and he gently traced his finger across it. Jaedin was quite taken aback by that gesture. It was like Fangar even saw his taints as beautiful.

Fangar pulled Jaedin to him and kissed him fiercely.

"There isn't much we can do about that blemish," Fangar conceded. "But something needs to be done about those locks of yours…"

*   *   *

Jaedin did feel a bit sentimental when Fangar sat him down in a chair and began to hack off chunks of his hair with a dagger, but he tried to hide it. It felt like the final stripping away of his identity. Circumstances forced him to give up his billowy black clothes for more practical attire when he lost his home and mother. He had to start tying that scrap of linen over his forehead after they sliced him open and turned him into something inhuman.

Now, he was an outlaw, and another part of him was being snipped away.

Delicacy was not in Fangar's nature, and he kept pulling too hard. Jaedin winced, but he bit back the urge to cry out.

Once Fangar had finished, he showed Jaedin his reflection on the flat of one of the silver plates he pilfered. Jaedin gasped. It wasn't the change to his hair that caused him such a shock – for he had been expecting that. The alteration caused Jaedin to see other, subtler, changes that he had been too busy recently to notice. His face was losing its roundness, and his jaw was more defined. He had lost weight. He was getting older.

"Now, let's go," Fangar said, swinging a bag over his shoulder.

"Where?" Jaedin asked. They had been sleeping in the same abandoned house in one of Shemet's slums for a few days now. It was far from glamorous, but Jaedin had become accustomed to it. They had not been chased out by any of the Synod patrols yet, so it was suitably neglected.

"Out of town. Just for a few days," Fangar replied. "It's best we lay low for a while. Don't worry, I've packed food, and the rest of the things we need I'm going teach you to *hunt* for."

Jaedin gathered his things, and they made their way out of the city. The sight of them racing down the street – with their legs swishing at a rate that must have seemed implausible – caused a few stares, but once they reached the farmlands outside, there were not as many eyes. Jaedin relaxed again. He then realised that a part of him had missed the rural wilderness and its privacy.

They built a shelter beneath the dangling leaves of a weeping willow, and then Fangar told Jaedin to grab his sword and follow him to the clearing outside.

"I want you to try to hit me," Fangar said.

It had been a while since Jaedin had wielded a weapon. Baird had been teaching him how to fight while they were on the run, and in that time, Jaedin had reached a level of swordsmanship he believed at least passable. He had not had any chances to practice since the Synod locked him away.

Jaedin hefted his blade. He had taken it from the Sentinel they killed, so it was still new to him and he was yet to accustom himself to its weight and balance, but the boy who would have once complained about such things was long dead.

"But you're unarmed," Jaedin said.

"I don't need a weapon," Fangar smiled. "Go on! *Hit me!*"

Jaedin swung his blade. He pulled the blow at the last moment – just as Baird taught him to do when engaging in a friendly duel – but it turned out that he needn't have bothered; Fangar had already dodged out of sight.

"I said, *hit me!*" Fangar growled, appearing behind him and tightening his wrist around Jaedin's neck. "Stop treating me like *them!*"

Jaedin twisted out of the headlock and circled his sword in one, fluid motion, but Fangar had already leapt away again. Jaedin gritted his teeth and charged, swinging the blade back and forth, but every time Fangar would spin, duck and dodge out of his reach.

"What's the use?" Jaedin yelled. "This isn't helping me learn *anything!*"

"Exactly!" Fangar spat. He squared up to him, snatched the sword from Jaedin's hands and tossed it aside. "Baird's been teaching you a way of fightin' which makes the fact you're small a weakness! That sword is bigger than the arms that are holding it! Swinging that bloody thing around is just slowing you down! You're trying to fight like a *human*, Jaedin, but you're not. No more than I am."

Fangar reached into the inside of his cloak and drew a pair of daggers. "You might be faster with a sword now than you used to be, but you could be even faster with daggers. You should use your speed to your advantage!"

He handed the blades over, and Jaedin examined them.

"With these, I can teach you to open throats before they even see you coming," Fangar grinned. "And dance around them so swiftly that you'll never need to block a blow ever again!"

"That doesn't sound honourable..." Jaedin said.

Fangar's eyebrows drew together. "Do the Zakaras know honour? Was Shayam honourable? What about the bastards who butchered me? There is no honour left in this world, Jaedin. The weak die. The strong live. And I can make you stronger."

*   *   *

When Astar entered the parlour early the following morning, he found Elita sitting at the table, tucking into a hearty breakfast.

"Made yourself at home, I see..." Astar commented.

"How is your father?" she asked. "I didn't see you last night."

"Sorry, I had other things on my mind," Astar said. "I don't think he has long left..."

She grimaced. "Is there anything I can do?"

Astar shook his head.

One of the doors opened, and Veldra shuffled into the room carrying a steaming plate in her hands. She looked at him with her shrewd eyes.

"Got her' so hurry yer left yer manners a' yer rear," she said. She placed his breakfast in front of him, but Astar wasn't hungry. "Leave ol' Veldra ter see ter yer guests – don't worry!"

"Give me a break," Astar groaned. "You do know *why* I've come back, don't you?"

"Veldra 'ears all tha' goes on these walls," she responded with no hint of apology. "Yer goin' t' be Lord soon, and yer actin' a lil boy. Man up!"

Astar glowered at her.

"Don't yer dare give me t' evil eye!" she screeched. "Or I'll tell th' lady 'ere how yer waste tha' gift t' gods gave ye, on vain shamshams."

Astar flinched, realising he had forgotten to remove his glamour.

"Oh, don't worry," Elita said, raising her cup to her lips. "I already know about *that*."

"And she ain't no lady," Astar cut in.

Veldra ignored his last comment and made her way towards the hearth to add more logs to the fire.

"I like her," Elita laughed.

Astar scowled. It seemed it had not taken Elita and his nanny long to start ganging up on him, and he was short on patience that day.

"Why don't you just bugger off…" he muttered.

Elita was so surprised by his reaction that, for a moment, her cool demeanour slipped and her face betrayed her. She felt unwelcome and dejected.

"Fine!" she said, rising from the chair and tossing her napkin on the table.

"She ain't goin' no-w'er," Veldra called. "Si' ba' down, gerl."

"It's okay," Elita said. "I know he's just upset. I'll go for a walk… maybe I'll find myself a nice farmer boy to play with…"

Her final comment stung him, but Astar didn't let it show until she had left the room and he and Veldra were alone.

"Tha' lass has spirit," Veldra nodded her head approvingly. "You'll do well wi' her."

"It's not like that," Astar grunted. "To be honest, she's starting to piss me off."

"Oh, I see…" Veldra said. "Gave yer the bump, di' she? Well, a' least one o' 'em ha' sense."

Astar bristled. "I'm going to see my father…" he said, reaching for his coat.

"Yer might need ter wait," Veldra said. "He's go' himself visitors."

"Who?" Astar asked.

"Yer not heard? Lor' Jarvis come this morn'. Wi' an escort. There 'er eight o' them! *Eight!*"

Astar frowned. "Jarvis?" he repeated. "Oh… I didn't realise."

"Don't yer worry," Veldra smiled. "Veldra saw ter yer

guests. I think they're 'tending ter stay."

"Thanks, Veldra..." Astar said. "I'll go welcome them."

When Astar entered the courtyard, he saw a group of men dressed in green robes standing outside the entrance to his father's quarters.

"Hello," Astar dipped his head. "Welcome to Llamaleil. Sorry I wasn't around to greet you this morning. I was engaged in other duties."

He waited for a response, but none of them said anything.

Astar frowned. There was something peculiar about these men. Nobles were known for their eccentric habits, and one of the more recent ones was donning their men in distinctive uniforms. Green robes were one of the more bizarre choices Astar had seen, though.

He couldn't shake the feeling that these men were somehow familiar, but he couldn't place exactly where it was that he had seen them before.

"Can you excuse me, please," Astar eventually said, pointing at the door behind them.

They rearranged themselves to let him past, and Astar squeezed through the door and into the solar to find Lord Jarvis there.

"Astar," he said, walking up to him and shaking his hand.

"Greetings, Lord Jarvis. Welcome to Llamaleil," Astar said, already hating all these formal greetings he was going to have to get used to giving. It felt strange to be the one to welcome Jarvis into the keep. Lord Jarvis was an old friend of Oren's, and Astar had known him since he was a child.

"My, you've grown!" Jarvis said, stepping back and looking at him. "I hear you're enlisted at the Institute now," he said. "Grav'aen spoke quite highly of you."

"Did he?" Astar asked, mildly surprised. He could only guess that those favourable words came *before* the incident with Bovan.

"Yes. He did mention that you have a tendency to get

into scuffles, but what youth doesn't?" Jarvis chuckled. "You're one of his most promising, from what I've heard."

"Well... I *was*..." Astar shrugged. "It seems I'm going to have to stay here now..."

"Oh, Astar," Lord Jarvis said. "I'm sorry about your father – that is why I came here as soon as I heard – but please, don't give up hope, yet. Oren is a fighter, and I have brought a very talented healer with me."

Astar swallowed a lump in his throat, struggling to think of a polite way to respond.

How could anyone believe there was any hope for his father?

"Have you... seen Lord Oren yet?" Astar asked tactfully.

Lord Jarvis nodded, which only astounded Astar even more. "Like I said," Lord Jarvis continued. "My healer is *very* talented. If anyone can bring Lord Oren back to life, it's him. You may make it back to the Institute yet, Astar."

"I was just on my way to go see him," Astar said. This conversation was beginning to make him feel uncomfortable. One only needed to take a fleeting glance at the state of Astar's father to know that there was nothing anyone could do for him.

"I'm afraid that it is best he is not disturbed," Jarvis said. He put a hand on Astar's shoulder. "Please, give him a chance... You can come back later. If anything changes, you'll be the first to know."

"But I–" Astar began.

"Please," Jarvis repeated insistently. "Just let him *try*. You do want him to live, don't you?"

*   *   *

Four days after the others left for their mission, Baird and Sidry began a new training regimen.

"Are you ready?" the burly mentor asked when he called upon Sidry's room in the morning.

"Almost," Sidry said and went to put his boots on. "Just give me a moment…"

"You won't be needing that," Baird grunted when Sidry reached for his sword.

Baird led Sidry through the Academy ground and then through a stone archway, reaching a large wooded area on the other side.

"What is this place?" Sidry asked.

"The hunting grounds," Baird replied. "It's part of the Academy."

"Why are we here?"

Baird looked at him. "To prepare for battle."

"Battle?" Sidry repeated.

He nodded. "It's coming, Sidry. Sooner or later. And when it does, we need to be ready."

"You have a plan for me, don't you…" Sidry said.

"No," Baird shook his head. "And *that's* the problem, Sidry. I *don't*. And I need one. All I know is that you and Jaedin are going to be important. We need to prepare. We need to *practice*. Find out what we can do and what we are capable of. And then, maybe, if I can get everyone back together again, *then* we can work on a plan."

"Okay…" Sidry said. The mention of his friends triggered a surge of motivation. He wanted to protect Bryna and to make Rivan proud of him. "I'm ready."

"Do it, then," Baird said. "Summon your Avatar."

Sidry clenched his fists, and the Stone of Gezra burst into life. White light replaced his surroundings, and energy coursed through his body. His limbs grew.

When the light faded, he was back in the same grove, but it looked different. He could see everything more clearly and in finer detail.

There was another flash of light. Baird vanished, and another glowing being appeared in his place. To Sidry, it was like seeing a mirror image of himself. A horned, alien entity. The only noticeable difference between them was a slight variation in colour; Sidry's scaly flesh – more similar to armour than tissue – had a green hue, whereas Baird was bluer.

First, they warmed up. They leapt around for a time and lunged at the trees. Some of them toppled over. Sidry began to gain a better sense of his strengths and limitations. How fast he could move. How much force he could exert. How high he could jump. How far he could leap.

These were things Sidry had never had time to consider before. In the past, he had only ever assumed his Avatar form when circumstances forced him. Chiefly when he was fighting for his own life, or the lives of loved ones.

Eventually, Baird squared up to Sidry, and they began to grapple with each other. They didn't unleash their blades, though. They fought with their fists.

It was only after Sidry reverted into his human form again – what must have been hours later – that he noticed the sky had turned dark. He realised that most of the day had passed without him even noticing.

"That's enough," Baird said after he also – with a flash of light – changed back to human guise. "Go sleep. We will meet again tomorrow."

This became their routine. Each morning, Sidry and Baird went back to the same glade and trained vigorously.

One day, they encountered a group of Academy students out on patrol. Most of them fled at first sight of two shimmering immortals fighting amongst the trees. For some of them, however, fear gave way to curiosity, and Sidry and Baird drew a small audience of open-mouthed youngsters. Even their mentor stared for a while before he drilled his students back into order.

Overall, they seemed less shocked by that scene than Sidry would have expected them to be, which he guessed meant that word had already spread about his and Baird's abilities.

When Sidry was in his Avatar, he felt like he was invincible. He would always pay the price when he reverted to his real self again, though. He was too exhausted most evenings to do anything after it was over. Sidry would generally eat a brisk supper in the mess hall and then go back to his room and fall into bed. He would think about Bryna, Rivan, Kyra, and Jaedin. He would wonder where they were, what they were doing, and whether they were still alive. Sometimes, he would think about his parents or Aylen, but was usually given a merciful release from those bleak thoughts by drifting to sleep. Keeping busy was good for his peace of mind. It cut the cycle of anxiety and torment.

Baird raised the scales each day. By the fourth, they summoned their blades as they duelled. They fought for a while but, eventually, Sidry missed a blow, and Baird's blade-arm bore through his chest.

It was a strange sensation. Not a visceral, human pain; more a dulled, uncomfortable awareness that a foreign object had infiltrated his body. Sidry fell, and then there was a burst of light.

*   *   *

"Are you okay?" Baird asked.

Sidry opened his eyes to see Baird leant over him. The two of them were both back in human guise now.

Sidry realised he must have fainted.

He looked down at his chest – to make sure he was intact – and then nodded. He had been wounded as an Avatar before, and so far, the injuries never carried over to his human self.

"Let's go back," Baird said. "That's enough for today."

"Okay…" Sidry said as he got up. He felt a bit dizzy, so he grabbed hold of a tree and stabilised himself.

"Can you walk?" Baird asked.

"I think so…" Sidry said.

"The same thing happened to me when we first escaped from Jalard, remember?" Baird said when they were strolling back to the Synod. "Seems that anything fatal makes us lose the power… we become human again."

Sidry nodded. "I remember. We thought you were dead…"

"But we *don't* die," Baird said. "That's the important

thing... maybe you should take a day off tomorrow, though."

"No," Sidry shook his head. "I want to practice. I'm fine."

Baird frowned. "You need to rest."

"And what would I do?" Sidry asked. "Sit in my room and stare at the walls? All my friends are *gone*..."

"You know it wasn't my idea to send them away," Baird reminded him.

"I know..." Sidry said. "I just wish I could have gone with them. It's horrible being stuck here. Just *waiting*..."

"You were too valuable to go on that quest, Sidry."

"Have they found any sign of Jaedin yet?" Sidry asked.

"No," Baird shook his head. "There have been odd reports of young men who look a bit like him thieving and looting around the city, but such claims always happen when someone's a wanted man. People get excited and want to be part of it. Greyjor is chasing some of them up, but none of them sound like anything Jaedin would do to me."

"He's with Fangar, isn't he..." Sidry said.

Baird nodded grimly. "I think so."

Sidry sighed. "Aren't you worried?"

"Of course I am," Baird said. "But what can I do? I can't control Jaedin anymore. He's a rule onto himself."

"Maybe if you just apologised–" Sidry began.

"I have *nothing* to apologise for!" Baird cut him off adamantly. "Since when were all of you so friendly, anyway? I seem to remember spending most of my time stopping the lot of you from killing *each other* when the Zakaras weren't there."

"Things change," Sidry said. "And so did Jaedin. We all did... I respect him now. He saved us, more than once. And I think we lost him because you keep treating us like children when we're not anymore."

"Jaedin was corrupted," Baird retorted, giving Sidry a warning glare. "By a *monster* – that is what Fangar is! A monster... and when I catch them, I'm going to kill him."

*   *   *

By the afternoon, Astar had grown weary of everyone being overly gracious to him, so he jumped onto the back of a horse and rode out of the castle. As he made his way through the town, he found himself scanning the faces he passed to see if he could spot Elita but never saw any sign of her. He wondered if she had kept faithful to her threat and was in the throes of intimacy with one of the local boys. The thought of it made Astar seethe with jealousy – and regret what he said to her.

He didn't realise how long he had been riding until he reached the top of one of the neighbouring peaks and saw the grey walls of his father's keep from a distance. He reigned to a halt and stared at it for a while.

The thought that he was soon to be sovereign to that, and all the hills and villages around it, felt surreal. Astar had always known it was going to happen but never thought it would be so soon. He thought he had already suffered his share of bad luck when his mother passed so early.

A part of Astar was relieved he would not be returning to the Institute. He could put all that trouble with Bovan, Frast, and Squad Three behind him.

But another part of Astar had developed a thirst for war. Astar had never understood why people were so eager to invade Sharma until the moment he saw his father on his deathbed. Was it really true that their lands were a green, fertile paradise, somehow immune to the bane of The Ruena? The thought that they were all living out their lives in an idyllic haven while their foreign neighbours perished by the dozens each day filled Astar with rage.

Elita's wellbeing was another matter of Astar's concern. He knew now that he should never have told her what he discovered about Squad Three. But now that he had, he needed to think of a way to protect her from Grav'aen.

What *could* Astar do to protect her? Elita had no family

to fall back on. If he kept her in Llamaleil, it would ignite an explosion of gossip, and the Institute would soon come looking for her.

Marrying her was an option. It would cause a brief scandal, but Astar would not be the first nor the last noble to put a ring on a common finger. And Elita had more than enough brass to earn people's respect over time.

Astar shook his head. He was getting ahead of himself. There was no saying that Elita would agree to such an arrangement. And he wasn't even sure *he* wanted to spend the rest of his life with her. There was no doubt that he would be pleased to have her warm his covers at night. And, despite how much she irritated him, there was something addictive about her fiery spirit. But he also worried that she might be too much for him to handle. Would he be able to uphold respect as a Lord if he took a common wife who dominated him?

He made his way home and was still lost for answers as he neared his father's keep. Astar drew upon some of his magic to make himself invisible as he rode through the town – the road was clear enough to alleviate the risk of someone bumping into him – and he didn't lift the veil until he reached the gate.

When Astar rode into the bailey, he noticed a peculiar atmosphere within the walls of the keep. The servants had a spring in their step as they ran around, performing errands, and no one paused to stare at him this time. In fact, they seemed too preoccupied to give him any heed at all.

"What's going on?" Astar asked, stepping into the path of a girl carrying a sack of grain to the kitchen.

"Master!" she said, dropping her burden and dipping into a curtsey. "I'm just–"

"What's going on?"

"Oh, Astar!" she said, a smile lighting up her face. "Have you not heard? It's a miracle! A miracle!"

"What miracle?" Astar pressed. He was beginning to lose his patience.

"Lord Oren!" she exclaimed. "Your father! He's alive!"

Astar frowned. "What do you mean?"

"He's been cured," she said. "Branner is preparing a feast to celebrate! Master, please, may I go now? He's waiting!"

Astar nodded, and she merrily hauled the sack back over her shoulder and scarpered away.

Could it be true that Lord Jarvis's healer had somehow cured Astar's father? It seemed implausible.

Jarvis *had* been involved in Grav'aen's project searching for a cure for The Ruena, Astar remembered, but the last Astar had heard that venture had reached a dead end, and they had given up.

Astar sprinted to the western tower and burst through the door. Lord Jarvis and his escorts were no longer there, so he ran straight up the stairs and into his father's room to find only a pair of maids there, scrubbing the floor and changing the bedsheets.

Astar eventually found Lord Oren in his study.

"Father?" Astar gasped when he saw him.

Astar couldn't believe his eyes. All signs of his father's illness had vanished. If anything, Lord Oren looked younger and healthier than he had for years.

"Astar," Lord Oren said, glancing at his son and then turning back to his papers. He was organising them. "You should get ready. They are preparing a feast."

"What?" Astar blurted. He struggled to find words.

"Is there anything you want?" Lord Oren asked. Astar couldn't stop staring at his face. A face which only hours ago had been riddled with putrid growths and rotting flesh.

"What did they do to you?" Astar asked. "How did they cure you?"

"I don't know, Astar," he replied. "They just did."

Astar then realised that in his rush to get to his father, he had forgotten to glamour his face. Astar had been hiding his resemblance to his mother for years. How had Oren not noticed?

"Father," Astar said. "Look at me."

At the sound of Astar's voice, Lord Oren's head jerked

up, and he stared at Astar.

"Get out…" he said. "You're wasting my time."

That is not my father, Astar thought, drowning in dismay. It just wasn't *him.* Something was missing.

It was just like what happened to Bovan.

Bovan! Astar realised. Was it all somehow connected?

Astar knew how to find out. He siphoned from the reserves of his *viga* and used it to create an illusion of a ring of fire around his father's feet. Orange flames rose, but Lord Oren merely continued working, oblivious to the apparitions of his son's sorcery.

Astar gasped.

I haven't escaped the Institute at all, he realised. Whatever dark secrets that place held had made their way into his home.

I need to get out of here. Now.

*   *   *

It was beginning to get dark when Astar stepped out into the courtyard. People were still rushing around preparing for the feast.

This is going to be difficult, he realised. *We're going to need horses. And food.*

He concealed himself with his magic as he made his way to the stables. And then, just before he entered, Astar drew upon more *viga* and gifted himself with the appearance of his father.

"Brin," Astar said, amplifying his magic to manifest an impression of his father's voice.

"Yes, M'Lord," Brin had a giant grin on his face. "My gods… it's good to see you! I mean, I heard, but I almost couldn't believe it!"

"Yes, yes…" Astar replied, carefully concentrating on impersonating his father's demeanour as well as sustaining the mirage. "Thank you… but Brin, I must admit I am becoming weary of everyone staring at me as if I was a ghost, and I'm hoping for a swift return to normality. Speaking of which. I have a task for you."

"What is it, M'Lord?"

"My son, young Astar. Please can you prepare two of our finest steeds for him and his lady friend."

"Tonight?" Brin asked.

"Yes," Astar nodded. "I know we have the feast and everything, but he's quite anxious to be getting back to the Institute, and I have disrupted his life for long enough."

"Of course, M'Lord," he said. "Right away…"

"Try not to let word of this reach other ears," Astar added. "Particularly those of our guests, Lord Jarvis and his men. You know what some nobles are like with their long-winded farewells and such. Astar wishes to quietly be on his way. No fuss."

"Don't worry," Brin said. "I'll keep it under me hat. The 'orses will be ready in the hour."

"Thank you," Astar said. "And I look forward to seeing you at the feast later."

"Oh, My Lord!" Brin exclaimed, bowing his head. "It would be an honour!"

"Well, this is a special occasion, after all," Astar said. "Now. Apologies, but I must leave, for I have duties to be catching up on."

Astar strode outside, making himself invisible again once he was out of Brin's sight. He leant against the wall to catch his breath and recover his wits for a moment. Brin seemed convinced by his trick, but that was just the easy part of Astar's plan. Getting his hands on some provisions whilst everyone was preparing for a feast would be a much tougher challenge.

Astar made for the parlour, hoping he would find Elita there. He didn't like the idea of running into Lord Jarvis in the guest quarters. When he was making his way down one of the corridors, a door opened, and he flattened himself against the wall.

It was Veldra, slowly making her way towards him with the aid of her walking stick. Astar held his breath. His magic would keep him hidden from sight, but there was always a chance that she might bump into him. As she drew closer, Astar began to feel guilty. Veldra was the only person he never dared to try and trick or manipulate with his gift. His respect for her was ingrained into his childhood, formed equally from love and fear. Hiding from her like this felt like a betrayal not only to her but also to himself.

"Veldra," Astar said as he revealed himself.

She yelped, slamming her hand against the wall to balance herself. "Astar!" she screeched. "Wha' the blazes yer thin' yer–"

"*Veldra*," he whispered, putting a finger to his lips. "Please be quiet. *Please!*"

Something about his demeanour must have made her aware just how serious his situation was, because for the first time in his entire life, she obeyed him. Her eyes widened.

"Wha's happened, Astar?" she whispered. "Yer in trouble?"

"Veldra…" he said, struggling to find words to explain. His heart was racing. He didn't have time for this, but he couldn't bring himself to lie to her. Not Veldra. "I can't explain – I don't have enough time – but please, listen to me. Trust me, just this once. I have to get out of here. *Now*. I'm in danger. You *can't* tell anyone you've seen me."

The wrinkles of her forehead drew together and, for a terrible moment, Astar thought she was going to give him away and call out to someone. "Wha' yer doin' sneakin' ran 'ere then?"

"I'm looking for Elita," Astar whispered. "Do you know where she is?"

"If yer lyin', I'm genna hide yer!" she warned, and then she took a deep breath. "Last I saw, she were headin' ter her room. Second one on ter right. There are other guests… but hidin' yerself wan' be a problem. Not fer yer."

Astar nodded.

"Yer got all yer need?" she narrowed her eyes at him. "It's late…"

"Brin is sorting the horses," Astar confided. "But food... it's–"

"Don't yer worry," she whispered. "Ol' Veldra will see ter tha'. I'll be waitin' by ther well for yer. Go ge' her."

"Thanks, Veldra," Astar said, not quite knowing whether to trust this sudden change in the relationship he had with his nanny. A part of him worried that this was a trick, and she was going to run straight to his father, but he had no choice but to rely upon her now.

Astar went straight up to his chambers and filled his bag. It didn't take him long because he had barely unpacked. By the time he got outside again, it was even darker but, as an extra precaution, he veiled himself as he made his way across the yard towards the guest quarters.

Please let this be her, he prayed when he reached her door.

He tapped on it, and a few moments later, it opened, and he saw Elita's face. She opened her mouth to say something, but Astar pushed his finger to his lips to signal her to be quiet. He then squeezed through and locked the door behind him.

"If this is an attempt to woo me, you're going to be *very* disappointed," Elita said.

"Give it a rest, Elita," Astar said. "This is not the time."

"What's the matter?" she asked, her face changing. "Your hands are shaking..."

"We've got to leave," he said. "Now."

"Why?" she asked. "Your father. The feast... they told me to dress–"

"That *thing* is not my bloody father!"

She frowned. "What do you mean?"

"Like Bovan," Astar said. "And Squad Three. The same thing's happened to him. You know that man who arrived this morning? Lord Jarvis? He's a friend of Grav'aen's."

Her face went white.

"Come on!" Astar urged. "We need to *go*!"

"Yes," she whispered. Something changed in her, and she became possessed by a calm and lucid bearing. She ran to the other side of the room and began stuffing her possessions into her pack.

"How long do we have?" she asked.

"Not long!" Astar warned. "Just get ready. Fast!"

"I told you. I am *always* ready, Astar."

"Stay close to me," Astar said when she'd finished packing and joined him by the door. "I'm going to use my magic to make it so they can't see or hear us, but there isn't much I can do about footsteps, so tread lightly. You understand?"

She nodded.

Astar opened the door and peered down the corridor to make sure it was clear before he stepped out. He then ushered Elita to follow and crept outside, his heart hammering against his chest. When he reached the archway and stepped into the moonlight, he let out a breath he didn't even realise he had been holding.

"Astar!" Elita whispered. She grabbed him by his cloak and pulled him up against the wall. "Watch out!"

She pointed to a pair of Lord Jarvis's men. They were heading towards the building he and Elita had just come from.

"It's okay," he whispered. "They can't see us. Come on, let's go."

"I swear one of them was looking at me..." she murmured.

"Impossible," Astar said as he led her away.

He made his way towards the well. It was a dark night, with just one horned moon glowing above them, but Astar still cloaked himself and Elita with his magic in case someone happened to cross their path.

"Now wait here a moment," Astar instructed.

Elita nodded, and he crept up towards the dais alone, catching sight of Veldra's outline. She was sitting against the edge of the well, staring up at the sky.

"Veldra," he whispered as he approached her. She remained perfectly still, but he saw recognition in her eyes. He put a hand on her shoulder. "Thank you," he whispered, his voice catching. He had spent most of his life convinced that he hated Veldra, but now he knew differently. The thought that he was leaving her behind, to an uncertain fate, and that he might never see her again, in some ways, felt even worse than finding out his father had The Ruena. "Now go. And be careful, Veldra. Don't let them find out you helped me. And don't trust Lord Jarvis. Or that *thing*… that thing is not my father…"

Her eyes widened. But just for a moment. She composed herself again and hobbled away with the aid of her walking stick. Astar loaded up the provisions she left into his bag and then signalled Elita to follow him again.

"Brin?" Astar called as they entered the stables.

"Yes, they're ready," he called back as he emerged from one of the stalls with a tethered horse.

"Thanks," Astar said. "That one is for you, Elita. Load him up. Where is the other?"

"Over here," Brin said, motioning Astar to follow. "Shame you can't at least stay for the feast, Astar. Bit strange to be ridin' off at night like this."

"Duty calls, I'm afraid," Astar replied, feigning a sigh as he prepared the horse. "I will come back soon. Thanks, Brin. Is the gate open?"

Brin nodded. "Don't ye worry. I've sorted that out."

Astar nodded. "Good."

He pulled himself up onto the horse's back and tapped it on the rump.

I can't believe I've pulled this off, Astar thought as he guided it outside. He was careful to make sure that Brin, at least, could still see him, but Astar drew upon more of his magic to make himself and Elita invisible to the eyes of others as they rode out into the courtyard.

"Astar," Elita hissed once they crossed through the gate. The keepers began to lower the portcullis.

"What?" he whispered back.

"It's those men again," she said, looking behind them. "The weird ones in the green robes."

"They can't see us," he reminded her.

"They're staring at me," she said. "Oh my god's! Astar, they're coming for us!"

227

Astar turned his head and caught sight of four figures marching towards them. It seemed like they were in pursuit, but how was that possible? Were these men somehow immune to Astar's illusions too?

"Go!" he yelled, spurring his horse into motion and speeding across the bridge. "Come on, Elita! *Go!*"

Chapter 12

Gavendara

Miles halted his horse and stared at the settlement in the valley below.

Sarok, he realised, when he recognised it.

*What am I **doing**?* came his second thought as a prickly sensation crept down his spine.

It had been over ten years since Miles passed through here, and he had done a decent job of disguising himself. It was unlikely anyone would recognise him

Yet Miles couldn't help but feel apprehensive. They were about to step into their first Gavendarian town. They had made it across the icy peaks, but it was now that the truly treacherous stage of their mission began.

They were going to have to tread carefully from here.

"There are some things we are going to need to discuss before we go to that place," Miles said once the others had gathered around him.

"Like what?" Kyra asked.

"Well... first of all, *who* are we?" Miles began.

The three of them turned to each other.

Miles drew a breath. "You need to stop calling me Miles. From now on, I will be Kevan."

"We get new names now?" Rivan asked.

Miles shook his head. "No. For you, it's probably not necessary, but it is of the utmost importance that *I* am not discovered."

"So this is all just to save *your* neck?" Rivan asked, crossing his arms over his chest.

"Oh, are you under the impression that, if I were to be discovered, it would bode well for *you*?" Miles raised one of his eyebrows. "That they'll let you skip away back home?"

"What if we handed you over?" Rivan turned to Kyra, and they both smirked. "We could bag ourselves some lannies! What *is* the price on your head, anyway?"

"First of all, lannies are not going to be of much value once we get deeper into Gavendara... I will give you a quick lesson on Gavendarian currency shortly. Secondly, for someone who questions *my* loyalties, you seem very confused about whose side *you* are on..." Miles said, wiping the grin from Rivan's face. Miles felt a small measure of satisfaction in that. Rivan's lack of respect was beginning to vex him. He needed to find a way to put the young man in his place, and soon.

"He's just scitting you," Kyra said. "Go on then, *Kevan*. What else do you have to tell us?"

"We need a story," Miles said. "If we lie – and say you're all Gavendarians – then at some point, we'll be caught out. You do not know enough about this place, and not many Sharmarians cross over the border. The few who do are mostly traders, but we do not have any wares to back that story up. Do any of you have any suggestions?"

"Well, *you* are clearly Gavendarian," Kyra pointed out. "No offence, but I always thought you talked a little funny, and when I met Shayam, I realised that all of you must speak like that. So you have got to be Gavendarian because you sound like one."

"You two look like you could be mercenaries," Miles pondered out loud as he eyed Kyra and Rivan. His gaze then shifted to Bryna. "But Bryna does not."

"Me and Bryna could be sisters," Kyra said, grabbing her hand. "And you..." she turned to Miles. "Are our Gavendarian father." She then pulled a faux-sad expression. "The war tore our family apart... and, being of mixed blood, we never felt like we truly belonged anywhere..." she added with a woeful sniff. "And recently, our mother passed away, so we have come in search of our long-lost Gavendarian family."

Miles was mildly impressed by Kyra's quick thinking. Even the way she delivered the story sounded convincing.

She's a good liar, Miles realised. *It could make her a*

valuable asset to this mission.

"That could work," Miles agreed. "Many families *were* torn apart during the war. But what about Rivan?"

"He could be… our cousin?" Kyra pondered out loud.

Bryna burst into a fit of giggles, which caught everyone by surprise. "Sorry," she said, putting a hand over her mouth. "Jaedin thought that was funny."

"Jaedin is with you at the moment?" Miles asked, feeling a pang in his chest. He wished Jaedin would speak to him. He had tried to communicate with him through Bryna a few times now, but on every occasion, Jaedin had made it quite clear that he had nothing to say.

She nodded.

"Does he have an opinion about our plan?" Miles asked. "I would be interested in hearing his thoughts."

Bryna's eyes flickered for a few moments and then cleared. "*I look like I could be your daughter because we are both pale-skinned, but nobody will believe that Kyra and I are sisters. Rivan being our cousin doesn't make any sense either. He says that, therefore, I should be your daughter, and Rivan and Kyra should be a pair of mercenaries we have hired as an escort. Although, people might think it a little strange that a man and woman work such a profession together, unless…*" Bryna then put her hand to her mouth and began to laugh again. "No! *Jaedin…*"

"What's he saying?" Miles asked.

Bryna blushed and then composed herself again. "He says that Rivan and Kyra look like they could be–"

"No way!" Kyra exclaimed before Bryna could finish the sentence. She shook her head and made a huffing noise.

"What?" Rivan frowned. "What does she mean?"

Yes… Miles thought, trying his utmost to not laugh out loud at the hilarity of the revenge Jaedin had just served up for him.

"How much does this mission mean to you, Rivan?" Miles asked, assuming a pragmatic tone. "I'm not asking the two of you to *sleep* with each other. I am saying that to maximise our chance of success, you need to put on a show when we are in the public eye."

Rivan looked at Kyra, and his eyes widened as he finally realised what Jaedin was proposing. His face turned red. "No!" he shook his head and folded his arms across his chest. "I'm *not* doing it!"

Miles feigned an exasperated sigh – but, inside, he was secretly revelling in this opportunity to make Rivan squirm. "Maybe you should head back to Shemet then…" Miles said softly. "I don't think you realise quite how serious this mission is… or the danger we are entering here. If you're going to let petty little neurosis get in the way of ensuring the success of our mission…" Miles shook his head. "Baird said you were ready for this, but I guess he was wrong."

Rivan's mouth fell open in dismay.

That's it, Miles thought smugly. *Strike them where it hurts. That's how to get what you want from people.*

A long time ago, Miles learnt that the best way to influence others was to find out what they craved most and exploit it. Rivan's foremost impetus was that he was Baird's favourite, and others admired him. If Miles were to hazard a guess, he would surmise that Rivan's parents didn't give him enough attention during his formative years. That was the usual cause for someone to have such a strong desire to prove themself to the world.

"I'm not going back!" Rivan said defiantly.

"Well, in that case. Do *you* have any better ideas on how we are going to get through this stage of the mission?" Miles challenged.

Rivan scratched his head.

"Well…" Miles said after giving Rivan a few moments. "If that's all, then I propose we get a move on."

Feeling very pleased with himself, Miles spurred his horse back into motion and continued along the trail before the others could make any further objections.

*   *   *

When Miles reached Sarok a few hours later, he found it remarkable how little things had changed in the years since he was last there. It was just as he remembered it. The buildings were grey, built from irregularly-shaped rocks – and they had that slightly crude, haphazard appearance about them which often prevailed in mountain territory.

The streets were reasonably clean. Most of the people had the flat noses and pale skin that were more reminiscent of a Gavendarian heritage, but there were a few whom Miles guessed to have some Sharmarian blood flowing through their veins; they were the ones who were more olive-skinned and had sharper features. Such intermixing was quite common among peoples who dwelled near the border.

Unexpected guilt began to creep into the back of Miles' mind, and it intensified with every face he saw. It had been a long time since Miles had been in his homeland. Being among Gavendarians again made it a reality that these were his people.

And he was betraying them.

Miles tried to push these thoughts out of his mind, but they lingered. Most of these people were just civilians. They had no idea what dark deeds a small but influential minority of their overlords were up to. Had Miles chosen the right side? To Selena, Baird, and the Synod, *all* citizens of Gavendara were the enemy. It did not matter to them that most of the population were not at fault.

"What kind of town is this, anyway?" Kyra murmured as they passed through one of the more dissident streets, where a group of lewd-looking women stood outside a somewhat thinly disguised brothel.

"That sort of thing is… typical of a border town," Miles uttered once they were safely out of earshot. "You'd be surprised what traders will get up to once they've scaled a mountain and are far away from the arms of their wives."

"Are *all* Gavendarian towns like this?" Rivan asked, pulling a face. "Don't you have *rules* here?"

"Believe me, you can find all sorts of things in Sharma, too, if you know where to look," Miles said, feeling defensive. "Gavendara is just more... open about these things. They don't hide it away like a guilty secret."

In the silence which followed, thoughts began to crawl back into Miles' mind again. He tried to remind himself of his reasons for betraying Grav'aen. He tried to think about the people he cared for. Jaedin, Bryna, Meredith, Kyra. Even Baird to some extent. But it was hard to tip the balance of those scales when he was back in his homeland and surrounded by his people again. Jaedin wasn't even speaking to him. Bryna, while not necessarily being unpleasant, was emotionally distant with him these days. Meredith was dead. Kyra made it perfectly clear that she no longer trusted him every single day. And Baird. *Baird* had handed Miles over to the justice of the Synod, despite all the things Miles did to redeem himself.

It was hard for Miles to remind himself where his allegiance lay when it appeared that even the people he had sided with loathed him.

He took in the sight of the market and the numerous gambling taverns as he went by. Despite Kyra and Rivan's searing comments, Miles liked Sarok. Beneath all of its vices, it was a lively place. A melting pot of cultures. The Ruena was less common here too, but it still prevailed. These people were still slowly dwindling, just like the rest of Gavendara, for no other reason than being guilty of being born on the wrong side of the border. Miles wished he could do something to help them, but his hands were tied, and he knew that Rivan and Kyra would jump at any excuse to do away with him if he strayed.

"I think we may have found a place to settle for the night," Miles said, eyeing up a reasonably large inn at the end of the street. It seemed suitable. There were even some stables annexed to the side.

A man came out to greet them as they approached. "Hello, travellers," he said. "Just made it across the mountain?"

Miles nodded. "Yes, and what I wouldn't do for a comfy bed and a warm fire. Do you have room for us?"

"We have three left," he said, eyeing the four of them. "So two of you'd have to share. For eight bruntas, they're yours. I can even throw in a plate of my wife's stew for each of you."

"Perfect," Miles said, grinning. "Now… let's talk about the price. I am sure you can do it for six. We *are* just taking three rooms, after all."

*   *   *

"Just imagine there is a line here," Kyra said, running her hand along the centre of the bed. "No one crosses!" she said sharply. "Actually, I have a better idea…"

She gathered some of the pillows and began to arrange them across her imaginary line.

Rivan watched her. Hating the awkward atmosphere that had filled the room the moment they shut the door behind them.

"Kyra…" he groaned. "Look, just stop *stressing*. It's okay. Calm down and stop making a big deal out of this. Please."

She smiled thinly. "Okay… but can you turn around a moment? While I change."

"Gladly," Rivan said, turning his back to her.

"I'm going to kill Jaedin when I see him…" Kyra said. He could hear her shuffling her clothes off behind him. "This has got to be some kind of scit. He could have suggested you being Bryna's betrothed or something."

Rivan didn't know why, but the thought of sharing a bed with Bryna unsettled him even more than *this* arrangement.

"What's the matter?" she asked. "You flinched then… you can turn around now."

"Nothing," Rivan said. "Close your eyes for a moment."

He removed his boots and leggings and picked one of his tunics from his pack to wear and, after changing into

235

it, walked to his side of the bed and peeled back the blanket.

They lay in silence for a while. Rivan turned on his side, so he was facing away from her, but he could still hear her breathing. A small part of him could see the funny side to this. He imagined somebody telling him a year ago that he would be sharing a bed with Kyra. That they would be comrades on a mission together. He would have laughed at the idea. Things had certainly been very different back then. He used to loathe Kyra, but now she was like a sister to him. A sister he couldn't stand most of the time, but still a sister.

"I miss Jaedin…" she whispered. "Gods… I even miss *Sidry*. I wish they were here."

He sighed heavily, wondering if she was ever going to let him sleep. "Me too…" he admitted. "And Aylen."

That name was followed by a long silence.

"Rivan…" Kyra said. "There is something I need to tell you… about Aylen."

"What?" he said, turning his head. Kyra's eyes were open, but they were a little shiny. He couldn't tell whether it was from tears or tiredness.

"It's my fault that he died," she said.

Rivan sat up. "What do you mean?"

"We…" she hesitated. "We had sex. And he loved me. And I think that, when he died, he did what he did for me."

Rivan stared at her. Could it be true? Her and Aylen? If it was, how had he not known?

He'd noticed the two of them became friendly towards the end, but he'd never guessed it had been in *that* way. Did Aylen really sacrifice himself for her? The thought of it filled him with rage.

For a brief moment.

But then the anger subsided, and Rivan rested his head back on his pillow. He took a deep breath.

"It's not your fault," he said. "So stop flattering yourself… if it makes you feel better, I think I'm more to blame than you."

She turned over and looked at him. "What do you mean?"

"Aylen was always trying to impress me," he said. "Like all the other kids back home. And I kind of liked it. Gods, I think I even *encouraged* it. I used to think it was great because I was their hero, and they all looked up to me. I think Aylen might have done what he did to prove himself to me. Like he always was... and I just wish I could go back and tell him that he didn't need to do things like that to make me like him, because I liked him anyway. And I wish he was here now."

Those last few words came out as a croak, almost as if he was holding back tears, but then he composed himself. "Go to sleep, Kyra. And stop thinking that everything is about you."

*   *   *

"Are we going to talk about it yet?" Elita asked.

Astar looked at her from across the fire. After riding for almost an entire day, they had finally stopped so they could rest and tend to their horses. He was weary. "What about?" he asked.

"About what the fuck is going on?" she placed her hands on her hips. "You didn't say much before we left."

"That's because I didn't have time," Astar groaned. He was tired, but he knew she was justified in her want of an explanation. "Look. All I know is that they've done something to him. My father."

"And now your magic doesn't work on him?" Elita clarified.

Astar nodded. "But it's not just that... something wasn't right. When he miraculously recovered, there was something different about him. There was this emptiness to his eyes... and it reminded me of Bovan."

Elita nodded sombrely. "And those men in the green robes were the same... they could see us despite your illusions. Who are they, anyway?"

"They were Lord Jarvis's men," Astar muttered.

"Never liked that git."

"Who is he?"

"Why all the bloody questions?" Astar asked. "Can't you see I'm tired?"

"Well, I'm sorry, little lordling," Elita snapped back. "But after running off with you in the middle of the night and then riding for an *entire* day, I think I have earned it … Look, I know you've got some really weird shit going on with your father and your home and all but, *I* am a part of this now. We need to bring everything we know out into the open and talk about it. See if we can figure out what's going on."

Astar ran a hand through his hair. "Jarvis is an old friend of my father's. The Lord of Casteldron. A regency north of here. He's an old friend of Grav'aen's, as well."

"And your father," Elita added. "He was buddies with Grav'aen too, right?"

"No," Astar shook his head. "My father didn't really know Grav'aen personally… I don't think they ever even met. It was through Jarvis that my father got involved in all this."

"In what?" Elita frowned.

"The research into finding a cure for The Ruena," Astar replied.

Elita narrowed her eyes at him.

"You don't know about that, do you?" Astar realised. "Okay, look, *before* Grav'aen took over the Institute, he was in charge of a project trying to find a cure for The Ruena. A lot of noble families donated money and were involved in it. My father was one of them."

"And what happened to it?" she asked.

"Nothing," Astar shrugged. "The last I heard, it reached a dead end and was disbanded."

Elita frowned. "But what they did to your father… they *did* cure him. I mean, I know it wasn't in a good way," she added when Astar opened his mouth to respond. "But they did, *technically*, cure someone who was dying from The Ruena. Maybe the project wasn't disbanded at all, maybe–" she gasped and put her hand to her mouth.

"Maybe Grav'aen moved to the Institute for a reason. Oh my gods... Astar, don't you see? Squad Three. Your father. The 'cure' for The Ruena... it's all connected. Maybe they *did* find a cure, but it wasn't in the way they expected."

"But that doesn't explain Squad Three," Astar said. "Why would they use it on people who *aren't* dying?"

"The members of Squad Three are freakishly strong and very obedient, but they are missing something... well *human*, I guess. Don't you see, Astar? They are perfect soldiers. Maybe whatever it was they found when they were trying to cure The Ruena is now being used to make Gavendara's fighters stronger."

"This is giving me a headache," Astar said. "Can we just sleep now, please? I feel like I am losing my mind, and I need to rest. We'll talk about this tomorrow."

*   *   *

When Astar opened his eyes the following morning, three figures were standing on the other side of the remains of the fire.

"Elita!" Astar yelled as he jerked out of his blankets. His vision began to clear, and he saw these men were clad in green robes and were Lord Jarvis's vassals. "Get up! They're here."

Elita groaned and turned over. As soon as her mind cleared and she saw the intruders, she scrambled to her feet.

"What are you doing here?" Astar asked them as he rose.

The one in the middle smiled coldly. Astar began to wonder just how long the three of them had been standing there, waiting for him and Elita to wake. Or even how it was that they had found them. Astar thought he had done a good job of getting away; he had even gone to the trouble of riding up the streams of several rivers to disguise their trail.

"Your father and Lord Jarvis have asked us to escort

you back home," one of them said.

A tense silence followed, and Astar and Elita turned to each other. Astar had no intention of going back.

Also, if it was *really* his father who wanted him back, then why was it *Lord Jarvis's* men who had come for him?

"We're not coming," Elita said. Standing beside Astar and handing him his spear. "So you'll just have to go back and *tell* him that."

"With all due respect," the one in the middle replied. He seemed to be their leader. "You *are* outnumbered."

"We are Blessed," Elita warned. "I'm worth at least twenty warriors if you get on the wrong side of me – and so is Astar. I'd turn away if I were you."

My magic doesn't work on them… Astar remembered. He drew upon some of his *viga* and tried to make Elita and himself invisible – as a test – but, just as expected, it didn't work.

"I'm afraid our orders were quite specific," their leader said. "We will use force if we have to…" He turned to Astar. "Jarvis said that he is willing to talk. He will explain everything if you come back. Just give him a chance and listen to what he has to say. I am sure you will understand. You are both valuable assets to the Institute. And Gavendara. We are willing to trust you. Tell you our secrets."

Astar hesitated. He felt tempted. He wanted answers, and they were inviting him into the inner circle. He could relieve his mind from all the questions which had plagued it since he had encountered Squad Three. He could go back to the safety of his father's keep instead of sleeping by fires in the wilderness and living on the run.

But, in his gut, Astar knew that something wrong was afoot here, and he didn't want to be a part of their sinister world. If he went back with them now, that would be it. It was unlikely that they would ever give him another opportunity to escape.

He turned to Elita to see what her thoughts were, and he could tell from the expression on her face that her feelings mirrored his.

"No," Astar turned back to their leader and shook his head. "We're not coming."

The man in the middle sighed. "It is… regrettable that you say that."

The men on either side of the leader advanced. One of them came for Elita, the other for Astar.

Astar swung the butt end of his spear at the man as he neared, aiming for the side of his head – Astar wanted to knock him out, not kill him – but the man raised his fist and caught the full blow on his forearm without even flinching. His other fist came out and punched Astar in the gut. Astar fell back, winded.

Elita stepped in front of Astar, extending her arms as she drew upon her *viga*. She summoned a gust of wind that sent the three men falling back.

The gale ended, and Astar took that moment to catch his breath and gather his wits. He wasn't going to hold back any more.

He charged at one of the men, twirling his spear. The man was still in the process of righting himself and narrowly missed Astar's opening thrust. He leapt away and then flipped himself back onto his feet in one swift motion, but Astar caught him on the backlash and drove his spear into his collar.

It was the first time Astar had intentionally wounded someone, and he could barely believe what he was doing as the tip of his spear gouged into the man's flesh. He saw blood and winced at the sight.

Pull yourself together! Astar thought.

He yanked the spear out, and the man fell facedown to the grass.

"See!" Astar said, turning to their leader. "Now back off! I mean it!"

The leader stared at Astar. Something about his eyes sent chills down Astar's spine. He didn't seem to feel any concern over what had had just happened to his comrade.

Astar noticed movement by his feet and turned his eyes down to see the man he had just hurt was now writhing. Astar stared at him, at first thinking he must be having a fit.

But Astar's instinct was telling him that something more ominous was going on.

As the man convulsed, black tentacles emerged from his spine, breaking free from his robe, each one wriggling and squirming independently.

Astar backed away. He couldn't believe what he was seeing. This was more bizarre and frightening than any illusion he had ever conjured.

"Elita…" he called, but his friend didn't answer. Astar wanted to check on her – see how she was faring – but he was too scared of what was going on before him to tear his eyes away.

The man used his tentacles to help push his body from the ground, and then Astar saw his face. It was blue. His eyes were a pair of bulbous black orbs, and a strange yellow fluid was oozing from his cadaverous features. He stretched his arms out, and his fingers grew into claws. There was not a trace of the wound Astar had dealt him anymore. The being standing before Astar no longer resembled a human.

Its body jerked, and a pair of its dark, leathery tentacles jutted out towards Astar. Astar dived, narrowly missing their reach but, whilst regaining his balance, the monster whipped its rubbery appendages again, and Astar didn't have time to dodge the next blow. A tentacle coiled around his arm.

Astar screamed. He didn't even know his vocal cords were capable of such a hoarse wail, but the sound that came from his throat was one he had no control over. The black tendril tightened. In an act of desperation, Astar drove the point of his spear into it, tearing into the dark flesh. The monster's ichor was brown. It was sticky too. Astar bit back his revulsion as it coated his hands. He pulled the spear out and struck again. This time the tentacle went limp, and Astar freed himself.

Astar ran while he had the chance. He caught sight of Elita a dozen paces away and raced towards her.

"Get behind me!" Elita yelled.

Astar could hear footsteps behind him. The monsters

were pursuing. He ran for dear life.

Once he reached Elita, she clenched her fists and drew upon her *viga.* Her hands began to spark with blue static, and she stretched her arms out towards the monsters to direct the blast of energy towards them. The monsters quivered. She gritted her teeth, and the air between herself and them crackled. Their bodies began to turn black.

Astar watched, realising then that during all those times they had fought each other at the Institute, Elita had been holding back. Her Blessing was much more potent than he had ever assumed.

She continued until there was nothing left of the three monsters but charred remains.

*   *   *

Baird advanced, his blade-arm swinging, and Sidry danced away from his mentor's opening blow.

Once Sidry had braced himself, he blocked each strike that followed. He was too occupied following the movements of Baird's blade to form any counter at first, but eventually, he saw an opportunity.

Sidry leapt towards a tree, grabbing its trunk and using it to anchor his momentum. He spun himself around it and launched from the other side, kicking out with his foot as he flew through the air.

Baird saw the move coming, though and dived out of the way.

Sidry landed somewhat clumsily and rolled across the ground. Righting himself, he twisted around just in time to catch sight of Baird's blade bearing down upon him. Sidry blocked but did so whilst crouching, which left him vulnerable.

Baird then paused for a moment – giving Sidry some time to raise himself.

Baird's blade came swinging again. Sidry tried to parry the blow – doing so in a fashion which had worked the previous day but, this time, Baird saw it coming and rebuffed, circling his blade. It was a motion Sidry didn't recognise – a new manoeuvre – and he braced himself.

By the time Sidry had figured out the destination of Baird's blade, it was too late; Baird struck him, burying his blade into Sidry's abdomen.

Shit! Sidry thought as Baird's blade entered him.

He knew what would happen now.

This was the part Sidry *hated*. The part where he fainted.

No! Sidry suddenly thought, possessed by wilful determination. *I will **never** get better at this if I **keep** passing out!*

The crystal at Sidry's forehead responded to his plea and flashed.

A burst of white light illuminated the forest, and Sidry felt a wave of energy course through his entire being, invigorating him.

The opening Baird had torn into Sidry's mid-section then closed itself.

Sidry stared down at it in disbelief.

He had just healed himself. How was that possible?

He looked at Baird, and the two of them stared at each other with the mere slits they both had for eyes.

Baird then positioned himself into a fighting stance again. Sidry understood the signal; they would talk about what had just happened later. For now, they would continue fighting.

Sidry went on the offensive this time, newly fuelled with adrenaline. He rushed Baird, flashing his blade. Baird was almost caught off guard but managed to block. Sidry then brought his second blade swinging – this time from above – and Baird took a step back. Whilst Sidry was righting himself, Baird leapt back in and kicked Sidry in the chest, sending him flying backwards.

Sidry collided with a tree. Baird strode towards him. He did so slowly, to give Sidry plenty of time to right himself, and then began to swing his blades again. Sidry blocked the first six blows. And then the seventh. And the eighth. But then Baird caught him with the ninth across his throat.

And then everything went white.

*   *   *

Sidry woke up to the sight of sunlight glistening through the canopy above him; a sight which had become all too familiar to him recently.

"You're awake?" he heard Baird's voice.

Sidry turned to his mentor and saw he had sat by the trunk of a tree with his back resting against it.

"How long was I out for?" Sidry groaned as he sat up and stretched his arms.

"A while…" Baird said. "I was getting worried I might have broken you…" Baird stood up and regarded Sidry with a hand on his chin. "What did you do back then? When I wounded you? Your crystal flashed, and you healed yourself. Did you see it?"

Sidry nodded. "I'm not sure *how* I did it… I just wanted to carry on fighting. I'm sick of being beaten. I will never get better if I keep passing out."

"Two odd things happened," Baird said. He raised his fist. "First," he said, extending one finger. "You managed to heal yourself and carry on fighting. And two," he then raised a second finger. "You were unconscious for longer than usual. I think these two events must be connected."

"So, basically, we can push our limits, but there is a cost," Sidry pondered out loud. "I guess it makes sense."

Baird nodded. "You need to be careful, Sidry. If you push it too far… well, that's the thing. We *don't* know what could happen."

"We've always changed back into ourselves and been fine," Sidry shrugged. "I don't see why being asleep a bit longer is an issue. We can practice for longer now. You can just carry me back to my room if I'm down for too long," Sidry joked.

Baird frowned. "You're not taking this seriously. What's got into you, Sidry? You've not been yourself of late."

"I just want to get better," Sidry shrugged. "You *always* beat me."

"I've got twenty years of experience on you," Baird

said. "It's to be expected. Anyway, *you're* the one who's discovering new abilities."

"What, for when we fall?" Sidry laughed. "Yeah, well, I've had a lot of practice. Anyway, it's still early. Shall we fight again?"

Baird stared at him for a while. "No..." he said. "Go back and rest. We'll continue tomorrow."

Chapter 13

New Objective

Kyra guided her horse around a bend and then, on the peak of the hill before her, saw a settlement.

"There's another village here," she called over her shoulder. "Do you know *this* one, Miles?"

Miles spurred on his horse a little to catch up and then squinted his eyes. "I'm not sure…" he said. "I don't think so."

Kyra sighed and continued riding. Miles kept promising them that they would be out of the highlands soon, but it never seemed to actually *happen*. She was getting frustrated.

This part of the Valantian Mountains was so sinuous you could never see more than a few hundred feet ahead of you at any given time. Each time Kyra neared a corner, she prayed it would be the last. She was looking forward to reaching flatter terrain.

She scanned the settlement as they entered it. It looked the same as all the other mountain villages they had passed over the last couple of days; a small collection of homes, a little market, and an inn.

As Kyra was riding, something caught her eye. Two figures were walking down the street, hand in hand. She gasped.

"Don't stare!" Miles said, appearing in front of her and giving her a look of disapproval. "It's rude."

"But they're…" Kyra stammered. "They're…"

"This is normal in Gavendara…" Miles explained, hushing his voice.

"You mean they're a…" Kyra stammered. "They're *coupled*?"

Miles shrugged. "Probably…"

Despite Miles' reprimand, Kyra couldn't help but continue watching the two men as they walked down the street together. She tried to be discreet about it, though. They seemed perfectly comfortable and at ease.

"Why?" Kyra asked Miles. "Why is it like *this* here?"

"Who knows…" Miles said. "It's just cultural… if I *were* to hazard a guess, I would probably say that religion plays a part."

"Religion?" Kyra repeated. "But we have the same gods as you."

"Yes. We do share pantheons…" Miles agreed. "But you Sharmarians only worship the Ancients and their scions. You only revere the gods that represent the forces of nature and vilify 'The *Others*' – as you call them. Here, in Gavendara, *all* gods are worshipped, including the less primal ones. In fact, Gazareth is our most revered deity of all."

"*Gazareth*!" Kyra hissed. "But he's–"

"Our creator?" Miles finished for her. It was not what *she* was about to say. "If it weren't for Gazareth, *none* of us would exist. He is our father, and Lania is our mother. We, as humans, are the children of both the Ancients and the Others."

"But isn't he supposed to be evil?" Kyra asked.

Miles shook his head. "That's just what *you* were taught. *Our* stories and myths are different. Who knows… maybe it's your people's demonisation of Gazareth that is the source of your prejudice. Gazareth himself was a lover to both women and men."

"Maybe…" Kyra said. In the tales she was told as a child, Gazareth was almost always depicted as a malevolent force. A troublemaker. He often seduced women, but sometimes men too, and it was always the stories where he coupled with men that she remembered as being the most shocking.

"'Soddy'. That is the word you Sharmarians use to describe people who are… of certain persuasions," Miles said. "And it is derived from 'Soddar'; who, in the myths, was Gazareth's mortal lover. In *your* stories, Soddar was punished by the Ancients for – what you Sharmarians perceive to be – his 'unnatural inclinations', but in

Gavendara, Soddar is an archetype for liberty. When he died, he was exalted and allowed to enter the realm of the gods to be Gazareth's lover for eternity. We even have shrines for him."

"Are you telling me that here you tell *children* stories about men coupling with each other!?" Rivan entered the conversation. Kyra wasn't sure how long he had been listening. "Like it is normal?"

"Yes," Miles replied.

"Isn't that a bit…" Rivan began but never finished the sentence. He scratched his head.

"We are told stories about men and women making love when we are young," Bryna said. "Is it so different?"

"Exactly," Miles smiled at Bryna. "I know it may sound odd to you, but that is just because of your upbringing. Maybe it is *because* we tell our children different stories – stories where that," Miles gestured behind them to where the couple had been – they had vanished from sight now, "isn't wrong, that people are more tolerant here. We don't use harsh-sounding words like 'soddy' to describe them, either… think of it this way, do you think *you* would have picked on Jaedin so much if you were taught differently when you were young?"

"I…" Rivan grimaced and turned his face downward. For a moment, Kyra could have sworn she saw guilt in his eyes.

"So what *do* you call people like Jaedin here, then?" Kyra asked. "What word do you use?"

"We don't have any…" Miles said.

* * *

Miles flicked his reins, spurring the horse ahead and taking the lead.

What were they expecting? he wondered as he built some distance between himself and the others. *That once they crossed the border, they would find themselves in a land of savages and villains?!*

249

They've been taught to see the world in blacks and whites, rather than variations of grey, Miles reminded himself a few moments later. *They can't help it.*

He knew that. But still, it was frustrating for him to have to constantly defend his former people. It vexed him that whenever Rivan and Kyra asked him questions about Gavendara, they always seemed to expect the answer to be something malign.

Miles rode on ahead for the rest of the morning, enjoying a little peace and quiet. Shortly after the midday sun passed, he crested a hill and saw a settlement in the valley below.

"We're here," Miles called behind his shoulder. He recognised it. "That's Leera," he said, pointing. "The final village on this road. After we pass through that, we'll enter the Folds."

"The Folds?" Kyra repeated.

Miles nodded. "It's a rather barren region... there are a few scattered villages and farms, but that's all really. It will take us a few days to cross it. Leera has a market, so I suggest we load up on some provisions."

They rode down the final mountain and entered the village. Miles scanned his eyes up and down the first street, looking for an inn or mess hall, but it appeared they were on the wrong side of the town for that. He was in the process of trying to recall where the market was when he noticed a pair of men in red uniforms marching towards him.

Miles' heart lurched within his chest. He recognised that uniform. These men were members of the Royal Guard.

Act natural! Miles told himself as they approached him. He composed himself, assuming a neutral, relaxed expression. Miles had always been good at acting. The trick was to convince yourself you really *are* who you are pretending to be – and Miles had spent so much of his life pretending he was not quite sure who the *real* him was anymore.

At this moment in time, he was Kevan, the recently

widowed tradesman on a quest to find his long-lost family. He had nothing to hide. Nothing to feel guilty about.

He just hoped his three companions could keep their wits about them too.

"Excuse me," one of the Royal Guards said as they approached Miles. Miles eyed the emblem on the left breast of his surcoat and saw it was indeed the sigil of the King. "Could you come with us, please?"

"Me?" Miles said. He kept his bearing calmly surprised – although, in reality, his heart rate was swiftly escalating. "Why, yes. Of course. Can I ask *why*?"

"Just come with us..." he said.

"Ok..." Miles stammered. He turned to his three companions. Kyra was at least *trying* to act nonchalant, but Rivan was visibly gawping. Bryna was just the same as she always was; distant and uninvolved.

This isn't good, Miles thought as they escorted him towards a small hut by the side of the road. *This isn't good at all. What are the Royal Guard even **doing** here? This far west?*

They opened the door and ushered Miles inside. A man was sitting at a table clad in the same red uniform.

"Sit," the man said, gesturing to the chair opposite him.

Miles pulled an expression on his face that he thought most fitting for an unworldly man feeling a little bewildered. "How long will this take?" he said, adjusting his accent a little to sound more common. "Sorry, but my daughter is outside and–"

"Neither of those young women are yours..." the man at the table said. "You do not have any children..."

Miles frowned. "What do you mean? I think you've got the wrong person... my name is Kevan. I'm–"

"I know who you are, *Miles.*"

Miles' heart lurched within his chest at the sound of his name. He was lost for words.

What *could* he say?

"Now, will you stop the pretence and sit down, please..." the man said, pointing to the chair.

I'm done for… Miles realised as he seated himself.

"Who are you?" Miles croaked.

The man smiled. It was a cold smile. One that put Miles on edge and made him suspect that it wasn't truly a man he was speaking to, but something else.

A Zakara.

"An old friend…" they said, making the hairs on the back of Miles' neck stand up. "Did you really think that if I saw you, I wouldn't recognise your face? I have eyes and ears *everywhere,* Miles."

Grav'aen! Miles realised.

The Zakara laughed throatily. "Well… this *is* an unexpected surprise. Now, the question is, what should I do with you?"

Miles turned his head down and stared at his knees.

"You see… you have caught me in a rather tight situation…" Grav'aen said, through the lips of the Zakara. "The vessel who is speaking to you right now, and the other three here," he gestured to the other members of the Royal Guard who had escorted Miles to this hut. Miles realised that they must all be Zakaras too. "Are the only agents I possess in this area, and I have some rather important errands for them to fulfil. They could *try* to kill you – and maybe they will succeed – but, considering your Blessing and the fact that you are not alone, it is also very possible they will not. Plus, the locals around here would witness a scene that would ignite rumours. And I do not want that."

Grav'aen paused and stared at Miles. "If you had Jaedin, Sidry, or Baird with you, then it *might* be worth me trying, but those three you have out there," he shrugged. "The witch is a force I intend to subdue eventually, but she doesn't mean all that much to me… certainly not enough to risk exposing myself here, anyway. No…" Grav'aen shook his head. "These Zakaras have *much* more important things to be getting on with than dealing with the four of you."

The Zakara leant back in his chair. "You've come here to snoop on us then?" he asked. "Find out what we're up to?"

Miles nodded, realising that there was no point in denying it.

Grav'aen laughed. "Look all you like... you're not likely going to find anything. And even if you do, I doubt it would make much difference anyway. Remember, Miles, I am *always* one step ahead. If I were you, I would turn back. As I just said, my resources in this area are limited right now, but that could soon change."

"Then why are you even speaking to me?" Miles asked, growing weary of this monologue. It was clear by now that Grav'aen had some manner of scheme up his sleeve. "Just tell me what you *want*."

The Zakara leant forward and placed his elbows on the table. "I would like to make a deal with you."

"What... makes you believe I would be willing to make *any* deals with you?" Miles asked.

"Because I have information you may find valuable..."

"I doubt it could be valuable enough for me to betray my..." Miles stumbled upon the last word because he wasn't even sure it was true. "Friends."

"What if I told you that Jaedin is in danger," Grav'aen said. "And that, unless I tell you *why*, it is very probable that he will die? I have information that could very well save his life."

Miles hesitated.

"Ah-ha!" the Zakara pointed a finger right up to Miles' face. "I *knew* I had found your weakness! That time I penetrated Jaedin's mind... I saw things. I saw things when I glimpsed Dareth's mind too... as well as others. I know all sorts of things about you and the people you are with. I possibly know you all better than you know yourselves."

"I don't believe you," Miles shook his head. "You're bluffing."

He shook his head. "I am willing to prove it to you. You can *psycalesse* with me."

"You must think I am really stupid," Miles crossed his arms over his chest. "Why would I risk that?"

"You, of all people, are not at risk whilst in a

psycalesse with me," Grav'aen said. "You are more than capable of protecting yourself during such a union. I know you are. Please, just humour me."

Miles fought an inner battle. It was true that he could easily block Grav'aen from doing him any harm whilst in a *psycalesse*, but did he *want* to go down this path? Grav'aen was clearly going to try and blackmail him, and Miles doubted very much that this 'deal' he had in mind – whatever it was – would be a benevolent one.

But then an image of Jaedin's face came to Miles' mind.

Was it really true that he was in danger?

"Fine," Miles said through gritted teeth. He knew it was a bad idea – and he already knew this was something that he would almost definitely live to regret – but he couldn't stop himself. Miles had risked Jaedin's life in the past, and now Jaedin hated him.

Miles owed it to Jaedin to do everything he could to help him.

The Zakara smiled. "I thought you would, Miles. Close your eyes. I will be waiting for you."

*   *   *

Miles slowed his breathing and tuned into his *psysona*. The *aythirrealm* opened up to him, and he became aware of Grav'aen's presence – a projection of his consciousness – hovering nearby.

Miles took a quick moment to reinforce his shields – to make sure Grav'aen wouldn't be able to harm him – and then reached out to Grav'aen. Their *psysonas* began to merge.

It was never a pleasant experience when someone entered your mind. Particularly when it was a Psymancer as powerful as Grav'aen. Neither of them trusted each other enough to establish a full joining, so they merely merged enough to allow them to communicate mind to mind.

Hello Miles, Grav'aen said. It had been years since

Miles had heard that voice in his mind. Most of the communication they had shared when Miles was a spy had been via a series of letters. It had been too depleting to Grav'aen's *viga* to communicate this way when Miles was stationed in Jalard.

For Miles, hearing that voice thundering within his mind again was another reminder that they were not so far apart now.

What do you know? Miles channelled back.

Grav'aen sent a nebula of thoughts spiralling into Miles' consciousness. They didn't bear any specific information as such – more a conveyance of sentiments and emotions – but, through them, Miles knew that Grav'aen was telling the truth.

Jaedin's life *was* in danger. And it was something to do with the Stone of Zakara that he possessed. Its powers. There was something Jaedin could do with the artefact which, if he did, could kill him.

What is it? Miles channelled back.

*You will have to do something for **me** before I tell you that*, Grav'aen said.

I don't see how I could be any help to you, Miles said truthfully – for in this form of communication it was impossible to lie anyway. *Not even the Sharmarians trust me. What could I possibly do for you?*

Oh, there are a couple of things you could do. Believe me... Grav'aen said. *Once you have completed them, I will tell you how you can save Jaedin.*

*But how can I trust you will fulfil **your** side of the bargain?* Miles asked.

I am going to make a bloodoath, Grav'aen said, sending Miles another wave of his consciousness. When it coursed into Miles' mind, Miles could see that, during that very moment, Grav'aen was drawing a dagger across the palm of his hand. Drawing blood.

I swear. By the gods, Grav'aen said, as he made the oath. *That once Miles has completed the two requests that I ask of him, I will tell him the danger the Stone of Zakar's powers pose to the one he cares about. Jaedin.*

Miles watched the act as if seeing it through Grav'aen's own eyes.

A bloodoath was no trivial thing for someone to make. It was a binding that most people wouldn't even dare contemplate.

If Grav'aen broke this vow, he would die.

Do we have a deal then? Grav'aen asked.

Gods forgive me... Miles thought to himself, privately, and then he opened up to Grav'aen again.

What do you want me to do? Miles asked.

*   *   *

"We should go in," Kyra whispered, for what must have been the fiftieth time. "He's been in there for *ages*. Why have they kept him so long?"

"*No*, Kyra!" Rivan uttered back. "Not yet! Just... stay calm."

"*Calm*?" Kyra rasped. "How can you expect me to be *calm*? You *do* know where we are, don't you?"

Rivan was far from calm himself – his heart was hammering against his ribcage – but he was almost certain that interrupting whatever was going on in that hut would be a very bad idea. They were in a foreign land. Perhaps uniformed men pulling people aside for interrogation was something completely normal in Gavendara. There was a chance Miles had been taken in there for reasons they were unaware of. If he and Kyra were to burst in there with their weapons drawn, it would almost certainly blow their cover.

"Just wait and see what happens," Rivan urged quietly. "There are only three of them, Kyra. That's it. We can deal with them if we need to. Just *wait*."

She paused. "Okay, *fine!* But we should... Wait! *Look*!" she pointed. "He's coming out!"

Rivan watched as Miles stepped out of the hut. He was alone. "Just act natural..." Rivan uttered to Kyra through the side of his mouth. "They might still be watching."

"Come on then," Miles said once he reunited with them. "Let's get going…"

"What did they want, Kevan?" Kyra asked.

"Oh, nothing really," Miles replied cheerily as he mounted his horse again. "They were just doing their job. No harm done."

Rivan leapt back onto his saddle and gripped the reins. Even though Miles seemed relatively calm, Rivan still felt a strong desire to get away from those men as quickly as possible.

"What happened? *Really*?" Kyra asked a few minutes later, once they had built a comfortable distance.

Miles shrugged. "Nothing much… they asked me some questions about what we were doing here because they didn't recognise our faces… I think I managed to convince them. I had to make a few changes to our story, though."

"How so?" Kyra asked.

"They seemed convinced that Bryna and Rivan were a couple for some reason so eventually I just went along with it. Bryna is still my daughter, and you are still our hired mercenary, but it appears I have acquired a son in law."

Kyra laughed. "So does that mean I get my *own* bed now? It sounds like a good story to me!"

She winked at Rivan, but he didn't find it funny at all.

He looked at Bryna – wondering what *her* thoughts on the new arrangement were – but she didn't return his gaze.

* * *

Baird found Selena in the Academy gardens. She was sitting on a marble chair by one of the flowerbeds.

"You wanted to see me?" he said.

"Yes," she said and patted the space beside her. "Sit, please. Sorry to have to summon you all the way here. I don't trust the Synod grounds at the moment. Too many ears and eyes."

Baird nodded.

"I think I've found something," she announced.

"Yes?" he asked. He had guessed as much when he got the message. "What is it?"

"It wasn't easy," she began. "A certain *someone* made the process rather difficult for me… but I managed to pull some strings."

Baird didn't need to ask who that 'someone' was. "What did you find out?" he asked.

"Not a single member of the Synod left the city during the night in question," Selena said. "So, I decided to look into the Academy, but none of its teachers nor students left the grounds that night either. There was, however, a squadron from the barracks dispatched."

Baird clamped a hand over his mouth. "How many?" he then asked.

"A hundred men," Selene said.

"This is not good…" Baird shook his head. "This is not good at all…"

"They were sent to Seeker's Hill," she added.

"*Seeker's Hill*?" Baird repeated. He knew that place. It was a training ground to the north. "Why send fully trained men up *there*? We should be sending our forces to the border! That's where we need them! Who gave that order?"

Selena turned her eyes to the ground. "Keep your voice down, Baird," she reminded him.

"Greyjor!" Baird realised, slapping his forehead. "It was Greyjor, wasn't it? Gods… can't anyone from the Synod see what he's doing?"

"I don't know what excuse he used, Baird," Selena shook her head. "Military matters are nothing to do with me, so there is no reason for them to tell me anything. I only found out what I did through some of the connections I have. As I said, there *are* others who have grown suspicious about Greyjor, but we have to be very careful. He's still powerful."

"So what are we going to do?" Baird asked.

Selene shook her head and placed her hands on her lap.

"I don't know, Baird..." she admitted. "I would *like* to send someone out there to investigate, but I don't see Greyjor letting that happen."

"Me and Sidry will go," Baird decided.

"No," Selena shook her head. "You can't. You–"

"Greyjor doesn't scare me," Baird muttered. "I'd like to see him *try* to stop me."

"But's it's too dangerous," Selena whispered. "You and Sidry are–"

"If me and Sidry can't handle a few dozen men, then what use are we going to be to you when the *real* war comes," Baird said. "If there is a Zakara among that troop we have to deal with them."

Selena inhaled deeply and then nodded. "I will arrange supplies... when will you leave?"

"Tomorrow," Baird decided. "In the morning."

"Be careful," she said. She looked at him, and to Baird's surprise, she seemed genuinely concerned.

"I'll be fine," Baird said. He rose to his feet. "Just sort me out with some supplies. I'll be back."

Selena nodded. "I know you will."

*   *   *

Fangar had given Jaedin an afternoon at his leisure.

At first, he didn't know what to do with himself; it had been a while since he'd had the luxury of idle time. Ever since he'd escaped from the Synod, there had always been some lesson Fangar wanted to teach him, or thieving that need be done so that they had enough coin to fill their bellies. On this particular day, however, the rogue had told him to do as he pleased.

Jaedin wandered through the streets of Shemet for a while. He didn't know where he was going, at first, but his feet seemed to be leading him towards The Academy grounds.

The Library, Jaedin realised. ***That** is where I am going.*

He knew it was risky, but that only made the idea of it even more alluring.

Eventually, Jaedin reached the wall, but such barriers were not much of an obstacle for him anymore. There were cracks, and he used them as grips, vaulting himself up a few feet at a time. He made it up to the top within moments and leapt over the other side, breaking his fall with a roll.

Leaping and climbing were some of the first lessons Fangar taught him and, under the rogue's guidance, Jaedin was becoming artful in roaming the upper reaches of Shemet's cityscape. No longer was he restricted to roads and paths and alleys. Sometimes, the rooftops were faster anyway and, being a wanted man, they were the best means of escape if he was ever recognised.

Jaedin hid behind a bush and peered around it to make sure that nobody had witnessed his intrusion. Once he was satisfied the coast was clear, he made a break towards the nearest pathway. After that, he didn't bother to hide anymore, but he kept his face obscured beneath the wide-brimmed hat that he was wearing. He strolled towards the Academy buildings, walking with confidence. He already knew – from past experience – that once you were inside the grounds, there was very little scrutiny.

It didn't take long to find the library, and for a while, he just stared wide-eyed at all the shelves filled with books.

He had always dreamed of seeing this place.

He began to look around. His initial thoughts were to visit the historical sections. But Jaedin knew that such frivolous use of his time would serve him no purpose. He browsed for a while, not knowing what he was looking for until he came across a range of books about locksmithing.

That *could be useful*, he realised, selecting a few volumes. Fangar had been teaching him how to pick locks. Jaedin could bump open most of the doors in this city by now, but there were still some that eluded him. And he suspected they were the ones where the *real* treasures lay. Maybe, learning a bit more about how they worked would help.

Later on, he found a section on human anatomy. Fangar had already told Jaedin which places to slit a man would make his blood run quickest, but there was always room to discover a few more. He picked out a tome called *Observations from Beneath the Human Skin* and added it to the pile he held to his chest.

He found a few more he thought might be worth a browse and then went to a desk in a quiet corner to read.

Before he sat down, Jaedin scanned his surroundings; counting how many windows were near enough to make a swift exit if he had reason to make a sudden escape. There were three. *Always know your exit strategy*, Fangar's voice echoed in his head. It was one of the many mantras the rogue had ingrained into Jaedin's consciousness over the last few aeights.

Jaedin began with one of the books on locksmithing. He found it quite interesting, especially the opening chapter about the origins of locksmithing and its evolution throughout the ages. After a few pages, he sternly reminded himself that he was not here to prattle, though, and turned over a few pages to reach the more practical information. It didn't take him long to figure out the basics. The author had filled the book with diagrams, which broadened Jaedin's awareness of the internal mechanics. He soon found himself thinking of new ways to manipulate them.

"Jaedin?" he heard someone say.

Jaedin flinched, his hands reaching for a pair of daggers hidden within his sleeves as he twisted around.

But then he saw that it was only Sidry.

"You scit!" Jaedin hissed, seating himself again. "You scared me to death."

"I thought it was you…" Sidry said, edging closer and sitting upon a chair nearby.

"How did you find me?" Jaedin asked.

"It was just a hunch," Sidry shrugged. "I just thought; Jaedin… libraries… you know…"

"That's… actually quite clever," Jaedin said, closing the tome he had been reading. "So… what are you going

261

to *do*, now that you have found me? If you try to hand me in, I'll put up a fight."

"Don't worry," Sidry said, sighing. "I'm just relieved to see that you're okay. You *are* okay, aren't you?"

Jaedin nodded. "Better than ever."

"Baird's worried about you," Sidry said gently. "And so am I. You should come back."

"No way…" Jaedin replied. "I'm fine just as I am."

"Where's Fangar?" Sidry asked. "Are you with him still?"

Jaedin signed. *Why is everyone so obsessed with him?* "We're fine. Don't worry about us. We can look after ourselves."

"You're different," Sidry said, crossing his arms over his chest and staring at him.

"It's the hair," Jaedin explained, pointing to his scalp. "I don't want people to recognise me."

"No…" Sidry shook his head. "It's not that. It's… I don't know. You just seem–"

"What do you want, Sidry?" Jaedin asked, pulling a frank expression.

"Me and Baird are leaving tomorrow," Sidry said. "He told me just now. Selena thinks that the Zakara that got away was part of a squad that was sent north. We're going to check it out."

I should go with them, Jaedin initially thought but then remembered that he needed to protect the city. If Zakaras made their way into Shemet and spawned more of their numbers, it would be catastrophic. Plus, Jaedin didn't like the thought of having to cooperate with Baird again. Jaedin had had enough of being told what to do by Baird. "I am sure you two will be fine," Jaedin said. "But good luck. Oh, and by the way. The others are well. They reached Gavendara."

"How do you know?" Sidry asked.

"Through Bryna," Jaedin replied. "We can speak mind to mind now. Long story."

"How is she?" Sidry asked, his eyes lighting up.

"Fine," Jaedin shrugged. "She thinks about you a lot…

it's actually quite gross."

This news only made Sidry's smile stretch even wider, making him look even more idiotic.

Yeah… still don't get what she sees in him… Jaedin thought.

"I suppose you should give the good news to Baird," Jaedin said. "But don't tell him how you found me."

Sidry opened his mouth to reply and then closed it again.

Jaedin sighed. "Okay, look. I'll cut you a deal. I will come here once every four days. That way, when you return, you get to see that I am okay, *and* I can pass on messages between you and Baird and the others. But *only* if you promise to never tell Baird this is where we meet."

"Okay, fine."

They both shook hands.

"Make sure you come back in one piece," Jaedin said.

"You too," Sidry replied. "And just… be careful with Fangar, Jaedin."

"You don't need to worry about Fangar anymore," Jaedin said. "He… listens to me. As long as I'm with him, I can keep him under control."

*   *   *

Later on, when Jaedin returned to Fangar, the rogue began to quiz him with the usual series of questions.

"What did you find today?"

Jaedin reached into his cloak and drew a book. It was just a small one, faded and crumpled.

Fangar's face fell in disappointment.

"Is that *all*?" he asked, frowning.

"You *said* I could have the afternoon off…" Jaedin shrugged. "I didn't realise I–"

"Never mind," Fangar huffed.

He then asked the second question.

"Where did you find it?"

"The Academy Library," Jaedin answered. "I snuck into the grounds of the Synod."

Fangar's lips parted in surprise. Jaedin began to worry that he was going to scold him for taking such a risk.

But instead, Fangar grabbed him by the shoulder, pulled him in close and ruffled his hair.

"*Well done*, Jaedin! You're learning well!"

*　　*　　*

When Rivan was forced to share a room with Kyra, he thought *that* had been an awkward experience, but it was nothing compared to the atmosphere which filled the room when he shut the door behind himself that evening, and he and Bryna were alone.

"Right then... so..." Rivan mumbled. He didn't actually have anything to say in mind. He was merely trying to fill the silence. He looked at the bed and then at the window, the walls – anywhere but at her.

"Me and Kyra have been doing this thing," he then said, walking over and grabbing a couple of pillows. "It's like a line–"

He finally dared to look at her. She was staring at him.

"Actually," he said, changing his mind. "I'll sleep on the floor. Just... let me have these," he gathered the pillows again. "And one of the blankets."

He arranged the pillows on the floor to assemble his make-shift bed. And he took his time doing so. It gave him something to focus on so that he didn't have to worry about coming across as rude by not looking nor speaking to her.

By the time he finished, he looked over and discovered that Bryna had already undressed and slipped beneath the covers. She stared at the ceiling. Her dress was draped across the nearby chair. She had done it all silently. Without any warning. Without him even noticing.

"Thank you, Rivan," she said. "*I* will sleep on the floor tomorrow. It is only fair."

"No, you won't," Rivan said. "Sidry would kill me if he found out I let you sleep on the floor. Don't worry. It's not so bad."

Another awkward silence followed, and Rivan couldn't help but feel that it had been caused by the mention of Sidry's name.

"You don't have to feel bad, you know," Bryna said eventually.

"About what?" Rivan asked.

"About the way you feel," Bryna said. "They are just feelings. You can't control them. No more than I can. It is your actions that decide the person you are. We both love Sidry – in different ways, but it is still love – and I know that you would never intentionally do anything to hurt him… as neither would I. I know that, Rivan. So try to not feel bad. I don't want to be the reason for you to feel guilty. You haven't done anything wrong."

"O-okay," Rivan stammered. He then turned over. "Good night."

"Goodnight, Rivan."

He tried to sleep, but for a while, all he could hear was her voice in his head repeating the same words, over and over again.

They are just feelings. You can't control them. No more than I can.

*　　*　　*

In the morning, Dareth quietly slipped out of Carmaestre's bed.

Why do I keep coming back? he wondered as he looked at her. Her mouth was hanging open, and one of her arms dangled over the side of the bed. For someone who spent so much time preening herself for the daylight hours, Carmaestre was far from a glamorous sleeper. Sometimes, she reminded Dareth of his mother, with her drunken, sottish ways.

This was the first time he had seen her for a while. Recently, she had been busy with her rituals: fusing a select few of Grav'aen's most trusted fellows to the remaining Stones of Zakar. Now, there were six others who had the ability to control Zakaras; they would be the generals who would march the creatures across the border when they invaded Sharma.

Dareth kept telling himself he would stop making these visits to her chamber. The two of them had near to nothing in common. Dareth had never been with a woman his age. Only her. He had never known how to talk to girls, and Carmaestre just made it all too easy for him.

What Dareth would not admit – even to himself – was that he was lonely. A part of him was still grieving over the loss of Aylen, and these short trysts with Carmaestre, while they never healed the void inside him, gave him brief moments of comfort.

Dareth began to put his clothes back on. He would have to report to Grav'aen soon, like he did most mornings, to find out what the Master of the Institute wanted from him.

'Master of the Institute' was a misleading title for Grav'aen these days. Everyone clued up enough knew that Grav'aen more or less had control of the entire Gavendarian army now. If not Gavendara itself. The generals were all under his charge, as were most of the Lords and their bannermen. King Wilard was a figure Dareth had never met, and Dareth could only guess that he was merely a puppet who didn't hold much genuine power. It was Grav'aen pulling the strings.

Dareth made his way to the main headquarters to find Grav'aen. As usual, the man was in his study, and he hailed Dareth before he even reached the door.

"Come in, Dareth!"

He stepped inside. Grav'aen was smiling that day, which made it immediately clear that he wanted something.

"And how are you this morning, Dareth?" he asked.

"Fine," Dareth replied, crossing his arms over his chest. Why did Grav'aen always feel a need to begin with pointless pleasantries when he had a task for him? Dareth wished he would just get to the point sometimes.

"I see that you are not in the mood for chit-chat,"

Grav'aen said. He turned in his seat. "Fine then. Sit down. I need you to do something for me."

I knew it, Dareth thought as he claimed a chair.

"Oh, don't be like that," Grav'aen grinned. "I think you'll enjoy this little venture… I have tracked down some old friends of yours."

"Who?" Dareth asked.

"Four of them," Grav'aen said. "They had the gall to tread upon Gavendarian soil. They're snooping around… I think the Synod sent them to spy on us."

"But *who*?" Dareth repeated.

"Miles, the traitor. He used to work for me, you know," Grav'aen said.

Dareth nodded. He knew about that. Miles had admitted it himself shortly after the others escaped from Jalard. "Who else?"

"Rivan, Bryna, and Kyra," Grav'aen said.

Dareth went through an entire journey of cascading emotions when he heard those names.

Rivan was someone Dareth used to consider a friend, but he didn't hold much affection for him anymore. When he heard about Bryna, the hairs on the back of his neck stood on end; she still spooked him, but now he could summon an Avatar of Gezra, the thought of encountering her didn't scare him as much as it used to.

It was the last name that evoked the strongest reaction.

Kyra!

Dareth's fists tightened when her name entered his consciousness. He remembered his last encounter with her. The grim triumph on her face as she sent his dagger flying from his hand and then kicked him in the stomach, sending him reeling. She humiliated him, and the memory of it still made his blood boil. She probably would have killed him if Carmaestre had not intervened.

It was also *her* fault that Aylen was dead.

"Where are they?" Dareth asked.

"I will tell you if you first *calm down*," Grav'aen said. "This is something which has to be handled carefully."

"But I can kill her, right?" Dareth checked. "Kyra."

Grav'aen nodded. "I would have killed the lot of them myself... but it was only by chance that I spotted them, and they were in an area where I lack resources. They are still by the border, but I think they are heading east. If you're going to do this, there have to be rules, Dareth."

"Like?" Dareth asked, realising that he would agree to almost anything for a chance to kill Kyra.

"First of all, you need to try to be discreet. No public sightings. I don't want any civilians to see you in your Avatar form if you can help it. I have to tread very carefully at the moment; some of the Lords in the west are not very supportive to my cause yet, and they would jump at the chance to point their fingers at me."

Dareth nodded. It seemed simple enough.

"Secondly: after you have dealt with them, you will come straight back to me," Grav'aen said. "I know you want to kill Jaedin... and I promise you that, one day, you will. But going off into Sharma by yourself is too dangerous. You're too important to risk yourself that way."

"Fine..." Dareth said reluctantly.

"Thirdly," Grav'aen said. "If you are to come across any of my Zakaras, you are to leave immediately. Do not interfere. I have some operations underway in that part of Gavendara, and they need to be handled delicately."

Dareth nodded.

"And, finally, whilst I realise that you have a vendetta against Kyra, I also want you to kill Bryna too. If it is possible to do so without risking yourself."

This request surprised Dareth. He opened his mouth to respond but then hesitated.

"Is that a problem?" Grav'aen asked, raising an eyebrow.

"No," Dareth said, clearing his throat. He didn't know why, but he felt reluctant to do such a thing. He had never killed a woman before.

Dareth longed to kill Kyra, but that was different. Kyra was a warrior, and they were – despite how much it pained him to admit it – evenly matched. Bryna wasn't a warrior.

Dareth knew he would get no joy out of killing her.

"Good," Grav'aen said. "And also, you *can't* tell Carmaestre about Bryna being in Gavendara. Nor that I ordered you to kill her. Ever." Grav'aen shook his head. "She has an unhealthy obsession with that witch. If Carmaestre were to find out she was here, she would drop everything to try to take that bloody stone she's always yapping on about, and there are much more important duties I need her to be focussing on. *If* you do manage to kill Bryna, please don't be collecting it, either. Just leave it. I don't want her distracted, and this world doesn't need any Descendants of Vai-ris."

"That's fine," Dareth said. In truth, he didn't feel much loyalty to Carmaestre anyway. "Is that all?"

Grav'aen nodded. "Just one more thing. You *should* be able to deal with these four – if you summon your Avatar – but if at any point you think you are going to fail or your life comes into danger, you *must* abort and come back to me."

Dareth nodded again.

"So, to summarise…" Grav'aen said. "You are to be *discreet*. *Find* them. *Kill* Bryna if you can. *But* if at any point you encounter any of my Zakaras or come into danger, you are to *flee*. These are all *direct orders*, Dareth. Do you understand?"

The moment Grav'aen said those words, the scar on Dareth's wrist flared. He put his hand to it.

The *bloodoath*.

Dareth was starting to regret making it now. It had been a part of the bargain when Grav'aen bequeathed him the Stone of Gezra. Dareth didn't think it a big deal at the time – as he thought the legends surrounding the Bloodsworn were little more than a myth anyway – but now he knew different.

The oath Dareth had taken was to never break a direct order when it was given to him by Grav'aen. Since Dareth became Bloodsworn, there had been a few occasions where he had felt tempted to defy Grav'aen, and, each time, the scar had warned him by throbbing.

Dareth nodded.

"As I said before, you are extremely valuable," Grav'aen said. "If you don't manage to kill them, it is not the end of the world. I have also put a backup plan into motion. Even if they *do* survive, I have made one of them still useful to me sometime down the line."

Chapter 14

The Pillars of Parchen

After their encounter with those creatures, Astar and Elita gathered their possessions, saddled up their horses, and rode away as fast as they could.

For the first few hours, they didn't even know where they were heading. They were acting upon instinct alone. They just wanted to get as far away from that place as possible.

"Astar!" Elita eventually yelled. "Where are we *going*?"

Aster drew his horse to a halt and looked at her. "Warling," he realised. That was where his instinct was drawing him to. "We're heading there."

"*Warling*?" she repeated. "Where in Verdana's crack is *Warling*?"

"It's my uncle's regency," he said. "North-east from here."

"Are you sure it's safe?" she asked.

Astar hesitated. In truth, he wasn't sure. But Lord Marven was the only relative he had who was not in some way connected to Grav'aen.

"It's the safest place I can think of," he replied. "I... don't know of anywhere else *to* go. Do you?"

She shook her head. "As far as I am concerned, I don't have a family, Astar... so Warling it is," she said. "We should be careful on this road, though. I think it runs to Mordeem, doesn't it? You never know who we could bump into..."

Half of the roads in Gavendara lead to Mordeem! Astar almost exclaimed but held back. It wasn't really *her* that he was angry with. "Don't worry," he said. "We'll turn off and take a different route soon."

They rode on and eventually found a path that led in a more northerly direction. They passed a small hamlet later in the afternoon, and Astar – disguising himself with his magic so that he wouldn't be recognised – asked one of the locals where they were and which road would take them to Warling.

All three moons were in the sky that night, so they carried on riding well into the evening. When they did settle down, they discussed the things they'd seen, but neither could come to any conclusive answers. They knew that those creatures must be somehow linked to Grav'aen, and Squad Three, but exactly *what* they were was still a mystery.

They both agreed that they should sleep in shifts so someone could keep watch. Waking up to those robed men standing over them the previous morning had been a sobering experience. They were going to be much more cautious from now on.

With nightly watches in practice, and days full of riding, they didn't have many opportunities to talk over the days that followed. When they did communicate, it was mostly for pragmatic reasons. Where they were going to cross a certain river. Which road seemed like it would be the most discreet. What they were going to eat.

They didn't speak about those creatures again. There wasn't any point. Neither of them knew enough to make any educated guesses, so all they had to go on was an endless stream of wild speculations. Astar most often thought about them when he was staring into the fire at night. With his extraordinary ability for recollection, he could recall everything about them to the tiniest detail. He used to think his memory a blessing, but now he wasn't so sure. The images made him shudder.

He thought about his father, too. The way he looked when he was ill, and the miraculous transformation to good health he'd made. It was the latter image Astar found more disturbing. The deadness in that being's eyes as it had moved, spoken, and even to some degree acted like Lord Oren but somehow did not ring true.

On the seventh morning, Astar and Elita ascended a mountain pass, and he saw Warling below them. It had been over ten years since Astar had laid eyes upon this place, but he could still remember it vividly.

It had not changed much. A few new rooftops had cropped up around the main keep, and the mountains behind it were a little greyer than they used to be, but apart from that, it looked the same.

"I've been here before..." Elita said, her eyes widening.

"When?" Astar asked, looking at her.

"When I was a child," she said, and for a moment, there was a haunted look in her eyes. As if she was reliving something that pained her. "I'm actually from the north, you know."

Now *that* was a surprise. Astar stared at Elita for a few moments. The dwellers of the Valleshian Mountains were the butt of many jokes in the lower lands of Gavendara because they had coarse accents, and many of them worked as miners.

"Anyway," Elita said, spurring her horse on. "Are we going to meet your family or not?"

They made their way down the mountain and towards the keep. For an area with no farmsteads – nor any other production industry Astar was aware of – Warling was surprisingly lively. Some of the goods Astar glimpsed as he passed through the market seemed exotic and could only have come from places afar.

"Hail!" someone yelled from the tower when they reached the gate. "Who's there?"

"Astar. Of Llamaleil!" he yelled back, turning his head up. "I'm Lord Marven's nephew!" he added.

"You shouldn't yell your name so loudly," Elita uttered beside him. She seemed on edge.

Astar ignored her and waited for an answer.

"What's taking them so long?" Elita asked after a while. She looked around them suspiciously. "You don't think–"

The gate began to rise, and her voice trailed off. Astar stared as the wall of iron lifted. A handful of people were waiting on the other side, and Astar didn't even recognise the man in the middle as his uncle at first. His hair had greyed a little, and he had more creases around his eyes than Astar remembered.

"Welcome, Astar!" Lord Marven said as he came forward. "See to their horses, please!" he said, turning to a pair of men standing behind him.

Astar leapt from his steed and walked over to greet his uncle. "Lord Marven," he said, briefly dipping his head. He wasn't sure how to regard this man anymore. It felt strange to address a family member so formally, but it had been many years since they last saw each other.

Lord Marven, however, smiled and took Astar's hand, pulling his nephew into an embrace. "It's good to see you," he said into his ear. He then turned to the young woman beside Astar. "And I believe introductions are to be made?" he said enquiringly.

"Elita, this is Lord Marven of Warling. My uncle," Astar said.

If Astar's uncle was surprised that Elita had no title, he was tactful enough to mask it. He smiled at her and kissed her hand, as a gentleman would any other lady.

"Come inside…" he said. "We'll see you both get rooms and baths. Food is already being prepared."

*   *   *

After being treated to a much-appreciated hot bath, Astar found a clean set of clothes waiting for him in his room. They were a little fanciful for his tastes – bright blue, with white frills around the neck and collar, and ornamental buttons – but he slipped them on out of politeness. At least they were clean.

He left his room and looked for his uncle. Astar knew what the usual formalities were when nobles visited a family member – a feast was to be made, and while it was being prepared, Astar was expected to wait in his quarters and spend his time making himself presentable – but he didn't have time for such trivialities. He needed to speak with his uncle. Soon, and privately.

"Where can I find Lord Marven?" he asked a serving girl he passed in the corridor.

"M'Lord," she said, making a little curtsy. "Lord Marven is just preparing for supper. He will see you in the–"

"No," Astar shook his head. "I need to see him *now*. Where is he?"

"I…" her face went red. "I… I'll go speak with him."

"I'll wait for you here."

She scarpered off, almost tripping down the corridor as she ran. Astar considered using his magic to follow her without being seen so that he could save more time but decided against it. He didn't know his uncle well enough to be getting up to antics like that.

She returned a few minutes later. "Forgive me, Sir," she said. "He said he will see you in his quarters. Follow me."

She led him through a series of corridors and then up a spiralling staircase.

"Astar," Lord Marven said when they arrived. He nodded at the girl, and she left, leaving the two of them alone. "My you've…" he looked him up and down and then hesitated. "How long has it been?"

Ten years, Astar thought, guiltily. "A while…" he went with. "I would have come sooner, but my father… he…"

Marven shook his head. "Don't you worry. I know what your father is like. I send letters to him every year, but he seldom replies."

Astar looked down. He felt like he should defend his father, but he didn't know what to say. Lots of the ways Oren acted *were* rude and neglectful. It was just the way he was.

"He loved your mother so much…" Marven said. "It is surprising that he doesn't want to see us more often."

"I think that's the problem," Astar said. "We remind him of her…"

Marven nodded sombrely. "You look like her, you know."

Yeah. I know, Astar thought.

"Who is the lady you've brought with you, then?" Marven said.

"Elita," Astar shrugged. "She's… one of the girls from the Institute. A friend."

Marven pulled a face. "I hope you know what you're getting yourself in for."

Astar frowned.

"I mean. If you love her, and she's *really* worth it," Marven shrugged. "I'll support you. But you'll get a lot of stick for marrying a commoner, you know. People will talk. It'll be harder for her than for you."

"No," Astar shook his head. "It's not like that."

"Then why else have you come running here?" Marven said.

Astar crossed his arms over his chest. "Wait… do you think I've come here because–"

"Am I wrong?" Marven asked. "First time I see my nephew for years, and he turns up with a girl and they're on a pair of horses which have almost been run into their graves. And you've also demanded to speak to me about something which is so damn important that it can't wait until later this evening."

"I wish it was as something as trivial as that… believe me." Astar sighed.

Maybe I was wrong coming here, he realised.

"Then why *are* you here?" Marven said.

"It's… complicated," Astar said, running his hands through his hair. "I don't even know where to begin… it's about the Institute. And my father. And this man called Grav'aen. You might not have heard of him, but–"

"Wait…" his uncle's eyes widened, and his entire manner changed at the mention of that name. "Did you just say Grav'aen? What business do you have with that man?"

From the tone he used when he uttered that name, Astar realised then that maybe, just maybe, he and his uncle shared a common enemy.

"It's a very long story…" Astar said.

"Sit down," Marven said, pointing to one of the chairs.

He walked over to a dresser on the other side of the room and picked up a pitcher of wine and two cups. "Supper can wait. I need you to tell me everything."

*   *   *

"This is not good..." Marven said once Astar finished explaining. "This is not good at all..."

Astar feared his uncle would not believe him about the monsters, but Lord Marven didn't seem nearly as shocked as Astar expected him to be.

"What do you know?" Astar asked.

"I have caught wind of lots of peculiar things lately," Marven said as he poured them both more wine. "Warling is the main gateway to the north, and lots of people pass through here, so you hear things. I happen to know that Grav'aen and many of his cohort – including Lord Jarvis – have shown an interest in the Valleshian Mountains during the last decade or so."

"Really?" Astar said.

He nodded. "They have passed through here quite a few times... Grav'aen, Lord Jarvis, an associate of Grav'aen's by the name of Shayam, and a woman with very strange purple eyes. As well as others..."

"Grav'aen was supposed to be searching for a cure for The Ruena," Astar said. "Why would that draw them *here*?"

"I knew of that project," Marven mused. "Initially, I thought their interest in this area was merely because fewer people from the north die from The Ruena than in the south, but... shortly after they started coming, I began to hear tales of strange things."

"What kind of things?" Astar asked.

"People vanishing. Mostly," Marven replied. "And also rumours that they were building mysterious outposts in the middle of nowhere, where people kept hearing bizarre noises. I sent some of my liegemen over to investigate, but some went missing, and the ones who *did* return didn't find much. Only the remains of buildings that had either been burnt to ashes or just completely abandoned. Whatever it is they are doing, Astar, they have worked very hard to cover their tracks. They even destroyed some of Valleshia's most ancient monuments."

"What monuments?" Astar asked.

"There are lots of old temples and monasteries up in those mountains," he explained. "Most of them were abandoned hundreds of years ago and are now buried under earth and snow. The Valleshian Mountains used to be a holy place. If one wanted to study lore, magic, or devote themselves to the gods, it was the place you would go. The north was not always the iron-mining land of peasants it has been reduced to today."

Astar sensed that the downtrodden status of the northern lands was something his uncle felt passionate about. He had not come here for a history lesson, though, so he didn't comment and merely nodded to limit the risk of being given a long-winded lecture. He primarily wanted to find out everything his uncle knew about Grav'aen. "So, what were they doing at these temples?"

"They obliterated some of them," Marven shook his head. "Took them apart till there was nothing but rubble. I don't know why they did it, Astar, or what they were looking for, but I think they found something there... something which would have been better left alone. And now, hearing your story, I have a feeling it must be connected. Your experiences at the Institute. Your father."

"That man is not my father anymore," Astar said. "Don't trust him."

That statement lingered heavily in the air between them, and for a time, neither of them said anything.

"Trust him or not, I have to tread very carefully," Marven said. "Things happen to those who oppose Grav'aen too openly... I have tried to seem neutral by keeping my head low."

"What about King Wilard?" Astar asked. "Hasn't anyone gone to him about it?"

"King Wilard..." Marven shook his head. "He has

become quiet over the last few years. He hasn't made all too many public appearances, and it's been a long time since I heard of him exercise any power... I fear he is not the man he used to be. I can only assume that Grav'aen has wrapped him around his finger somehow. There are very few you can trust during these times, Astar. I know a few others who are suspicious of Grav'aen – I can't tell you who they are, because rumour has it Grav'aen is a powerful Psymancer and he can read people's thoughts," Marven tapped the side of his temple. "Therefore, I can only trust people who have ways of concealing their thoughts from him."

"I can do that," Astar said. "I... used my Blessing to create an illusion once. I think it worked."

"You really *do* take after your mother..." Marven said, his mouth parting for a moment. "But whether you can do that or not, it is paramount that Grav'aen doesn't catch you..." he shook his head. "I am sorry, Astar, but you cannot stay here. For both *your* safety *and* mine. We will feast together, and you can sleep in comfort tonight – we'll act like everything is normal – but, early tomorrow morning, you will have to slip away. Too many people saw you enter my keep. Eventually someone will catch wind of it."

"Where shall I go?" Astar asked.

"South," Marven said without a moment of hesitation. "The southern provinces are the places where Grav'aen holds the least sway, and there is also the Jungle of Babua. Gavendara has never quite managed to subdue the tribes there."

"Can't I just go north? Surely, you must know someone up there I can hide out with?"

"The north is too obvious," Marven said. "And also, that is where I am going to *say* you went when people come here looking for you."

"But I would have to go past Mordeem to get to Babua!" Astar said.

"No," Marven shook his head. "Not if you take a different route. Here, I will show you..." he then went over to a nearby desk and rummaged through one of his drawers, pulling out a map. "Everyone thinks that Holliston is the only way to get to the south, but it isn't," he said as he unravelled it and spread it across the table. "A tight vigil is kept over gates at Holliston. They are fussy over who they let in or out. If you try to go through, you'd likely face difficulty. Possibly even be caught. There is another way, though. One which cuts through the Levian Mountains."

Lord Marven then pointed to a location on the map. It was a place called Falam, sandwiched between the Valantian and Levian mountain ranges. "Not many people know about it," he said. "The man who controls access to this pass – Lord Galrath is his name – is loyal to Grav'aen, but there is something which he is even more loyal to, and that is money. He is a crook, and it is one of Gavendara's worst kept secrets that he makes deals with smugglers and will let almost anyone through if they slip him enough coin. I have a friend who often makes such deals with him, and I am sure he could arrange it for you. He lives in Sarok."

"*Sarok!*" Astar exclaimed. "That's on the border! It's about to turn into a war zone! Are you trying to get me killed?

"Of course not!" Marven seemed offended. "On the memory of your mother Lysadie, I am trying to keep you *alive*, Astar."

Astar scratched his head.

"I know it's a risk," Marven conceded. "But it's the best I can do for you. The border isn't a warzone yet. You'll make it way before that happens if you travel with haste. I will give you and Elita clothes. Humble ones, which won't draw attention to you. I will also give you money, supplies, and new horses. Those you've been riding are good steeds but they need some rest and care. Head to Sarok. And then, when you get there, go to an inn called The Pearl and Jackdaw and ask for a man named Ilarn. He and I go way back, and he owes me a favour or two. If you tell him I sent you, he will help you out."

*   *   *

When Bryna first woke up, she was alarmed, for she was in a room that was unfamiliar to her and could hear snoring. She sat up and looked around herself.

Her mind cleared, and she realised the noises were coming from Rivan; he lay in a nest of pillows and blankets on the floor.

Bryna watched him for a while. His mouth was hanging open and, every time he exhaled, his head tilted ever so slightly. It reminded her of Fraknar. When he almost died. She had watched him sleep for hours back then. Night and day. Not that there had been much difference between the two in that dingy underground dwelling.

He had slept very differently back then. Silent and inert. Vulnerable.

It was a special bond, the one formed when you nursed someone back to life. Bryna's mother had warned her about it when she began to train her as a Devotee of Carnea. She told Bryna that it could sometimes be painful once the patient woke up, and you realise that they did not remember all those moments you had shared whilst they were delirious and at death's door. All those times you held them, coaxed them to drink your potions, tended to their wounds. Therefore, they did not feel the same affinity.

Bryna knew now that she would never be a fully-fledged Devotee of Carnea. She would never be a medicine woman of her mother's calibre. Her life had taken a different path.

Bryna rose from the sheets and slipped her clothes on, careful not to wake Rivan as she left the room. She held herself as she walked towards the parlour. Not because she was cold but more to comfort herself. Ever since they had entered the Folds, Bryna had felt on edge. There was a feeling in the air which she couldn't explain but didn't like.

It wasn't an omen. Bryna knew all too well what *that* felt like. It was more an ambience. Something about this place simply didn't feel *right* to her.

They had been there for five days now, and Bryna would be glad to leave it behind.

She stared out of the window. Bryna had become accustomed to being the first to wake; she didn't seem to require as much sleep as most people. Usually, she made use of the extra time by venturing off with her basket to forage for leaves and other things, but she had not done this since they entered Gavendara. She was a little wary of wandering alone, and besides, the Folds were a barren place.

"Early bird?" a voice said, interrupting her thoughts.

Bryna turned her eyes away from the brown, flat landscape outside the window and looked at Edra.

Edra was the landlady of the farmhouse they were staying in. A short and plump woman with bright blue eyes. When she smiled, there were gaps where she was missing teeth, but it was still an expression that put Bryna at ease in a strange place and made her warm to her.

"Nee had I moment to rustle up breakfast yet," Edra said, as she carried a bucket filled almost to the brim with milk towards the kitchen. "Just come from tendin' the cows. There's leftover stew if you take fancy?"

Bryna shook her head. If the stew Edra was referring to was the same that she had served the previous night, Bryna did not feel inclined. It had not been to Bryna's liking, and she suspected that her companions had not taken a shine to it either. Edra, however, had seemed very proud of it.

"Thank you," Bryna said. "But I can wait. The others should be up soon."

Edra cleared her throat and continued to hobble towards the kitchen, shutting the door behind herself and leaving Bryna, once again, alone to her thoughts.

Bryna closed her eyes and briefly called out to Jaedin in an attempt to connect with him. She didn't get any response, which she guessed meant that he was either busy or sleeping. She could have probed a little more insistently if she wanted to, but thought better of it. She reminded herself that if he were in danger or pain she would know about it regardless.

But she still worried about him. Often.

She got out a needle and thread and busied herself with some darning. Kyra and Rivan had left her with a small pile of clothes that needed mending, so she occupied herself with that. In the background, she could hear Edra tinkering around in the kitchen.

Miles was the first to emerge from his room. And he was shortly followed by Kyra. They both sat at the table, and Edra began to place bowls in front of them.

Porridge. It was thick and gloopy, with dark little spots Bryna guessed to be a grain she was not familiar with.

"Gods, this is *awful*," Kyra said once Edra was safely out of earshot. "And I thought the stew was bad..."

"I am afraid this part of Gavendara is not known for its cuisine," Miles said, grinning as he plunged his spoon back in his bowl. "I find it tastes a little better if you close your eyes..."

"Nor *any* part of Gavendara, to be honest," Kyra said. "Ever since we crossed the border, I can't think of a single meal I have actually *enjoyed*. The meat always tastes funny."

"Your lands are more fertile than ours," Miles reminded her. "Farming methods are different."

"But didn't you say the Folds are mostly farmland?" Bryna said. "I haven't seen much growing around here."

"Come to think about it, you're right..." Kyra pondered out loud. "Where are the actual fields and crops, Miles? We've been riding through here for days."

"It's mostly livestock they produce in the Folds," Miles said.

"So where are all the animals then?" Kyra asked.

Just as Miles was about to answer, Rivan emerged, stretching his arms out and yawning as he joined them.

"Do you *have* to make such a racket?" Kyra muttered as Rivan sat himself down at the table, rubbing his eyes.

"How else is the nice old lady to know she needs to bring my food over?"

"You may live to regret that…" Kyra muttered.

"What did you say?" Rivan asked.

"Oh, nothing…" Kyra said, grinning sheepishly as Edra entered the room with another bowl of porridge and a proud grin on her face. "Where are we riding to today, Kevan?" she asked, turning to Miles.

"Nowhere," he replied. "We are taking a break."

"What?" Kyra narrowed her eyes at him, and everyone stopped eating. "Why?"

"The horses, for one," Miles said. "They need a rest and some care. We've been running them into the ground."

"I agree," Rivan said as he accepted the bowl from Edra, who then walked back to the kitchen. "We've been stretching their limits. Mine could do with a little grooming too."

"Speak for yourselves. I don't know how *you* lot have been treating your horses, but Swifty is doing just fine," Kyra said. She, like Bryna, had taken to the habit of naming her mount and found every excuse she could to use it since.

"There are other reasons," Miles said quietly.

"What is it?" Kyra whispered, leaning towards him.

Rivan put his first mouthful of porridge into his mouth and then spat it back out. Kyra briefly frowned at him and then turned back to Miles.

"I do not know where to head next," Miles admitted.

"So *where* have we been heading all this time!?" Kyra hissed.

"We are in the right region. So to speak," Miles reassured her. "I *do* know that some of Gavendara's armies are often stationed somewhere to the northeast of here. I just don't know exactly *where*…"

"Why not?" Kyra asked.

"I never had any reason to," Miles shrugged. "Military matters were never my concern. If I had shown too much interest in them it would have been suspicious. Anyway, I was speaking to Edra last night, and she mentioned that there is a market just a few miles away. I thought that if I went there I might be able to find out something."

Kyra eyed him suspiciously. "If you think I am going to let you go off on your own then–"

"You can come with me if you wish," Miles offered. "Maybe we can both ride on 'Swifty' if you think he's up to it," he suggested.

"Your mount needs some care, too," Rivan said to Miles. "His coat is all–"

"Is that an *offer*?" Miles asked, smiling at Rivan. "Thank you for being so kind. It *would* be a good way for you to occupy yourself whilst Kyra and I are out gathering intelligence."

Rivan scowled at him. "You think I'm here to do your dirty work?"

"You consider the care for the creatures which carry us on their backs all day 'dirty work'?" Miles asked. He frowned at Rivan, but Bryna could tell he was secretly savouring this opportunity to get one over the younger man. "I am merely thinking of ways that we, as a group, can be more effective with our time. *I* have an important task to carry out today, *Kyra* has nominated herself to keep an eye on me, so it is only fair *you* pitch in too… I am sure you would do a much better job of grooming that horse than I would anyway. Perhaps, you could tend to Bryna's as well, while you're at it, as she *is* being kind enough to mend your clothes…"

Rivan looked at Bryna, and his face turned red. She could tell that he wanted to argue the point further, but the mention of her name seemed to change his mind.

"Well… now that that's settled," Miles said curtly. "Let us finish this delicious breakfast and get on with our day."

*   *   *

Shortly after Miles and Kyra left for the market, Rivan stomped off towards the stables, muttering a string of curses under his breath, and Bryna once again busied herself with darning. Miles had added a few more clothes and the pile had grown.

285

It took Bryna most of the morning to get through them all. By the time she had finished, Edra's husband, Jev, returned from tending to the farm to eat his midday meal. Edra offered to prepare something for Bryna too, but Bryna tactfully declined. She did however accept a cup of mulberry-leaf tea. After Jev left, she and Edra sat together for a while.

"Going to gather the eggs soon," Edra said, after downing the last dregs from her cup of the slightly over-brewed concoction. "You'll be alright on your own for a while, lass?"

"Actually… I could help. If you would like?" Bryna offered. "I would like to see the farm."

"Alright," Edra said, smiling as she got up from her chair.

Bryna went to her room to put on her coat and boots and then went outside, where Edra was waiting for her with a rather large wicker basket cradled beneath her arm.

It took a little longer to walk to than Bryna had anticipated. She began to wonder where exactly these chickens were. Back in Jalard, most families – even ones who weren't farmers – kept at least a few chickens. They roamed the gardens, and children would check their nests for eggs each morning.

Edra led Bryna towards a large wooden building. It almost looked like a barn, with its crude, haphazard structure, but the roof was much lower.

Bryna felt an ominous feeling in the pit of her stomach as she approached it. It felt like a phantom hand was in there, squeezing at her insides.

And it was getting worse with each step she took.

"This is the pen," Edra said over her shoulder. "Well, one of them. We have eight in all. I check two of them each day. The–"

She continued talking, but Bryna wasn't listening anymore. She felt like crying, and she didn't even know why. The foreboding feeling – the one she had been experiencing ever since she had entered the Folds – was escalating with every step she took. They were very close now. A fetid stench hit her nose. It carried the scent of rotting flesh and other things. Bryna covered her nose with her hand.

Edra opened the door. At first, the inside was dark, and all was silent, but then Bryna's eyes adjusted and she saw eyes and beaks. Dozens of them.

And then a loud cacophony erupted as they all began to squawk.

"Oh, shut it!" Edra groaned as she picked up her basket again and stepped inside. "Sorry," she then said, turning to Bryna a moment. "They make an awful racket when I let the daylight in!"

"Why?" Bryna croaked.

"Who knows?" Edra shrugged.

"Why do you keep them *here*?" Bryna said, raising her voice. She was unable to hide her horror that moment. Bryna took another step inside – even though she knew she would live to regret it – to get a closer look.

The hens were all crammed into cages. They looked weak and sickly. Many of them lacked feathers, and the skin beneath was red and inflamed. Some of them even had wounds – which Bryna could only guess was from them pecking at each other.

"How else am I to keep them close to the Pillar?" Edra asked.

"The Pillar?" Bryna repeated. She covered her mouth because the smell was so bad that she could almost taste it.

Edra pointed, and Bryna followed the direction of Edra's finger and saw a large wooden object in the middle of the barn. It rose from the ground, and there were mysterious symbols etched upon the length of the outer bark.

"What is *that*?" Bryna whispered. She could feel an energy emanating from it. One that sent chills down her spine.

"A Pillar of Parchen!" Edra said, shaking her head. "Are you going to help me gather the eggs, or are you going to stand there gawping?"

*   *   *

When Bryna returned to Edra's house, she ran to her room and, once the door was safely shut, planted herself upon her bed and cried into her pillow.

"Bryna?" Rivan said, peering through a crack in the door a few minutes later. "Are you okay? Edra said you have taken sick."

"No," Bryna whispered. "I am not sick... I just... I don't like it here, Rivan. We need to leave."

"What's happened?" he asked.

Bryna began to explain. Well, she tried to, but she was so upset she struggled to express herself. She kept stumbling on her words. Stopping and starting. She knew that much of it must have sounded like an incoherent babble, but Rivan was supportive anyway. He sat next to her. He seemed to be wary about maintaining a certain amount of distance with her but put a hand on her shoulder. She could tell he wanted to do more to comfort her but was afraid.

"Don't worry," he said as he rubbed her shoulder. "We're leaving in the morning. Miles and Kyra just got back. They found out where the armies are stationed."

"Did they?" Bryna asked, looking up at him.

He nodded. "Why don't you come out? You can ask them about their day?"

"I will..." Bryna said. "Just... give me a few minutes. I need to fix myself."

He patted her on the shoulder one more time and then left the room.

Bryna sat up and gathered her wits for a while. She knew there was nothing she could do to change what she had just witnessed. She was just a visitor – worse, a spy – in a foreign land. She had to leave this place behind as inconspicuously as she had entered it.

She went over to the bucket on the other side of the room and splashed her face with cold water to refresh herself.

When she went to join the others, she found them

gathered around the table. Neither Edra nor Jev was anywhere to be seen, but Bryna could hear faint sounds coming from the kitchen, so she guessed they were busy preparing supper.

"Why didn't you tell us?" Bryna whispered to Miles once she had sat.

"Rivan told us you were upset," Miles said. "What's troubling you?"

"The Pillars of Parchen," Bryna said. "What are they?"

Miles' eyes widened a little.

"I was hoping you wouldn't discover them…" he admitted, turning his head down. "As I knew it would upset you… things are different here, Bryna. Try not to judge. As you already know, our lands aren't as rich as yours, and we have a large population to feed."

"What are you two talking about?" Kyra asked.

Bryna explained to Kyra what she had seen that day. She was feeling more composed now, so she was able to explain it much more lucidly than she had to Rivan earlier.

"That's disgusting!" Kyra exclaimed. She pulled a face and looked at Miles.

"Shhh," Miles brought a finger to his lips. "Be careful. They might hear you."

"How could they do such a thing?" Kyra hissed.

"As I *tried* to explain to you," Miles said. "We don't have as much fertile land as you do. If it weren't for the Pillars, many people would starve."

"But it's *wrong*!" Kyra whispered back.

"And to someone from Gavendara, many things in Sharma – which you take for granted – are also seen as wrong. Trust me on that…" Miles said. "You said to me earlier today that you liked Edra. You know she isn't a bad person, don't you? It's just the way things are here."

Everyone stared at the table for a while.

"What *are* Pillars of Parchen?" Bryna asked.

Miles drew a deep breath. "They come from the area around Mordeem. You do know who Parchen was, don't you?"

"It sounds familiar," Kyra said. "Is he one of the gods?"

"Okay, remember when you were children and you were told all those stories about how wicked and evil Gavendarians are?" Miles said in a slightly sarcastic tone. "How we destroyed our sacred forests and been cursed with barren lands ever since? Well, there is *some* truth to that. We *did* destroy one of our forests. It was the Forest of Parchen, which was in the area where Mordeem now stands. It happened many hundreds of years ago – when our population was expanding, and we were being somewhat reckless with our resources – but it didn't make our lands barren... *that* bit was a lie fabricated by, guess who? Sharmarians..." Miles shook his head and sighed. "Anyway, sorry, I have digressed... Most of our lands were arid *before* we cut down that forest, and we used much of the timber from the Forest of Parchen to create the civilisation we have today. The Pillars of Parchen are what remains. They were created from the last vestigial trees from Parchen's forest. Some of our greatest Enchanters discovered that certain symbols, when carved upon the trunks of the trees, create a space around them where things grow at an unprecedented rate. Crops and animals."

"So they don't need feeding?" Kyra gasped.

Miles nodded. "And that is why those chickens are cooped up so tightly around those pillars. I know it seems cruel, but it *is* the fastest way to raise livestock..." He cleared his throat. "In the space that exists around each Pillar of Parchen, Edra – and other farmers like her – can produce more than five times the amount of food than the laborious and time-consuming methods you Sharmarians use."

"Why are they all hidden away, though?" Bryna asked.

"Yeah," Kyra said, turning back to Miles. "I thought it was strange you never actually *see* any animals around here."

"Well..." Miles grimaced. "Believe it or not, most Gavendarians are not completely comfortable with it either. It makes it easier for them to not think about it when it is out of sight. Also, it is considered unhealthy to spend too much time around a Pillar of Parchen, so farmers adopted a practice of keeping them at a distance from their homes."

Just then, the door opened, and everyone went quiet. Edra hobbled into the room, carrying a large steaming pot with an unpleasant aroma.

"I have made a lovely soup. Lots of vegetables," she said as she placed it down on the table. "Something hearty for the young lass, who's feeling a little sickly."

Edra ran her calloused hand over Bryna's forehead, and Bryna feigned a smile.

Edra then stirred the soup with a ladle and began to fill each of them a bowl. "I have roasted a hen for you as well," she added. "I will bring it out in a tick, just waiting for Jev. He shouldn't be long…"

"I think I will pass on the chicken, thank you," Bryna said as she picked up a spoon and blew upon the soup to cool it a little. "I am not feeling up to meat…"

Chapter 15

Flash

Sidry and Baird set off early in the morning, leaving Shemet behind via the woodlands at the rear of the Academy. They avoided the main roads at first because Baird was worried Greyjor might try to stop them when he caught wind of their departure.

Later in the afternoon, they passed a village, and the sky was beginning to dim. Sidry suggested they find somewhere to stay for the night, but Baird shook his head.

"We're not staying here," he decreed. "We ride further. And camp."

Sidry was surprised by this. Selena had provided them with enough coin to fill their bellies and see them sheltered for several aeights along the road, but Baird's reasoning became clear later when, after they had ridden well beyond that town and set up a shelter beside a river, Baird instructed Sidry to follow him to a glade nearby.

"Change," Baird then said. "Summon your Avatar."

They both transformed in two flashes of light which, in the gloom of dusk, must have been visible for miles.

Sidry understood then. Baird intended them to continue with their training while they were on the road and, to do so, it was wise to keep away from the public eye.

For a few minutes, they warmed up. They circled each other, swinging their blades. Through the last few aeights, they had developed a unique language they used to communicate with each other when they were Avatars. Their mouths, when they were in this form, could only produce polyphonic noises and lacked the capacity for full speech, but their perceptions were heightened. Their augmented eyes could pick up everything around them in much finer detail, smells were more acute, and their ears could distinguish between sounds with an accuracy that was sometimes distracting. All of these enhancements meant that every voluntary movement or noise each of them made – no matter how small – was that much more noticeable. Over time, their vocabulary was growing and becoming more refined, and things such as the slight tilting of the head, the raising of an arm, or even the barest twitch of a muscle could be used to convey meaning between them.

After a while, Baird strode up to Sidry and spread out his arms, baring his chest.

Sidry paused. This gesture was a new signal – one Baird had never used before – so it took him a while to realise what he meant.

He wants me to hurt him, Sidry realised.

At first, Sidry refused. He shook his head. It went against his every instinct to knowingly hurt his mentor. But Baird was insistent. He patted his abdomen – indicating where he wanted Sidry to strike him – and then spread his arms out again.

Sidry eventually gave in to his wishes, raising his blade and positioning the point of it to Baird's belly. The area Baird requested the blow was one of the Avatar's weak spots: a place where two of the glowing thews merged.

Sidry carefully applied pressure, and the end of his blade sank into Baird's midriff. Baird legs shook a little – which Sidry perceived as him suppressing his instinct to fight back.

At least he's not in pain... Sidry thought. He knew from his own experiences that one did not feel pain when they were an Avatar. Not pain as a human would know it, at least. It was uncomfortable but not visceral. It never impaired your ability to function or concentrate. It was one of the things that made the Avatars of Gezra such formidable fighters.

Once Sidry's blade passed through to the other side, he retracted it, took a step back, and waited to see what would happen.

The injury Sidry just inflicted upon Baird was usually enough for an Avatar to reach its limit and the host to revert to human form but, instead, Baird clenched his fists and, in a flash of light, regenerated. Blue energy flared, coursing towards the hole Sidry made in his abdomen, and it began to close.

Once Baird had healed, they began to spar again. But this time, Sidry noticed a difference in his mentor. Baird seemed to be reacting slower than usual. His movements were sluggish, and he struggled to keep up.

For one of the first times, it was Sidry who dealt the finishing blow. He caught Baird at the end of his blade whilst the older man was attempted to block but missed. It bore through his chest. Baird fell back with a thud, reverting to his human guise in a flash of light.

*　　*　　*

It was a peculiar reversal of roles for Sidry to have to care for his mentor whilst he was unconscious. He carried Baird's limp body back to their camp and built a fire.

Once lit, Sidry sat and stared into the flames. His thoughts turned to his friends – like they often did when he was alone and unoccupied. He thought about Bryna. Rivan. Even Kyra. Now he had left Shemet too, it felt like they were even further away – which didn't make any sense because, if anything, they were closer.

Baird woke up after a while. It was dark by then, but Sidry caught sight of him stirring by the other side of the fire.

"It worked," Baird said, sitting up and scratching his beard.

Sidry nodded. "You healed, but you weren't quite the same after. You were slower. Probably explains why I beat you for once."

"There was a burst of light, wasn't there? I think I remember seeing the same thing happen to you when you did it… I think we should call this ability '*flash*'," Baird suggested.

Sidry nodded. "It seems fitting."

*   *   *

Throughout the days which followed, Sidry and Baird experimented more with *flash*.

They didn't avoid civilisation altogether. They often visited settlements but used them as places to purchase supplies rather than rest. This way, they didn't need to worry about hunting nor foraging for food. And yet, they had privacy.

Every evening, once they had finished journeying for the day, they pitched their tent in a secluded place so that they could practice fighting.

Sidry began to gain some leverage in their brawls, but he suspected Baird was going easy on him to help build his confidence. Or maybe Baird just wanted more opportunities to practice using *flash* to regenerate. Sidry tried to not let it bother him. He knew now that he would never best his mentor when it came to combat technique. And why should he? Baird had decades of experience over him. Instead, Sidry took pride that he seemed to have a better grasp over *flash* than Baird did. Sometimes, Baird failed to use it in time and would fall unconscious. Sidry, however, was its discoverer and seemed to have more of an instinct for it.

During Sidry's youth, Baird had encouraged competition between him and the other boys of Jalard – and it had been effective in pushing them all to their limits – but Sidry was an adult now, and he knew he needed to rid himself of that mindset. Baird was not his enemy. The Zakaras and those who created them were.

One night, Sidry discovered another use for *flash.*

Baird had wounded him fairly early in their bout that evening, forcing Sidry to use *flash* to heal himself. He, as usual, became a little languid after that. Sidry had learnt by then that the process of regenerating had consequences beyond an extended downtime once one changed back to human form: it also made you, as an Avatar, less effective and impaired your reflexes. This frustrated Sidry. What use was he ever going to be against an army of Zakaras if he was in a state like *this* when he faced them?

And, just as Sidry was having these thoughts, he found himself unconsciously drawing more *flash*.

It wasn't something Sidry had never tried before – using *flash* when he didn't need to heal himself – so he wasn't expecting it to work.

Nobody was more surprised than him when a rush of energy coursed through his body, invigorating him.

Baird must have noticed it, too, because he froze for a few moments and stared at Sidry.

Sidry then charged at Baird, reigniting the brawl. He felt rejuvenated. Giddy. Drunk almost, but not in a way that was ungainly or clumsy. Sidry's body seemed to work faster than his mind, and it knew what to do.

His mentor backed away. He stumbled. Sidry had to consciously slow himself down – which, for some reason, was a difficult thing for him to do because he was so rallied. Baird struggled to keep up with him, and it wasn't because he was bewildered by what just happened – for he had had more than enough time to recover his wits by now – he simply wasn't fast enough. Sidry swung his blades. He felt empowered. Elated. After all this time, he *finally* had the upper hand over his mentor.

He caught Baird with a blow to his side, and the blade went in. Sidry then withdrew. There was a burst of light as Baird restored himself, and Sidry took a step back to let his mentor heal.

The fight didn't last long after that. Sidry engaged again, but Baird's movements became lethargic and heavy. Sidry caught him with a second blow to his head, and Baird fell.

*   *   *

Sidry woke up to see stars twinkling above him. It was one of those rare nights where only one moon was present, so it was darker than usual.

There was a source of warmth nearby. Sidry turned his

body towards it and saw Baird sitting by the fire with his thighs pulled up to his chest and his arms crossed over his knees. He seemed pensive.

"What did you do?" he asked.

"*Flash...*" Sidry whispered as the delirium of being newly awake ended, and he remembered his last conscious moments. He sat up, excited by the revelation. "We can draw upon it even when we're not hurt!"

"You need to be careful..." Baird said.

"But it makes us stronger," Sidry said. "Didn't you see? I was faster, and I was *beating* you for once! I never–"

"Do you know how long you've been asleep for?" Baird interrupted him.

Sidry shook his head.

"Hours!" Baird said. "And that is not even counting the time that passed until *I* woke up and dragged you back here. Imagine if Zakaras – or someone else – had found us then? Both of us dead to the world!"

"Has it really been *that* long?" Sidry asked.

Baird nodded. "We need to be more careful, Sidry. Who knows. Maybe one day, if we push ourselves too hard, we won't wake up at all!"

"I doubt that," Sidry shook his head. "I trust the Avatars. They haven't let us down before, have they? Why are you upset about this? We've just discovered something that makes us stronger! You saw it, didn't you! We have to try it again. See if–"

"No," Baird shook his head. "We're going to take a break for a few days."

"But–"

"No buts," Baird decreed, making it clear that his decision was final and he was not up for discussing the matter. "You're getting reckless, Sidry, and you won't be any help to anyone if you're dead. We'll take a break for a few days, and then we'll talk about this another time."

* * *

Rivan was glad to leave Edra's house behind. Being stuck there for an entire day while Miles and Kyra went to that market had left him feeling restless and fidgety.

They left early in the morning. By midday – just as Miles promised – they reached the end of the Folds, and the transition was quite dramatic. The flat, barren plains became replaced by precipitous green hills. They made their way along a road that twisted through a valley and saw something they had not seen for some time: trees. Everyone began to feel a little more at ease, and even the air seemed to change, becoming fresher.

"So where are we going, anyway?" Rivan asked Miles when they stopped to eat lunch.

"North," Miles replied.

Rivan huffed. He knew *that* much. He, like every other youth from Jalard who was worth his salt, was perfectly capable of discerning direction – as well as the time of day – by the position the sun held in the sky.

Miles was just patronising him, as usual.

"I mean *why*," Rivan groaned. "What makes you think there are armies up this way?"

"Follow the food," Miles said.

"Follow the food?" Rivan repeated.

Miles nodded. "When Kyra and I went to that market yesterday, it wasn't to ask questions. After all, two strangers snooping around asking dubious questions would have been highly suspicious. I was noting what directions the carriages of food were heading. Think about it, an army comprises thousands of men, and every one of them needs to be fed."

"Judging from the tracks, it does seem like a lot of horses and carts have been this way recently," Kyra said, eyeing the road.

Miles nodded. "And I happen to know that this is a very lowly populated area of Gavendara, so *why* are they going this way? If that much food were being sent to Darlesh, Mordeem, or Chillin, it wouldn't be mysterious at all, but the fact that it is all being sent *here* – of all places – is very peculiar. Also, this area does make sense, strategically, as a place for an army to be stationed for a few reasons. Firstly, because it is sparsely inhabited – so it is discreet, and thus easier to keep anything that goes on around here under hush – and secondly, because it is close to both Llamaleil *and* the Folds; which are both abundant food sources. And it is also not too far away from the path one would tread if they were marching to Sharma from Mordeem anyway. So, it is my belief that we are on the right path."

They got back onto their horses shortly after that and rode on, stopping later at an inn stationed by the side of the road.

Bryna, once again, refused to eat meat that night. A habit she seemed intent on sticking to for the rest of their time in Gavendara. She was also steering away from butter, cheese, and eggs and only accepting vegetables, grain, and fruit. And even with those, she ate them meagrely.

Rivan didn't like the sound of the Pillars of Parchen either but saw little sense in compromising his health over something that was beyond his power to change. He worried about Bryna; Baird had taught them that a balanced diet was vital to keeping healthy and strong.

Miles did a little eavesdropping over a few mugs of ale in the lounge that evening, listening to the conversations of the other travellers. Many of them were merchants, and two of them had just returned from transporting grain to a garrison stationed a couple of days north.

It seemed they were on the right path.

They left early the following morning. The terrain was similar to that of the previous day, but the road narrowed and the hilly copses became so steep and rocky they were forced to skirt around them. It felt like, even though they rode for hours, they weren't covering much distance.

By late afternoon, they reached the top of a mountain and found themselves at a crossroads. It was unclear which way they should go, and it was nearing the end of the day anyway, so Miles decided it best they search for somewhere inconspicuous to make camp. They veered away from the path and explored the wooded areas nearby, finding a grove.

They pitched their tents, and then Kyra climbed one of the trees to see if she could get a high enough vantage to spot anything.

"I think I saw smoke coming from behind one of the hills," she said when she returned. "It could just be a village, though."

"I doubt it," Miles said. "I don't think there *are* any villages here."

"Well, it might be a good place to head to tomorrow then," Kyra said as she sat down.

Miles nodded. "I look forward to hearing your findings when you return."

"You're not coming?" Rivan asked.

"I think we're close now," Miles said. "Far too close to be roaming around as such a large group. I think we should use this place as a base so that the two of you can venture off alone and see what you can find."

"But what about *you?*" Rivan asked.

"It would be unwise for me to attempt any scouting," Miles shook his head. "It requires you to be an accomplished rider and have good tracking skills. I have neither."

"I don't like the idea of leaving you alone," Rivan crossed his arms over his chest.

"I would not be alone," Miles said, turning to Bryna and smiling. "Bryna will be with me."

"You know what I mean," Rivan said flatly. "Someone needs to stay here so they can keep an eye on *you*. Break your legs if you try to do a runner or something. No offence, Bryna…" he added, looking at her. "But you're not the type for breaking legs."

"So what you're saying is, after all this time, you *still* don't trust me?" Miles said.

"Of course not!" Rivan exclaimed.

"I would advise that, for us to get this done as swiftly and effectively as possible, the two of you should *both* go out. Separately," Miles said, looking at Rivan and Kyra.

"You can cover more ground that way, and we'll be out of here sooner. I don't know about you, but I don't like the idea of attempting to cross the Valantian Mountains when winter hits. If you think crossing it was tough a couple of aeights ago, think about what it will be like after the Festival of Manveer. We might not be able to pass at all. We would be forced to stay in Gavendara for the winter."

"I'll take my chances," Rivan said. "Better than coming back one afternoon and being jumped on by a gang of your buddies."

"The idea that I would have the means to arrange that – even if I *wanted* to – is, quite frankly, absurd," Miles said.

"It wouldn't exactly be the first time you've schemed a little ambush upon us, would it?" Rivan said.

"That was… different," Miles said.

"Even if I *do* find an army, how am I supposed to count them all anyway?" Kyra asked, changing the subject. "Didn't you say there could be *thousands* of them? That would take me hours. And what if they're moving–"

"No one is expecting you to have an exact figure," Miles replied, turning to her. "There are methods to estimating numbers that I will give you instruction upon later this evening. I would advise you against getting close enough to see each person individually anyway, as it is too likely you'd be caught."

"What makes you think that it is *you* that gets to go off scouting?" Rivan asked, looking at Kyra.

"Well, *you're* the one who wants to keep a watch on him so much," Kyra replied, gesturing to Miles. "You trust him just as little as I do!" Rivan said. "And you got to be the one who went off the other day when I was stuck in that ruddy farm, grooming his scittin' horse for him!"

"Oh, come on, Rivan," Kyra rolled her eyes. "Let's be honest here. I know we've had that whole rivalry thing going on for years, but we both know that I am a faster rider than you. And I am smaller. I'm better at climbing trees and making my way around unseen. I tell you what, I am willing to admit that you may be *slightly* better with a sword than me, and you're stronger. There you go! Are you happy now? I have *finally* admitted that – but you *know* I have the better skillset for scouting."

Rivan scowled at her, trying to think of a counter-argument, but he couldn't.

Because he knew she was right.

It just irked him that Kyra was, once again, getting to venture off and do the exciting stuff while he got left behind.

"Fine!" he exclaimed as he grabbed his bow. "Have it your way! As fucking usual!"

He walked off to cool his head for a while. It seemed like he was now stuck here for a while, so he explored the area around them to familiarise himself with the surroundings. He noticed some blackberries growing nearby. He didn't have a gathering basket with him, but he memorised its location to tell Bryna about it later.

Goats lived in the ridges of the mountain – or at least Rivan believed they were goats, for they looked a bit different to the ones native to Sharma. They probably took to living out on those crags because it was safe from predators, Rivan guessed, but for him – with his bow – they were easy targets. When he loosed his first arrow, he missed, and they all scattered – leaping to different ledges to get away – but there were no trees for them to hide behind, so Rivan caught one of them with his third arrow, and it fell, its body tumbling down to one of the fissures below.

It took Rivan a while to claim his quarry. He had to climb down a steep ravine – whilst clinging to a series of tree trunks – and then clamber through bushes and shrub. He scratched himself on several brambles in the process but eventually reached the ledge where the goat had fallen and hauled it onto his shoulders.

By the time he returned to the camp, the others had already stoked a fire, and Kyra was busy chopping more wood. Rivan placed the goat on the ground and began to skin it in preparation.

It was worth it in the end. When the sky turned dark,

and some of the meat was ready, he managed to coax Bryna into eating some. She seemed grateful.

*   *   *

Kyra left the following morning as the sun was still rising, and Rivan watched as she prepared. It seemed she was making provision for every scenario that could possibly unfold: taking her bow, a quiver full of arrows, her sword, and a burlap sack loaded with enough supplies to feed both her and her horse for at least two days.

Finally, she unravelled the roll she kept her daggers in and began to slip them into all the secret pockets and pouches she had in her sleeves, boots and leggings.

"I don't think you have enough daggers," Rivan remarked as she attached another one to a strap on the inside of her thigh. "Maybe you could stuff a few into your armpits too."

"Hey, it was one of these which got us out of Shayam's encampment, remember?" she retorted, just before she leapt upon her horse.

"Good luck," Rivan grunted. "Don't do anything stupid."

"Like I would," she huffed and rode off.

*   *   *

Rivan was anxious about Kyra that first day, but he would never admit it. He occupied himself by dealing with the rest of the goat carcass, putting aside some of the meat for them to eat the following evening, and then cutting the rest into strips. He rubbed the strips with salt and suspended them over the fire so that both its smoke and the sun would help dry them.

Bryna went off with her basket to gather those berries and returned later with not just that, but a selection of leaves and some thin rubbery tubers. Rivan didn't recognise them, but Bryna was insistent they were edible. She began to prepare a stew, using some of the leftover meat.

Miles mostly talked. He waffled on about the history of the area they were in. Then, he started to give Rivan a lecture about all the other regions of Gavendara. The friendly, light-hearted manner he assumed was as if they were old friends. It was irritating. It felt like Miles was trying to soften him up so that he could manipulate him. Rivan eventually told the other man, quite firmly, to pipe down, and got a brief period of respite, but it did not take long for Miles to begin orating again. His topic transitioned to the machinations of Gavendarian noble politics. Rivan's head soon began to ache.

Later that afternoon, the stew was ready. It was the best thing Rivan had tasted for aeights. He praised Bryna and filled himself a second bowl.

As the sun began to come down, they all went silent. None of them spoke, but Rivan knew that they were all wondering the same thing.

Why had Kyra not returned yet?

Just when Rivan was about to suggest that they go out and search for her, Kyra strolled into the camp, guiding Swifty by his muzzle to the cluster of trees they were keeping their steeds tethered. She then joined them by the fire, reporting that she had not found anything of note that day.

*   *   *

The following morning, Rivan suggested Kyra borrow his steed so that hers could take a rest. He expected her to flare into one of her irrational outbursts – for she seemed very proud of the bond she had with 'Swifty' – but on this occasion, her pragmatism prevailed, and she agreed.

She returned a little earlier on her second foray, riding into the camp when there was still an hour of sunlight left. She solemnly reported that she had not come across a single soul that day. She did, however, discover a set of tracks that seemed to have been left by a large group on the move.

It was on the fourth day Kyra came across the first conclusive sign of an army.

"I found something!" she exclaimed before she had even tethered her horse.

"What is it?" Miles asked, getting up and walking to her.

"The remains of a camp," she said. "A big one. They didn't clean up after themselves very well!"

"Were there still tracks?" Rivan asked. "Did you see where they were headed?"

She nodded.

"That's great! Miles began, but Kyra spoke again.

"Best hope it doesn't rain tonight, though… they were starting to fade."

*   *   *

Rivan felt apprehensive the following morning when Kyra left; if she *did* find that army, skirting so close to it would be the most crucial and dangerous stage of their entire mission.

Bryna was fidgety that day – she had her needle out and was sewing something which didn't even look like it needed mending – and even Miles was unusually quiet.

Later in the afternoon, Rivan's nerves got the better of him. The sky was beginning to go dim. Why hadn't Kyra returned yet? He climbed a tree to gain a better vantage point and see if he could spot her. He waited there for a while, scanning their surroundings, but the only movement he saw was a large flock of starlings making an aerial display as they flew back to one of the neighbouring hills to roost.

"Boo!" a voice exclaimed, interrupting his thoughts.

Rivan almost fell from the branch he was sitting on and looked down to see Kyra standing at the base of the tree with her arms crossed over her chest.

"Kyra!" he exclaimed. "What the blazes are you doing?"

"Were you looking out for me?" she asked chidingly. "Don't tell me you were *worried*."

"No…" he said. "I was watching the starlings. They were–"

"Nice try," she said. "But I'm not buying it. You're not the kind of guy who watches starlings."

"How long have you been back?" Rivan asked.

"Just arrived," Kyra said. "Didn't you see me from all the way up there? I guess I must be a good scout then. Anyway, are you coming down or what? I have news, and I don't want to have to repeat myself, so I'd appreciate it if all three of you were there when I tell it."

She then walked off, and Rivan scrambled down the tree to catch up.

"I found them," Kyra said once they had all gathered. "Well, some of them, at least. They were marching. I tried to count them," she turned to Miles. "But it was difficult cause they were on the move, and I didn't want to get too close. I think there were about two hundred."

"That's not many," Rivan uttered. "That's not even a proper army!"

"I don't think it was all of them," Kyra said. "I also found another abandoned camp today and snooped around… I don't think it was the first time the site had been used – there was too much crap there – so I think they must be following a bigger group."

"Did you find out where they were going?" Miles asked.

She shook her head. "It got too late, and I had to turn back. Their tracks should still be there in the morning, though. I think I'll take a tent with me tomorrow. Might have to stay somewhere overnight."

"I don't like the idea of that," Rivan said. "We'd have no way of knowing how long you'd be. What if you get caught?"

"Do you have any other suggestions?" she asked.

"If I may interject," Miles said, raising his hand. "We could all, as a *group*, move to a different site. Somewhere closer… Kyra, can you think of somewhere we could set up our tents which would be close enough to this trail you're following and yet hidden enough to limit the risk of being discovered?"

She sniffed. "I think so…"

"Well, that's settled then," Miles said. "We'll leave in the morning."

* * *

They rose at the crack of dawn.

Rivan was glad to be on the move again. He'd begun to feel a bit claustrophobic on that mountainside. Even the prospect of danger – of heading closer to an area where, Kyra suspected, multiple waves of an army were crossing – was somewhat welcome.

Kyra led the way, and they rode discreetly, avoiding the main paths. On a few occasions, she asked them to wait and rode on ahead for periods to survey the area in front of them and confirm the coast was clear.

Later that afternoon, they reached their new base. It was smaller than the last place they had settled, and the only source of water was a spring that trickled so gently it was a great test to Rivan's patience to fill his waterskin. Kyra seemed confident in the location, though, pointing out that with it being on the far side of the mountain they could probably get away with lighting a small fire.

"I don't like it here," Bryna said to Rivan.

"It's not ideal," he admitted. "But we'll just have to make do."

"That is not what I mean," Bryna shook her head. "I can *feel* something."

"What?

She paused. "People have died here."

"When?" Rivan asked.

"I do not know," Bryna said. "I sense no souls... just energy. It lingers when people pass. There is a lot of it here."

"Can't you find out what happened to them?" Rivan asked.

She shook her head. "That would be unwise... I should save my *viga*. You may need my help."

"We'll be careful," Rivan patted her shoulder. "Just let us know if anything changes."

*   *   *

Kyra left the following morning and, initially, Rivan felt a sense of optimism as she rode off. It seemed like everything was drawing to a head, and they were getting closer to fulfilling their objective. Everything they had been through since they left Shemet had been leading to this final, crucial stage. As long as everything went to plan and Kyra didn't get caught, it was quite possible they would be heading back to Sharma soon.

And that was a very welcome prospect.

But soon after she vanished from sight, Rivan's anxiety returned. Once again, he could do nothing but simply wait. He hated it. He had no idea when Kyra would return. Or even if she would return at all.

It came as a great surprise to him when she rode back into the camp shortly after noon.

"What happened?" he asked, running to meet her as she dismounted.

"Nothing *happened*…" she said. "I *did* find them, though. They're actually not that far away."

"What, the entire army?" he asked.

Kyra shook her head. "No, just the group I saw a couple of days ago. They've set up camp in a ravine… it's really quite odd…"

"How so?" Miles asked.

"I think it would be better if I showed you," Kyra said. "Get your horses ready. We'll ride there."

"Is it safe?" Miles asked.

"I think so," Kyra replied. "I found a ridge overlooking their camp, so even if they *do* spot us, we'd have a decent head start."

"But how far away is it?" Miles asked. "Would we make it back here by sundown?"

"That's the other weird thing," Kyra said. "It's quite close if you take the direct route… Whoever is in charge of this army has been leading them around in circles."

*   *   *

Kyra had not been exaggerating when she told them it wasn't far away. Even with Miles and Bryna on tow, it didn't take them long.

"Let's tether the horses here," she said, tugging upon her reins and drawing Swifty to a halt. "We're close now."

They dismounted and guided their steeds to a nearby tree. Once tethered, Kyra gestured for them to follow her further up the hill by foot.

"Now get down," Kyra said, crouching as they neared the top. She crawled forward, and Rivan followed.

Reaching the edge of the precipice, he peered down into the ravine below and saw a series of brown circular tents. He could also see movement. There appeared to be dozens of people down there. It was too far away for his eyes to discern what they were doing.

"See what I mean?" Kyra said. By then, Miles and Bryna had caught up and crouched beside them. "It's just *weird*. Why would they stop *here*? It's a really vulnerable position."

"I wish there were more of us," Rivan said. "It would be *so* easy to ambush them. Just two small groups, come at them from both sides, and boom," he clapped his hands together for effect. "We'd wipe them out. Easy."

Kyra nodded. "It just doesn't make any sense... And like I said, they spent a day marching them around in circles before they arrived here. I found a much more direct route."

"I don't like it here..." Bryna whispered, tugging upon Rivan's sleeve. Rivan looked at her, and he could tell from her expression that she was terrified. Her face was even paler than usual, and her hand – still on his coat – was shaking. "Can we go? Please..."

She isn't suited for all of this, Rivan realised. "Don't worry," he said. "I'll take you back."

"I'll come too," Miles said, drawing away from the edge of the canyon. "I think I have seen enough. You're right, Kyra. This is a very odd place for them to set up camp. From a strategic point, anyway. And I'm not sure I like the idea of us crossing this ravine ourselves. It's in plain sight, so if any other squads were to pass this way, we'd be sure to be seen. I think we're going to have to discuss how we proceed from here. I would prefer to do it back at the camp, though."

"I'll join you later," Kyra said, not taking her eyes away from the sight below them. "I'm going to keep watch for a while… see if anything happens."

"Good idea…" Miles said. "I am sure Rivan can figure out the way back for us. Just be careful. And make sure to come back before it gets dark."

"I won't be too dark tonight anyway. Teanar and Lumnar are both waxing at the moment," Kyra reminded him.

"I think you should still come back before sundown," Rivan advised.

Kyra shrugged. "If you wish."

*   *   *

Rivan spent most of the journey back to camp pondering over what they had just discovered. He couldn't figure out why anyone, in their right mind, would settle a migrating group in a location like that. It made him uneasy. A voice in the back of his head was screaming at him to try to convince the others to pack up and leave, but he couldn't justify it. That squadron was vulnerable in that position – and even if they did discover Kyra's presence, the four of them would have a significant head start at fleeing.

When they reached the camp, Rivan tended to the horses – making sure they were suitably fed and watered – while Miles retired to his tent. By the time Rivan finished, Bryna had stoked the fire and was sitting by it, staring into the flames. She still seemed on edge. Not quite as shaken as she was at that gorge, though.

He busied himself by chopping more wood for the fire. They already had enough to get them through the night, but he didn't know how much longer they were going to be there and wasn't in the mood for being idle. Bryna began to prepare supper.

At some point, Rivan looked over and noticed Bryna had stopped. Her hands were shaking.

"Bryna?" he said.

There was a delayed reaction, but she turned to him eventually. Her eyes seemed to look *through* him rather than at him, and her mouth was agape.

"What's the matter?" he said.

"They're dying…" she whispered.

* * *

At first, the newcomers appeared as a series of dots Kyra could see in the distance, further down the vale. She watched as they drew closer, gaining shape. They were men, she realised. They were still not close enough for her to accurately count their number, but there appeared to be several of them.

Probably just a small party. Sent away to scout or gather food, she thought, as she watched them approach the camp.

Behind the migrating figures, the sun was creeping towards the horizon. Kyra knew she should head back to meet the others soon, but she wanted to stay and find out more. After all this time spent waiting, something was *finally* happening. She wanted to see how it panned out.

It was a slow process, waiting for this small convoy to reach the camp. She cast her eyes across the rest of the area while she waited.

And then, she saw them. Another group. This one was coming from the other side of the ravine.

They probably just sent two parties out, Kyra thought, not quite able to explain the chills going down her spine. Or her strong urge to turn and run. Somehow, she knew this was important, and she should sit this one out and see what happened.

As the two groups closed in, some of the soldiers within the camp came out to meet them. Kyra's eyes darted between the two scenes, trying to keep an eye on what was happening on both sides at once as the events unfolded. The air was beginning to dim. The sun was merging with one of the mountains in the distance, making the sky blur into an orange haze. But, as Kyra predicted, Teanar and Lumnar both appeared that night, bestowing further luminescence upon the valley.

There was a sudden flurry of movement. Kyra gasped. It happened on both sides of the encampment all at once. The figures below – the two groups of people who had approached the camp – seemed to wriggle and grew in size.

They were no longer men, she realised.

She clamped her hand over her mouth and watched, hopelessly, as Zakaras descended upon the men.

*   *   *

Bryna fell back, screaming and convulsing.

"What's wrong?" Rivan asked, dropping the axe and running to her. He hesitated for a moment over whether he should touch her, but she was so clearly in need of help, he grabbed her shoulders. She continued writhing.

"Bryna!" he yelled, pinning her arms to the ground and holding her down. "What's wrong?"

"It hurts!" she cried, tears streaming down the side of her face. "It hurts! It hurts! It *hurts!*"

"What hurts?" Rivan asked, looking her up and down. "What's happened?"

Bryna looked at him then – as if she had only just noticed he was there – and her eyes momentarily cleared and became coherent again. "Rivan... help me..." she pleaded.

"How?" he asked. "What do you want me to do?"

"Give me your dagger," she said.

"Why?"

She winced as another wave of whatever was affecting her seemed to hit her. "Just do it! *Please.*"

Rivan momentarily let go of her – she seemed to have

313

calmed down a little anyway – reached into his belt for one of his daggers, and handed it to her. She grabbed it from him with greedy fingers and turned away.

"Now go," she said.

"Why?" he asked.

"Because you will not like what I am about to do."

"What do you mean?" Rivan croaked.

"Just *go!*" she cried, turning her head to look at him, and that moment, her expression was so pained that it hurt him too. "Please! Leave me!"

"What are you going to do, Bryna?" Rivan asked. He crawled towards her. She had her back to him now, but when he reached her, he saw that she had rolled back her sleeve and pressed the edge of the dagger to her arm.

"No!" he yelled, grabbing hold of her wrist. "What are you doing?"

"It's the only way," she said. "I have to."

"Don't!" Rivan yelled. "Please!"

He wrapped his arms around her. He did not understand what Bryna was going through, but the thought that she felt she had to harm herself to endure it was more than he could bear.

When Rivan embraced her, Bryna's body froze up at first – almost as if she was in disbelief – and then, after a few moments, she relaxed again. She gave in, pressing herself against him.

She rested her chin on his shoulder. He held her tightly.

"Don't Bryna," he whispered, and to his utter disbelief those words come out as a croak.

He was *crying*. Rivan had never cried before. Not that he could remember anyway. If he had, it must have been when he was a child. "Please don't. Just hold me if it helps."

They stayed like that for a while. Both of them crying. Bryna's hand clawed at Rivan's back. The tips of her fingernails dug into his flesh as another wave of pain passed through her. And then it passed. She ran the palm of her hand down the contour of his spine, and Rivan let out an involuntary sigh.

His lips were against her neck, and he found himself doing something he never imagined he would.

He kissed her.

At first, the sentiment behind it was fairly innocent. He brushed his lips upon her cheek, but she responded, shifting her body and pressing herself closer to him. He kissed her again. This time it was upon her lips, and it lingered. They looked at each other.

They both knew, during that moment, they were about to do something they would come to regret.

But they couldn't stop it either.

Bryna needed him. He needed her. It was a tide they could not stop, for it had already swept them away, and they were drifting. Drowning. Together.

*   *   *

Miles watched from the opening of his tent as Rivan and Bryna made love under the moonlight. Neither of them seemed like themselves. It was like they were both possessed.

Was this part of your plan, Grav'aen? Miles wondered.

It had seemed a strange request when Grav'aen asked Miles to engineer events that forced Rivan and Bryna to spend more time together. Miles found it difficult to fathom what the other man's motivations were.

But it certainly seemed to have had an effect. Tangible chemistry had grown between the two of them, and the scene now playing out before Miles was the next stage of that. Miles wondered what Grav'aen's reasons were for wanting such a thing to happen. How could two people becoming enamoured with each other be of any particular consequence?

However hard Miles tried, he could not figure out what Grav'aen's reasoning was.

Besides, Miles was much more worried about the second thing Grav'aen had asked of him.

Chapter 16

The Lost Squadron

They descended upon the camp like waves breaking across a shore. It was dark. The humans were surrounded. Men ran, but there was no escape. The Zakaras, like a tide, swept upon them, hewing flesh, and men screamed and bayed and fell as they were swathed in a sea of blood.

*   *   *

For Bryna, it was agony. A pain that overwhelmed all her other senses. She had never, since the day she'd been reborn as the Descendent of Vai-ris, had to cope with something so severe before.

Not even during the siege in Fraknar.

Then, most of the citizens died *before* Bryna graced the city. All that had been left upon her arrival was lingering energy and restless souls. If anything, it had been invigorating. A splash of cold water that woke her from her psychosis.

She was fortunate enough to miss the massacre that time. Some died during the night they stormed the castle, but during the Festival of Verdana she was empowered. She had a focus – somewhere to channel all that energy – so she didn't have time to *feel.*

But *now*, on this occasion, she had to endure it all. Quietly. Passively. She had to hold back or risk her presence being discovered, so she fought with all her will to block out the flood of souls who, freshly cleaved from their mortal coils, were sharing their torment with her. They called out to her. Begged for deliverance. It was paralysing. She existed in a sphere of torment. One where she was not even fully aware of herself anymore. She was not Bryna, the daughter of Meredith, sister of Jaedin, and friend to others. She was only the Descendent of Vai-ris. There was no room for anything else.

Between it all, she kept seeing a face.

Rivan.

It was him who pulled her through. Through her suffering, she reached for him. He gave her the strength to endure.

During a moment of clarity – between floods of torment – she begged him for a way to give herself relief, but he wouldn't let her.

He held her instead.

It was a shock, feeling his body against hers.

Maybe a shock was what she needed because, for a few moments, it made her forget. She escaped from it all. His arms became her sanctuary.

But then, in the distance – but all too close for Bryna – another man died. Another soul screamed out in celestial suffering, and it was like a bolt of lightning striking her very core.

She pulled Rivan in tighter. It helped, but it wasn't enough. She clung to him. Pressed her fingers into his flesh. She needed him closer.

She felt his lips on her neck, and it was like an inferno. It drove away the pain and enflamed a series of other sensations. Ones that she had never experienced before but craved. Awakened. She tugged upon Rivan, pulling him in closer.

What happened after that was hazy. A distant part of her knew what was happening – and that it would have consequences – yet Bryna couldn't stop it. Her mundane, mortal life, and all of its petty concerns, seemed so meaningless and trivial during those moments. She became a crazed creature of desire and impulse. She didn't care about anything else because, for a while, nothing else existed. Nor mattered. She had an anchor now.

Rivan.

*   *   *

When it was over, neither of them could even look at each other. Rivan held her. Bryna thought that she should shuffle away but couldn't bring herself.

They both stared up at the sky, and Bryna experienced a moment of déjà vu. This wasn't dissimilar to the night she and Jaedin were conceived. When Bryna witnessed it, she had been shocked by Meredith's behaviour. She never thought her mother could be so compulsive and reckless.

Maybe we are not so different... she realised. A tear formed in the corner of her eye and smeared down her cheek. She fought back the urge to wipe it away. She didn't want to move. She knew she would come to regret this. She and Rivan both would.

Rivan opened his mouth to say something.

"Don't," she whispered. "Don't speak. I–"

"I think I can hear Kyra..." he said.

"Really?" Bryna said.

"Yes... can you hear that?"

And then Bryna heard it. Hooves. Galloping towards them.

They both lurched upright and hurriedly began to dress.

Bryna thought that it must have been obvious what had just occurred between herself and Rivan when Kyra emerged from the trees. Rivan was still in the process of fastening his coat, and Bryna was struggling to straighten her breeches.

Kyra, however, was oblivious. "We've got to go!" she exclaimed.

"What's happened?" Miles said, rubbing his eyes sleepily as he emerged from his tent.

"Zakaras!" Kyra said. "They killed them all!"

*   *   *

Jaedin awoke, his dream disturbed by a peculiar feeling. He sat up and placed his hands upon the floor as he steadied his breathing.

"Bryna..." he whispered.

319

It was his sister. Whatever it was that he was feeling, it was coming from the link he shared with her.

But it felt different to all the other times they had communicated this way.

Bryna? he called out to her. He closed his eyes and focussed upon reaching her, but she did not reciprocate the connection. Despite her lack of response, Jaedin was still on the receiving end of sensations from her. They were incoherent, and he couldn't glean much, apart from that she was in distress and wasn't channelling to him consciously. Feelings were leaking out from her uncontrolled.

Jaedin wrapped a blanket around his knees to warm himself and listened for a while. Fangar was sleeping beside him. They were in a barn. Usually, when Jaedin felt cold during the night, he would curl up against him, but he didn't want to wake the rogue.

Jaedin tried to make contact with Bryna again. Still nothing. He could sense she wasn't in any immediate danger – that the source of her torment, whatever it was, was emotional rather than visceral – which came as some relief.

He sighed. Bryna had always been a much better Psymancer than him. The only reason Jaedin could hear her now was because her 'voice' was so much louder than his. He wouldn't be able to commune back unless *she* initiated it.

He lay down and tried to shut her out. Tried to get back to sleep. Eventually, he was successful.

And, just as he was slipping back into unconsciousness again, he heard her.

Jaedin?! she called.

Bryna! he channelled back. Sitting up. *What's happened? I kept hearing you...*

He saw something then within Bryna's mind's eye – Rivan's face – but then Bryna shut him out.

Jaedin, she said. *Kyra just came back from a scouting mission, and she saw them turning a squad of soldiers into Zakaras!*

How many? Jaedin asked.

There was a brief pause. *About two hundred,* Bryna said. *She thinks there may be more. There is a ravine near us, and they're using it as a place to infect them.*

Did any of them see her? Jaedin asked.

Another pause.

She doesn't know, Bryna replied.

How close did she get? Jaedin asked.

Bryna then sent a mental image from her mind to Jaedin's. It was of the ravine as she had seen in earlier that day, with the men camped out below them.

Which way was the wind blowing when Kyra saw them? Jaedin asked.

Hold on. I will ask... Bryna said. *Everyone is shouting and arguing. It is hard to get a word in...*

Do you want me to intervene? Jaedin asked. *Let me speak through you?*

No, don't worry. It's fine, Bryna said. For Jaedin to take control over Bryna's voice, he would need to immerse himself deeper into her mind, and Jaedin suspected there was something there right then which his sister didn't want him to see. *Kyra said she doesn't know which way the wind was blowing.*

Run, Jaedin said to her. *Get out of there!*

But it's the middle of the night, Bryna responded. *We're–*

Run! Jaedin yelled. *Zakara noses are much keener than ours. They may know you're there. They could be chasing after you right now!*

But Miles said we're supposed to find out the numbers of the armies... Bryna said.

That doesn't matter! Jaedin said. *You won't be able to bring back any information to the Synod if you're all dead. Go! **Now!***

Okay, Bryna said. *We're leaving.*

Let me know what happens, Jaedin said. *And don't worry about the Synod. I will write to them and tell them what you've seen.*

*   *   *

Almost three aeights after they left Warling, Astar and Elita finally reached Sarok.

It was a lively town, but not as big as Astar expected it to be. Most of the people there seemed to be in transit: guiding laden carriages from one side to the other, or hauling heaped wagons loaded with goods towards the market. The actual residents were brassy and gregarious individuals – yet, for all their zeal, they were not unfriendly. Astar had never been this far south before but Sarok, it seemed, was the sort of place where one would not last long unless they possessed some sass.

Elita fitted in well. Of course. As they made their way through the market, searching for The Pearl and Jackdaw, she flitted between the stalls, bartering for goods she neither needed nor intended to buy. Flicking her hair, laughing, and flirting.

"Can't we just get going?!" Astar muttered after curtailing a rather lengthy discussion with a silk trader. "We're supposed to be inconspicuous, remember!"

"I thought you were glamouring me?" Elita said. "Aren't I supposed to be a plain-faced brunette right now?"

"Yes," Astar said. He had, shortly after they left Warling, taken to using his magic to alter Elita's appearance. At least while they were in the public eye. It was far less taxing upon his *viga* than making the two of them invisible. "But it's not effortless, you know. When you swish around, it drains me!"

"Well, you've had plenty of practice…" she uttered. Astar did not know whether she was insinuating that he also had a tendency to 'swish' or commenting on his habit of glamouring himself. He did not bother to find out either. He had long accepted by then that Elita simply *always* had to have the last word, and conceding that privilege was the quickest way to buy her reticence.

For Astar's own disguise, he was simply *not* casting an illusion around himself. He was making sure *Elita* still saw him as he liked to be favoured, of course, but the rest of the public now saw him as he truly was. Most people knew him as the favourable haze he lived through anyway, so it was the easiest way not to be recognised. The only people who knew what he actually looked like were Veldra and Grav'aen.

And Elita, to his vexation. Not only had she seen him that night at the Institute, but now she had seen him sleep many times whilst on the road together.

It took them a while to find The Pearl and Jackdaw. It wasn't on the street where most of the other inns were, but down one of the alleys. On the outside, it looked rather tired and dingy, but once they stepped through the door they found themselves in a warm alehouse that was in fairly good shape and had a rather large fireplace.

The man behind the bar was polishing tankards. At first, he pretended not to notice their presence.

"We are looking for a man called Ilarn," Astar said, approaching him.

The barkeep frowned at him and then turned his attention back to polishing. "Ilarn is busy…" he said. "Come back this evening."

"We need to see him as soon as possible!" Astar said. "I was sent here by someone. We–"

He was cut off by Elita, who put a hand on Astar's arm and breezed past him. "Hello," she said to the stranger, crossing her arms over the counter and leaning towards him. "We have come from very far!" She smiled. "And this is a *very* lovely town, isn't it?"

She carried on talking. And then, she began to flutter her eyelashes, flick her hair, and break up parts of her speech with the occasional giggle. She even, at one point, stroked the man's beard.

She seemed to have once again forgotten that – thanks to Astar's magic – she currently possessed the appearance of a girl much homelier than her usual self. But the strange thing was it that didn't seem to matter. The barkeep became allured by her anyway. Astar came to realise then that Elita's looks were only a part of her appeal. It was her presence that truly beguiled people.

Astar knew what Elita was doing. The barkeep was probably all-too-aware of what she was doing too, but it didn't make it any less effective.

Astar decided to lend Elita some assistance. He altered the mirage he was casting around her and gradually lifted it, restoring her face to its usual splendour. He kept her hair brown, though. To change it back to its usual blonde would have aroused suspicion – and even though they were not on the road anymore, they still needed to be cautious. Elita's hair was one of her most distinctive features.

"Take a seat," the barkeep grunted and gestured to one of the tables in the corner of the room. "I'll get Ilarn for you."

*   *   *

The barkeep poured them both a cup of ale and wandered off, leaving them alone in the foyer. It was strange that the place had no customers. It was still the morning hours, but Astar suspected the residents of Sarok were not the sort to be opposed to having a tipple at this time of day.

While they waited, Elita tried to initiate small talk, but Astar just gave her abrupt replies that did nothing to advance the conversation. He was wary of speaking too much in this place as, for all they knew, people could be listening, and Astar was worried Elita might let something slip. He sipped upon his ale and watched the door, waiting for something to happen.

The barkeep returned, with a man following him.

"Greetings," he said, introducing himself to Elita first. "My name is Ilarn."

Astar stared at him as he shook Elita's hand. He wasn't quite what Astar expected from a smuggler. Not that Astar had ever met one before. He'd imagined someone scruffier, but Ilarn was clean-shaven and his hair was cut short and styled in the current Mordeemian fashion of combed-back sides. He was wearing a rather elegant red waistcoat over a white tunic.

As Elita shook his hand, she abandoned her alias and gave Ilarn her real name. Astar wanted to kick her for that. Since they had left Warling, she'd been calling herself 'Racha', and Astar had been 'Lew'.

Astar knew this man was supposed to be a friend of his uncle, but he was still wary over whether to trust him.

"And you?" Ilarn enquired, turning to Astar.

"I am…" Astar hesitated. "A friend…" he went with. "Of Lord Marven of Warling."

Ilarn's eyes widened a little at the mention of his uncle, but not in a hostile manner. "Oh…" he said, seating himself. "And do you have proof of this affiliation?"

Astar brought out a scroll from the inside of his coat and passed it to him. Ilarn examined the seal – his eyes widening briefly – and then opened it and began to read.

Astar did not know its contents. His uncle gave it to him just before he left and said it was for Ilarn's eyes only. Astar had been tempted, on more than one occasion, to open it, but he didn't want to break the seal. Its sigil was one that Astar had never seen before but was certainly not the official stamp of the House of Warling. Astar suspected it carried some weight with the smuggler sitting before him.

After a few minutes, Ilarn placed the scroll back on the table and laid his hand upon it. "I am afraid I have some bad news…" he said.

"What is it?" Astar asked.

"Your uncle has requested I see you get passage through the Levian Mountains," Ilarn said. Astar inwardly cursed, realising that, somewhere in that letter, Marven must have given away his identity. Astar wasn't sure if he was ready to trust this man yet, but Elita and his uncle seemed to have made that decision for him. "And, until very recently, I was the man to come to if you wanted to arrange such things," Ilarn said. "But there have recently been some complications."

"What kind of complications?" Astar asked.

"The Levian Mountain Pass has been blocked," Ilarn said. "Access was cut off several aeights ago. Under the order of King Wilard himself."

"I…" Astar began and then paused to consider his next words carefully. Even though this man knew his identity now, Astar was still wary. "Am Blessed. I could probably get us past a few guards."

"Unless your Blessing – whatever it may be – includes the ability to fly, I very much doubt you would make it," Ilarn said. "King Wilard sent a group of mages down from Mordeem to conjure a series of landslides to make sure the trail would be impassable. Rumour has it they did a pretty thorough job, too."

Astar cursed.

"So, what are we to do then?" Elita asked. "Is there *any* other way you could help us?"

"Do either of you know how to use waystones?" Ilarn said.

Astar shook his head. As did Elita. Astar had never even *seen* a waystone, let alone used one. Rumour had it that there were very few Enchanters in Gavendara with the skill to make them, so they were rare.

"That's a shame," Ilarn sighed. "I happen to know Lord Galrath has been secretly hoarding up quite a supply. Some were smuggled across the border, and they were all headed in his direction."

"*Sharma* can produce waystones?" Astar said.

Ilarn nodded. "Not quite as many as we can, but they have Enchanters too. Very skilled ones, from what I hear."

Astar was surprised by this. Enchanting was a highly skilled craft. One that required many years of study before one became adept enough to produce items as complex as waystones. Astar had assumed that, with such a high proportion of the Sharmarian population being farmers, they wouldn't have the means to produce such things.

"Anyway," Ilarn said, leaning forward and rubbing his hands together. "That 'skill' you said you have –

whatever it is – would it be enough to get inside the keep at Falam and find those waystones? You could make a lot of money off waystones, kid. Even if you don't know how to use them yourself."

"I have no interest in making any damn money!" Astar exclaimed. "If I was, do you think I would have run away from Llamaleil?"

"In all respect, I do not know much of your circumstances," Ilarn said.

"Not even in that bloody biography my uncle wrote about me?" Astar exclaimed, gesturing to the scroll on the table.

"Your uncle was actually suitably discreet and did not reveal much about you at all," Ilarn said, lifting the paper. "You can read it if you like. I only guessed he was your uncle because I happen to know that he is childless, and you bear a resemblance to him. It was *you* who confirmed my suspicions."

"We have some very influential men looking for us," Elita said in an attempt to rescue the situation. "And we need to get away. If you can't get us to Babua, where else do you suggest we go? Is there another way you could help?"

Ilarn stared at the table for a few moments before he answered. "I could possibly get you across the Valantian Mountains," he said. "But I would need to discuss in further detail just what kind of 'skill' this young man has."

"Across the Valantian Mountains!" Astar exclaimed. "That's in *Sharma*!"

Ilarn nodded.

"No way!" Astar said. "I'm not going to that bloody place. That's like jumping into a pit of snakes to escape from the wolves!"

"There is another option," Ilarn said. "Another way to get you to the south… but it does have its own risks…"

"What is it?" Astar asked.

"There is a small dock to the south of here in a place called Dotto. I could find out if any boats are leaving there for Inez but, as I am sure you are already aware, sea travel comes with risks. And if the moons are not in favourable cycles right now, there won't be any leaving anyway. But I *can* make enquiries for you if you like."

Astar turned to Elita.

"It's your call," she said, pulling a face. She didn't seem thrilled by the idea. "It seems we're stuck between a rock and a hard place…"

Astar sighed. He had never been on a boat at sea before – not many people ever did such a thing – but it was said to be a very uncomfortable experience. Very few inlanders attempted it, and there were reasons for that. Seafarers were said to live short lives.

"We will think about it," Astar said. "How long would it take you to find out if it is possible?"

"A few days," Ilarn shrugged. "In the meantime, I could find a place for you to stay if you like. We do have a few rooms here but suspect they won't quite live up to the standards of a little lordling like yourself. Plus, The Pearl and Jackdaw has a somewhat muddied reputation, so it's one of the first places people come to when they are looking for fugitives. I would therefore suggest you find somewhere else."

*　　*　　*

When Dareth stepped into the inn, a cacophony of voices greeted him. It was late, but people were still drinking. A particularly rowdy group were sitting around one of the tables, listening to a man with a rather bushy beard tell a story and, at the moment Dareth walked past, he brought the tale to its final punchline, and they burst into a fit of laughter.

Dareth didn't care to listen. He strolled straight up to the innkeeper.

"Are you staying here?" the innkeeper said. "Sorry, but I don't know your face…"

Dareth shook his head. "No, I've just arrived."

The innkeeper seemed somewhat taken aback by that

answer. He turned his eyes to the window and frowned.

Dareth could guess what he was thinking; it was past midnight, and this inn was a waystop for traders and in the middle of nowhere. There was only one moon in the sky that night, and it was dark. Way too dark for a man to be riding alone.

But Dareth was not just any man.

"Do you need a bed?" the barkeep asked. "I've only got one berth left... it's small, but a young man your size could squeeze into it."

"No," Dareth shook his head. "I'm not staying. I'm looking for some friends of mine."

"Many faces pass through this place," the man replied, casting his eyes across the bar. "It's tasking to remember them all... how long ago would they have been here?"

"A couple of aeights ago, I believe," Dareth said. "And they're not the sort forgotten easily. There were four. Two girls, both about my age. And two men."

The man's eyes lit up. "Was one of the lasses a little strange looking?" he said. "Dark hair and spooky eyes? I think they were purple. If you can believe that!"

Dareth nodded. "Yeah, that's the one. She's quiet too. Her friend isn't, though. She's loud."

"Yes!" he said. "I remember them well! They came here twice."

"Twice?" Dareth repeated.

He nodded. "The first time was a couple of aeights ago – like you said – and they were heading north. But then they were back again seven days later."

"Why?" Dareth asked.

"Who knows?" he shrugged. "They seemed in a rush though as they didn't stay the second time. Just bought some bread and other snippets and jumped back on their horses. They were heading south."

"And they didn't say where they were going?" Dareth asked.

The man shook his head. "They didn't, but the Folds be that way."

Dareth was familiar with the Folds; he had just come

from there. "Okay…" Dareth said as he turned and walked away. "Thank you."

"You're not riding off again, are you?" the barkeep asked. "It's the dead of the night!"

Dareth didn't respond. He just continued walking.

When Dareth returned outside, he joined the road again and headed south, back the direction he'd just come.

Usually, turning back like this would be frustrating. But, on this occasion, Dareth was feeling rather smug.

The distance between him and those he was pursuing had just halved.

I'm getting close… Dareth realised.

The first aeight of his search had been utterly fruitless. No matter how many people Dareth questioned, he failed to find any sign of them.

Earlier that day, however, he had finally received his first clue.

An old lady called Edra, who lived in a farmhouse within the Folds, had seen them. She had even remembered their names.

Bryna, Kyra, Rivan, and Kevan, she had said, when Dareth asked her. *They went north, they did.*

It didn't take much stretching of Dareth's mind to deduce that 'Kevan' was likely just an alias Miles was using. The others had been foolish enough to travel by their real names.

Once Dareth had cleared a fair amount of distance between himself and the inn, he summoned his Avatar of Gezra and began to sprint. The road streaked by in a blur. His feet made the ground shudder with each stride he made.

Dareth had ditched his horse a couple of aeights ago and begun to travel this way instead. It was faster. He could clear many times more distance than any steed could carry him.

It meant that he had to travel at night instead – so as to not be seen – but the darkness was not a problem for him. Not with his enhanced sight.

Despite only travelling at night, Dareth had crossed

paths with several people, and they had witnessed him in his Avatar form. He wasn't too worried about that, though. Grav'aen had ordered Dareth to be 'discreet'; a vage stipulation that was open to Dareth's own interpretation.

Dareth had become well accustomed to stretching the limits of his bloodoath. Whenever he came close to breaking it, the scar tingled. As if it to warn him. This way, Dareth always knew how much he could get away with.

Even if people did see Dareth in his Avatar, what exactly could they do about it? Dareth was near invincible.

The only thing he was concerned about right now was finding Kyra.

Because he was going to kill her.

*   *   *

"We're getting close," Baird announced to Sidry.

"Really?" Sidry asked.

Baird nodded, pointing to a settlement that had just appeared in the valley below. "I recognise that place," he said. "We should reach Seeker's Hill by the afternoon."

"And what's the plan?" Sidry asked.

"I don't think we *can* have a plan, as such," Baird scratched his head. "We're going to have to just call in."

"We're not going to at least take a look around first?" Sidry asked. "Make sure it's safe?"

Baird shook his head. "The location for Seeker's Hill was chosen for a reason, Sidry; it is a place which is difficult for outsiders to get a glimpse inside. Also, it's a *training* ground, so they'll have patrols and maybe even be scouting exercises going on. I don't think it'd go down too well if they caught us snooping around there, so we're going to have to just call in and talk to them. We're not exactly in a position to go storming in and making accusations. We have no authority here."

"But there might be a Zakara among them…" Sidry

reminded him. He began to feel uneasy.

"Yes… that is true," Baird said. "But let's not be brash. It's possible the creature Jaedin detected is not even a member of this squad and went somewhere else. We're just going to have to go in and see what happens. But be wary, Sidry, and don't do anything reckless. *I* will do the talking."

*　　*　　*

After riding a while, Baird decided it best they make the last leg of the journey by foot, so they tethered their horses to a cluster of trees and left most of their gear behind.

When they ventured deeper into the woodland, Sidry scanned the ground to see if he could spot tracks or any other signs that this area was inhabited. He didn't find anything. Baird seemed sure that they were heading in the right direction, though, so he didn't question it. It came as a great surprise when a wattle-style fence appeared before them. Sidry stared at it. It seemed to have come from nowhere; he had still not seen any footprints, heard any noises, nor come across any other signs that there were people here. The weave of the fence's wooden strips was so tight he couldn't see anything past it.

Sidry and Baird crept their way around it until they came across a gate.

Baird hailed. At first, there was no response, so he called out again. Sidry then heard footsteps on the other side, followed by a hatch opening. A face appeared in the aperture.

"Who's there?" a man asked. His eyes went from Baird to Sidry.

"I would like to speak to your captain," Baird said, stepping closer. "His name is–"

"Stay back!" the man warned.

Baird halted, lifting his hands to demonstrate that he was unarmed. "We have come from Shemet…" he said. "And there is a matter I wish to discuss with you. If you would just let me explain–"

"We take orders from Greyjor! Greyjor, and no one else!" the man said.

Baird frowned. "But that is not–"

"*No one but **Greyjor**!*" the man screamed, and this time his voice came out as a rasp and saliva sprayed from his mouth. "We wait for *him!*"

The hairs on the back of Sidry's neck stood on end.

He had a bad feeling about this. A very bad feeling.

"What in damnation is going on here?!" Baird asked. "This is supposed to be a–"

The gate began to rattle.

Baird and Sidry turned to each other, their eyes widening. Sidry could hear noises coming from the other side.

Baird took a step closer to peer through the aperture. He gasped. Backed away.

The gate flew open.

Everything happened so fast Sidry didn't have time to think. He acted upon instinct, summoning his Avatar. When the flash of light ended, a hoard of Zakaras burst out from the opening, some of them colliding into each other as they poured through.

Baird charged at them, making a gesture with his arm as he did so.

Split up! the signal said.

Sidry complied with his mentor's wishes, bending his knees and launching himself over the fence.

Zakaras awaited on the other side. Too many for Sidry to count.

He unleashed his blades and twirled them, felling two of the creatures as he landed. He ducked, narrowly missing a pair of claws. Sidry swung his blades again, bisecting the Zakara before him. The two halves of its body fell, innards still wriggling. Sidry was surrounded – Zakaras were coming at him from all sides and closing in fast – so he launched himself into the air again.

He landed, and waves of Zakaras rushed to meet him. Sidry charged towards the nearest group, cutting through the neck of the first and then driving his blade into the path of the next. His blade bore into its abdominal flesh and, whilst still buried in its guts, Sidry somersaulted, his feet going up into the air. As his body flipped, his blade twisted through the creature's insides, cleaving through its ribcage, neck, and then its head.

Sidry struck his other blade upon the ground before him as he landed, dealing a mortal blow to the next Zakara in his path.

Claws raked his back.

Shit! he thought as he righted himself. He shoved the creature away and leapt to the nearest free space to recover.

Once Sidry landed, more came for him. He spun around. They were coming from all sides. Closing in. He cursed. He shouldn't have jumped so far. He was deep within their base now, and Baird was far away.

Sidry charged to meet the nearest drove of Zakaras. They were stampeding towards him. He swung his blades – he dealt no fatal injuries, but he bought himself enough time to leap away again. He needed to reunite with Baird.

He landed amidst another cluster of the creatures. Sidry flattened one to the ground and drove both of his blades into its eyes. It shrieked. It had a scaly green body and six arms. It struck Sidry on the side of his head, but Sidry ignored the blow and drove the points of his blades deeper into its eye-sockets and its head. It went limp.

Tentacles coiled around Sidry's arms and tightened. They tried to reel him in, but he resisted. He summoned upon all his strength and stretched the creature's leathery appendages until they snapped.

But it came at a cost. While occupied, another monster came up from behind and stabbed Sidry in the back. He felt a peculiar sensation and looked down to see that a large chela had emerged from his stomach. The forceps flexed and then tightened again, searching for purchase.

Sidry disengaged himself, feeling the pull of the claw as it dragged through his insides. It passed through. He was free. He ran, drawing upon *flash*. It was a grave injury. It took a while for Sidry to regenerate.

Another Zakara leapt at him, wrapping its arms around Sidry's neck and sinking teeth into his shoulder. Sidry fell. It was on top of him, a bearish creature with a fanged mouth. It went to bite him again, and Sidry wasn't fast enough to stop it. He could only jerk his head away so that the teeth went into his neck instead of his face.

I need more! Sidry realised.

He drew upon *flash*, and there was another burst of light. The creature was propelled away, its legs and arms flailing.

Sidry leapt back to his feet, noticing that not just one but a few Zakaras within his radius had just been pushed back by the flash of light when he drew *flash*.

Had he just discovered another new ability?

Sidry didn't have time to dwell upon it; Zakaras were closing in again.

One of them leapt over the heads of its comrades to get at Sidry, its arms swinging. But Sidry twisted away from its path and, as the creature landed, drove his blade down upon its neck, beheading it. Another Zakara leapt upon Sidry's back, raking its claws. Sidry grabbed one of its arms in each hand and pulled them apart. He had a larger arm span than the creature, and he was stronger too, so he tore it in two. Sidry dropped the two halves. He drew more *flash*. Not because his most recent wound needed healing. He just wanted more power.

Sidry circled his blades to stop the Zakaras from closing in. The creatures drew back, but not for long. One of them sent its tentacles jutting towards him, and Sidry leapt away, landing upon another creature and driving his foot into its skull until it cracked open.

A tentacle coiled around Sidry's heel, and he didn't have time to fight free. Another Zakara leapt upon him. He tried to shake it off. A second tentacle came. And another. Sidry managed to free himself from the Zakara clinging to his back, but another tentacle wound around his other leg.

And then all four of the tentacles began to pull at him.

Sidry panicked. He didn't know what to do, so he drew more *flash*, causing a flare of white light. Some of the creatures closest to him fell back. Sidry saw it properly this time and witnessed the moment that a wave of energy burst out from his body and repelled them.

It felt *good*.

It didn't buy him much time, though: the Zakaras righted themselves and came at him again.

*I need **more**!* Sidry thought, summoning another wave of *flash*. This time, the creatures were driven back further and more violently. One of them didn't even rise.

The rest of them, however, crawled back to their feet. Sidry met the nearest cluster head-on, swinging his blades. He beheaded one. Dismembered another. He spun around to face the next. He was charged with *flash* now – glowing brighter than he ever had before – and his blades seemed to be working faster than his mind. He twirled and twisted, cutting down Zakara after Zakara. Never letting any of them get too close. They were all around him, but he managed to keep them at bay.

For a while.

Eventually, Sidry became aware of a peculiar sensation in his arm. He held it up to his face. The blade was covered in a dark, sticky ichor and melting – dissolving before his very eyes in a cloud of smoke.

The Zakara Sidry had just struck had corrosive blood. It had been a long time since Sidry had encountered one with that trait. It was a rare one.

Sidry drew upon *flash* again. He knew he had already drawn too much, and Baird had warned him to be careful, but he had no other choice. It was either that or let himself be defeated.

He used the fresh burst of energy to regenerate his arm. It grew back.

Sidry cast his eyes around himself. He was still surrounded. There were Zakaras everywhere. He knew he was dangerously close to being overwhelmed. He looked for Baird, but his mentor was nowhere in sight.

Sidry gathered more *flash*. He needed to be stronger.

Better. He needed to kill them **all**. Every single one.

More!

His whole body began to glow. The energy was intoxicating. Overwhelming. Hard to contain.

He stared at the monsters. He wanted to kill them. Kill them *all!*

More!

The *flash* grew. Sidry became a being of it. He knew nothing else, and he couldn't contain it anymore.

It consumed him.

Chapter 17

An Old Friend

The Valantian Mountains were whiter than they were a few aeights ago. Of that, Miles was certain. An encroaching, jagged outline in the distance. One could not describe its icy peaks as 'on the horizon', for they towered towards the sky and inhabited a space above that.

They had almost reached Sarok. Miles recognised the contour on the summit before them. The town was in sight.

We need to hurry, Miles thought, eyeing the mountains behind it. He knew its crossing was going to be much more arduous than the previous occasion. Not just considering how much colder it was, but Miles and his group were in a weakened physical shape.

Over an aeight had passed since Kyra witnessed the massacre, and they'd been on the run ever since. Kyra's account had been nothing short of terrifying. All of them knew what the implications were. Those men were Zakaras now. They would soon rise again.

And Jaedin warned them they might have caught Kyra's scent.

They left many of their possessions behind, only loading the bare essentials onto their horses in their rush to escape. They rode for the entire night and a day without stopping. It wasn't until the second evening they permitted themselves any rest. And even that was a short respite; they pitched only one of their tents to save time, slept in shifts, and packed up again as soon as the sun rose.

None of them slept much in the days which followed, but they managed to cross the Folds in almost half the time it took before.

The horses were in bad shape. Miles felt guilty every time he flicked the reins, urging his steed to pick up the pace, but he had no choice.

They were close to the border now. Miles felt some relief in that. Once they reached the gatehouse on the Sharmarian side, they would be safe. Miles was hoping he might be able to talk the guards into giving them fresh horses so they could ride to Shemet with better haste.

As they rode into the outskirts of Sarok, Miles checked the sun's position in the sky. A few hours of daylight remained. He held an inner debate with himself as to how to proceed. They could rest comfortably here. Or, if they pushed themselves, they could ride on further. Possibly even reach Passerskeep, which would give them a better head start for the challenging climb which lay ahead for them the next day.

But Miles was also aware that such a course of action could be risky. Passerskeep had a garrison. It had soldiers.

Miles reminded himself that there were a couple of small villages on the road between Sarok and Passerskeep. Perhaps that would be a safer compromise. One of them may have an inn they could stay in. Miles could even try to buy their silence by slipping them a few extra coins.

"Let's make our way through here as quickly as we can," Miles said through the side of his mouth as they approached the first street of Sarok. "But don't look too rushed. Speak to no one unless they approach you. Just try not to be noticed…"

Miles had already braced himself for the usual tirade of insolence from Rivan – and even Kyra's customary sequence of annoying questions – but they were both surprisingly compliant that day and made no comment.

Miles led them into the town, warily casting his gaze up and down as they passed the outskirts and made towards the centre. He noticed, almost immediately, there seemed to be a rather sullen ambience in the air. Something was off. Sarok was usually a vibrant place. The kind of town where every passer-by was encouraged to engage. But the people weren't radiating their chronic exuberance that day. And, even more telling, nobody tried to coax them into an inn or sell them anything.

Miles didn't know the reason for this – perhaps a resident had recently passed, or their taxes had been raised – he just hoped it was nothing that would cause them any delay. He wanted to pass through as swiftly as possible.

Initially, it seemed like luck was on their side. They got through the market quarter without any issues, but then, just as they were about to leave, Miles caught sight of a blockade in the middle of the road where a queue of carriages had formed.

Miles gasped, and his heart jerked within his chest. The men forming the blockade were wearing the regalia of the Royal Guard, and there were ten of them.

"This way. *Now…*" Miles muttered, steering his horse down one of the side streets. The others followed him and, once they had cleared a few paces, Miles drew to a halt.

"What was that about?" Kyra asked.

"I'm not sure. But you saw them didn't you?" Miles said. "Those men blocking the road."

Kyra and Rivan both nodded.

"It's the Royal Guard again," Miles said.

Kyra's eyes widened. "The Royal Guard?" she repeated. "I didn't realise… wait… does that mean *the King* is here?"

"No!" Miles hissed, pressing a finger to his lips. "And lower your voice. The Royal Guard are not *literally* guards – well, not all of them – they're patrollers. They're retainers of the King. They enforce his will."

"So what are they doing here?" Rivan asked.

"I don't *know!*" Miles muttered. "But if I'd known they *were* here, we wouldn't have come."

As Miles was speaking, he saw movement by the junction they'd just come from. It was one of the carriages from the blockade. The man guiding it was turning back, and he seemed rather disgruntled.

"Wait here," Miles said as he dismounted.

"Where are you going?" Kyra asked, putting a hand on her hip.

"To find out what's going on," Miles said. "Keep an eye on my horse."

Miles was cautious about approaching the man in the chariot. To do so within sight of the Royal Guard may have aroused suspicion. At first, he followed him for a while – making himself seem occupied with other errands – but after clearing a safe amount of distance from the blockade, Miles spoke.

"Any news from across the border?" he asked.

The sour-faced rider cleared his throat. "How would I ruddy know?"

"Oh…" Miles said, feigning surprise. The man's use of the word 'ruddy' was telling – it was a curse usually cast from the lips of Sharmarians. *He's probably a trader*, Miles thought. Almost all who made a living carting goods from one side of the border to the other were from Sharma, as it was much easier for them to enter Gavendara than it was for Gavendarians to go the opposite way. "Sorry, I just assumed you came from… well, never mind," Miles said, whilst assuming his best imitation of a Sharmarian accent.

The man looked at him and drew his reins, bringing the carriage to a halt. "You're from Sharma?" he asked.

Miles nodded. "Torna, born and bred."

"Why didn't you say before?" the man said, his entire bearing towards him changing. "The bastards won't let me through! I've got a whole wagon full of goods here and a family to feed back in Chandra! What are they expecting me to *do!*?"

"Did they say *why*?" Miles asked. "Me and my companions were just about to saddle up home ourselves."

He spat upon the road and shook his head. "Nope. They wouldn't tell me a ruddy thing. Thank the Gods I have a friend here, that's all I can say. Would be kipping rough otherwise. Do *you* have somewhere to stay? I can ask around if you like. I know a few here… one of them might be able to put you up. They're quite friendly. Most of them."

"It's okay," Miles said. "I have others with me, and we already have beds for the night. But thank you. Can I ask what you are planning to do?"

"Guess I just need to wait," he shrugged. "Got no other ruddy choice, have I? Hope they sort it soon cause I'll be stuck here all winter otherwise. Can't lug this ruddy thing up the mountain when the snow hits, can I?" he thumbed behind his shoulder to the main body of the carriage.

"Yes, that would be difficult..." Miles grimaced. "Anyway, I best be off. Good day to you and good luck."

"Aye," he said, starting up his carriage again and then waving. "And you too."

This is bad, Miles thought as he made his way back to the others. *Very bad.*

Sharma had always kept a tight regimen over their side of the border – with particular care being taken over who they let *in* – but Gavendara had not closed off their side for years. It seemed a rather drastic move. The trade of goods between Sharma and Gavendara was a mutually favourable arrangement that benefitted both nations. Cutting it off almost seemed like an act of war.

We knew war was coming... Miles reminded himself.

He never thought it would be so soon.

Whatever happens, I lose... Miles realised, remembering the terrible deed Grav'aen asked him to do when he returned to Shemet.

He'd thought it peculiar when Grav'aen let him off the hook, but Miles knew better now. Grav'aen only struck that deal as insurance. To engineer the game so that, even if Miles somehow managed to achieve his objective and return to Sharma unscathed, Grav'aen still benefitted. It did not mean he'd left Miles unfettered.

A part of Miles felt relieved by the thought he might not be able to return Sharma – and do what Grav'aen expected of him – but then he thought about Jaedin. He remembered that it was the only way to save him. That thought reinforced Miles' conviction.

*We **have** to get back to Sharma!* Miles decided. *Somehow…*

When Miles reunited with the others, even Bryna seemed on edge.

"I have some bad news," Miles said. He saw little point in dallying, so cut to the chase and told them about the exchange he'd just had with the trader.

Rivan swore. A little too loudly, so Miles gave him a reproachful look, and the younger man covered his mouth.

"Can't we just sneak past them?" Kyra said.

"No," Miles shook his head. "That would be impossible. This town is surrounded by crags. And even *if* we did manage to get past those guards, we would later have to go near Passerskeep, and that place is swarming with soldiers. They're not letting anyone through, so we would stick out like a sore thumb."

"What about the other passes?" Rivan asked. "You said this wasn't the only way to cross the border, didn't you?"

"Yes," Miles replied. "There are two other crossings… the nearest is a few days away, and it is regulated much tighter than this one. *This* one is actually the more discreet option – the one often used by crooks and outlaws, believe it or not – so if the border is being blocked *here*, it is almost certain the others are too."

"So what are we going to do?" Kyra asked.

"I don't know…" Miles said, quite honestly. This was the first time since they'd left Shemet that he felt stuck for options. He couldn't think of a plan. It seemed they had nothing at their disposal. "Let's just turn back, for now… leave this town and find somewhere to camp further down the mountain. Gods know we all need the rest – and the horses do too – so we might as well make the most of this little snag to recover our strength. We'll think of a plan in the morning when our heads are a bit clearer."

None of them argued, but Miles could tell they were far from satisfied.

They seemed dispirited and made their way back through the town sombrely. Miles knew he needed to think up a course of action and do it soon, or his tenuous hold as the foremost decision-maker of this group could be at stake.

As they rode, Miles caught sight of a face. One which caught his eye and caused him to jolt in his saddle. He pulled his horse to a halt and looked at her again.

The girl on the other side of the road seemed familiar to him.

It took a moment for Miles to realise where it was that he recognised her.

Whilst he was staring at her, she seemed to notice and looked back at him. Her eyes widened.

It can't be... Miles thought.

"What's the matter?" Kyra asked, appearing in front of Miles. "You've stopped."

"I... recognise her..." Miles whispered.

She was in her late teens – which would make her about the right age to be the one whom she resembled in Mile's mind's eye – and yet something was not right. Her hair was a dull shade of faded brown, and it drooped limply from her scalp: whereas the girl Miles had known, all those years ago, had had the palest, most vibrant hair of anyone he had ever met.

She turned away and began to speak to her companion: a young man clad in a brown cloak.

"How do you know her?" Kyra interrogated, her hands tightening upon her reins until her knuckles went white. "Does she–"

"No," Miles shook his head. "Don't worry... it's not her. I was mistaken. Let's go..." he said, turning away and tapping his horse on the rump to spur it into a trot again.

A few moments later, someone called his name.

"Miles?"

He drew his steed to a halt again and looked over his shoulder. It was the young woman. She had followed him. "Miles," she said, looking him up and down once she had caught up. "Is it... is it really *you*?"

He was so surprised he couldn't hide it. "Elita?" he gasped.

"Yes..." she smiled. "Oh my gods! Where have you *been*? It's been so long. Grav'aen said that you were–"

Grav'aen. That name sent Miles into a state of panic, and his horse must have noticed it because it buckled beneath him. Elita backed away.

When Miles calmed his steed down, he and Elita looked at each other. This time, with a hint of suspicion.

Miles was at a loss over what to do. He was so surprised at seeing her that he had forgotten the connection Elita had to Grav'aen.

"What are you doing here, Elita?" Miles asked. "Why aren't you at the Institute?"

Her face fell at the mention of that establishment. Not only that, but her companion – the short young man standing behind her – leant into her ear and whispered something.

Elita listened to his counsel and then turned her attention back to Miles.

"Miles, you *can't* tell Grav'aen I'm here..." she said. "*Please*... if you care about me, forget you ever saw me. Something happened, and I had to leave."

Is this some manner of ruse? Miles wondered. There had been a time, once, when he and this girl shared a bond, but that was long past. She was a woman now.

Miles realised – with a wave of regret – that he had missed seeing her grow up.

But he also knew that it was very possible Grav'aen had polluted her mind in the time since then and moulded her into an agent to use against him.

"I'm sure you are already well aware that Grav'aen and I no longer see eye to eye..." Miles said. He prepared himself to draw upon his *viga* – just for in case he had a need to use it.

Elita seemed surprised. Her eyes widened.

"What happened at the Institute?" Miles asked her.

"I can't tell you," Elita whispered. She turned her head down and looked around them self-consciously. "Not here..."

"Do you want to talk?" Miles asked. "We can find

somewhere more discreet."

She stared at him for a while.

"What is going on, Miles?" Kyra asked, interrupting them. It was only then Miles noticed that she, Rivan, and Bryna had all halted and were watching the exchange.

"Be quiet," Miles shushed Kyra, putting a finger to his lips.

"I think we need to find somewhere to talk…" Elita said.

*　　*　　*

Sidry couldn't remember exactly when it was that he woke up, for it was a fitful shift he made back to consciousness. A hazy, flickering sequence experienced between reveries and ephemeral delirium. He could dimly recall that, for a period of time, he kept opening his eyes and seeing a thatched, sloped ceiling above him, bordered by beams.

Aches and pains were the most acute sensations, though. His whole body was stiff and heavy. It hurt when he tried to move.

Between it all, there were voices. And faces. One of them was Baird, but most of the time, it was a stranger.

The first occasion Sidry could remember being lucid was when, after staring at the ceiling for some considerable time, he had a sudden thought.

*Where **am** I?*

It was an ordeal for him to turn his head. He bit back the pain, strained the muscles in his neck to will them to move, and his head rolled across the pillow. The world seemed to sway. He felt dizzy, but then it steadied. He was finally able to take in the room he was in.

It was a bare place. The walls were brown wooden panels. The only other feature – apart from the bed he was laid upon – was a single chair. The door was closed.

He panicked. The last time he had awoken to find himself in a strange room – with no memory of *how* he got there – was when Shayam kidnapped him.

The day his life took its harrowing turn.

If Sidry had the strength to move, he would have got up and attempted to break free, but he couldn't. He could only scream. He didn't even know what it was that he was shouting. He was crazed.

The door opened, and a man rushed in. Sidry didn't know him, which only escalated his panic. The stranger approached the bed and placed a hand on Sidry's forehead. Sidry cringed. He was still unable to move at first, but hysteria imbued him with a moment of strength, and he shoved the stranger away.

The man fell, his arms flailing as he tumbled back. He then crawled to the other side of the room and placed his back against the wall. Sidry took his first proper look at the stranger then; he was a skinny man in his middle years.

Sidry relaxed a little. His thoughts were beginning to clear, and he was thinking more rationally.

He could tell that, whoever this other man was, he was no threat.

Baird entered the room.

"Sidry!" he said. "Are you awake?"

"Baird!" Sidry exclaimed. He tried to sit up, but pain clenched in his chest. He winced. "Where am I?" he said.

"I will make him something to drink…" the stranger said, rising to his feet. Baird thanked him.

"That is Larn," Baird said after the other man left. "He's a Devotee of Carnea, and he's been looking after you. How are you feeling?"

Sidry remembered his last conscious moments and gasped. "We're *alive*!?" he whispered. "But how did we… what *happened*?"

His mentor grimaced. "I can't really tell you…" he said. "Well, not yet, anyway. You need to rest first. You've been asleep for five days."

"You're scitting me?" Sidry said. Five *days*? He didn't even know it was possible to sleep for that long.

Baird shook his head. "No, I'm not. It could well have been longer as I don't know how long I was out for."

"What happened?" Sidry asked again. "Just tell me. I want to know."

"It's not that I don't *want* to tell you," Baird said, and he pulled that same expression again. It was almost a wince. "It's just… hard to put into words. I can't think of *how* to explain it, so I will just have to *show* you instead. But you are not fit to go outside yet."

"What about the Zakaras?" Sidry asked. He didn't have to strength to argue. "What happened to them?"

"They're dead," Baird said. "All of them."

*   *   *

"Are you sure about this?" Astar whispered to Elita.

She nodded, but he could tell she wasn't as confident as the air she presented. "Let's just hear them out," Elita said. "It's not like we have any other opportunities up our sleeves right now."

"But why do we have to leave town?" Astar asked, glancing behind them as they walked. Sarok was almost out of sight now.

"That's a silly question," Elita said. "You *know* the Royal Guard are there, and I didn't want anyone to hear us talking. You seem to forget the situation we're in, Astar."

"The Royal Guard serve *King Wilard*. Not Grav'aen…" Astar said.

Elita rolled her eyes. "Same thing, these days. It's well known that Grav'aen is the one pulling the strings now. He's got Wilard wrapped around his finger."

"Has it not occurred to you we might be walking into a trap?" Astar asked. He thought he had spoken quietly, but one of the strangers seemed to hear. The young woman with the stern face and brown hair. She turned and narrowed her eyes at Astar in a way that made it clear she trusted him as little as he did her. He watched her for a few moments as she continued riding. She was heavily armed, with a longbow, a quiver full of arrows, a sword, and what must have been a least half a dozen daggers strapped to her belt. She seemed like she knew how to use them all too. "How well do you even know this guy, anyway?"

"Miles was like a father to me," Elita said, her expression softening. "He saved me once… I don't know who the others are, but I trust *him*."

"You didn't answer the question," Astar said. "*How* do you know him?"

"You're not going to like it…" Elita warned.

"Grav'aen!" Astar guessed, and the look in her eyes confirmed his fear. "Shit! *Elita*, what the fuck do you think–"

"It was years ago," Elita interrupted. She grabbed Astar's shoulder, and the two of them drew to a halt. The four strangers didn't seem to notice; they were mounted on horses, whereas Astar and Elita were on foot.

Elita leaned into Astar's ear and whispered. "Miles just said that he isn't in cahoots with Grav'aen anymore. And I got a very strong impression from the way he acted when he saw me that he's hiding from him. Maybe he knows what Grav'aen's been up to and has turned against him too."

"Or maybe Grav'aen sent him to lure us!" Astar said. "Did you not think of *that*? This is a pretty big gamble you're making!"

"I don't think so…" Elita said. "How would Grav'aen even know we're here? Unless your uncle betrayed us."

"Marven wouldn't do that!" Astar said.

"Well, I know Miles better than you know that damned uncle of yours!" Elita said. "Marven was the one who sent us here, and look what good it's done us! We're stuck at a border that is about to turn into a warzone! Come on, Astar… we need to hear them out. Even if it's a risk, we've got to take it. Miles might know some of Grav'aen's secrets."

Astar couldn't argue with that point. "You still haven't told me exactly *how* you know him, though," he said, crossing his arms over his chest.

"Miles and Grav'aen were the ones who found me and took me to the Institute when I was young. There were these old ruins near the village I grew up in, and Miles, Grav'aen, and a load of other southerners were studying them. Or something... I can't really remember what exactly it was they were up to, to be honest, but it was something to do with those ruins... Anyway, it was Miles who saved me from my family and took me to Mordeem. He talked the Institute into taking me in, and he used to come visit me every Veyday," Elita smiled nostalgically. It was a peculiar expression for Astar to see on her face. "But, one day, he just disappeared... he told me that he had to go away because he had something very important to do. I never saw him again–"

Elita was then interrupted by a voice.

"Are you coming or what?"

Astar and Elita both turned around. It was a man who had just spoken. Not Miles, but the younger one. He was brown-skinned, had a thick beard and was built like a tree. He reminded Astar of Bovan.

"Could you be a little politer to this lady and gentleman?" Miles said to his companion. "One of them happens to be an old friend."

The younger man scowled at Miles. There was an air between them that gave Astar the impression they didn't care for each other all too much. It made Astar wonder what kind of circumstances had forced them together.

"I think we have ventured far enough from civilisation to speak now," Miles then said. He turned his eyes to a cluster of trees by the side of the road. "Let's tether the horses and talk over there."

The others all dismounted and led their horses towards the trees.

"Astar," Elita said as they followed them. "Are you still glamouring me?"

"Yes," Astar replied.

"Can you stop it now?" Elita said. "It's not necessary here. I want Miles to see me as I truly am."

Astar's initial instinct was to refuse, but he couldn't think of a solid enough justification so he complied, lifting the veil, returning Elita to her natural beauty, and letting her platinum hair shine. At the same time, Astar made it so that the others – not just Elita – saw him as he usually liked to be favoured; taller and more imposing. These were new people – and potentially dangerous ones, too – so he wanted to make an impression.

Miles seemed to notice the change straight away. "Elita?" he said, looking her up and down. His eyes then shifted to Astar, and they widened even more. "How?" he said, looking between them again. "You look–"

"He is Blessed," Elita said, making Astar want to kick her. He never gave her permission to reveal *that* detail about him. "He can make people see things."

Miles turned back to Astar and smiled. "You're Blessed by Maja!" he said. "My... I haven't met one of *you* for quite some years..."

"Maja?" the stern-faced young woman with brown hair asked. "Who is Maja?"

"She's a goddess," Miles answered, turning to her. "One of the Others. Those who have her Blessing can conjure illusions. It's a rare one."

Astar had never known his Blessing had a name.

"Shall we cut to the chase?" the younger, bearded man asked. He crossed his arms over his chest. "Who are these people, Miles? And how to do you know them?"

"I have known Elita since she was a girl," Miles said. He smiled at her warmly, but there was also something guarded in his expression. It gave Astar the impression that whilst he was genuinely glad to see her again, he was also suspicious. "Would you like to introduce us to your friend?"

"This is Astar," Elita said, making Astar want to kick her again. Recently he had been known as 'Lew' when they were in public. Why couldn't she have just stuck to that name?

At least she didn't tell them where I am from, he thought.

"Greetings, Astar," Miles said. "My name is Miles, and these are my companions. Rivan, Kyra and Bryna," he said, gesturing to each of them.

It was when Miles introduced the last one – the smaller lady with the black hair – that Astar found his attention drawn. She tilted her head up, and Astar saw her face properly for the first time. Her eyes were purple. Astar had only ever encountered one other person with irises that colour before. A peculiar woman he used to see wandering around the grounds of the Institute sometimes.

"Now that introductions are over…" Miles said. "My first question is this; why did the two of you feel the need to travel in disguise?"

Elita and Astar looked at each other. *This was your idea!* Astar thought as he glared at her. ***You** speak to them!*

"We ran away," Elita said, turning back to her old friend. "Grav'aen is looking for us, Miles… you can't tell him you've seen us."

The other members of the group shifted uncomfortably at the mention of that name.

Maybe she's right, Astar realised. *Maybe we **do** share an enemy…*

"I can assure you, quite firmly, that that wouldn't happen," Miles grimaced. "As we are avoiding him ourselves… but why are *you*? What happened?"

"Astar," Elita said, gesturing to him. "We were sent to his–"

"We escaped from the Institute," Astar interrupted her. He didn't want Elita to tell them where he was from. Not these people. "Something weird is going on here… it's… hard to explain…"

"Just try," Miles coaxed. "You might find we understand more than you think."

"They've been doing something to the students," Elita said. "There's a group called Squad Three, and one of them used to be my friend… but he's not the same person anymore. All of them have changed, and there's something not right about it…"

Elita paused as she struggled to find the right words, so Astar pipped in.

"When we escaped, we were attacked by these

creatures," he said. "You wouldn't believe me if I–"

"Zakaras…" Rivan said in a rather tired manner.

"What did you say?" Elita asked.

"Zakaras," Rivan repeated. "That's what those creatures are called. And I bet that's what happened to your buddy too. They're Zakaras now."

"Zakaras?" Elita said the word out loud. She then turned to Miles questioningly.

"I'm afraid it sounds like he is right…" Miles said, sighing. "The Zakaras were created by Grav'aen, and he's assembling an army of them. He wants to use them to attack Sharma."

"So the people who are acting all strange *and* the monsters – they're both the same?" Astar asked.

Miles nodded.

Astar thought of his father and experienced a terrible feeling in his chest. "Is there a cure?" he asked. "A way to change them *back*?"

Miles shook his head. "No, not that I know of… and, from what I *do* know, I would say the chances of it even being *possible* are unlikely. I'm afraid it is best to think of anyone who has been changed into a Zakara as already dead. A creature is using their body, but it is not truly *them* anymore."

Astar turned his eyes to the ground, and a few moments later, Elita placed a hand on his shoulder.

Damnit! Astar thought. Usually, when he was upset, he used his magic to hide his emotions, but he'd forgotten this time.

"But *why*?" Elita asked, removing her hand and turning her attention back to Miles. "I can understand why the people in the Institute are being changed into these 'Zakaras' – as you call them – because they are going to be part of Grav'aen's army… but there have been others. People who are not even going to be part of this war; we think that they might have been changed too. What about *them*?"

"Are these people you speak of in positions of authority? Or influence?" Miles asked.

Elita was about to reply, but Astar beat her to it. He didn't want these people to know about his father.

"Yes," he replied guardedly. "Some of them are."

"Then I know exactly why," Miles said. "Grav'aen can control people who have been turned into Zakaras."

"How?" Astar asked.

"It's complicated..." Miles said, rubbing his hands together. "Think of it as a form of Psymancy... a person who has been turned into a Zakara is essentially an empty husk disguising itself as a human. There is no soul, and their minds are utterly void of conscious thought. Grav'aen, and a few others like him, can control these creatures telepathically. And that is why they are creating an army of them. They are the perfect, most obedient soldiers."

"How do you know all of this?" Elita asked. "And *where* the blazes have you been all this time? It's been over *ten* years, Miles!"

There was something in her voice then that surprised Astar. Elita seemed almost vulnerable that moment. Like her glacial shell had cracked.

Astar realised that, whoever this Miles person was, Elita cared for him deeply. His absence had affected her.

"I have been in Sharma," Miles said.

Elita gasped. "But *why*?" she asked. "What's in Sharma for you?"

"It's a long story..." Miles replied. "The short version is that Grav'aen sent me there to act as a spy, but when I realised that he was creating Zakaras, I had second thoughts and turned against him."

When Miles delivered that account, the young man beside him – Rivan, his name was if Astar remembered correctly – frowned. Which made Astar suspect there was much more to this story than Miles was telling.

"And what about all that time since?" Elita asked. "What were you doing? And *who* are these people?" she waved an arm at his three companions and pulled a face. It almost seemed like she was jealous. "They don't talk much, do they..."

Miles turned his eyes to the ground. "They're not usually as quiet as this…" he said with a grimace. "I can assure you… quite the opposite, actually…"

"Stop changing the subject," Elita said and then repeated her questions. "What are you *doing* here? And *who* are these people?"

"Don't tell them!" the brown-haired woman spoke up. She stepped in front of Miles. "Don't you *dare*!"

"Calm down, Kyra," Miles said measuredly. "I'm sure–"

"*No!*" she yelled.

"I agree with Miles," Rivan interrupted their quarrel. "I think it's worth a shot… it seems we share a common enemy, so just tell them and see what they say. If it goes down the wrong way, what can they do? There's two of them and four of us. They're outnumbered! It's not like they're anything we can't handle."

You clearly don't know **who** *you're speaking of*, Astar thought, but he didn't say anything; he *wanted* Miles to tell them his secrets.

"Fine!" Kyra exclaimed, stepping away and crossing her arms over her chest. "But be it on *your* heads when it goes wrong!"

"The truth is, Elita…" Miles said once he had composed himself again. "We came here as spies. To see what Grav'aen is up to. To find out whether he has started building his army yet."

"But who have you been spying for?" Astar asked.

Miles fidgeted with his hands. "Sharma."

"You're fucking kidding me!" Elita yelled.

"*Sharma!*" Astar exclaimed, his whole body tensing with rage. "You *traitor*!"

"Hey, you're the ones who created the fucking Zakaras!" Kyra screamed.

"I didn't create shit!" Astar yelled back. He looked at her, noticed her coppery skin, and a realisation dawned upon him. "Wait, are *you* from Sharma?" he asked.

Suddenly, it made sense. Both Rivan and Kyra were darker in complexion than most Gavendarians. Astar had barely noticed it when he first met them. Mordeem was very multicultural and home to people from the provinces south of Holliston, so he had been surrounded by lots of different skin tones recently. Now he realised that Kyra and Rivan looked different to the people from Gavendara's southern peninsular; their noses were sharper, and the shape of their eyes more rounded.

"Can everyone just *calm down*!" Miles raised his voice. He strode forward, positioning himself between Astar, Elita, and the other three. "Elita, *please*," he then said, turning to her. His expression softened. "Just let me explain–"

Elita frowned; for the first time in her life, it seemed she was unable to think of anything wise to say.

"I'm not betraying Gavendara," Miles said. "This war is not about Sharma against Gavendara. It's bigger than that! Do you agree with what Grav'aen is doing?" he asked, shifting his gaze from Elita to Astar.

Neither of them said anything.

"Well?" Miles pressed. "*Do you*? You said yourself that you are on the run from him. Because you didn't like what he was up to. Well, that's exactly what *I* did!"

"We wouldn't even be having this war if it wasn't for them leaving us to die from The Ruena!" Astar yelled, pointing at Kyra.

"We didn't know about The Ruena," Kyra said. "Not many from Sharma do… I only found out when Miles told me."

"What the fuck do you think we should do?" Rivan challenged. "Let your ruddy army come over and turn us all into fucking Zakaras?"

"It's not *my* army!" Astar yelled.

"No!" Miles agreed, pointing at Astar. "Exactly! It's not your army. And Grav'aen does not represent the wishes of the Gavendarian people. Don't you see? It's *him* we are trying to stop. This is not about Sharma against Gavendara!"

"But you've sided with the bloody Sharmarians!" Astar crossed his arms over his chest.

"Grav'aen is sending an army of Zakaras across the

border. What in Gazareth's name do you suggest they do?" Miles challenged.

"I don't care," Astar shrugged. "They can look after themselves. I just think you're a traitor for siding with them. We should fight Grav'aen *here*. In Gavendara. Find others who are against him, and join together. Spread the word so that everyone knows what he's up to. Get Gavendara to deal with Grav'aen, not the bloody Sharmarians!"

"As wonderfully optimistic as that sounds, I think you already know such a thing is not possible," Miles said. "Grav'aen is a powerful Psymancer, and he has risen to such influence that starting a rebellion against him within Gavendara would be futile. He has King Wilard wrapped around his finger. I even suspect Grav'aen has turned him into a Zakara, and is now controlling him... meanwhile, an army of Zakaras is being gathered, this very moment, and it is going to cross the border and take over Sharma. Do you think they should just lie down and take it?"

"Why do you keep saying it's a whole army of Zakaras?" Astar challenged. "It's just one of the squads from the Institute and a few other people so far. I would hardly call that an 'army'."

"There *is* an army!" Kyra spoke up. "I saw it! They're on the other side of the Folds. And anyway, Zakaras multiply fast. Anyone who is killed by one becomes infected and turns into one too."

"Really?" Astar gasped.

He didn't know that.

Kyra nodded. "Yes, it happened to my village. The Zakaras came and killed everyone. And then, when we came back, the bodies rose again. It happened in Fraknar as well."

"You have Zakaras in Sharma?" Elita asked.

"Not anymore," Kyra shook her head. "We killed them all."

"But how the blazes did Zakaras get into Sharma?" Astar asked, turning back to Miles. "I thought you said Grav'aen created them?"

"*That* is an even longer story," Miles said. "But yes, there were Zakaras in Sharma. Grav'aen sent them. And Kyra, Rivan and Bryna here are the survivors of a village that was slain by them."

When Miles revealed that, something happened to his companions. It was like a gust of cold wind swept the air around them, and all three of them shifted uncomfortably. They all had a haunted look in their eyes.

Astar realised then that he believed them. Well, at least *that* part of their story. They were about the same age as him, and yet they possessed the air of people who had endured burdens well beyond their years.

These were the first Sharmarian people Astar had ever met, and they were far from what he expected.

"Can Astar and I have a moment to speak alone, please?" Elita asked.

"Sure," Miles said. "We're not going anywhere."

"Come with me," Elita said, gesturing for Astar to follow.

They walked away together. "It's okay," Astar said once they had cleared a few paces. "We don't have to walk *that* far. I can use my magic to make it so that they can't hear us."

"Some people can listen by watching the movement of lips," Elita warned.

"I can sort that out, too," Astar said, drawing upon threads of his *viga* to blur himself and Elita a little. "So, what's your take on all this, then?" he asked. "Do you really think they're assembling a whole army of those things?"

Elita shuddered. "I don't know…" she said. "I've always thought Grav'aen was a crafty snake… but to be capable of what Miles is saying… it's hard to believe, isn't it?"

"And what about *him*? Astar asked, gesturing to Miles. "Do you trust him?"

"I think so…" Elita said, eyeing him thoughtfully. "I want to hear more of his story. That's for sure. I think he and his companions know plenty more than what they've just told us."

"But they're Sharmarians…" Astar said.

Elita grimaced. "I know… I don't like it either but they *do* seem to be in the same boat as us… trapped here and on the run. Maybe we could help each other."

"What are you suggesting?" Astar said. "I hope you don't want us to join them… They're spies, Elita! For *Sharma*!"

"I know that!" she snapped. "But what other options do we have? It doesn't feel like Gavendara is particularly on our side right now either."

"I'm not going to Sharma with them," Astar shook his head. "No bloody way!"

"I'm not saying we should," she replied. "And quieten your voice!"

"They can't hear us anyway!" he reminded her. "I told you… I'm taking care of that!"

"I'm not saying we should team up with them," Elita said. "Not yet, anyway. I *do* think we should talk to them more. I want to find out more about Grav'aen and those creatures. Who knows? Maybe they can help us escape."

"I think we should leave them…" Astar said. "Fuck them! We don't need them! And do you know what? Fuck that Ilarn guy, too! We can find our own way to Babua. Or just go somewhere else."

"No," Elita shook her head defiantly. "Since the moment we left Mordeem, *you* have made all the decisions, and I have blindly followed. And where has it got us? We're stuck, and *you're* the one who got us here! It's *my* turn…"

Elita then shouldered past him and marched back to Miles. "Lift the spell, please," she said. "I'm going to speak with them."

Astar tried to argue, but she ignored him. He cursed. Elita had already made up her mind, and she was stubborn as a bull. There was nothing he could do to sway her now.

He lifted the veil.

"Hello Miles," Elita said as she reunited with them.

"Have you reached a decision?" Miles asked, smiling at her.

"Almost..." Elita said. "But I have a question for you... do you know how to use waystones?"

Astar's heart skipped a beat.

*What the fuck are you planning, **Elita**?!* he wondered.

"Why do you ask?" Miles asked, frowning.

"Answer the question," Elita said. "Do you know how to use waystones?"

"It has been a while... but yes. I do," Miles replied. "Why? Do you have one?"

"No," Elita shook her head. "But I think I know where we can *get* some."

"Really?" Miles' eyes brightened. "Where?"

"I will tell you about it," Elita said. "But *only* if you agree to help us."

Miles' face fell as a thought seemed to occur to him. "But Elita," he said. "Waystones can only carry a maximum of five people. We are six."

"We're not going to Sharma with you," Elita rolled her eyes. "No offence, but that's just not for us. When we get the waystones, we'll part ways. You can go to Sharma, or wherever you want, and me and Astar will go to Babua. I will need you to show us how to use them *before* you whisk yourselves away, though. Could you do that?"

"It would take a bit of time..." Miles said, playing with his hands thoughtfully. "But it should be possible... where are these stones then? And are you sure you can get your hands on more than one?"

"Yes," Elita nodded. "We have quite reliable information that someone not too far away from here has recently got his hands on several of them," Elita said. "Do you know a place called Falam? There is a man there called Galrath."

Miles burst into a fit of laughter and turned his head up to the sky. Everyone stared at him.

"What's the bloody matter?" Astar asked.

"Sorry," Miles said, turning his eyes back to them. There was still a big grin on his face. "I was just... oh, Elita!" he laughed again. "It must have been fate which brought us back together! It really must have been!"

"Why?" she asked

"I should have guessed it would be Galrath squirrelling away all the waystones," Miles chuckled again. "The rapacious, pinch-fisted git!"

"You *know* him?" Elita asked.

"Know him? Yes, I know Lord Galrath quite well..." Miles smiled. "I also happen to know the layout of his keep!"

Chapter 18

Boom

Kyra did not like this turn of events at all.

"So I guess that settles it," Miles said as he rubbed his hands together. "The next question is; how do we proceed? Personally, I would suggest that we leave as soon as possible."

"Elita and I are going to need to get our things first," Astar said. "They're back in Sarok. Our horses are there too."

Miles nodded. "And there isn't much daylight left either... so how about we camp here tonight?" Miles said, looking at the space around them. "This seems as good a place as any... We are hidden from sight and yet close enough to the road to be swiftly on our way tomorrow. I don't know what it's been like for the two of you recently," Miles added. "But my three companions and I could do with some rest."

Kyra was too shocked to think of anything to say at first, so she watched the rest of the exchange without commenting. She had already made her objections very clear, but it seemed she had been out-voted.

Why couldn't her companions see how dangerous this was?

"Okay," Elita said before she and Astar walked away. "Astar and I best get going if we want to return before sundown."

Kyra clenched her fists as she watched them leave; it all seemed to be spiralling out of control, and there was nothing she could do about it.

"What the blazes do you think you're doing?" she asked Miles once the two strangers were out of earshot.

"It appears we have found a way to get ourselves out of here!" Miles grinned in an attempt to buoy the situation to her, but Kyra wasn't going to fall for it.

"And how do you know they're not just going to rat on us?" Kyra challenged.

"Why would they?" Miles raised his hands. "Even if they *wanted* to, they couldn't. They're on the run from Grav'aen too."

"Unless they lied," Rivan pointed out. He scratched his beard thoughtfully.

"And don't even get me started on *you*!" Kyra exclaimed, turning to Rivan. "What the blazes were you thinking, siding with him," she gestured to Miles. "And letting him tell those two strangers our secrets?!"

It was going to take Kyra a while to forgive Rivan for that little stunt.

"Yes, I did," Rivan said, crossing his arms over his chest. "And I still stand by it. We're short on options right now, and they might be able to help us get home. Doesn't mean I trust them, though."

"*I* trust Elita," Miles said. "And their story does make sense… and anyway, did you not *hear* them? They're going to help us get *waystones!* We could be back in Shemet like that!" he clicked his fingers.

Kyra and Rivan looked at each other. The thought of being whisked back to Shemet did sound tempting.

But that was the problem; it seemed too good to be true.

"It's just suspicious," Kyra said, shifting the weight of her body from one foot to the other and then back again. "Is it really worth the risk? Maybe we should just do a runner… get away before they come back with a dozen of those Royal Guards or something."

"No," Miles shook his head. "Elita wouldn't do that… not to me…" he put a hand to his chin, and an idea seemed to occur to him. "I know… how about one of *you* accompany them on their trip back to Sarok? To keep an eye?" he asked. "Would that make you more comfortable?"

"Yes!" Kyra said. "You know what, I think I will!"

She was just about to get on her horse when Rivan stepped in front of her. "I'll go," he said. "You got to go scouting for days while I was left waiting. It's my turn!"

*   *   *

Kyra was agitated the whole time they were away. She kept watch while Miles and Bryna made camp. Every sound caused her to startle.

It was a tremendous relief when Rivan returned a couple of hours later with Astar and Elita riding behind him. He seemed calm.

"They just grabbed their things and then we came back," Rivan shrugged when Kyra quizzed him.

"Were they ever alone?" Kyra asked.

Rivan frowned. "They went up to their room briefly to get their things…" he said. "I waited outside."

"How long were they in there for?" Kyra asked. "Did they talk to anyone?"

"Kyra, relax," he said. "It all went fine. Stop worrying."

Kyra watched as the two newcomers tethered their horses. *Someone has high connections…* she noted when she eyed their steeds. They were robust destriers. Warhorses. Well cared for, bred for speed and stamina.

After pitching their shelter, Elita and Astar joined them by the fire, and everyone ate supper together. Miles tried to get them to engage in a bit of small talk but was unsuccessful. The atmosphere was awkward. Everyone kept staring at each other as if sizing one another up.

When they finished eating, Miles coaxed Elita and Astar to tell a more detailed account of their story. Kyra listened to it closely and asked lots of questions. She tried to catch them out – discover inconsistencies or gaps – but was unsuccessful.

When it began to get dark, Elita and Miles cosied up together by the fire and began to talk fondly about all these old memories the two of them shared. It was a strange interaction for Kyra to witness; it reminded her of the way Miles used to act around her, Jaedin and Bryna. Jovial. Paternal and caring. Almost playful.

Before he betrayed them.

Kyra soon grew weary of Miles and Elita's idle chit-chatter, so she moved away and sat on the other side of the fire where it was a bit quieter.

She glared at Elita. Kyra didn't like her at all.

Kyra's feelings towards Miles were complicated, but he was a presence she'd grown accustomed to. Now, there were two *more* people she didn't trust in her midst. Two new cats in a bag that had already been somewhat twitchy and clamorous.

She's Gavendarian! Kyra thought as she stared at her. *And you're telling her **our** secrets!*

But Kyra's dislike for Elita went beyond the fact she was Gavendarian. The other woman irritated her. Her voice was too loud. It was a pitch that abraded Kyra's ears. She was too brassy. Too gregarious.

Kyra watched Elita as she placed a hand on Miles' shoulder and whispered into his ear. It seemed almost flirtatious. When she finished telling whatever story or anecdote she was sharing, they both burst into a fit of giggles, and her laughter rang through Kyra's ears.

It was going to take Kyra a while to get used to that sound.

She hoped this situation didn't last long enough for her to have need.

Kyra narrowed her eyes at them. Her eyelashes blurring the sight until all she could see of them was a faint outline beyond the dancing flames.

She then heard footsteps. Ones that sounded unfamiliar so immediately triggered an impulse within her. She jerked and twisted around.

It was Astar returning to the fire.

"Hello," he said as he approached Bryna. He sat next to her, and Kyra couldn't help but notice that he did it in a way that was a little too familiar.

Bryna shifted uncomfortably and turned her eyes to her feet.

"So, tell me…" Astar said as he stretched his arms out so that one of them was behind Bryna's back. He tried to make it seem like an accident, but it clearly wasn't. "Are many of the ladies in Sharma as beautiful as you?"

Kyra clenched her fists.

"What are you doing?" Bryna asked him softly.

"Sorry if I seem a little dazzled," he said. "It's just not every day one meets a lady like you. Maybe we could go for a moonlight walk together… it's a beautiful night."

"Who would I be walking with?" Bryna asked. She lifted her head and looked him directly in the eyes – something she rarely did with anyone. "The visage you wear? Or the person beneath?"

Elita cackled with laughter, breaking the moment. "Now *that* was a putdown!" she applauded, clapping her hands. "You did the wise thing there, trust me. I've seen both, and neither were all *that* impressive…" she then turned her attention back to Miles. "I like her. She's smart! What's her deal, anyway? How did she see past his–"

"I'm going to bed," Astar uttered as he got up and left the fire. He said it so loudly that Kyra didn't hear the rest of Elita's sentence.

They have a strange relationship… Kyra noted.

"What was all *that* about?" Rivan asked.

Kyra shook her head. "I don't know."

* * *

Kyra and Rivan kept turns to keep watch over the camp that night. Miles did suggest that they share the duty with the newcomers, so they could all get more rest, but Kyra was far from comfortable with that idea. She took the first shift, and it coincided with Elita's. The girl blathered, but Kyra didn't engage. She knew Elita was trying to soften her up, and she wasn't going to fall for it.

When, halfway into the night, Rivan came to take over, Kyra joined Bryna in their tent, but the rest of the dark hours were far from restful. She was anxious, and she tossed and turned fitfully. When she heard the dawn chorus, it seemed like the night had gone rather quickly.

They packed up and left. Miles seemed to know the lay of the land rather well and began to lead them towards

Falam. He said the journey was going to take them a few days.

"So, what's the plan?" Kyra asked, levelling her horse beside Miles.

"Did you not *listen* yesterday?" Elita asked chidingly. "We're going to get those waystones and get the fuck out of this place."

"I know *that*," Kyra said through gritted teeth. "I mean *how*. You said that they're being kept in a fortress," she turned back to Miles. "That means we need to get *in*. And even after that, we're going to have to search the entire ruddy place to find the things."

"I'm pretty sure I know where Galrath is keeping the waystones," Miles said. "So don't worry about that part. I think that between us, we have more than the skills required to pull this off. We'll think of something."

"If we can get them to open the gates for long enough, I can get a handful of us in there without them seeing," Astar said.

"What, by making us invisible?" Miles asked.

He nodded.

Miles whistled. "That's impressive. I've only ever met one other who was Blessed by Maja before, and she couldn't pull off anything as advanced as that."

"But if you make us all invisible, won't we bumping into each other?" Rivan asked.

"No," Astar shook his head. "I can isolate the illusion so that *we* can all still see each other. It's just other people who won't."

Miles whistled again. "Good thing you're not on Grav'aen's side anymore. That's all I can say…"

He clearly meant that as a joke, but Kyra sensed that it didn't go down very well. Astar and Elita looked at each other sheepishly and went quiet.

"So what's with this 'Blessing of' business?" Kyra asked Miles a few minutes later. "I thought people were just Blessed or not Blessed, but recently you've been giving them all names."

"Some people, who are particularly gifted in a specific

form of magic, are considered Blessed by a god who shares that particular trait," Miles said. "So, for example, someone who is particularly good at manipulating fire would be a 'Blessed of Ignis'."

"How come I have never heard of this before?" Kyra asked

Miles shrugged. "Because you grew up in Jalard, and there were no people there who could claim such a title. Apart from Meredith, of course, but she was a Devotee of Carnea, which is a title in itself. Oh, and me. But I was... well... you know..."

Keeping it secret. As part of your lie, Kyra almost said, but she decided it was best to not be too open about her dislike for Miles in front of the newcomers. Division was something that they could exploit, so she wanted to present a united front.

"You had a Devotee of Carnea who was *Blessed*?" Elita said, turning to Miles. "Didn't you say they were from a tiny village?"

"Yes," Miles smiled. He seemed happy for an excuse to change the subject. "And I don't think they realised quite how lucky they were..." he then turned back to Kyra to explain. "Most Devotees of Carnea who are Blessed end up moving to bigger towns. They can share out their skills among more people that way. You were rather privileged to have a healer as gifted as Meredith in a village as remote as Jalard."

"So people who are *not* like you, Meredith, and Astar," Kyra said. "Why do you still call them 'Blessed' when it doesn't appear to be by any particular god?"

"Now *that* is a big question," Miles began. He turned his eyes to the sky as he gathered his thoughts. "I guess it's just the way language and terminology develop over time. It is said by many historians that back in Ancient times, many more people were Blessed, and the Blessings were stronger. The annals and accounts which have survived from that period do appear to support that theory... there certainly did seem to be much more magic back then."

"But why would such a thing happen?" Kyra asked.

"My guess would be as good as any other," Miles shrugged. "Some people think it is because people are not as devout as they used to be. One only needs to explore the relics of our past, such as the ones in the Valleshian Mountains, to know that we were once far more devoted to the gods than we are now. Remember when we went to Shemet, and you saw all those temples along the side of the river? Those cults are the last remaining glimmers of traditions that go back thousands of years. Their monuments used to be much bigger and grander."

"I remember..." Kyra said. "All those people in robes... it seemed like it would be a boring life, becoming a devotee."

"Not all do it for the entirety of their lives," Miles explained. "These days, a lot of young ladies just join a temple for a year or so because they hope they will earn enough favour for their offspring to be Blessed."

"That sounds like a waste of time," Kyra said. "Spending an entire year worshipping just for the off-chance something *might* happen."

"To some, it seems worth it," Miles said. "If it *does* happen, and your child is Blessed, it is very likely your youngster will be enrolled at the Academy – or, if you live in Gavendara, the Institute – and not only will they receive a good education there, they will also be helped to reach their full potential. Some of them may even go on to study Enchanting, and there is a lot of coin that can be made from that. Do you know how much items like waystones, glowstones, or even just Enchanted doorways cost? Being Blessed is pretty much a guarantee to a more comfortable and affluent life."

"How does Enchanting work?" Kyra asked.

"It is not an area I know all too much about," Miles said. "As I was always more drawn to history... if I *had* taken to the study of Enchanting, I would likely be a very rich man by now!" He laughed. "I *do* know some things about it, though. Anyone who is Blessed, no matter how weakly, can become an Enchanter. But it takes a lot of study and practice to be good at it. Maybe it's what Jaedin would have ended up getting into if he had enrolled at the Academy."

Kyra stared at the ground for a while and thought of her friend. It had been a while since she had communicated with him through Bryna, or Bryna had given them an update on his wellbeing. They'd been too busy running away from those Zakaras. Kyra had asked Bryna a few times, but Bryna was cagey about it, claiming she didn't want to trouble him. *He's fine*, Bryna had said, the last time Kyra had nagged her. *If anything were to happen to him, I would be the first to know. Don't worry.*

"If the Blessings really do come from the gods, then why do we have people like Jaedin?" Kyra asked Miles. "Who don't seem to have been favoured by any particular one?"

"Well, we can never know for *sure*, but there are some theories," Miles said. "There are actually more people like Jaedin than there are people who are gifted enough to claim they're Blessed by any particular deity these days. The most popular notion is that people like Jaedin are descendants of those who were Blessed by a particular god but, over the generations since then, the bloodlines have mixed and become watered down."

Kyra almost asked Miles another question then but stopped herself because it was going to be about Bryna. She realised that it was probably best not to reveal too much about her friend in the presence of Astar and Elita. Bryna inheriting the powers of Vai-ris was something they were trying to keep secret.

"To be honest, all these labels are just an attempt to simplify something which is far more complicated than we make it seem," Miles said. "For example, we haven't even touched upon the subject of Psymancy yet... Psymancy is mysterious. *All* people who are Blessed – no matter how weakly – are capable of Psymancy, but some are more gifted at it than others. And how gifted people are at Psymancy doesn't seem to bear any relation to how powerfully they are Blessed, either. Jaedin is a good example of this; although he is weakly Blessed, he does seem to have quite an acute aptitude for Psymancy." After a short pause, Miles then looked at Elita. "And then you have people like Elita," he said. She smiled at him. "Who is a grey area as far as definitions go. She can conjure both wind *and* water, summon rain and thunder. Is she Blessed by Manveer, or by both Vaishra *and* Ta'al?"

Kyra stared at the other girl. She didn't know all that much about sorcery, but she could guess that meant Elita was someone to be wary of.

* * *

It took a few days after Sidry's awakening for him to gain his strength back, and they were the most frustrating of his life.

At first, he could barely move. Larn, the Devotee of Carnea caring for him, had to spoon-feed him his first meal. Sidry hated that. He made a stubborn attempt to feed himself, but within mere moments of clasping his hand around that spoon, he dropped it, scalding himself with hot soup. He had no other choice but to allow Larn to feed him after that, and it was humiliating. Even worse, whenever Sidry needed to relieve himself, it took the efforts of both Baird and Larn to assist him during visits to the privy outside.

Larn kept making Sidry potions. Most of them were foul, but Sidry quaffed them with little complaint, hoping they would help speed up his recovery. He suspected Larn was lacing them with sedatives because he often felt drowsy after imbibing them.

He drifted in and out of sleep the first two days.

The third day was marginally better. Sidry could at least sit up in his bed by then. He could feed himself too. Albeit slowly. His legs were a bit wobbly, though, so he still needed help reaching the privy outside, but he was able to carry out the rest of that deed unaided.

"Why is it taking so long?" Sidry asked Baird while

Larn was cooking supper that evening. It was one of the first occasions they had been alone since Sidry first woke up. "What happened to me?"

"I will show you when you're fit enough to ride again," Baird crossed his arms over his chest. "You're lucky to be alive, Sidry. We both are."

"I hate being like this," Sidry muttered, clenching his fists. Even that was a tough thing to do because it hurt the joints in his hands. "Can't he do something to make it faster?" he asked. He remembered when he had a fever as a child, and even the touch of Meredith's hands seemed to have this mysterious way of making him feel better, but Larn never did such a thing.

"I doubt it," Baird shook his head. "Larn *is* a Devotee of Carnea, but he's not a Blessed one. The only thing he can do is speed up nature's process by using his botanical knowledge. And the best *you* can do is eat, rest, sleep, and drink all the potions he makes you."

"How did you find him, anyway?" Sidry asked. "Where are we?"

"We're on the outskirts of a village. About a quarter of a day away from Seeker's Hill."

"How did you get me here?" Sidry asked.

"It wasn't easy, trust me."

*   *   *

On the fourth day, Sidry managed to go for a brief walk outside. The village Larn lived in was even smaller than Jalard. Sidry could see a few cottages on the other side of the river, but not much else. It seemed a rather dismal place, but that may have been just because the sky was overcast, and it was gloomy that day.

It was on the fifth morning when Sidry finally convinced Baird to take him to Seeker's Hill.

They rode out after lunch. If Sidry had his way, it would have been earlier, but Baird insisted they eat a proper meal first. After eating a broth with lots of vegetables and barley, Baird prepared the horses. Sidry watched from the window and fidgeted.

They rode out. They didn't speak much during the journey, only communicating when Baird needed to tell Sidry which turn to take when they reached crossings. They passed a few cottages and hamlets upon the way. One of the men they crossed paths with seemed to recognise Baird and waved.

"A friend?" Sidry asked.

"He helped us when you were unconscious," Baird grimaced. "He told us where to go… where to find Larn."

"How much further is it?" Sidry asked.

"We're about halfway," Baird said, casting his eyes around them. "Or at least I *think* we are… it's all a little hazy. When I rode through here, I was a bit dazed and confused."

An hour later, they reached the woodland and rode into it. Sidry began to feel apprehensive. He wondered what it was they were going to find.

He found out much sooner than he expected to. As he was riding, he saw something beyond the trees that made him gasp. He tugged upon the reins and drew his steed to a halt.

They had reached the edge of a precipice.

The landscape before them was black. A deep abyss of charred earth. That's all there was, apart from the remains of a few trees around the edges, which were scorched to a cinder and lay upon their sides.

"What happened?" Sidry whispered. It looked like a colossal ball of fire had fallen from the sky.

"*You* did this," Baird said.

"No," Sidry shook his head. "That's impossible… I couldn't."

"You did…" Baird said, looking at him. "I don't know *how*, but it was you."

Neither of them spoke for a while.

"Do you remember what happened?" Baird asked.

"Not really…" Sidry muttered. "I was surrounded – trying to fight them off… but there were too many."

Baird nodded. "They had me clogged in too… I was

374

trying to reach you – I knew you were in trouble – but I couldn't. I'm sorry."

"It's okay…" Sidry mumbled.

"You were using *flash*, weren't you?"

Sidry nodded.

"I need you to tell me how it happened," Baird said.

"I don't remember."

"It may come back to you," Baird said. "And if it does, you need to tell me. We have to make sure this doesn't happen again."

"What happened after the light?" Sidry asked, turning to his mentor.

"I don't know," Baird said. "I passed out. I woke up eventually. Somewhere in that," he said, pointing into the depths of the crater before them. "And you were just lying there, right in the middle of it… I thought you were dead." Baird hesitated. "Before I passed out, the last thing I remember seeing was a burst of energy. It expanded outwards. Like this," Baird drew his hands together and then pulled them apart again, extending them outwards. "It was just like that. *Boom*."

Chapter 19

A New Terrain

As Miles led the party further down the mountain, the climate began to warm a little. By the third day, the scenery became sparse, and grassy hillocks replaced the woodlands and groves. The only vegetation which seemed able to thrive in this terrain was wildflowers, bracken, intermittent thickets, and gorse.

Kyra had never seen anything like it before. It was an odd place, but it possessed a desolate beauty.

"I think we're going to have to find somewhere discreet to make camp," Miles said shortly after midday.

"Why?" Kyra asked. "Isn't it a bit early?"

"See those?" Miles asked, pointing ahead of them. Kyra squinted her eyes. It was a little foggy, but she could see a faint outline ahead. "Those are the Levian Mountains," Miles said. "And I happen to know that Falam sits upon the ridge of two of those two peaks – there, in the centre – so we are currently on a path which leads right to it. It won't be long until we're able to see the towers of Galrath's keep. And it wouldn't be long after that, that *they* would also be able to see *us*. So I suggest we set up camp, somewhere out of sight, and begin to plan what we are going to do tomorrow."

Kyra scanned the area around them, realising that finding a discreet place to settle might prove difficult in this terrain. Since they had entered Gavendara, they had got into the habit of pitching their tents beneath the cover of trees, something this moorland seemed to lack.

"What about over there?" Kyra said, pointing to one of the nearby hills. Dark vegetation covered its peak, and it was the only place in sight that showed promise of offering some form of camouflage.

"I was thinking the same thing," Rivan said. "Let's check it out."

They rode towards it, veering away from the trail and cutting across the back of one of the bluffs. There was a river on the other side of the peak, and it took a little coaxing for Kyra to convince Swifty to cross it but, once they passed, they skirted around the next slope and towards the hill beyond.

"That's not going to be able to hide us!" Elita exclaimed as they ascended. "I can see it from here! They're just bushes! They're not high enough."

"Let's just take a look," Miles said measuredly. "We've come all this way... I can't see any other options right now."

When they reached the top of the peak, Kyra hated to admit it, but Elita was right. The shrubberies barely reached her waist, and they were certainly not high enough to hide their tents. She wondered what was on the other side of them, though. "Let's check over there," Kyra said, urging her horse forward. She rode on, navigating through a series of knolls and patches of heather dotted with purple flowers. When she reached the other side of the ridge, she found herself looking down upon an empty valley.

"Come here!" she called. "I think I've found something."

She heard a series of hoofbeats, and a few moments later, the others appeared.

"What do you mean?" Elita asked, frowning as she drew her horse to a halt. "You can't be suggesting *here*?"

"It's not perfect, but I think we're going to have to make do," Kyra shrugged. "We're on the far side of the peak to Falam, so we'll be hidden from view. The wind is blowing that way, too," Kyra pointed down the valley. "So I think we could even get away with having a fire, as long as it's small."

"I am quite aware of which way the wind is blowing," Elita huffed as she pulled up her sleeves. "What about a source of water? Have you thought of *that*?"

"What were you expecting us to find out here? A fucking palace from the tales of old?" Kyra asked, putting a hand on her hip. "Look, Princess, not all of us are as delicate as you! If you can't hack it, then why don't you just bog off?!"

"Let's have a little calm, please..." Miles interrupted their quarrel. He turned to Elita. "I think Kyra may be right... I can't see any *other* opportunities around here."

Elita sighed. "Okay... hold on, let me just check something..." she said, and then closed her eyes. The features of her face stiffened a little – as if she was concentrating deeply – and Kyra recognised that expression. It was similar to the one Miles, Bryna, and Jaedin pulled when they were conjuring.

"What is she *doing?*!" Kyra asked, turning to Miles. Her whole body stiffened in alarm. "Stop her!"

"Chill out!" Elita droned, briefly opening one of her eyes. "I'm doing something for *all* of our benefit, so don't worry..."

"Don't worry?" Kyra repeated. "Don't fucking *worry?* Some witch is summoning gods-knows-what and telling me not to fucking worry!"

"I am *trying* to find a source of water," Elita muttered. "Oh wait, correction," she opened her eyes again. "I have just *found* a source of water... it's over there," she pointed to some crags further down the hill. "There's a little spring beneath those rocks. It may be a good place to tether the horses to as well. And you're welcome, by the way," she added, looking at Kyra and smiling sweetly. "It was a pleasure."

Kyra's hands tightened around her reins.

"How about we go and check it out," Rivan suggested as he spurred his horse into motion. His stirrup knocked against Swifty's side as he passed. "Come on, Kyra."

Kyra huffed. She could feel everyone staring at her, waiting to see her reaction. "Fine!" she exclaimed and reluctantly followed Rivan.

"What's your problem?" he said once they were out of earshot.

"She's a scitting little shrew!" Kyra exclaimed.

"Oh, I know that," Rivan said. "And I don't trust her as

far as I can throw her either. But why are you making everything so difficult?"

"I can't stand her!" Kyra yelled. "And that ruddy Astar too! What kind of name is that, anyway? They both flounced their way in like a pair of swans, and now they act like they're in charge. Elita's got Miles wrapped around her scrawny little finger! I *hate* it!"

"Even more reason to cooperate with them," Rivan said. "Sooner we get this done, the sooner we can part ways. We'll get back to Sharma, and they'll go to that Baba place, or whatever it's called. You'll never have to see them again."

"That's *if* this all isn't just some spawny trap," Kyra muttered. "What are we *doing*, Rivan?"

"We've already talked about this," Rivan sighed. "Like them or not, they're our best chance of getting ourselves out of Gavendara. It's a risk, and we're taking it. So let's just get it done."

"I know…" Kyra exhaled through her teeth. "She's just *so* annoying! She talks *all* the bloody time! She always has to have things *her* way! And she *always* has to have the last word!"

"I agree," Rivan said as he rode on with his back turned to her. "That does sound rather annoying… perhaps, with time, you'll get used to it, though…"

They reached the crags shortly after, and true enough, there was a little pool on the other side. Kyra unsaddled Swifty and led him to it, stroking his mane for a while as he quenched his thirst. It helped calm her down too.

After Kyra and Rivan had filled their water bladders, they went back to join the others and began to set up camp.

"So, what's the plan?" Kyra asked Miles the moment he sat.

"Be patient, Kyra," Miles said, looking over to where Astar and Elita were still building their shelter. "Wait until everyone is ready."

"I don't see why we need *them*," Kyra muttered. "I'm sure we could pull this off by ourselves…"

Miles raised an eyebrow. "You think that the four of us could get into the walls of a keep, past dozens of guards and witnesses, *and* find some extremely valuable items, alone? And then escape too?"

"Why not?" Kyra shrugged. "There was only four of us when we broke into Shayam's base and saved your hides. We managed that, didn't we?"

"Actually, if I remember correctly, things didn't go so well for you that time... *I* saved your life, and Baird killed most of those Zakaras for you," Miles reminded her. "And we don't have any Avatars of Gezra with us this time, Kyra. We *do*, however, happen to have two very powerful mages..."

A few minutes later, once everyone was gathered around in a circle, Miles brought out a dagger and began to carve a series of lines and circles into the ground.

"What are you doing?" Rivan asked.

"I am drawing a plan of Galrath's keep," Miles said. "Or at least how I remember it... not only has it been a while since I was there, but it may have changed a little..."

He carried on carving, and Kyra watched. The outer wall appeared to have three sides, and Miles carved out a little circle at each corner, which Kyra guessed to be the watchtowers. Miles then began to add a series of boxes to the interior, followed by some other details she didn't quite understand.

"Now, Galrath's keep is of a moated, triangular design," Miles said. "And it sits just before the entrance of what was once – until very recently – the Levian Mountain Pass, which could be accessed at this point, here," Miles indicated one of the watchtowers on the far side. "*We* will, however, need to find a way to get in through the main gate at the front, which is *here*," Miles finished, poking the end of his blade to the centre of the largest outer wall.

"I'm guessing that's not going to be easy..." Rivan grimaced.

Miles nodded. "There is a bridge, followed by a

gatehouse with a portcullis – which has to be drawn up from the other side, of course – and there is also a barbican on each side of the gate. And I think there is a murderhole too."

"What's a murderhole?" Kyra asked. "That doesn't sound very nice…"

"It does not matter," Miles shook his head. "The point I am trying to make is; this is not a place we are going to be able to fight our way into."

"I could create an illusion to trick them into opening the gates," Astar suggested.

"Such as?" Miles asked.

"I don't know…" Astar scratched his head.

"Could you make it so that Lord Galrath sees a friend of his?" Miles suggested. "Or a family member? Someone he *would* let in."

Astar shook his head. "For me to conjure an illusion of someone, *I* have to know what they look like too. I need to know the way they speak and how they behave. Plus, I am already going to be using my magic to hide myself and whoever is coming with me to find those waystones too. Doing that *and* sustaining the illusion of someone to distract them – all at the same time – would drain my *viga* very quickly."

"So we need to find another way to get them to open those gates," Miles concluded.

"Let me handle that," Elita spoke up.

Everyone turned to her.

"What is it you are suggesting?" Miles asked.

"You said you needed a distraction," Elita shrugged. "And I can give you that. I will find a way to get them to open those gates, trust me. I can talk my way into *anywhere*. Astar will vouch for me on that."

"She can be rather… convincing," Astar said.

"I will do my damsel in distress act… I'm good at that," Elita said. "I may not be highborn, but there were lots of noble brats and little lordlings at the Institute, so I know how to *act* like one. And we all know pretty girls find it easier to get into places."

"Maybe I should do it," Kyra suggested. She didn't like the idea of Elita and Astar taking *both* of the critical roles in this plan.

Elita glanced at Kyra, smirked, and then turned back to Miles. "Anyway… as I was saying, *pretty* girls have a way of getting into places which others… may find difficult. I can get them to open those gates–"

Kyra interrupted her. "I'm not letting you–"

"*Kyra!*" Miles said. "Let Elita finish what she was saying, and *then* you will have your turn to speak. I will consider all ideas…" He then turned back to Elita and gestured for her to continue.

"As I was saying," Elita glared at Kyra. "I will not *only* get them to open the gates, but I will do everything I can to keep them distracted while the rest of you are looking for those stones. Maybe we could devise some form of signalling system? I could use my magic to make something happen to the air around the castle if I sense something is wrong or they are onto us, and Astar could use his magic to give me a signal when you're done and you've found the stones. That way, I will know when to get them to open the gates again and let us out."

"Sounds like you've thought this through," Miles said.

Elita nodded. "I have been thinking about it a lot over the last few days… while we were riding. Another idea I had is I could use my magic to manipulate the weather and make it foggy around the castle so people can't see very well. Or I could even conjure a storm if you like… people are always a little distracted when the weather's off."

"A storm might be pushing it a bit far!" Miles chuckled. "We don't want to make things difficult for *ourselves* too – we're the ones who are going to have to leave the castle eventually, after all – but I can see what you're saying. We'll discuss the finer details later. Let's sort out some of the bigger things first."

"But I thought you were going to listen to *all* of our ideas?" Kyra said, but no one seemed to hear her.

"And also…" Astar added. "About getting into the

castle… I don't think it's a good idea to take *all* of you with me."

"Why not?" Rivan asked.

"Because it would be difficult to hide *everyone*," Astar said. "It drains my *viga*… and anyway, with so many of us, we'd be bumping into people in the corridors and stuff. It'd be chaos. No," Astar shook his head. "I will take *one* other person with me. That's all."

Kyra and Rivan looked at each other.

"I'll go," Kyra began to say."

"No!" Rivan exclaimed. "I'm sick of being left behind!"

"But I–"

"With all due respect," Miles raised his voice. "I think it is best if *I* go."

"On my dead body!" Kyra exclaimed.

"Do either of you know which part of this keep the waystones are in?" Miles challenged. "I am the only person here who has ever been there before, and I think I have a good idea where Galrath will be keeping them."

"But–" Kyra stammered.

"What's the problem?" Astar frowned at Kyra.

"He's a traitor!" Rivan yelled, gesturing to Miles. "That's the ruddy problem. I'm not letting you go off alone! You'll lure us into a trap, and the Gavendarians will have our heads!"

Elita's eyes widened. "Wow… sounds like they have some serious trust issues…" she murmured.

"It's… a long story," Miles grimaced and sighed. "Rivan…" he said, turning to him. "Can you sit back down, please? Let's have some calm and speak of this rationally. Can't you see that, for us to have the best chance of pulling this off, it makes more sense for it to be me who goes??"

"The Synod sent us to keep an eye on you," Kyra said to Miles. "Make sure you don't betray us again…"

"And you've done a great job," Miles praised. It sounded almost patronising. "We have gained the information we came for, and now it is of the utmost importance we get *back* to Sharma to deliver that information…" He cleared his throat. "Me being the one who goes on this mission is the best way to ensure we get this done. Unless you have any better ideas? Can you think of a plan to get those waystones, which is better than the one Elita and Astar have just come up with?"

Rivan just scowled at him.

"What about you, Kyra?" Miles asked, turning to her.

Kyra bit down upon her lip. She had nothing.

But still, the idea of her safety being put into the hands of these three people – while she, Rivan, and Bryna sat idly by – was something she couldn't stand.

"Let's just go!" Kyra suggested, turning to Rivan and Bryna. "Leave them. The three of us'll make our own way back to Sharma."

"Kyra…" Miles said with a great amount of concern for her in his voice. Kyra wasn't sure if it was genuine or not. That was the problem. She knew Miles was a slippery snake. And a great liar too. "Let's not be brash about this. I mean, for a start, I don't think Jaedin nor Baird nor Sidry would forgive me if I returned to Shemet without you…" he chuckled softly in an attempt to lighten the mood.

"I'm not letting you go free," Rivan grunted. "No way…" He turned to Kyra. "And I'm not leaving him here, either! Not unless it's his dead body…"

"*Rivan*?" Miles gasped.

"The Synod told us to kill you if you turned on us," Rivan said.

"You'd have to get through *me* first!" Elita said, her posture stiffening.

"Everyone, stop this!" Miles said. "This is all getting out of hand! Let's talk this through…"

"Let him go," Bryna spoke up.

Everyone turned to the young woman in surprise. It was the first time her lips had moved throughout the whole exchange.

"What?" Kyra asked.

"Let them go ahead with the plan. As they suggested,"

Bryna said. She spoke softly, but as always, there was a calm authority to her manner. "I think it is the right way."

"But it's *Miles*!" Kyra reminded her. "Don't you remember what he did to us? We can't let him go off on his own! What if he turns on us again?"

"He won't," Bryna said.

"You *trust* him?" Rivan asked.

"No…" Bryna said. "Not entirely… but on this occasion, I think his interests are in harmony with ours. He *wants* to return to Shemet just as much as we do. Even though it's for different reasons… I sense that Miles will do the right thing this time," Bryna concluded. "And I think you should let him go ahead with the plan."

*   *   *

Shortly after the heated discussion was over, Elita wandered away from the camp for a while to get some peace and quiet, passing through a series of knolls covered in heather.

She soon found herself looking upon the Levian Mountains.

That was rather intense, she thought as she sat.

She felt relieved to get away. When Rivan had threatened Miles, she had been ready for a fight. She had even drawn upon her *viga* and primed herself for it.

She was glad it had not come to that, but the incident raised some questions in her mind.

Why was it that the others distrusted Miles so much? He had turned his back upon his own people to help them, had he not? Those Sharmarians didn't seem to appreciate the sacrifice he had made. It angered her.

But yet, she also suspected there was much to the story.

Elita gazed at the mountains. The sky had cleared a little, and she could see an outline in the distance. She squinted. A manmade structure lay perched on the col of two peaks. She wondered if it was Galrath's castle.

Elita closed her eyes and steadied her breathing, summoning her viga.

386

Tuning into her magic, she listened to the currents. Air and water were all around her, in many forms. Rivers. Streams. Clouds. Vapour. A gust of wind swelled across the hill she was sitting on and caressed her face. She harmonised with it as it swept through her hair, deciphering its origin and source. It had come from the east, birthed from the dew of cold peaks, far away.

Elita connected with the essence of that place. Even though it was far away, she still achieved unity and could wield influence over it. She called upon the mists drifting between the ridges of its mountains, the clouds hovering above, the water surging from the rills, and she stimulated them. Drew them towards her. Beseeched them to animate and cohere.

It felt good to finally be able to use her magic without restriction and fear of admonition. When she'd been taken to the Institute as a child, her teachers had focussed on suppressing her powers. They had their reasons. Elita's Blessing had manifested, wild and unfettered, when she was young, and the consequences had been grave. It was still painful for her to think about that period of her life.

It took years for Elita's mentors to trust her enough to allow her to utilise her gift and, even then, it had been in a controlled manner. Every feat they permitted her to perform was a mere gentle stretch of her full potential.

But now Elita was, for the first time in years, flexing her wings again.

The Institute couldn't stop her anymore.

It was only when she brought herself out of her state of trance that Elita realised Miles had sat beside her.

"I thought we were going to discuss things before you started meddling with the weather?" Miles said.

"Was it that obvious?" Elita asked.

"You've been sitting there for quite a while," Miles said, drawing one of his knees up and resting his arm upon it. "I even called your name a few times, but you didn't hear me. One has to be channelling a lot of *viga* to reach a state of trance that deep."

"Don't worry," Elita said. "I haven't summoned the apocalypse or anything… we will have plenty of time to get to Falam before the fun begins if we leave early enough. And there won't be violent thunder or anything like that. Unless I change my mind and decide I *want* there to be, of course," Elita winked at him.

"I suppose that is acceptable," Miles said, smiling. "Maybe it would be better for you to consult me next time, though."

"There isn't going to be a next time…" Elita realised, feeling a wave of sadness. "Tomorrow, if everything goes to plan, we will part ways."

They both sat in silence for a while.

"It doesn't have to be like that," Miles said. "Are you *sure* you don't want to come to Sharma with us?"

Elita shook her head. "Sorry, but I can't. Going to Sharma is… something I'm not even going to consider. I don't like those guys," she added. "What are you doing with them, anyway? The way they talk to you…" she shook her head. "I wouldn't put up with that."

"It's… complicated," Miles said.

"It always is," Elita said wistfully. "Come to Babua with me and Astar," she implored. "What is there for you in Sharma, anyway?"

"Now *that* is even more complicated," Miles said. He shook his head. "I don't have choices anymore, Elita. I am part of something much bigger than myself now."

"So that's it then?" Elita looked at him. "After all these years, you're leaving me again."

"That's unfair," Miles said. "I had to leave Gavendara all those years ago, Elita. Grav'aen gave me no other choice. I know you were a child, and it was difficult for you to understand. But, this time is different. We are both adults now, and we are both choosing to go separate ways. Neither of us is at fault… the natural courses of our lives have pulled us in different directions, that's all. It is sad, but it's just the way it is. I often think about you, Elita," he added.

Elita looked back at him. It had taken her years to get

over Miles' departure. He was her link to her past – during a turbulent time of her life when everything changed, he had been her anchor. She had never forgotten about him, yet, as she got older, he almost began to feel like a dream. "Fine," she said and then leaned over and draped her arms around his neck. "Just promise me we will meet again, one day," she said.

"You know that such a promise would be an empty one..." Miles said. "I can only promise that I very much *hope* we will meet again."

"I hope whoever she is, she's worth it," Elita said.

Miles smirked. "You're a little off the mark there..." he said. He then rose to his feet and offered Elita his hand. "Come, you beautiful young woman. Let's get back to the camp. Before people start talking..."

Chapter 20

Lord Galrath

The atmosphere was tense the following morning as the party of three prepared to leave. When Astar ventured to the stream to gather the horses, he passed Rivan and Kyra, and the two of them glared daggers at him. He used his Blessing to cast an image of himself with his head held high and seeming imperious but, the truth was, the way those two pairs of eyes bore into him – full of loathing and distrust – made him feel nervous. It was an image that lingered in his mind.

When they left, the sky was clear, and the air was fresh, but the weather soon began to decline as they approached Falam. Astar could feel the humidity rising. Clouds loomed in the distance.

"I think you should start making yourselves invisible soon," Elita said eventually. "I can see the castle now."

"Let's get a little closer first," Astar suggested. "I want to conserve my *viga*."

"We need to find somewhere to hide the horses, too," Miles said. "Let's ride on a little further. I doubt we're close enough to draw attention just yet."

Shortly after, they spotted a series of crags and furrows on the side of the road and investigated them, finding an old quarry hidden from view.

"This'll do," Miles said. "Let's leave them here."

"But there isn't any water," Astar said.

"We won't be gone for long," Miles said.

Let's hope not anyway, Astar thought, feeling a little guilty as he tethered his horse to one of the rocks. He brought out a few apples from his sack and fed them to his steed as he stroked his mane.

Miles tethered his horse too, and then the three of them ventured back to the road. Elita was still on horseback, but Astar and Miles were now making their way by foot.

Astar prompted his *viga* shortly after that, casting a shroud around himself and Miles. "Just try not to ride too fast," he said to Elita as he finished winding the mirage. "We need to keep up."

Elita nodded and continued riding towards the castle. It began to rain shortly after that. At first, it was gentle, but it swiftly accelerated. Astar cursed. He had not dressed appropriately for this weather.

Miles conjured a shield to protect them from the worst of the downpour.

"Stop it," Elita said over her shoulder. "I *want* to be wet when I arrive. It's part of my plan."

"Did s*he* cause this?" Astar asked, turning to Miles.

Miles grinned. "She's brilliant, isn't she?"

As they approached the castle, mist seemed to cascade from the mountains, drowning everything in a grey brume until Astar could no longer see any of its walls or towers. It didn't matter. He knew they were close. Within moments, they were crossing the bridge, and he could see it again. He quickened his pace to catch up with Elita.

"Hail!" Elita called, lifting her head and directing her voice to the gatehouse. "Is anyone there?"

No one answered. Astar and Miles turned to each other.

The rain continued to pour. Elita was soaked through by now. Her coat, boots and the blue gown she was wearing were drenched and clung to her body. She hugged herself as if to keep warm, and Astar wasn't sure if it was genuine or part of her act.

"Hello!" she called again, this time with a hint of impatience.

"Who's there?" a voice answered. It seemed to be coming from one of the windows above, but Astar couldn't tell which one. "Show me your face."

Elita pointed her head up. "Let me in!" she wailed.

"Who are you?" the voice asked.

"My name is Jenla," Elita said. "Let me in!"

"I do not know of any Jenla…" the man yelled back. "What are you doing here? The Levian Pass is closed."

"I don't want to go *there*!" Elita said. "I'm on my way

to Chillin! Please let me in... my father is Lord Layren of Jolden, and he said I could stop here."

"Lord Layren of *where*?" he asked.

"*Jolden!*" Elita repeated. "It's near Dohgan. If you just let me in, I can draw you a bloody map if it pleases you! Just open the gate!"

"Wait there," he said. "I need to ask Yen. He–"

"I'm *drowning* out here!" Elita exclaimed, gesturing to her sodden clothes. "Can't we carry on with all this jibber-jabber *inside?*"

"Yen said–" the guard began.

"*Look* at me!" Elita yelled. "I'm just a girl! What are you scared of?"

The man didn't respond to that.

"Well?!" Elita yelled again. "What's your problem?"

She opened her mouth as if to say something else, but then there was a sudden movement, and she jumped.

The portcullis was rising.

*   *   *

Dareth could scarcely believe it at first when he saw their faces, but there they were. He had found them.

Rivan, Bryna, and Kyra.

Dareth stooped low upon the crest of the hill he was watching them from and observed for a while. He wasn't sure if crouching was necessary, but he wanted to be careful. He could see *them* from this far away, but he was in his Avatar form, with enhanced vision. It was unlikely that they, with their human eyes, could spot *him* from this distance.

There were only three of them. This was puzzling; he had been following a set of hoof prints that belonged to a party of at least six. Where were the other three? And, more importantly, *who* were they? Dareth was reasonably sure that Miles – or 'Kevan' as he seemed to be known these days – was one of them, but the identities of their other two companions was a mystery.

Dareth had not been expecting to find them so soon. The last confirmed sighting of a group matching their description had been four days ago in Sarok. Since then Dareth had been running on guesses, following random sets of trails, all of which had led him to a dead end. He had begun to worry that they had somehow eluded him.

But he had found them now.

The three of them sat around the remains of a fire, talking. Bryna was doing something with her hands, but Dareth was not quite close enough to discern what it was. It seemed that the three of them were idly passing the time. That was good. It meant they would be unprepared when Dareth decided to strike.

Kyra and Rivan were nothing for Dareth to worry over. Not anymore. He was an Avatar of Gezra. Two mere humans couldn't stop him.

Bryna, however, was a different story. Dareth was wary of her. He was far from forgetting what the witch had done during the siege in Fraknar. The mere thought of it sent chills down his spine. She was someone that, though he would never admit it, Dareth was scared of.

But he wanted to kill Kyra, and he wasn't going to let that stop him.

I need to deal with her first, Dareth decided, studying Bryna. *If I can surprise her before she has a chance to do any of her scitting magic, I can kill Kyra after...*

Dareth rose to his feet and began to make his way down the mountain.

*   *   *

The portcullis rose, and Elita rode through the archway. A man came over to meet her on the other side.

"Thank you," Elita said. "For *finally* letting me out of that dreadful weather! Do you have somewhere suitable for my horse?"

The man gestured to a stableboy, who hurried over.

"What a handsome young man," Elita praised as she handed him the reins. She ruffled the boy's hair, and his face turned as purple as a carrot. He ran off, taking Elita's steed with him.

"Now, *who* did you say your father was?" the man asked Elita.

"Can you just hold this for me a moment, please?" Elita changed the subject as she removed her coat. The man accepted it but held it at arm's length to stop the water from dripping over him. "I am just *so* wet!" Elita exclaimed, stretching her arms out. The gown she wore beneath clung to her skin and didn't leave much to the imagination. The man stared, his jaw hanging open. "I mean, *look* at me!" Elita continued, acting like she was oblivious to the man's reaction, but Astar was wise enough to know she was all-too-aware. "Can you believe that weather outside? It just suddenly came down. *All over me!* I had no time to prepare!"

The man blinked a few times and then seemed to remember himself. "So… can you tell me again, what is your–"

"Don't worry. I will tell you everything soon. I promise," Elita said, placing a hand on his shoulder and beaming at him. "Can you just let me get out of these clothes, please?" she asked. "I fear I will catch a death of cold."

"Your clothes?" the man mumbled, his eyes widening.

Elita nodded, and then she seemed to realise something and slapped her forehead. "Oh! I mean I want to change into *other* clothes! What kind of lady do you think I am?" she laughed. "Could you tell me where I could do such a thing?"

Miles tapped Astar on his shoulder. "Come on!" the scholar hissed. "We need to find those stones. She seems to know what she's doing…"

Miles began to lead Astar through the castle ward. The air around them was thick with fog, and Astar could barely see anything more than half a dozen paces away.

"How does your Blessing work?" Miles whispered as they passed through an ornamental garden. He seemed to know where he was going, so Astar followed him without question. "Do I need to be careful what I do whilst you hide me?"

"You can talk, as long as you do so quietly," Astar replied. "The louder you are and the more sudden your movements, the harder it is for me. And try not to knock anything over or bump into anyone, either. I can hide us from ears and eyes, but if you touch someone, there's not much I can do. Where are we going?"

"The Magest Tower," Miles replied, pointing ahead. Astar couldn't see anything but fog at first, but they continued walking and, a few moments later, a four-storey hexagonal building appeared out of the mist.

"Is that it?" Astar asked. There were two guards standing outside the entrance. "Looks like it might be difficult getting past those doors…"

"It's probably the busiest building in the entire keep, so I am sure someone will have reason to enter or exit it soon… when that happens, you can hide us, and we'll sneak in behind them," Miles said. "Galrath only uses his Great Hall when he has guests. He spends most of his time in *this* tower. His living chambers are on the top floor. Below that is the parlour and the library. And the treasury is in the cellar."

"And you think that is where he is keeping the waystones?" Astar said. "Isn't that a little obvious?"

"Yes, it is completely obvious. And that is the entire point," Miles replied. He indicated a spot nearby sheltered from the rain, and Astar followed him. "Let's wait here," he said and then continued explaining. "You see, like many men of noble stock, Galrath is somewhat a peacock and thus prone to grandiose posturing. Essentially, he likes to collect costly novelties as a way of bragging, and what better way to show them off but have them stored in a place that is visibly guarded? Even the act of having guards posted outside it night and day is a way of exemplifying his status and wealth because it proves he can *afford* to keep men occupied in such a way. Think about it; Galrath isn't even Blessed, so what use does he have for those waystones? He probably only bought them because he knows the price of them is going to catapult soon with the war coming."

"The price of waystones goes up during war?" Astar asked.

Miles nodded. "Of course. War can be very lucrative if you're crafty enough. Luxuries that people take for granted during times of peace become scarce, and where there is scarcity, profit can be made. Waystones are not only valuable, but they are incredibly useful."

"I'm surprised King Wilard – or Grav'aen – hasn't ordered everyone to hand them over," Astar said.

"No doubt they've already tried," Miles surmised. "But *telling* everyone to cooperate with such a demand and *implementing* it are two very different things… and I suspect Grav'aen has much more immediate things to deal with right now than chasing up waystones. They aren't all that useful to the invading side in a war anyway – as they can only carry a maximum of five people, so you can hardly shift armies with them – but they can be lifesavers for individuals who happen to be on the losing side of a battle. I can't even begin to tell you the number of historical sieges that have ended by some Lord or Lady using a waystone to escape, leaving their poor servants and wardens behind. Anyway, I am digressing…" Miles said. "The point is; I think Lord Galrath got those waystones as an act of indemnity because he is beginning to worry about his wealth. The tolls he charged people for them to pass through the Levian Mountains was one of his main sources of income – not to mention all the bribes he took from smugglers on the side – so I imagine he was pretty mad when it was closed…" Miles chuckled. He then noticed something going on behind Astar's shoulder and pointed. "Look," he said. "I think the doors are about to open."

Astar turned around and saw a pair of girls walking towards the entrance of the tower, carrying platters. The rain had paused, so it seemed they were taking the opportunity.

"It seems it is Galrath's lunchtime," Miles smiled. "Come! This is our chance."

"Okay," Astar said, drawing upon more of his *viga* and

gathering his wits. "Just be careful!" Astar hissed. "Don't bump into them!"

Astar crept up behind one of the girls while Miles trailed the other. The guards opened one door each, smiling at the young ladies as they passed through.

Timing was crucial. If Astar was too premature and the girl he was following made an unexpected movement, he risked bumping into her. Yet if he was too hesitant it could be even worse; he could block the door as the guard closed it again.

However, he and Miles passed through without any incident and, as soon as Astar was safely on the other side, he let out a sigh of relief.

"Quick! This way!" Miles whispered, grabbing Astar's arm before he had any time to take in their new surroundings. He followed Miles without question, simply concentrating upon making sure the two of them were invisible as Miles dragged him across the room.

"This will do," Miles then said, coming to a stop. Astar then looked around them. He and Miles were on the far corner of the chamber. There was another man in the room, standing in front of a panelled door. He was clad in chainmail and holding a spear.

"That's where the waystones are, isn't it..." Astar muttered dryly.

Miles nodded. "Behind that door is the stairs leading down to the treasury."

"This is going to be difficult," Astar thought out loud as he rubbed his hands together.

"Maybe not... that is not the *only* passage he is keeping watch over," Miles said, pointing to an opening on the other side of the room that led to a corridor. "That leads to a stairway which goes all the way up to Galrath's chambers. And that one," he added, directing his finger to another opening on the opposite corner. "Leads to his drawing-room. And let's not forget the main entrance, where we just came from," Miles finished, pointing to the large pair of wooden doors which led back outside. "That makes four. It should be fairly easy to distract him."

"I guess…" Astar said. "But once we get inside that cellar, how are we going to get back *out*? He seems to like standing in that space. It'll be hard to open it a second time without him noticing."

Miles scratched his beard thoughtfully. "How about *I* go down there, alone, and you stay up here to keep an eye on him? Once I've found the stones, you can find another way to distract him so that he moves out of the way. I can open the door a second time then and escape."

"How will I know when it's the right time?" Astar asked.

Miles paused. "Or, I could just *not* close the door behind me. Could you create an illusion to make him *think* it is closed?"

"That would be risky," Astar said. "I can trick his eyes and ears, but if a draught comes up from that cellar he will feel it and there is nothing I can do about that. What if he decides to lean on it or something and falls down the stairs?"

"I guess we'd just have to just deal with those things *if* they happen," Miles grimaced. "I am sure you could improvise something… you seem like a bright lad. And as to the draught, there are no windows in that treasury. It's underground…"

"This is going to be dicey…" Astar said.

"Yes," Miles agreed. "But we knew that from the very beginning. I think we're just going to have to clench the arrow. We need to get this done quick. As capable as Elita is, we don't want to keep her waiting too long."

"Fine," Astar said. "Let's do it."

Astar drew upon his *viga* and took a few deep breaths, priming himself. He knew that these next few moments were pivotal to the success of this mission, and he was going to have to concentrate hard to pull it off.

He began by conjuring a knocking sound, isolating it as an audial illusion that only the guard could hear. Astar made it seem like it was coming from the doors leading outside.

The guard cocked his head and looked around the

room. His gaze then settled upon the doors, and he frowned.

He then began to walk over. Astar gave Miles a thumbs up.

"Go," Astar whispered. "Now."

Miles crept towards the treasury door and carefully lifted the latch. As he opened it, the hinges groaned, making a sound that was so grating it made Astar flinch.

But Astar didn't let it cause him to flounder. He kept his focus firmly upon beguiling the guard, making sure that he could not hear the door.

The guard was now conversing with the men stationed outside.

"Hearin' things again, are you, Kivran?" one of them teased.

"Or did you just want to enjoy the weather?" the other one said. The three of them laughed.

It took much concentration on Astar's part to hide what Miles was doing from all three of them; isolate the individual sounds so that they could still hear each other's voices yet not hear nor see what Miles was doing.

Miles slipped through the opening and made his way down the stairs, leaving the door wide open. Astar recalled in his mind how that door had appeared a few moments ago when it was closed and projected that image. So that all other eyes, aside from his and Miles', would see it that way.

The guard then closed the door and returned to his post. Astar's heart was in his throat as the man positioned himself in front of that opening again. Despite Miles' assurances, Astar was still worried the man might notice a change in the temperature now that the door wasn't in place, but the man seemed oblivious. He crossed his arms over his chest and resumed his watch.

Astar waited.

It seemed a long time. He focussed all of his attention upon the guard; watching his movements. Sustaining the illusion.

Eventually, Astar heard footsteps.

Shit! he thought, at first believing it must be Miles on his way back up the stairs. He drowned out that sound from the guard's ears, making him deaf to it.

But then, Astar realised that the sounds were coming from a different stairway.

"Elsa!" the guard said as a young woman stepped into the chamber. Astar recognised her face; it was one of the girls who had carried those platters up to Galrath's chamber. "Didn't hear you then…"

The girl blushed and made her way outside. As she opened one of the doors, she must have let in a draught because the door down to the treasury – hanging invisibly open – wobbled.

Astar's heart lurched in his chest. The door rocked back and forth a few times. He held his breath, praying it would stop.

It didn't. It struck the wall and then rebounded, gradually veering towards the guard.

Astar rushed to stop it, conjuring more layers to his illusions to cover up the sight of himself, as well as the sound of his footsteps.

He caught the door just in time. It was a mere few inches away from the guard's face when Astar curbed its momentum. Astar let out the breath he had been holding in, enjoying a brief moment of relief, but he didn't let himself relax; he was way too close to that guard now to be comfortable.

Astar drew away, pulling the door so that it was wide open again and flattening it against the wall.

And it was during that moment when Miles appeared again.

Astar heard him walking up the stairs. A sound he immediately hid from the guard's ears. *That* part was easy; it was how to proceed next that he was nervous over.

He needed to get the guard to move out of the way so Miles could get past him.

***Think** Astar…* he coached himself. *Think fast!*

He summoned a pair of bats. It was the first illusion

401

that popped into Astar's head. To the guard, they seemed to suddenly fly into the chamber from the stairway the serving girl had just emerged from, flapping their wings as they careened into the room. Astar conjured one of them to make a shrieking noise and swerve right in front of the guard's face. The man ducked and covered his eyes.

"What the–" he began to say, but Astar then made the other bat swoop in from the opposite side, forcing the guard to leap out of its path. This time, to Astar's satisfaction, the guard moved *away* from the door to the treasury.

"Now," Astar uttered to Miles. "Quick!"

Miles stepped through and then hurriedly bolted the treasury door shut behind him.

In the meantime, Astar kept up the mirage of the bats. The creatures were flying around the chamber, making shrill cries as they darted from wall to wall, and the guard opened the doors to the outside. Daylight streaked into the chamber, and the two guards posted out there turned their heads. When they saw the bats, they stared with wide eyes.

"Come on!" Astar said to Miles as he made his way to the exit. "This is our chance!"

"Bloody cavecreepers!" one of the guards exclaimed. "How did they get in there?!"

Astar marched towards them, drawing more *viga* to amplify his magic as he did so. "You go first," he said to Miles between gritted teeth. Sweat was gathering on his forehead. It was taking every shred of his capacity – and his *viga* – to keep himself and Miles hidden from the guards while simultaneously maintaining the illusion of the bats. "Walk between them. Just don't let them touch you. *Hurry!*"

Miles complied without comment, but Astar could tell, from the expression on the scholar's face, that he was nervous. Astar was nervous too, but he tried not to let it show. He followed Miles, and they made their way out of the tower. At one point, Astar had to squeeze through the narrow gap between two of the guards; neither of them more than a few inches away, but thankfully, they didn't seem to notice. They were too busy arguing over what to do about the bats.

We made it! Astar realised when he noticed the change in temperature, and a cool breeze caressed his face. He continued walking and didn't look back, maintaining the illusion.

Once clear, he then turned around.

Time to bring this to an end, he thought as he made the pair of illusory bats fly out of the doors of the tower, flapping their black wings as they ascended, making one last shriek as they vanished into the fog. The three guards all jovially cheered, still completely unaware of what had just occurred whilst they were all distracted.

"Give Elita the signal," Miles then said. "It's time to go."

"Fine by me," Astar said as he summoned one last final mirage: a bolt of thunder tearing across the sky above the castle.

Miles looked upwards as the clouds seemed to rumble. He then gave Astar a nod of approval.

They made their way back to the gatehouse and waited outside one of the barbicans. Miles seemed agitated and shifty.

"Where is she?" Miles said after a few minutes had passed.

"Be patient…" Astar said. "I'm still keeping us hidden. No one can see us."

"I know…" Miles said, casting his eyes around them. "I just… hope they don't notice."

"Notice what?" Astar asked him.

"There was another door at the bottom of the stairs," Miles said. "I had to break it open."

Astar cursed. "Is that what took you so long?"

Miles nodded. "The lock wasn't too difficult… but the Enchantment on it took me a while to figure out."

"I thought you said you didn't know much about Enchanting?" Astar said.

"I don't know anything about *making* Enchantments," Miles responded. "But I can sometimes figure out how to cease them. It's quite intuitive as long as you know Ancient. The—"

"She's here," Astar interrupted him. He didn't know which gave him more relief when Elita emerged out of the mist, the prospect of getting out of this place or an excuse to bring one of Miles' lengthy orations to an end.

"Thank you *so* much!" Elita said to the man now strolling beside her like an eager puppy, his eyes all bright and wide as he stared at her.

"Are you *sure* you have to go back out there?" he asked. "Why don't you stay a little longer?"

"I have to!" Elita said, feigning regret as she ran a hand across her brow. "But don't worry, I will be fine. I have Padleg with me!" she said, tugging upon the reins of her horse as she urged him to follow her towards the gate. "And I have supplies now, too, thanks to you."

Elita pinched the man's cheek, and he blushed. It was one of the most bizarre interactions Astar had ever witnessed.

"Now, can you be a dear and get your friend to open up this gate for me, please?" Elita asked.

"Yes, of course!" he said, running into the gatehouse.

Once the man was out of sight, Astar momentarily lifted his veil of invisibility to Elita – so that she, alone, could see him – and waved. She smiled through the side of her mouth but made no other acknowledgement of his presence.

A few moments later, the portcullis began to rise, and Astar and Miles scrambled towards it, eager to get out.

As they were making their way, Astar found his eyes drawn to the window of one of the buildings nearby. A man stood there, and for a brief moment, Astar could have sworn that he was staring at himself and Miles.

He's probably just watching the gate, Astar thought to himself.

He crossed the bridge, feeling a little more relief with each step he took.

*   *   *

After Lord Galrath of Falam had finished his luncheon, he called for one of his servants.

"Belise."

A few moments later, she appeared and began to clear the table. She was his favourite. He smiled at her as she stacked the plates and utensils onto one of the platters.

"Can you bring me some wine when you're done?" Galrath asked.

"Yes, M'lord," she said and walked away.

Galrath got up from his chair to stretch his legs and went to the window. *Strange weather…* he thought as he peered outside. He couldn't see the mountains like he usually could, or even much of his ward, just fog.

He sighed.

Galrath was restless. Ever since King Wilard had decreed the Levian Mountain Pass be blocked, he had felt unsettled. It was not just the money he was missing; it was the bustle. His life had been so much more intriguing when his home had been a place of passage. Without the flux of traders, smugglers, and wayfarers, Falam might as well be struck from the map. It had no purpose.

Damn you, Grav'aen!

He was no fool. He was well aware that, even though the men who had come to demolish the pass had been wearing the King's livery, Grav'aen had been the one to give the order.

You will be more than compensated, Grav'aen had promised. *I have plans for you. Ones which will make you even richer than you are today.* But Galrath was still waiting for that nest egg to hatch.

Galrath ran a finger down the centre of his forehead – where the scar was – as he thought about the pledges Grav'aen had made to him. He was beginning to suspect Grav'aen had duped him, though. Grav'aen was crafty fox; Galrath knew one when he saw one, for he was one himself.

The procedure will leave a small mark, was one of the

lies Grav'aen had fed him, just before he had that witch perform the ritual. Grav'aen had promised it would grant Galrath powers that would someday bring him great wealth and power, but that was another promise which Galrath had yet to see come to fruition.

'A small mark' was a rather unembellished choice of words on Grav'aen's part. The scar on Galrath's forehead was so ugly he had taken to wearing fedoras to cover it.

Master!

Galrath flinched. He still wasn't used to *that*. Hearing voices in his head. It came from one of the men Grav'aen had left behind after he and the witch departed.

There were six of them, in all, and they were strange creatures. Galrath was telepathically connected to each one.

Grav'aen claimed that their purpose was to protect Galrath, but he didn't believe that for a moment. They were watching him.

Yes… Galrath replied.

I have just seen a man, he said. The tone behind his persona as he communicated with Galrath was, as always, monotonous and free from any emotion. It was like these creatures didn't even possess souls. *He is on Grav'aen's list. We were ordered to hunt him down if we saw him and bring him back to our master. Alive, if possible.*

Who is this man? Galrath asked. Very few people passed through his castle these days.

The man projected an image into Galrath's mind, and Galrath gasped.

"*Miles?*" Galrath exclaimed out loud. "What is *he* doing here?"

Would you like me to pursue him? the creature asked.

Yes! Galrath replied. *Gather the others and find him! Find him now!*

Chapter 21

Flight

Dareth waited, crouched behind a rocky furrow near the bottom of the hill.

He watched them, waiting for the right moment to make his move.

Kyra and Bryna sat by the fire. They chatted, but Dareth was not close enough to hear any of the content. Not even with the ears of an Avatar.

Rivan was nearby too, but Dareth didn't see much of him. The burly giant of a man seemed to spend most of his time on the other side of the peak – out of Dareth's sight – but he did occasionally return to the fire for brief periods. He seemed on edge. Dareth got the impression that all three were nervous about something, but he had no idea what that something was. Rivan kept pacing up and down. Kyra was fidgety. Bryna was the same as she usually was, no matter the situation; serene and unreadable.

At one point, Kyra ventured down the hill to fill her water bladder at the stream, and she was little more than a few dozen paces away from the boulders Dareth had crouched behind. She gave the horses some attention whilst she was down there, making cooing noises as she ran her hands through their manes. It seemed more to comfort herself than them. She spoke to them, and Dareth heard some of it. It seemed she had given them all names, the witless cavecrawler.

It took much self-restraint on Dareth's part to not jump her there and then, but he held back. Kyra's ears were sharp, and her eyes were keen. She would almost certainly hear Dareth coming and put up a fight. She would probably even be sagacious enough to call for help.

And that would give Bryna a chance to work her sorcery before he could deal with her.

For what he intended to do, he would need to be patient.

The opportunity Dareth was waiting for eventually came. Bryna made her way down the hill. At first, Dareth assumed she was heading out to forage – that was the usual reason for the girl to wander off, in Dareth's experience – but she didn't have her gathering basket with her, nor a receptacle for storing water.

Instead, she crouched behind some gorse bushes and began to relieve herself.

Dareth had never been witness to a girl urinating before. It was a peculiar act to watch. Especially with it being Bryna, of all people. For some reason, it had never occurred to Dareth that her body had functions just as anatomical as his own.

Dareth summoned his blades, his fingers melting into a single tapered point as his hands grew, but he didn't rush her yet. He held back. He wasn't entirely sure why.

Maybe it was because, despite the grimness of the deed he intended to do, it only seemed right to let her finish.

But something happened that forced Dareth to hasten. Bryna's body suddenly tensed, and she gasped, her mouth parting and her eyes widening.

She turned her head and looked in Dareth's direction.

Shit!

He should have known that she would have somehow become aware of him.

Dareth charged, launching himself from behind the rock and crossing the space between them in just a few colossal leaps. She was too close, and he was too swift-footed for her to have a chance at making a run for it, but he would have expected her to at least scream.

She didn't make a sound. Not even as Dareth struck her.

He drove his blade into her chest and passed through with surprisingly little resistance. Within moments, the tip emerged on the other side through the centre of her back. Her mouth opened, and her face went as white as a snowdrop.

Dareth then withdrew his blade, and Bryna fell to the ground facedown.

It was only then that Dareth noticed that she had somehow – in the time he had charged at her – managed to pull her breeches back up, sparing herself some dignity. It seemed such a peculiar thing for someone to concern themselves with during their final moments.

Dareth turned her over to check if she was still alive. Somehow, she was. She looked at him with her ghostly eyes.

"You had a choice, Dareth," she whispered.

He paused. It wasn't that she was still able to speak which chilled him that moment. Or even the placid calm in her voice as she spoke.

It was that she knew his name. Somehow, she had seen past his celestial armour and knew *who* he was.

He raised his blade to finish her off but found himself hesitating. A strange feeling blossomed in his chest as their eyes met. Almost like he could feel her pain.

After a few moments, the scar on Dareth's arm – the one he made when he became Bloodsworn – flared.

Dareth realised then that, whether he liked it or not, he would have to see this through.

Besides, there was no need to prolong her suffering.

"The darkness triumphed in you…" was the last thing she said, just before Dareth drew his blade across her throat.

*　　*　　*

Afterwards, he stared at her for some time. Her – now, lifeless – face, contorted in pain. Her dead eyes. For some reason, there wasn't as much blood as Dareth expected.

It was the second time Dareth had killed. In some ways, it was easier – because he had done it before – but it weighed upon his conscience a little more on this occasion. When Dareth killed Tarvek it had been reactive. Dareth had snapped, and Tarvek had only got what was coming to him. He had *deserved* it.

But Bryna – while Dareth had never really liked her – didn't do anything to warrant this. Dareth got no pleasure nor catharsis out of killing her. It had just been necessary for him to fulfil his oath to Grav'aen.

He raised himself back to his feet and turned away. He did not doubt that what he had just done would come back to haunt his conscience, but he didn't see any point in dwelling upon it yet.

It was time to confront the one he had *really* come for. Kyra.

He raced up the hill. Despite Bryna's lack of cries, Kyra and Rivan must have noticed something because when Dareth approached the camp, they were ready for him, running towards him with weapons drawn. At the sight of him, they both halted.

"Baird?" Rivan blurted. His eyebrows joined together into one line. "Sidry?"

"It's not them," Kyra said. "That thing is the wrong colour."

Dareth wasn't interested in their chatter. He advanced on Kyra, readying his blade.

But then, to his utter disbelief, Rivan blocked his path.

*What's he **doing**?* Dareth wondered. He tried to step around him, but Rivan responded, skirting into his path again and pointing his sword at Dareth.

In a flash of light, Dareth reverted to his human form. Rivan and Kyra both stared, their eyes becoming wider.

"Move aside," Dareth advised Rivan. "I have no quarrel with you. It's *her* I've come for."

"*Dareth*?" Rivan gasped. "How did you become an Avatar?"

"Move!" Dareth repeated. "I won't ask again."

"No," Rivan shook his head and shifted his sword into a more defensive position. He edged closer to Kyra, so they were only a few feet apart. "It doesn't work like that. We fight together."

"*What?*" Dareth pointed at Kyra. "It's *her!* Since when did you care? Just move out of the ruddy way, Rivan! There's no need for both of you to die."

"Where's Bryna?" Kyra asked. She looked around them. "What did you do to her?"

"I... dealt with her," Dareth said. For some reason, he couldn't bring himself to be more explicit. "I had to..." His voice, against his will, croaked. "She was dangerous."

Rivan's face fell when Dareth said that. And there was a strange look in his eyes.

*Things **have** changed...* Dareth realised. More than he could have ever predicted. Not only did Rivan and Kyra seem to possess a new camaraderie, but also that look – the one Dareth caught in Rivan's eyes at the mention of Bryna – was one he had seen before.

It was the same one Aylen used to have when he spoke of Kyra. Shortly before he died.

I'm going to have to kill them both, Dareth realised. It was a shame. There had once been a time when Dareth looked up to Rivan. Considered him a friend, even.

But Dareth wanted to kill Kyra, and he wasn't going to let anyone – not even Rivan – stop him.

Dareth called upon the crystal in his forehead, summoning his Avatar of Gezra again. There was a flash of light, and a warm glow consumed his body. He shifted into a new shape while temporarily suspended in a dimension of white light.

When Dareth came out of it – transformed – there was a sudden movement. It occurred so fast there was nothing Dareth could do to stop it. The only warning he got was a blur of silver as Rivan's sword whistled through the air. It was followed by a peculiar sensation.

Dareth looked down to see that Rivan's had buried his sword into his chest.

He had never been stabbed before as an Avatar. It was a strange feeling. Not painful, but certainly uncomfortable.

Rivan still had both of his hands on the hilt. Dareth looked down at his face, now a mere arm span away from his. They stared at each other. From the look on Rivan's face, he was just as shocked by what had transpired as

Dareth was. Maybe he had only attempted to strike Dareth as a final act of defiance and never actually expected it to pay off.

When Dareth was an Avatar, he felt invincible. It had never occurred to him that someone – a mere human wielding a weapon – could cause him injury if they were swift enough.

Dareth eventually recovered his wits. He remembered who and what he was and summoned one of his blades.

You'll regret that! he thought as he raised it.

He swung it down upon Rivan. Dareth caught the moment of panic in Rivan's eyes when he looked up and realised Dareth's blade was on a course towards him. They both knew it was too late for Rivan to evade. Time seemed to slow. Rivan abandoned his sword – the one that was still buried in Dareth's chest – and let go of the hilt as he leapt away. He wasn't fast enough.

Dareth's blade bore into Rivan's side, passing through his ribs like a knife through hot wax and tearing through some of the organs beneath. Rivan screamed, and his legs gave way beneath him. Dareth then yanked the blade out again, and blood burst out from the wound in Rivan's side in an eruption of red. More followed.

"Rivan!" Kyra wailed as the man fell. She had been in the midst of nocking an arrow to her bow, but dismay had paralysed her.

You're next! Dareth thought as he raised his blade.

"Get away from them!" a voice rasped.

What is that? Dareth thought. He had not heard anyone coming, and that voice sounded like it was close.

He spun around.

Bryna.

Dareth gasped. He thought he must have been hallucinating at first, but there she was. Standing at the edge of the camp. There was still a thin red line at her throat – from where he had slashed her – but the flesh there seemed to have joined itself back together again.

Blood coated her dress, and her legs were shaking but somehow she was still standing.

Her trembling hand voyaged from the wound at her chest – which Dareth could see had somehow begun to regenerate too – to her necklace. She tightened her fingers around it, and it began to glow with purple light.

Initially, Dareth was too shocked by the sight of her to react, but then his wits returned to him. He charged, determined to get to her before she could finish whatever spell she was about to cast.

But then he remembered that he still had the sword stuck in his chest. It twitched achingly as he moved. Not only that, but the injury had affected him in other ways. He felt weaker and more lethargic than he usually did as an Avatar.

Dareth grabbed the hilt and pulled the blade out, his entire body quivering as the sword passed through his insides; he experienced a whole spectrum of peculiar and unpleasant sensations.

Once he freed himself from the blade, he tossed it aside. *Kill her, **now!*** he thought. *Kill her before she kills you!*

But then a familiar face appeared before his eyes. One that made him hesitate.

It was Aylen. Translucent yet glowing. He looked the same as all those beings Bryna had conjured during the Festival of Verdana, back in Fraknar.

He stood in front of Bryna with his arms crossed over his chest. Calm, yet protective.

"Don't do it!" Aylen said. "Leave them, Dareth."

You're not real! Dareth thought.

"I am real," Aylen said. As if he had somehow heard Dareth's thoughts. "Please, Dareth. Don't do this. You don't have to. Look what you've done to Rivan!"

But I– Dareth began to respond but then heard something. It was only a slight noise, but it was one Dareth's Avatar ears picked up.

A bow flexing.

Dareth turned, and just as he spun around – his vision twirling as he twisted not just his head but his entire body – a flash caught his eye.

413

As soon as Dareth saw it, he knew it was too late. There was a moment of blackness, his head jerked back from the impact, and then a ringing as the arrow tore through his brain.

Kyra, with a bow in her hand.

*   *   *

It was not long after they reclaimed their horses when Astar noticed they were being followed.

"Look!" he said, pointing towards Galrath's castle. The gate had lifted, and several figures emerged from the drawbridge. They were heading straight towards them.

"I count six," Elita said, covering her eyes with her hand to shield them from the rain as she observed them. "But they're not on horseback, so I don't think they're after *us*… maybe it's just coincidence, and they're just heading this way for some other reason."

"Let's just ride on," Miles suggested. His voice was outwardly calm, but Astar could sense that he was a little nervous. "They seem to be moving rather fast for people just on foot…"

They spurred their horses on. Although Elita and Miles had claimed there was nothing to be concerned about, Astar couldn't help but notice that both of them were now riding faster than before. As an extra precaution, Astar used his *viga* to cast a shroud around the three of them and hide them from sight.

"They're gaining on us!" Elita said a few minutes later. She seemed genuinely worried now. "I just saw them again. They're only a few hills away. How are they catching up so fast?"

"Hide us, Astar!" Miles said.

"I already have been!" he replied. "I started it earlier! When I first saw them."

Miles cursed. Astar had never heard the well-spoken scholar swear before. "Let's speed up! Come on! We'll veer off from the path and take another route."

"I'll summon some rain," Elita said. "It'll cover our

tracks and make it harder for them to follow us."

She closed her eyes, and a few moments later, the sky began to shower down upon them again. This time much heavier than it had before. Miles conjured shields above their heads to cover the three of them from the worst of the downpour, and they rode on. The trail beneath their feet soon became so wet the dirt turned into a thick mire. The horses kept kicking clumps of it into the air as their hooves drudged through. Miles led the way, and they broke off from the main path. He claimed he could see the hill where Kyra and the others were waiting, but Astar wasn't sure how one could see anything that far away in this weather. The clouds Elita had summoned around Galrath's castle were following them now, and the air was foggy.

"They're gaining on us!" Elita screamed after looking behind them again. "How is that possible?"

"They must be Zakaras!" Miles yelled back. He was unable to hide the panic in his voice now.

"I think he's right!" Astar replied. "It's why they can still see us. My magic doesn't work on them."

"What are we going to do?" Elita asked.

"Get back to the camp!" Miles shouted back at her. "We're almost there now. The higher ground will give us an advantage, and the others can help us fight them."

Astar swallowed a lump in his throat, urging his steed to pick up the pace as they galloped on. He was worried. They were going to have to confront their pursuers eventually and, if they really were Zakaras, Astar wasn't going to be able to help them much.

Astar just had to hope that Elita and Miles still had enough *viga* left to get them through this.

He could see the hill now. The one where the others were waiting. It was just ahead. Astar turned his head to check on their pursuers and saw that they were crossing the crest of a hill two peaks away and racing towards them with astonishing speed. Astar flicked the reins again, coaxing his mount to go faster. Even Elita's destrier seemed to be losing momentum now. Astar hoped they could keep it up a little longer.

Ahead of them, there was a sudden flash of light.

"What was that?" Astar exclaimed, turning to Elita.

"Wasn't anything to do with me!" she yelled back.

"I think I know…" Miles muttered. "But… how could it be possible…"

Astar was just about to ask Miles what it was that he meant when they came across a stream and had to coax the horses to cross it. Astar got splashed by Miles' horse as it trundled through the body of water, but he didn't complain. They rode on and began to ascend the final hill. Miles leaned forward on his saddle. "Quick! Come on! We're almost there!"

Just as they were nearing the peak, there was another flash of light. Astar looked around to try to discover the source, but Elita shrugged. She seemed just as confused about it as he was.

He flicked the reins a few times, urging one last burst of speed as they crested the top of the hill and wound through the mounds of gorse bushes to reach the others.

As soon as Astar reached the camp, he gasped at the scene he found. The first sight he found his eyes drawn to was of Rivan and Bryna.

Rivan was on his back. His eyes were closed, and Astar couldn't tell whether he was still alive or not, but the ground around him had pooled with blood. Bryna was weeping as she pressed a poultice to a wound on Rivan's chest. Her hands were completely red.

Astar leapt off his horse.

"What happened?" he asked, turning to Kyra, who appeared to be the only one still standing.

It was only then that Astar noticed there was someone else in the camp. A figure lay face down on the grass.

"Who's *that*?" Astar asked.

"What happened here?" Miles asked as he dismounted. "There's Zakaras coming!"

"Zakaras?" Kyra repeated. Before Miles had said that word, she had been staring at the figure lying on the ground, but then her eyes widened and she turned to

Miles. "Where? How many?"

"Six, I think," Miles replied. "They're following us."

"Shit!" Kyra exclaimed. "We were attacked, Miles! Rivan's down. I think he might be—"

"Who is this?" Astar asked as he walked over to the figure lying in the middle of the camp.

"Be careful!" Kyra yelled. "He's—"

Astar turned the body over – it was a dead weight in his hands – and saw the face.

"*Dareth*?!" Astar exclaimed.

"You *know* him?" Kyra said as she marched over.

"Yes!" Astar said, and then he looked at Dareth's face again to make sure. "Of course! He was at the Institute. How do *you* know him?"

"He's from Jalard," Kyra narrowed her eyes at the sight of his face. "My village."

"You're scitting me?" Astar said.

Kyra bit down upon her lip and shook her head. "Nope," she said.

She then unsheathed one of the daggers hanging from her belt.

"What are you doing?" Astar asked.

"Finishing off the job," Kyra said grimly. "I'm going to kill him, of course!"

"*Why*?" Astar asked as he blocked her from getting to him.

"I don't have time for this," Kyra said through gritted teeth. She tried to shove past Astar, but he pushed her back. "Move out my way, Astar! This isn't to do with you!"

"It is!" Astar yelled back. "I *know* him."

"No, you bloody don't!" Kyra screamed. "If you knew anything about him, you'd ruddy slit his throat *for* me. Now *move*!"

"Can I remind everyone that we have Zakaras incoming?" Elita spoke up. "Am I going to have to deal with them *alone*, or are you lot going to *help* me?!"

Astar and Kyra looked at each other.

"Trust me, Astar," Kyra said. "He ain't worth it. Let me

kill him. It was him who got Rivan and Bryna."

Kyra then seemed to see something behind Astar's shoulder, and her eyes widened in alarm.

Astar spun around and saw that Dareth was awake again. The young man opened his eyes, groaned, and used one of his hands to push the top half of his body up from the ground. He seemed a little dazed and confused at first, but then he looked around himself. When his gaze settled on Kyra, his whole body stiffened as if he was preparing to leap at her.

"Don't!" Astar yelled, positioning himself between Dareth and Kyra. "Stop this! There are *Zakaras* coming! We need to deal with *them*! Not fight amongst ourselves!"

Neither of them seemed to hear him. Dareth drew to his feet and tried to step around Astar to get to Kyra. She did the same. Astar had to dance between the two of them, both of his arms extended, to keep them from getting to each other.

And then he had an idea.

He called upon his *viga*.

"Where has she gone?!" Dareth asked a few moments later. He spun around in a full circle. "Where have *all* of them gone?"

"Where is he?" Kyra cried, almost mimicking him in action as she wheeled around, her dagger swinging.

"I've hidden them from you," Astar said to both of them. "I'm not going to let you hurt each other."

"Why?!" Kyra yelled.

"There's *Zakaras* coming!" Astar reminded her. He hollered those words so loud she flinched.

"Zakaras?" Dareth repeated.

"Yes," Astar said, turning back to him. He then made himself invisible to Kyra too, and stepped away from her to distance himself. "Help us!" he pleaded with Dareth. "We can talk about whatever bad blood there is between you and them later. Make it right."

"No," Dareth shook his head. "It's too late for me and them. Even if I *wanted* to, they'd never saddle up with me again. Not after what I've done. And not after what *they've* done, either. I… have to go…" he said. "I can't fight those Zakaras anyway. I made a *bloodoath* to Grav'aen, and he told me to leave if I encountered them. I'm sure you guys will get through this. Apart from Rivan…" Dareth said, and Astar detected a hint of regret when Dareth said that name. His voice softened a little. "I didn't *want* to kill him, I just…" Dareth shrugged and then looked back at Astar. "Don't trust those people, Astar. It's *their* fault my village was destroyed."

Dareth then turned, and there was a flash of light. He transformed into that horned being again – the one Astar had seen at the Institute – and fled.

*   *   *

What is taking them so long? Elita thought as she stared down the hill, waiting for the Zakaras to arrive.

Elita had been shocked when she saw Dareth too; she didn't know the man quite like Astar did, but she certainly recognised his face. She had seen him wandering around the Institute a few times, and witness him transform into a glowing being whilst fighting a member of Squad Three was not the sort of spectacle one forgot all too easily.

And it seemed the others knew him too. Another surprise. But it was not one Elita was willing to tarry over. Not yet.

The Zakaras were coming, and Elita began preparing for their arrival.

Drawing upon her *viga*, she began by clearing the fog. She had initially summoned it in the hope it would help them lose the Zakaras, but that had not worked; the Zakaras had found them anyway. Now, it suited Elita's purposes for the air to be clear so that their surroundings were more visible.

She coaxed the aerosols of mist to drift back up the sky and mingle amongst the clouds. They gradually merged, and the clouds became darker and more animated. They were the same clouds Elita had conjured above Galrath's castle that morning. When she learned that the Zakaras were on their trail, she had bidden them follow her back to the skies above the camp.

"How close are they?" Miles asked, appearing beside her.

Elita shook her head. "I don't know. The last time I saw them, they crossed that ridge over there. My guess is that they are on the other side of that hill," she pointed in the direction of the peak opposite them. "Unless they're making their way around the other side to surprise us, that is."

"Let's assume – pray, rather – that they are not," Miles grimaced. "Zakaras are not all that smart, so I doubt they would be that cunning. And if Galrath is aware that we have taken his waystones, he will have instructed them to chase us down as swiftly as possible to stop us having a chance to use them."

*Now **that's** an idea...* Elita thought.

"Where are the others?" she asked. "Have they brought their drama to a clinch yet?"

Miles shook his head. "I expect they'll join us soon. Hopefully, anyway."

"What about Bryna?" Elita asked. "Can *she* help? There are six Zakaras, I think. I took down three by myself once, but it drained the life out of me. I don't have so much *viga* left today. She's Blessed, isn't she?"

Elita watched Miles' face as he prepared to reply. As usual, where Bryna was concerned, Elita could tell Miles was hiding something. Elita had registered that Bryna had some manner of secret – something which she and Astar were not trusted enough to be privy to yet – quite early on and had tried getting to the bottom of it a few times by subtly probing them with questions, but it was a matter the others always skirted around.

Miles shook his head. "I just spoke to her... she's been hurt too, and said she will only have the strength to help us again if one of us dies... that is a rather sobering thought, isn't it?"

*Why would it take someone **dying** to enable her to help us?* Elita wondered. She didn't ask, though, because this was not the right time for interrogation.

"That moment might come sooner than you would like," Elita commented. She had seen the state of Rivan – and Elita was no devotee of Carnea, but even she could tell the man was unlikely to live much longer.

"I think you may be right," Miles said sadly.

Kyra appeared then, readying her bow as she joined them.

"Where are they?" she asked as she flexed the string to test it. She didn't seem happy with the tautness, so her hands went to the upper nock to adjust it.

"I don't know. I haven't seen them for a while," Elita said. "Where is Astar?"

"I don't know!" Kyra said, her face turning red with anger. "He vanished! Along with Dareth!"

"There!" Elita exclaimed, pointing when a group of figures appeared on the peak of the hill opposite them. "They're almost here!"

"I count six," Kyra said as she squinted. "That's not good odds, is it…"

"They're not in human guise anymore, either," Miles commented.

The figures were not close enough for Elita to see them in much detail yet, but even from this distance, she could discern that the six of them all had peculiar outlines. One appeared to be hurtling on several pairs of elongated limbs, giving it the appearance of a spider crawling over a mound as it descended the slope.

"I'm coming!" Astar yelled, and Elita turned to the sound of his voice to see him running to join them. "What's happening? Are they here yet?"

"Where's Dareth!?" Kyra asked him.

"Gone…" Astar replied.

"They're not far now!" Elita replied, in an effort to change the subject and remind them both of the impending threat. "And there are six of them… I don't think we can take that many."

"So, what do we do?" Astar asked.

"How long would it take to get one of those waystones ready, Miles?" Elita asked.

"A while…" Miles said and then frowned. "But it can only carry five."

"Get started on it…" Elita said. "Sit with Bryna and Rivan – you can protect each other that way – and call for us when it's ready."

"But it can only carry *five*," Miles repeated. "There are six of us."

Elita looked at him. "You saw Rivan, Miles. I don't think there is going to be six of us much longer."

"I hope you're not saying what I think you are?!" Kyra exclaimed. "We're *not* leaving him behind!"

"I'm being realistic!" Elita snapped back. "If these monsters kill us, we *all* die. Just get it ready," Elita turned her attention back to Miles. "Just in case. If Rivan is still alive by then… well… we'll cross that bridge if we come to it."

"I would rather take Rivan's corpse back than *you*!" Kyra shouted.

"Just get the bloody waystone ready!" Elita screamed at Miles, ignoring Kyra. "We don't have time to argue about this! Get it to take us to Babuton."

"It is of the utmost importance we get to Shemet as soon as possible," Miles said. "We–"

"*Fine!*" Elita snapped. "Shemet then! Just go, and bloody *do* it! You can teach Astar and me to use one of them to get to Babuton when we get there."

Miles ran off without saying another word.

"Rivan is a fighter," Kyra said. "He'll survive! We're not leaving him."

"Be quiet!" Elita said. "It's just a precaution. Hopefully, we won't need to."

"The Zakaras are getting close!" Astar pointed to the bottom of the valley. The creatures were now crossing the stream, and Elita could see their gruesome and morbid anatomies' clearer. She suppressed a shudder. "What are we going to do?"

"I am hoping I can take a few of them out before they get to us," Elita said.

"How?" Kyra asked.

Elita didn't respond. Instead, she turned her head up to the sky and called upon her *viga*. The clouds above were charged with energy, and Elita coaxing them to rouse, priming them.

Elita turned her gaze back to the approaching Zakaras. They had crossed the stream now and were crawling up the hill, passing through an area clustered with trees. In the path ahead of them lay an open space. Elita waited for them to reach that. When charged light struck from the sky, it was often drawn towards large objects such as trees on its way to the ground. Elita didn't want anything to interfere with what she intended.

"They're getting closer!" Kyra said.

I know! Elita thought, but she resisted the urge to scream at the other woman during this crucial moment. She had primed the elements above them, and they were ready to burst. She couldn't hold them back much longer.

The Zakaras passed through the trees and reached the open space.

Elita let go. There was a rumble as forks of light tore from the clouds. Elita focussed upon the Zakaras as she directed the terminus of the energy. Lightning struck two of the creatures, and they both jolted. Elita narrowed her eyes and drew upon more *viga* as she communed with the source of the discharge, urging it to bolster. The shafts of light rippled, and smoke rose from the jittering bodies of the Zakaras until they turned black.

"Only four now," Astar said as he readied his spear. "Can you do that again?

"No," Elita replied. The four other Zakaras continued bounding towards them. She cursed inwardly. She had intended to take three of them out with that strike, but she only caught two. She still wasn't used to manipulating these forces so capaciously. "There isn't enough pressure left in those clouds," she said. "It is going to take a while for them to gather enough force again."

Elita then realised that it might be possible for her to accelerate that process. She closed her eyes and connected with the clouds again, willing the forces within them to roil and meld.

"Can't you just conjure it from your hands like you did that other time?" Astar asked.

"I don't have enough *viga,*" Elita shook her head as she opened her eyes again. "For me to summon it from nothing takes much more effort than if the necessary elements are already available to me. What I just did was bend nature; the force of that thunder was already in the clouds. It is far less draining to do it that way." Elita then turned to Astar and Kyra and raised her voice. "Now, I need you both to prepare yourselves. I am going to separate one of those Zakaras from the others and, when I give you the signal, I need you to kill it as quickly as possible. And I suggest you ready your sword, Kyra. That bow isn't going to be much use here."

"But–" Kyra began to object, but Elita ignored her. She didn't have time for that girl's nugatory remarks right now. Elita began to channel again, drawing upon her dwindling supplies of *viga* to summon winds. Kyra and Astar both looked around themselves as they noticed new draughts swirling around them. Elita coaxed them to gather in the air above her and churn into a cyclone.

Elita then turned her attention back to the Zakaras – who were by now halfway up the hill – and extended her hands, directing the torrent of wind she had just gathered towards three of them with such force it made the air whistle. The creatures fell back. Two of them tumbled over, their grotesque bodies cascading down the hill in a flurry of flailing limbs, but the third dug its talons into the side of the bank and clung on.

The fourth Zakara – the one Elita had intentionally excluded from the burst of air she conjured – carried on charging. It was so close now Elita could see its immense outline. It was black, with leathery skin, bulbous eyes, and a pair of mandibles protruding from its mouth. It loped towards them on six legs.

"That one!" Elita yelled to Astar and Kyra. "Kill it now! I'll keep the others at bay!"

Astar and Kyra both charged towards the creature. Elita was happy to notice Kyra had heeded her advice and was now brandishing a sword. That was good; the winds Elita was channelling were causing a disturbance in the air around them, and it would have greatly affected the accuracy of Kyra's arrows.

Astar met the Zakara head-on, thrusting his spear. The creature jerked away, avoiding the point of the weapon by inches, and then reeled its head, swooping its mandibles upon him. He danced around the Zakara, twirling his spear and using the momentum of its motion to stab at the monster again. This time, he struck, but not hard enough to pierce through.

Meanwhile, as the creature was distracted, Kyra dashed around the side of the Zakara, her sword poised and ready. The blade turned into a whirl of silver, one that was followed by a burst of red as she hacked off one of its legs. The creature howled, and one side of its body dropped as it lost its balance.

Elita turned her attention back to the other Zakaras. The ones she was keeping at bay with the winds. One of them was still clinging to the side of the hill with its talon fastened to the ground; *that* creature wasn't going anywhere. Elita was much more concerned about the other two. One of them had tumbled so far down the hill it was almost free from the brunt of the winds.

It rolled a few more times and then righted itself. It looked at Elita as it crawled to its feet and began to charge up the hill again on four legs, building up speed and skirting around the main thrust of the winds. Elita adjusted the trajectory in an attempt to catch the creature within its flow again, but the creature continued flanking. It was on a path towards Astar and Kyra.

"Incoming!" Elita warned them. She turned her eyes to her two companions briefly to check on their progress. The Zakara they were fighting was now on its back, and Astar was standing over it, trying to get the point of his spear past the range of its pincers so he could stab the creature in the head. Kyra hacked off another one of its legs, and it howled. "Get ready!"

"Give us more time!" Kyra screamed.

"I *can't*!" Elita yelled back.

She turned her attention back to the other two Zakaras. There was nothing more she could do for her companions. She just had to pray they managed to pull through.

It was a good thing she did, because Elita then discovered that one of the other creatures had also freed itself from the torrent.

Shit! Elita thought, her heart lurching in her chest. The creature was bounding towards her and was now little more than a dozen paces away. She only had a few seconds left until it reached her. She closed her eyes and filled herself with *viga*, calling out to the elements to aid her, begging them for some way to get through these next few moments alive.

She found it in the clouds above. They were almost ready to strike again – they just needed a little more coaxing. Elita stirred them into motion, opening her eyes and directing the blast of energy at the incoming Zakara. It took so much focus on her part that she let out a groan, and the flash of light was so intense it stung her eyes. She covered them. She held onto her link with the clouds and let the forks of lightning sear through the creature until, eventually, the fetor of seared flesh hit her nose.

Elita drew it to an end, and the Zakara – what remained of it – toppled over.

And then Elita remembered that there was a second Zakara.

In the panic, she had forgotten. She had channelled all her focus into summoning thunder. In the process, she had let go of the winds which had been keeping the other Zakara at bay. It was coming for her now – she could see its outline. Its rawbone legs carried its body with incredible speed as it raced towards her. It spread its arms – all four of them – as it neared, its claws flexing. It was so close Elita could see its black, lizard-like eyes and its long yellow teeth.

She called upon the winds to aid her again, even though she knew it was no use. The creature was too close. She couldn't propel the Zakara away without sending herself tumbling down the hillside with it.

The winds coiled around her, waiting for direction, but Elita couldn't think of a way to command them that wouldn't also harm herself as well as the Zakara. She let them swirl around her. It was oddly comforting and made her feel less alone. The winds encircled her limbs, cocooning her within a cyclone of air.

Her feet lifted from the ground.

Elita jolted in surprise, and she almost fell from the loss of balance, but the winds caught her. Wrapped around her. Lifted her.

As the Zakara closed the final few feet, its claws swinging, Elita made a final plea. One last desperate attempt to save herself.

She launched herself into the air. The winds carried her, accelerating as they swirled around her entire body.

Wrap yourself in wind! she realised. ***That's*** *how you do it!*

She had always thought that the tales of Farlenna – the legendary Blessed of Manveer who could fly – were just fables of fancy, but maybe they were true.

Elita looked down at the Zakara as it raked its claws through the empty air. It spun around, confused by Elita's sudden disappearance.

Then, there was a sudden burst of movement, and the creature jerked as something long and dark passed through its back and emerged through the other side of its body.

Astar's spear. He had launched it at the creature while it was distracted. He and Kyra came running in, Kyra's sword shimmering in a flash of silver as it struck, hacking off one of the creature's arms.

The Zakara shrieked and twisted away. Astar tried to grab the heft of his spear and yank it out of its body, but

427

the creature swept its claws, forcing Astar to abandon his spear and duck.

Kyra ran back in from behind the creature, skidding the last few feet on her knees as her blade glimmered on a course for the creature's legs. The creature's limbs were thin and brittle, and both of them snapped in two bursts of brown ichor. The Zakara fell howling, its remaining limbs and the stumps where the others used to be lashing through the air blindly. The point of the spear still buried inside it caught the ground on its way down, and the creature ricochet.

It wriggled one last time as if preparing to right itself, but Kyra's sword returned, this time from above, cleaving the creature's head from its body.

"Are you okay?" Astar then asked, turning his eyes up to Elita.

It was only then that Elita realised she was still hovering above them.

She gently coaxed the winds to release her; at first, drifting down gently, but she fell the last few feet and landed a little clumsier than she would have liked.

After she steadied herself, she looked up again, and Astar was smiling.

"You can fly now?" he asked, pulling a bemused expression.

"Apparently…" Elita straightened her breeches and smiled at him. "I figured it out. There's a trick to it. You wrap yourself in the wind."

Elita then looked at Astar more closely and noticed that his tunic was torn and covered in blood. There were three parallel gashes across his chest.

"Are you okay?" Elita asked.

Astar nodded. He tentatively put a hand to his chest and touched the skin around his wound, wincing. "Don't worry, it's not deep…" he said. "Most of the blood isn't mine."

Elita looked at Kyra and noticed that she was covered in blood too, but it was clear, from her absence of wounds and the slightly off-brown colour of the ichor, that none of it was her own. She appeared to have come out of the ordeal unscathed.

She's a plucky one, Elita thought. But she wasn't going to say such a thing out loud as she was damned before she ever paid *that* woman a compliment.

Kyra peered down the hill, and her eyes widened. "Shit!" she said, her body stiffening. She hefted her sword.

"What is it?" Astar asked.

She pointed down to the bottom of the valley. "Look down there. Two of the corpses are moving!"

Elita ran to Kyra's side and looked in the direction the woman was pointing. The two Zakaras she had struck with the first blast of lightning were no longer charred and black. Their bodies were beginning to wriggle. Somehow, they had regenerated. One of them was in the motion of rolling over and crawling to its feet.

"Move!" Elita yelled as she turned back towards the camp. She grabbed Astar's shoulder. "We need to go!"

"We can take them out, can't we?" Kyra asked.

"No!" Elita exclaimed. "We *can't*. Not two at the same time. I have hardly any *viga* left, and there is *nothing* in those clouds for me to work with anymore!" she pointed upwards. "If those Zakaras have revived, then others might too. We need to go! *Now!*"

Elita began to race back towards the camp, and the other two followed. They returned to find the others huddled together.

"Miles!" Elita cried as she joined them. "Is it ready yet?"

The waystone was in Miles' hands, glowing with blue radiance as he stroked it with his fingers and stared into its depths. He turned to Elita briefly, and the break in his focus made the light within the stone dim. "Almost…" he said, and then gritted his teeth and turned his attention back to the magical implement again.

Elita looked at Rivan. His eyes were closed, and he wasn't moving. Bryna was pressing an old robe she was using as a makeshift bandage to the wound on his chest, and she was crying. Her hands, the robe, and the ground around Rivan had turned to a dark crimson.

"Is he still alive?" Elita asked. She said it softly, trying to be as gentle about the matter as the immediacy of their situation allowed, but the other woman didn't even seem to hear her.

"No!" Kyra screamed when she caught up. "We're *not* leaving him behind!"

"What do you suggest?" Elita asked her. "Leave someone behind to die so you can take back a bloody *corpse*?"

"I say we *fight* them!" Kyra yelled back.

"With what?" Elita argued. "I have hardly any magic left, and Astar's Blessing is useless against them! We can't take them on with just your sword and a few bloody arrows!"

"The waystone is almost ready!" Miles exclaimed, interrupting their quarrel. The light radiating from it began to glimmer, its inner light pulsating. He looked at Kyra and Elita. "I think she's right, Kyra," he said regretfully. "It's not nice to leave him here... but try to be practical!"

"No!" Kyra crossed her arms over her chest. "There's got to be another way! There has to be!"

"We don't have time for this!" Elita screamed. "The Zakaras will be here any moment! How does it work, Miles?" she asked.

"We all need to link hands," Miles said, turning to Bryna and putting a hand on her shoulder. "You need to let him go, Bryna..." he said softly. "I'm sorry, but he's gone. There is nothing we can do for him."

"He's not dead yet," Bryna cried. Her voice was so soft it barely came out as a whisper yet everyone heard her. "I'm keeping him with us."

*We're **all** going to bloody die if we can't decide what to do soon!* Elita thought.

What way was there out of this? According to Bryna, Rivan was still clinging to life, but Elita doubted he would last for much longer in the state he was in. In her opinion, the kindest thing they could do for him was a quick act of mercy and bring his suffering to an end, but the others didn't seem to see it that way. They were too attached. They were all too blinded by their emotions to deal with the urgency of their situation. The Zakaras were coming, and they were running out of time.

Elita then realised that there was another option.

"Fine!" Elita exclaimed. "You win, Kyra! Have it your way! Link up hands – all of you! Go without me."

Miles began to object, but Elita cut him off.

"Just do it!" she screamed. "Don't worry about me! I will be fine."

Miles opened his mouth to say something else, but the words never came because what he saw next made him gasp.

Elita summoned the winds again, drawing upon the last remaining shreds of her *viga*. They swirled around her, coalescing until her entire body became enveloped within their cool, comforting presence. Her feet parted with the ground.

"Go," Elita said as she rose. "I'll be fine. You don't have time to argue."

"But Elita!" Astar called. "What about Babua?"

"I will head there!" she said to him. "And wait for you. Once you get to Sharma, get Miles to teach you to use those waystones, and come find me. I will wait there for you in Babuton! For one aeight, Astar, no more! If I don't see you by then, I'll assume you're not coming and go my own way!"

"Take my hand, Astar!" Kyra said, reaching for him. Astar turned to the young woman from Sharma and hesitated. The others had all linked hands by now, and Astar was the only link missing in the chain.

"Do it!" Elita yelled at him. "*Now!*"

Astar nodded and then reluctantly turned around and grabbed hold of Kyra's palm.

He was just in time because it was that moment the Zakaras appeared. Two figures emerged from behind the mounds on the other side of the camp. They hurtled towards them. One of them opened its massive jaws and let out a shrill scream as it charged.

Elita tuned in to the winds which were spiralling around her, spurring them to quicken. She began to ascend, feeling a surge of euphoria as the breeze ran through her hair and across her skin. Nothing in her life had ever felt so liberating.

A flash of blue occurred below her as the others vanished in a burst of light.

Elita took to the sky.

Chapter 22

A War Coming

The moment Miles activated the waystone, Bryna felt it. A sudden lurch. Like the entirety of her being – not just her body, but her mind and soul too – were yanked from the earthly world. It felt like she was being stretched, and yet at the same time, she was spinning. Suspended. She could feel the *aythirrealm* pulling at her as she was wrenched from one breadth of physical space to another.

They were carried away from that hilltop in Gavendara. Four people, and one still, lifeless, body. Time seemed to slow down and speed up all at once. Bryna could still see Elita; the young woman soared towards the sky. Bryna could see the Zakaras too, as they dashed towards her – towards their prey – but, as they charged, they seemed to get smaller and smaller, and then they were lost within the prismatic dimension of light and spiralling colours.

Throughout the whole thing, Bryna clung to Rivan's body.

When it was over, it felt like she had been spat out by a gargantuan creature. Her body jerked as it felt the heave of arrival upon solid ground once again. Soft, slightly damp grass pressed against her knees. Her body assumed the weight of physical existence anew.

She cast her eyes around her surroundings.

They were in the courtyard at the back of the Synod. Bryna was still dizzy, and her mind was muddled, but she recognised it. It was daytime. The sun was a little brighter than it was back in Gavendara a few moments ago.

Jaedin! she called out to her twin. It was her first instinct.

I'm coming! he replied, almost instantaneously. For the briefest moment, Bryna felt Jaedin's presence in her mind as he peeked through her eyes to discern their location,

433

and when Bryna heard his voice, she sensed he was already nearby. She would usually have been able to discern more, but she was exhausted, and it was taking every shred of her remaining energy to keep Rivan's soul from leaving them.

I need more, Bryna realised. She was back in Shemet now, so that shouldn't be a problem. She closed her eyes and reached out. Sure enough, there were a few souls within Bryna's range who had departed the mortal world that day, and lingering remnants of their *viga* remained; Bryna absorbed it to rejuvenate herself.

She opened her eyes again, instantly feeling more alert and awake. She then noticed that there were other people in the courtyard beside herself and her companions. They were all staring.

Bryna should not have been surprised by this; she and the others had suddenly appeared from nowhere in a flash of light.

"Where is Selena?" Miles said. The first one of them to recover his wits. He looked around them but none of the people watching responded. "Are you going to stare or *help us*?" Miles asked, unable to hide his irritation. He raised his voice so that others could hear. "Do any of you know where Selena would be? Get her for us! Now! Tell her it is Miles, and we have returned!"

A few of them seemed to snap out of their stupor and ran off towards the main Synod building. Others scurried in different directions. Some of them merely continued staring.

"Do you need help?" a young woman said as she tentatively approached them. She seemed fearful, and Bryna couldn't blame her. Herself and her companions were covered in blood and must have been quite a woeful sight. The lady's eyes went from Rivan to Astar and then to Kyra. "I am training to be a Devotee of Carnea... I am just a novice, but I know some things."

Bryna held on to Rivan protectively. "Stay away from him!" she said.

The woman flinched and drew away.

"Help *him*," Bryna then said, gesturing to Astar and making a conscious effort to gentle her voice this time. "He's wounded and needs tending."

Jaedin arrived a few moments later. Bryna didn't even know how he managed to get into the courtyard – she had been too distracted to pay attention to the link she shared with her twin. He just appeared, striding across the gardens towards them. It felt like it had been a long time since Bryna had seen her brother, and she might not even have recognised him at that moment if she had not sensed his presence. He was wearing a long brown surcoat, and he pulled back the hood to reveal his face. His hair had been cut short. It wasn't just his appearance that had changed, though. It was his ambience. His demeanour. Even the way he walked.

"What happened?" he asked.

"*Jaedin?*" Kyra exclaimed as she looked him up and down. "Is that *you*?"

He didn't reply. He strode right up to Bryna and narrowed his eyes at Rivan. "You were hurt…" he said and looked at his sister. "I felt it so I came."

"I need your help," Bryna whispered to him. "It's Rivan! He's–"

Jaedin turned his eyes back to the figure whose head rested upon Bryna's lap. "What happened to him?"

Bryna opened her mouth to respond, but Miles cut her off.

"Selena's coming!" he exclaimed.

Miles pointed, and they all turned. A group of figures had just emerged from the postern doors of the Synod. Bryna recognised the lady in the middle as Selena from her blonde hair. She had an entourage of four Synod Sentinels with her.

"I suggest it's time you made a swift exit, Jaedin," Miles said through the side of his mouth.

"No," Jaedin shook his head. "Bryna said she needs my help. I'm not scared of those people."

"Miles?" Selena called as she approached, running the last stretch of the distance to reach them. Her escort rushed to catch up. "How did you get here?" she asked.

"We got our hands on a waystone," Miles replied. "We've just arrived."

"What happened to you?" Selena asked. She looked at the others. "And who is this man?" she added when her eyes went to Astar. The novice Devotee of Carnea was now tending to him and in the process of carefully removing his bloodstained tunic.

"His name is Astar, and it's a long story," Miles replied. "He helped us."

Selena nodded. "We will see to his injuries," she said, swiftly gathering her composure and becoming her usual poised self. She turned to one of the armed men behind her. "Tephor. Take this young man to the infirmary and watch over him as he is treated."

Tephor walked over to Astar and offered the young man a hand to help pull himself up. Astar just stared at him at first. He seemed bewildered. He cast his eyes across the scene around him, and Bryna realised that this place must seem very strange to him. He had never set foot in Sharma before, but now he was deep within the heart of its civic authority.

"Go with him, Astar," Miles coaxed. "It's okay."

Astar looked up at Tephor again, and after a few more moments of hesitation, reached for his hand. Tephor pulled Astar to his feet.

"Kyra," Selena said, turning to her. "Maybe it would be best if you accompany him."

"But I'm not wounded!" she began to protest.

"There are baths in the infirmary, too," Selena interrupted her. She said it mildly, but it carried a nuance of authority. "They will see you clothed into something more... presentable," she said, her eyes wandering across Kyra's bloodstained and torn attire. "We can talk properly once you've cleaned up. I am sure you have lots to tell us."

"Jaedin..." Selena then said, turning to him and raising an eyebrow. "Is that really *you*?"

Jaedin's body tensed as if he was preparing for

something – whether it was fight or flight, Bryna couldn't tell, but she sensed much dissent within her brother that moment.

"I need his help," Bryna said to Selena.

"He's an outlaw," Selena replied to Bryna coolly.

"He is the only one who can help me save Rivan!" Bryna argued.

"He's still alive?" Selena asked, unable to hide her scepticism when she looked down at Rivan's body. "We have some of Sharma's finest Devotees of Carnea here, Bryna. Let them handle it."

"They can't help on this occasion. It is beyond them," Bryna said. "I *need* Jaedin."

Selena frowned. "What is it that Jaedin can do which they cannot?"

"There is no time to explain!" Bryna exclaimed. As soon as she raised her voice, she felt everyone's eyes turn to her, staring. "We risked our lives going to Gavendara for you, and now we are back, and you *owe* us. *Let*. Jaedin. Help. Me."

As far as Bryna knew, her identity as the Descendent of Vai-ris was still a secret to the Synod; and therefore, to Selena, she was just the daughter of a medicine woman from a humble village. Nobody of particular note.

But something about Bryna's bearing that moment must have made an impact – or possibly, made Selena see something within her – because the expression on the older woman's face changed. She looked at Bryna in a way she never had before, her eyes widening.

Selena, after some consideration, turned to Jaedin.

"Jaedin was a young man with long hair and a rather timid manner..." Selena said. "You do not resemble him much to me..." she turned back to Bryna. "I will turn a blind eye and let him help you, for now," she said. "But I cannot say the same for other members of the Synod if they were to become aware of his presence. I will try to keep it hushed for as long as I can. Greyjor is out right now on a matter of national interest. I do not know when he will be back, but I would advise your *unknown* companion," she said, looking at Jaedin again. "Whoever he is, to be discreetly gone before Greyjor returns."

*　　*　　*

It was a rather surreal experience for Jaedin to be escorted by Selena and her entourage of armed guards into one of the Synod buildings. It was the very same building that he had been taken to and, very briefly, allocated a room to stay when he arrived in Shemet all those aeights ago.

Just before he had sensed Ne'mair was a Zakara and killed him.

That seemed like a long time gone now.

"Where is Fangar?" Miles whispered to Jaedin as he rushed to catch up with him.

"Oh, he's not far away," Jaedin replied coolly. He said it loud enough so that Selena could hear too. It gave Jaedin great satisfaction that the current situation allowed him to walk amongst a member of the Synod so brazenly. "I'm sure if there is any trouble, he will make an appearance…"

"This room," Selena said curtly a few moments later. It was clear, from her manner, that she had heard Jaedin's comment about Fangar but was choosing to not engage with it.

She opened one of the doors, and Jaedin stepped into the chamber. He circled the room with his eyes and saw that there was a window – one which was just big enough that he could leap out of it if he had a sudden need to make a hasty exit. Jaedin walked over to it and opened the shutters. He did it casually – making it seem like he was merely letting the light in – but in reality, he was observing his escape route.

Outside, Jaedin saw movement in one of the trees. Fangar on vigil. He smiled to himself.

Now I just need to find out what Bryna wants from me, Jaedin thought as he turned around. Selena's men were in the process of carefully placing Rivan upon the bed in the middle of the room. The young man's face was completely white.

Is he even still breathing? Jaedin wondered.

"I will leave some men outside," Selena said. "Hot water and dressings will be brought to you. If you need anything else, just ask them."

But mostly, they are being left there to watch over me, no doubt, Jaedin thought, but he refrained from commenting.

"Close the door behind you, please," Bryna said. "And tell them not to enter unless I ask."

Selena complied, and a few moments later, Jaedin and Bryna were alone.

"What's going on, Bryna?" he asked her

Bryna took his hand. *There is no time to talk*, he heard her voice within his mind. *Psycalesse with me.*

Jaedin could sense the urgency within his sister, so he did as she said immediately, closing his eyes and tuning into his *psysona*. It didn't take them long to achieve unity; his mind merged with hers within moments. Whether it was because they were twins – and already had that connection – or simply because of the urgency of the situation, Jaedin didn't know.

How do we save Rivan, then? Jaedin asked.

Rivan is already dead, Bryna channelled back.

Jaedin was surprised how much this news hurt him. It made him realise just how much they had all changed since they escaped from Jalard. He and Rivan used to despise each other, but somewhere along the way, Jaedin had learned to care about him.

Why are we here then? Jaedin asked after a short pause while he swallowed the bitter news.

Bryna showed Jaedin, drawing him to a place so deep within her psyche that he could feel her sensory experiences as his own. Jaedin became witness to the process of Bryna wielding her magic. It was peculiar for Jaedin to experience someone else channelling their Blessing. One he did not himself possess.

Bryna was using her power as the Descendent of Vai-ris to hold Rivan's soul in place and keep it from leaving his body. Which could only mean that what Bryna had just said was true; Rivan was dead, and his soul and body were no longer naturally joined to one another. It was only Bryna's intervention that was preventing his soul from crossing over to the spirit world. The strain it was having upon her was beginning to take its toll. She couldn't keep it up for too much longer.

Why are you doing this, Bryna? Jaedin said to her gently. *He's dead... you need to let him go.*

I can't, she resonated back.

Within that response, it wasn't just words that Jaedin perceived; it was her emotions too. They were so overwhelming it forced Jaedin to withdraw a little so that his secondary experience of Bryna's feelings didn't sting him.

*Do you **love** him?* Jaedin asked. *That night... it was a while ago now, but I **felt** something. You were upset, and Rivan was there. What happened?*

I can't talk about that right now! Bryna responded, and Jaedin sensed conflicted emotions flare within her.

What about Sidry? Jaedin thought.

No! Bryna cried. *Don't! This isn't the right time!*

You need to let Rivan go... Jaedin said softly. *I'm sorry... I know it's sad. I'm upset about it too. Can you believe that? I used to hate him, but after all we went through, we learnt to care for each other, didn't we? That's a nice thought, isn't it? Take comfort in that. You can't just keep him like this forever. I don't think it is what he would have wanted. Was it a Zakara that killed him?* Jaedin then added. *If it was, that means he is going to turn into one, and from the look of him, I think that is going to be soon.*

No... it wasn't a Zakara that killed him. But that is why I brought you here, Bryna said.

What do you mean? Jaedin asked.

Didn't Miles once say that those who possess a Stones of Zakar can reanimate a recently dead corpse and turn it into a Zakara? she asked. *Is it true?*

Bryna! Jaedin's inner voice came out as a shout then, and it echoed in the chamber of their shared consciousness. *That's crazy! Why would you want me to turn him into a Zakara?*

Let me finish, Bryna said. *I have an idea. One which I think may be able to save him... You also mentioned something the Stones can do once. Something you can do to Zakaras with them. 'Enhancing' you called it. When you make them smarter and give them more freedom. Why don't we try it? On him?* Bryna suggested. *I still have his soul. I am holding it in place. Maybe, if you open up his mind, he can access his memories and consciousness, and I can get him to stay. He can keep his soul. He would be a Zakara, but he would still be **him**.*

I don't like the idea of this... Jaedin said. *I'm not even sure it would work...*

Can't we try? Bryna pleaded. She sounded desperate.

What if it goes wrong? Jaedin asked. *What if I do what you're asking me, but Rivan **still** dies? When a Zakara is enhanced they're difficult to control. Sometimes impossible. What if he wakes up and becomes a monster?*

I think I can handle that, Bryna said. Although Jaedin could tell from the essence of that statement, she was not utterly certain. Bryna had restored her *viga* a little since returning to the city, but she was still weak. Jaedin also knew that she had been hurt earlier that day, but he had not had time to ask her the details of that yet; nor delve into that place within her mind where he could find out.

I still don't like the idea of this... Jaedin said. *I made a promise to myself that enhancing was something I would never do.*

This is different, Bryna insisted. *Please, Jaedin. We need to save him.*

That last message came with a nuance of feeling that cut so deep, Jaedin realised he couldn't refuse her.

Okay, fine, he said. *I will **try**, but I can't promise anything.*

Jaedin reached out to his Stone of Zakar. It took him a while to achieve harmony with it whilst maintaining a *psycalesse* with Bryna, but eventually, it came to him. He accessed the artefact's powers and then turned his attention to Rivan.

What now? Bryna asked.

I guess I need to turn him into a Zakara, Jaedin said, and his *psysona* shuddered at the thought. *You do realise this was something I promised I would never do?*

This is a special situation, Bryna said.

Yes, I know, Jaedin replied. *But I still don't like it... Before I proceed, I think we are going to need fuller unity.*

Yes... Bryna replied. *I agree.*

The two of them merged their *psysonas* even deeper into one another other. Delving further into each other's consciousness than they had ever been before. Not even when they were children had Jaedin felt Bryna's thoughts so acutely. They were almost as real as his own.

Jaedin then probed into the archive of memories he had taken from Shayam just before the Gavendarian noble had died. Jaedin had never imagined that the particular technique he was recalling was one he would ever put to use. He had only stored it – along with all the other things he had learned from Shayam – because he had thought it best he understood the ways that *others* would abuse the Stones of Zakar's powers.

He found it; the method for creating new Zakaras. It involved the transference of energy.

Almost all Zakaras – as they are known today – were spawned from one initial creature. The one Carmaestre created after years of 'failed' experiments that produced creatures she considered 'imperfect', such as Fangar. Once Carmaestre brought that original Zakara into existence, its energy became a template for all the others.

Jaedin, after a moment of hesitation, did something that other wielders of Stones of Zakar before him had done, but he never dreamed he would do personally.

He siphoned that energy into Rivan's lifeless body.

I can't believe I am going through with this... he thought.

Rivan turned soon after. Jaedin felt the shift within him. Within a few moments, his chest drew in a breath of air. And then, a few moments later, he exhaled. And then he drew another one. Each respiration he made was deeper. His body began to repair itself.

Jaedin intervened immediately – stilling Rivan's mind so that the monster within wouldn't awaken – and then, he began the process of enhancing him.

It was not something Jaedin had ever done before himself, but he knew the techniques from Shayam's memories. Jaedin roamed within Rivan's mind, crisscrossing through the labyrinth of his psyche and awakening all of its tiers. It was a rather eerie process. Rivan's brain, as a Zakara, was a dark, bleak place.

Throughout the process, Jaedin occasionally felt – within Bryna's mind – Rivan's soul twitching as it tried to wriggle free. As Jaedin repaired Rivan's consciousness – granting him back his skills, thoughts, and memories – Rivan seemed to become more restless but, thanks to Jaedin and Bryna having full unity through their *psycalesse*, Bryna was prepared for it each time and, whenever it occurred, Jaedin paused for a while to give Bryna time to stabilise Rivan again. The process was painstaking. Towards the end of it, Jaedin had no doubt that, had he and Bryna not been joined – and thus acting in perfect harmony – it would not have worked.

Indeed, he even suspected that it was only the bond they shared as twins that made this venture possible.

I think it is done... Jaedin said eventually.

Do you think it worked? she asked.

I don't know, he responded. *I guess we're about to find out...*

They simultaneously released him. Jaedin unleashed Rivan from the probing influence of the Stone of Zakar, and Bryna let go of his wriggling soul. They both waited for a while, observing Rivan closely.

I think we did it, Bryna said after a while.

We don't know that for certain yet, Jaedin replied. *Not until he wakes up.*

His soul is bound to his body now, Bryna said to Jaedin. *I am not holding them together anymore, but his soul has stayed... Zakaras don't have souls.*

Has it occurred to you that maybe Rivan might not **want** *to be this way?* Jaedin asked her. *That he might have preferred to have just died?*

She didn't respond to that.

Jaedin let go of her hand, ending the *psycalesse* as he drew back into himself.

Then he opened his eyes.

"I guess we're going to have to wait for him to wake now... only then will we find out what it is that we have created," Jaedin said, looking at the figure of Rivan lying on the bed. He could see now that, during the procedure, Rivan's wounds had healed themselves.

"We will..." Bryna grimaced. "Thank you, Jaedin."

They embraced, finally able to rejoice over being reunited. It was a tremendous comfort for Jaedin to know that his sister had returned from Gavendara in one piece.

"So, are you going to tell me what happened?" Jaedin asked after he withdrew. "Who hurt you? Earlier today, I felt this horrible pain here," Jaedin patted his chest. "And then–"

As Jaedin spoke, he noticed movement outside the window and brought his conversation with his sister to a halt. "Fangar?" he said, walking over. "What is it? Don't worry! You can show yourself. It's just Bryna here."

Fangar's face appeared in the frame, and he lifted himself onto the sill and grinned. "It seems the reekmoss has hit the hearth," he said, shaking his head. He seemed rather amused. "There's a brouhaha going on outside the Synod."

"What's happened?" Jaedin asked.

"Baird and Sidry have returned," Fangar replied. "And not just them, but that swineass Greyjor has just appeared too. And that Selena and a swarm of other Synod drones. They're all outside the Synod screaming at each other."

Jaedin frowned. "Did you hear what they were arguing about?"

Fangar shrugged. "I took a quick peek when I first caught wind but didn't stay long. Wanted to come back so I could tell you."

"I think we should go see," Jaedin said. Perhaps this meant Baird had finally got to the bottom of who the Gavendarian mole within the Synod was. Jaedin would be happy to have that issue resolved. "I'll come with you."

"Be careful, Jaedin," Bryna said as he climbed out of the window.

Jaedin turned to his sister just before he leapt out and chuckled. "Don't worry. I'll be fine. You keep an eye on Rivan."

Jaedin dropped down to the grass outside and sprinted to catch up with Fangar. The rogue led the way, racing towards the walled enclosure that surrounded the Synod grounds. Once he reached it, Fangar scaled his way to the top of it within a few seconds, but Jaedin had not quite mastered the art of climbing as swiftly as Fangar could yet – it was a technique he was still practising – so he decided to save some time by launching himself from one of the oak trees nearby. He jumped, grabbed hold of a branch, and let himself swing back and forth a few times to gain some momentum. On the third swing, he let go and jetted towards the wall.

He grabbed hold of the ledge: a little clumsily, but his grip stayed true. Fangar grinned at him as Jaedin pulled himself up.

"You slowing me down again today?" Fangar asked.

"Scit off!" Jaedin said.

The two of them then dashed along the top of the wall, both building up speed. The sandstone structure of the Synod passed them by in a blur of yellow, and then Jaedin saw the commotion Fangar had told him about. Outside the front of the building, people were yelling and pointing fingers at each other. They seemed to have drawn an entire audience of civilians who had gathered around the gate to watch, peeking their heads through the iron bars.

As Jaedin got closer, some of the people noticed him approach and stared at him.

"Wait here," Jaedin uttered to Fangar. "I'll go alone."

Jaedin leapt from the wall, dropping to a roll as he landed to break his fall. He then raced towards the crowd, climbing some of the steps along the front of the Synod so that he could approach them with the advantage of height.

"What are you waiting for!" a voice hollered. It was Greyjor. He pointed at Jaedin. His face was all red and creased up with anger. "Arrest him! That's *Jaedin*!"

"No!" Baird yelled, stepping in front of the Synod Sentinels to block their way. He then pointed at Greyjor. "Arrest *him*! He's the traitor!"

The Synod Sentinels – all six of them – turned to each other, at a loss over what to do with the conflicting orders.

"What happened, Baird?" Jaedin yelled.

"I have just returned from Seeker's Hill!" Baird said, raising his voice so that not only Jaedin could hear, but everyone else too. "A place where *he*," Baird indicated Greyjor. "Sent a squadron of soldiers a few aeights ago. Considering we are *supposed* to be preparing for war right now, I thought sending so many men to a site so far away from the border a bit suspicious, so I went there to investigate. They had been turned into Zakaras! *All* of them! Not only that, but just before they tried to kill me and Sidry, they said that they followed the orders of one man and one man only. And guess who that was? *Him*!" Baird finished, pointing at Greyjor again. "He's working with the Gavendarians!"

"Who are you doing to trust?" Greyjor challenged, also raising his voice. "I have served and protected you all as a valued member of the Synod for over ten years, while *he*," he gestured to Baird. "Comes bull-charging into this city, making the most outlandish claims and threats. He associates himself with *murderers*!" Greyjor finished his statement by waving his arm in Jaedin's direction again.

"Enough of this!" Selena intervened. Jaedin had not

even noticed she was present until that moment because she had her back to him. She positioned herself between Baird and Greyjor. "I am sorry, Greyjor," she said. "But considering the circumstances, I am going to have to insist you be taken away so that you can be questioned and we can get to the bottom of this. If you are innocent then you have nothing to worry about."

"You're trying to arrest *me*?" Greyjor asked incredulously. "I am the Head of the War Consil. I outrank you!"

"That may be," Selena agreed. "But in cases such as this, there are clauses I can invoke. You *know* that, so don't force me to recite them. As I said, if you *are* innocent, you have nothing to worry about. You will be judged fairly..." She then turned to the Synod Sentinels. "And arrest Jaedin too."

"On my dead body!" Jaedin yelled.

A pair of the Sentinels began to march towards him, so Jaedin drew a pair of daggers from his sleeves. "Stay back!" he warned. "*If* you value your lives... I don't *want* to kill you, but I will if I have to. You've heard about me. You know what I can do."

"I will willingly go with these men on one condition," Greyjor said as the Sentinels approached him. "You arrest Baird too and hold *him* for questioning. And Sidry," he added. "*All* of Baird's aides and accomplices. This is a plot against me, and when I have proven my innocence, I want them to be accountable for all the trouble they've caused!"

"Why are we even doing this?" Jaedin challenged, looking at Selena. "It's scitting obvious Greyjor is a traitor. How much evidence do you need? We all know it. Why, in Lania's name, are we wasting all this time?"

"Proper procedure must be followed," Selena responded.

"If those Zakaras Baird found said that they were following *his* orders," Jaedin said, pointing at Greyjor. "Then he *is* the traitor. He *has* to be. I know how Zakaras work! In the absence of someone who possesses a Stone

447

of Zakar – such as myself – Zakaras revert to a chain of command. It was *him* who sent those soldiers there, too!" Jaedin shook his head. "Ever since we got here, we've been trying to *warn* you and get you to prepare for the danger which is coming, but *he* has slowed us down every step of the way! It's *him!* He's the traitor! I am certain of it."

"And if you can testify that when this matter is brought to trial, your statements will be considered," Selena said to Jaedin coolly. "Therefore, the quickest and surest way to get this matter resolved is for you to surrender yourself to the Sentinels, Jaedin."

"No!" Jaedin shook his head. "I don't trust you."

"All you have is their word against mine!" Greyjor exclaimed, addressing all the other people around them. People whom – Jaedin guessed – were other members of the Synod. Their faces mostly read as uncertain.

"You're wasting time!" Jaedin yelled. This time he didn't just address Selena, but everyone. He raised his voice. "Gavendara is gathering an army, and you're all just *standing* here! *Talking!*"

"There's an army?" Selena asked. Her eyes widened in alarm. "You mean the others found one?"

Jaedin frowned at her. "Of course there is. Didn't you get that letter I sent to you?"

Selena shook her head.

"I wrote to you!" Jaedin exclaimed. He then realised that many of the people gathered around him probably didn't even know about the clandestine mission Bryna and the others had just returned from. "Selena sent a secret group of people over to Gavendara!" he explained, raising his voice again. "To scout for armies, and they found one. And it wasn't just any army, but an army of *Zakaras*. My sister was part of the mission, and she communicated to me through Psymancy about the army when she discovered them. I wrote to the Synod! I did it so that you could start preparing! What happened to my letter?"

Someone in the crowd then spoke up; young lady with

a crooked back. "I think I know of the letter you speak..." she said. "I was in the Solus about an aeight ago when a messenger arrived with it. They said they were looking for Selena but she wasn't there that day so Greyjor accepted it. He didn't let us see it, though. Or tell us of its contents."

Everyone looked at Greyjor again, and some of them began to mumble to each other. "I burned it!" Greyjor admitted, and several people gasped. "But it was only because we cannot let ourselves listen to the lies of murderers!"

"See!" Jaedin yelled, fury overwhelming him as he pointed at Greyjor. "Can't you see what he's doing?! He's dragging our feet. There's a war coming, and he is trying to stop us from preparing for it! You've just lost an entire aeight when you *should* have been mustering your armies! And now, he is going to make you waste even *more* time in a pointless trial!" Jaedin turned to Selena. "And I *know* how long you take to get things done in this ruddy place! Wake up! You don't have time for this! The Gavendarians are coming, and you need to prepare!"

Selena grimaced. "I can assure you we will seek to resolve this matter as swiftly as we can..." she said. "We will begin Greyjor's trial tomorrow morning."

Tomorrow? Jaedin thought, his fists tightening by his sides. ***Tomorrow!?***

Tomorrow wasn't soon enough for Jaedin. It seemed that none of them was listening. They didn't understand the urgency of the situation. None of them had ever even seen a Zakara. They didn't appreciate the danger they were in.

They're not prepared for this, Jaedin realised. *None of them are willing to do what needs to be done...*

Greyjor was guilty. It was clear he was the mole. And he was probably going to drag out that trial for as long as he possibly could, all to hinder Sharma preparing its defences.

They'll still be arguing over what to do about him as the Zakaras march into the city! Jaedin thought.

And it was during that moment – fuelled by not merely just anger, but a frustration more acute than Jaedin had ever known – Jaedin reached a decision.

*If **they** won't do what has to be done, I guess **I** will have to...* he realised.

Greyjor began to argue again, and Jaedin didn't even bother listening to the lies streaming from his mouth this time.

Jaedin leapt at Greyjor, his legs propelling him several feet above the heads of the other people. Everyone was distracted – still enraptured by the altercation – but some of them turned their heads as they noticed what must have looked like, to them, a sudden blur of movement. None of them had any time to respond, though. Jaedin was too fast, and they were unprepared.

Jaedin's initial leap wasn't enough to get him to Greyjor: as he came down, he realised he was on a course to impact with one of the Sentinels. Jaedin allowed that to happen, and the man broke his fall. The Sentinel yelped when Jaedin collided into him, and Jaedin grabbed his shoulder as they both went down, using it to steady himself.

Jaedin then raced towards Greyjor. The man was only a couple of strides away now. People had noticed something was going on by then – including Greyjor himself – but none of them was quick enough to react. As Jaedin approached, Greyjor's hand went to his waist – as if to draw his weapon – but he was too late. Jaedin had already drawn his dagger, and it turned a blur of grey as he drove it into Greyjor's neck.

The blade entered through the side of his throat – Fangar had taught Jaedin to do it this way, because it avoided all the tough cartilage at the front. There was a brief moment of resistance, but it was shortly followed by a pop – which Jaedin guessed to be Greyjor's windpipe opening to the tip of his blade – and then the dagger sank in deeper. Blood ran down the man's chest. Greyjor's eyes went up to the sky.

Jaedin then twisted around him, grabbing Greyjor's

shoulder with his other hand as he manoeuvred around him so that Greyjor's back was pressed against him. Jaedin yanked the blade across, and a spurt of red burst from Greyjor's throat.

The Head of the War Consil collapsed. The thud of his body flopping to the ground outside the steps of the Synod was the only sound he made. The man was already dead.

Jaedin then looked up. Everyone was staring. Frozen. As if they couldn't believe what had just happened.

Jaedin could barely believe it himself.

"The Zakaras are coming," Jaedin said.

End of Book 2

Acknowledgements

As usual, Roy Gilham; my primary beta-reader, and almost always the first person to glimpse anything I complete.

Pete, Alison, Sofia, and everyone else involved in Elsewhen Press for the incredible work they do.

Chuck Ashmore for his support, patience, and a lovely map.

All the friends and connections I have made in the SFF community. There are too many to mention you all (and if I try, I will end up forgetting people and feeling guilty for it) but Chris Nuttall in particular deserves extra gratitude on this occasion for his help getting this series to reach more people. I will also mention Anna Smith Spark, Joanne Hall, Allen Stroud, James Worrad, Craig Meighan, David Tallerman, S Naomi Scott, Francesca T Barbini, Pete Sutton, Bethan Hindmarch, David Craig, Sami, Mayri, Jayran Main, The Mole and KA Dore, all of whom have been kind enough to help promote this series in some way.

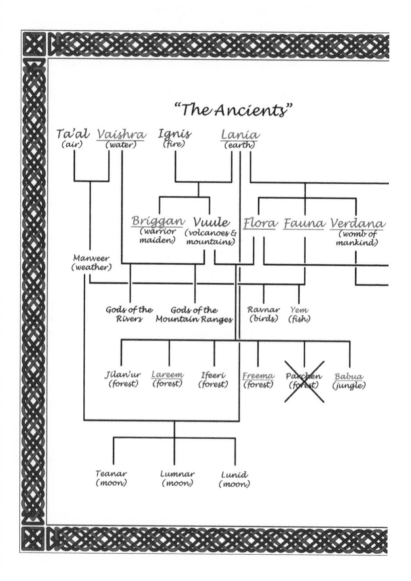

"The Ancients"

Ta'al (air)   Vaishra (water)   Ignis (fire)   Lania (earth)

Briggan (warrior maiden)   Vuule (volcanoes & mountains)   Flora   Fauna   Verdana (womb of mankind)

Manveer (weather)

Gods of the Rivers   Gods of the Mountain Ranges   Ravnar (birds)   Yem (fish)

Jilan'ur (forest)   Lareem (forest)   Ifeeri (forest)   Freema (forest)   Parchen (forest)   Babua (jungle)

Teanar (moon)   Lumnar (moon)   Lunid (moon)

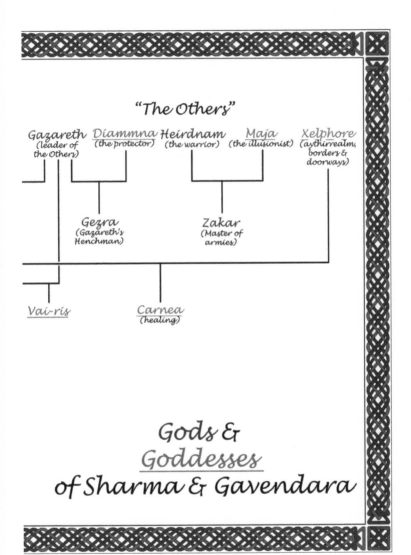

"The Others"

Gazareth
(leader of
the Others)

Diammna
(the protector)

Heirdnam
(the warrior)

Maja
(the illusionist)

Xelphore
(aythirrealm,
borders &
doorways)

Gezra
(Gazareth's
Henchman)

Zakar
(Master of
armies)

Vai-ris

Carnea
(healing)

Gods &
Goddesses
of Sharma & Gavendara

Elsewhen Press
delivering outstanding new talents in speculative fiction

Visit the Elsewhen Press website at elsewhen.press for the latest information on all of our titles, authors and events; to read our blog; find out where to buy our books and ebooks; or to place an order.

Sign up for the Elsewhen Press InFlight Newsletter at elsewhen.press/newsletter

By Tej Turner

Bloodsworn
Book 1 of the Avatars of Ruin
Tej Turner

"Classic epic fantasy. I enjoyed it enormously"
– Anna Smith Spark
"a stunning introduction to a new fantasy world"
– Christopher G Nuttall

Everyone from Jalard knew what a bloodoath was. Legendary characters in tales they were told as children made such pacts with the gods. By drawing one's own blood whilst making a vow, such people became 'Bloodsworn'. And in every tale where the oath was broken, the ending was always the same. The Bloodsworn died.

It has been twelve years since The War of Ashes, but animosity still lingers between the nations of Sharma and Gavendara, and only a few souls have dared to cross the border between them.

The villagers of Jalard live a simplistic life, tucked away in the hills of western Sharma and far away from the boundary which was once a warzone. To them tales of bloodshed seem no more than distant fables. They have little contact with the outside world, apart from once a year when they are visited by representatives from the Academy who choose two of them to be taken away to their institute in the capital. To be Chosen is considered a great honour… of which most of Jalard's children dream.

But this year the Academy representatives make an announcement which is so shocking it causes friction between the villagers and some of them begin to suspect that all is not what it seems. Just where are they taking the Chosen, and why? Some of them seek to find out, but what they find will change their lives forever and set them on a path seeking vengeance…

ISBN: 9781911409779 (epub, kindle) / 9781911409670 (432pp paperback)
Visit bit.ly/Bloodsworn

Coming soon:

Blood War
Book 3 of the Avatars of Ruin

By Tej Turner

Urban fantasy by Tej Turner
The Janus Cycle

The Janus Cycle can best be described as gritty, surreal, urban fantasy. The over-arching story revolves around a nightclub called Janus, which is not merely a location but virtually a character in its own right. On the surface it appears to be a subcultural hub where the strange and disillusioned who feel alienated and oppressed by society escape to be free from convention; but underneath that façade is a surreal space in time where the very foundations of reality are twisted and distorted. But the special unique vibe of Janus is hijacked by a bandwagon of people who choose to conform to alternative lifestyles simply because it has become fashionable to be 'different', and this causes many of its original occupants to feel lost and disenchanted. We see the story of Janus unfold through the eyes of eight narrators, each with their own perspective and their own personal journey. A story in which the nightclub itself goes on a journey. But throughout, one character, a strange girl, briefly appears and reappears warning the narrators that their individual journeys are going to collide in a cataclysmic event. Is she just another one of the nightclub's denizens, a cynical mischief-maker out to create havoc or a time-traveller trying to prevent an impending disaster?

ISBN: 9781908168566 (epub, kindle) / 9781908168467 (224pp paperback)
Visit bit.ly/JanusCycle

Dinnusos Rises

The vibe has soured somewhat after a violent clash in the Janus nightclub a few months ago, and since then Neal has opened a new establishment called 'Dinnusos'. Located on a derelict and forgotten side of town, it is not the sort of place you stumble upon by accident, but over time it enchants people, and soon becomes a nucleus for urban bohemians and a refuge for the city's lost souls. Rumour has it that it was once a grand hotel, many years ago, but no one is quite sure. Whilst mingling in the bar downstairs you might find yourself in the company of poets, dreamers, outsiders, and all manner of misfits and rebels. And if you're daring enough to explore its ghostly halls, there's a whole labyrinth of rooms on the upper floors to get lost in…

Now it seems that not just Neal's clientele, but the entire population of the city, begin to go crazy when beings, once thought mythological, enter the mortal realm to stir chaos as they sow the seeds of militancy.

Eight characters. Most of them friends, some of them strangers. Each with their own story to tell. All of them destined to cross paths in a surreal sequence of events which will change them forever.

ISBN: 9781911409137 (epub, kindle) / 9781911409038 (280pp paperback)
visit bit.ly/DinnusosRises

By Tej Turner

Existence is Elsewhen
Twenty stories from twenty great authors including
Tej Turner
John Gribbin
Rhys Hughes
Christopher Nuttall
Douglas Thompson

The title *Existence is Elsewhen* paraphrases the last sentence of André Breton's 1924 *Manifesto of Surrealism*, perfectly summing up the intent behind this anthology of stories from a wonderful collection of authors. Different worlds… different times. It's what Elsewhen Press has been about since we launched our first title in 2011.

Here, we present twenty science fiction stories for you to enjoy. We are delighted that headlining this collection is the fantastic **John Gribbin**, with a worrying vision of medical research in the near future. Future global healthcare is the theme of **J A Christy's** story; while the ultimate in spare part surgery is where **Dave Weaver** takes us. **Edwin Hayward's** search for a renewable protein source turns out to be digital; and **Tanya Reimer's** story with characters we think we know gives us pause for thought about another food we take for granted. Evolution is examined too, with **Andy McKell's** chilling tale of what states could become if genetics are used to drive policy. Similarly, **Robin Moran's** story explores the societal impact of an undesirable evolutionary trend; while **Douglas Thompson** provides a truly surreal warning of an impending disaster that will reverse evolution, with dire consequences.

On a lighter note, we have satire from **Steve Harrison** discovering who really owns the Earth (and why); and **Ira Nayman,** who uses the surreal alternative realities of his *Transdimensional Authority* series as the setting for a detective story mash-up of Agatha Christie and Dashiel Hammett. Pursuing the crime-solving theme, **Peter Wolfe** explores life, and death, on a space station; while **Stefan Jackson** follows a police investigation into some bizarre cold-blooded murders in a cyberpunk future. Going into the past, albeit an 1831 set in the alternate Britain of his *Royal Sorceress* series, **Christopher Nuttall** reports on an investigation into a girl with strange powers.

Strange powers in the present-day is the theme for **Tej Turner**, who tells a poignant tale of how extra-sensory perception makes it easier for a husband to bear his dying wife's last few days. Difficult decisions are the theme of **Chloe Skye's** heart-rending story exploring personal sacrifice. Relationships aren't always so close, as **Susan Oke's** tale demonstrates, when sibling rivalry is taken to the limit. Relationships are the backdrop to **Peter R. Ellis's** story where a spectacular mid-winter event on a newly- colonised distant planet involves a Madonna and Child. Coming right back to Earth and in what feels like an almost imminent future, **Siobhan McVeigh** tells a cautionary tale for anyone thinking of using technology to deflect the blame for their actions. Building on the remarkable setting of Pera from her *LiGa* series, and developing Pera's legendary *Book of Shadow,* **Sanem Ozdural** spins the creation myth of the first light tree in a lyrical and poetic song. Also exploring language, the master of fantastika and absurdism, **Rhys Hughes,** extrapolates the way in which language changes over time, with an entertaining result.

ISBN: 9781908168955 (epub, kindle) / 9781908168856 (320pp paperback)
Visit bit.ly/ExistenceIsElsewhen

Thorns of a Black Rose

David Craig

Revenge and responsibility,
confrontation and consequences.

A hot desert land of diverse peoples dealing with demons, mages, natural disasters … and the Black Rose assassins.

On a quest for vengeance, Shukara arrives in the city of Mask having already endured two years of hardship and loss. Her pouch is stolen by Tamira, a young street-smart thief, who throws away some of the rarer reagents that Shukara needs for her magick. Tracking down the thief, and being unfamiliar with Mask, Shukara shows mercy to Tamira in exchange for her help in replacing what has been lost. Together they brave the intrigues of Mask, and soon discover that they have a mutual enemy in the Black Rose, an almost legendary band of merciless assassins. But this is just the start of their journeys…

Although set in an imaginary land, the scenery and peoples of *Thorns of a Black Rose* were inspired by Egypt, Morocco and the Sahara. Mask is a living, breathing city, from the prosperous Merchant Quarter whose residents struggle for wealth and power, to the Poor Quarter whose residents struggle just to survive. It is a coming of age tale for the young thief, Tamira, as well as a tale of vengeance and discovery. There is also a moral ambiguity in the story, with both the protagonists and antagonists learning that whatever their intentions or justification, actions have consequences.

ISBN: 9781911409557 (epub, kindle) / 9781911409458 (256pp paperback)
Visit bit.ly/ThornsOfABlackRose

BY DAVID M ALLAN
QUAESTOR

When you're searching, you don't always find what you expect

In Carrhen some people have a magic power – they may be telekinetic, clairvoyant, stealthy, or able to manipulate the elements. Anarya is a Sponger, she can absorb and use anyone else's magic without them even being aware, but she has to keep it a secret as it provokes jealousy and hostility especially among those with no magic powers at all.

When Anarya sees Yisyena, a Sitrelker refugee, being assaulted by three drunken men, she helps her to escape. Anarya is trying to establish herself as an investigator, a quaestor, in the city of Carregis. Yisyena is a clairvoyant, a skill that would be a useful asset for a quaestor, so Anarya offers her a place to stay and suggests they become business partners. Before long they are also lovers.

But business is still hard to find, so when an opportunity arises to work for Count Graumedel who rules over the city, they can't afford to turn it down, even though the outcome may not be to their liking.

Soon they are embroiled in state secrets and the personal vendettas of a murdered champion, a cabal, a puppet king, and a false god looking for one who has defied him.

ISBN: 9781911409571 (epub, kindle) / 9781911409472 (304pp paperback)
Visit bit.ly/Quaestor-Allan

THIEVER

Change is not always as good as a rest

After the events in Jotuk at the end of *Quaestor*, Anarya is no longer a Sponger but is now a Thiever – when she takes someone's magic talent they lose it until she can no longer hold on to it. Worryingly, the power also brings a desperate hunger to take others' talents, just as the false god did. As Anarya struggles to control the compulsion, Yisul is fraught with worry and seeks help for her lover. But Jotuk is in upheaval; the Twenty-Three families are in disarray, divided over how the city should be governed.

In Carregis, the king seeks to establish himself as an effective ruler. First, though, he must work out whom he can trust.

Meanwhile, the priestesses of Quarenna and the priests of Huler are having disturbing dreams…

Thiever is the much anticipated sequel to David M Allan's *Quaestor*.

ISBN: 9781911409977 (epub, kindle) / 9781911409878 (386pp paperback)
Visit bit.ly/Thiever

About Tej Turner

Tej Turner does not have any particular place he would say he is 'from', as his family moved between various parts of England during his childhood. He eventually settled in Wales, where he studied Creative Writing and Film at Trinity College in Carmarthen, followed by a master's degree at The University of Wales Lampeter.

Since then, Tej has mostly resided in Cardiff, where he works as a chef by day and writes by moonlight. His childhood on the move seems to have rubbed off on him because when he is not in Cardiff, it is usually because he has strapped on a backpack and flown off to another part of the world to go on an adventure.

When he travels, he takes a particular interest in historic sites, jungles, wildlife, native cultures, and mountains, and so far, he has clocked two years in Asia and a year in South America. He also spent some time volunteering at the Merazonia Wildlife Rehabilitation Centre in Ecuador, a place he intends to return to someday. He also hopes to go on more adventures and has his sights set on Central America next.

Firsthand accounts of Tej's adventures abroad can be found on his travel blog on his website (http://tejturner.com). A place he also posts author-related news.

His debut novel *The Janus Cycle* was published by Elsewhen Press in 2015 and its sequel *Dinnusos Rises* was released in 2017. Both are hard to classify within typical genres but were semi-biographical in nature with elements of magical realism. They have often been described as 'gritty and surreal urban fantasy'.

He has since branched off into writing epic fantasy and has an ongoing series called the *Avatars of Ruin*. The first instalment – *Bloodsworn* – was released in 2021, and *Blood Legacy* is its sequel. He is currently engaged in writing the third instalment (*Blood War*).